the Queen's favorite Witch

PAPERCUTZ

MORE GREAT GRAPHIC NOVEL SERIES AVAILABLE FROM

PAPERCUTZ™

THE SMURFS #21

BRINA THE CAT #1

CAT & CAT #1

THE SISTERS #1

ATTACK OF THE STUFF

ASTERIX #1

SCHOOL FOR EXTRATERRESTRIAL GIRLS #1

GERONIMO STILTON REPORTER #1

THE MYTHICS #1

GUMBY #1

MELOWY #1

BLUEBEARD

THE RED SHOES

THE LITTLE MERMAID

FUZZY BASEBALL #1

HOTEL TRANSYLVANIA #1

THE LOUD HOUSE #1

MANOSAURS #1

THE ONLY LIVING BOY #5

THE ONLY LIVING GIRL #1

PAPERCUTZ.COM
Also available where ebooks are sold.

Melowy, Geronimo Stilton; © 2018 Atlantyca S.p.A; Bluebeard, The Little Mermaid and The Red Shoes © 2018 Metaphrog; Fuzzy Baseball © 2018 by John Steven Gurney; The Loud House © 2018 Viacom International Inc.; Manosaurs © 2018 Stuart Fischer and Papercutz; The Only Living Boy and The Only Living Girl © 2018-2019 Bottled Lightening LLC.; GUMBY ©2018 Prema Toy Co., Inc.; The Sisters, Cat & Cat © 2018 BAMBOO ÉDITION; HOTEL TRANSYLVANIA TV SERIES™ © 2018 Sony Pictures Animation Inc. All Rights Reserved. Brina the Cat © 2020 TUNUÉ (Tunué s.r.l.); Attack of the Stuff © 2020 Jim Benton; The Mythics © 2020 Éditions Delcourt. ASTERIX® · OBELIX® · IDÉFIX ® · DOGMATIX ©© 2020 HACHETTE LIVRE. School for Extraterrestrial Girls © 2020 Jeremy Whitley and Jamie Noguchi.

© Peyo - 2020 - Licensed through I.M.P.S. (Brussels) - www.smurf.com

the Queen's favorite Witch

#1 "The Wheel of Fortune"

Benjamin Dickson
Writer

Rachael Smith
Artist

PAPERCUTZ
New York

the Queen's favorite Witch

For Our Magical Nieces,
Rosie Dickson
and Karolina Keighren

BENJAMIN DICKSON-Writer, Logo Designer
RACHAEL SMITH-Artist, Colorist, Letterer
DEWI RHYS-JONES- Divine Language Consultant
LILY BILGREY-Production/Design
JEFF WHITMAN-Managing Editor
JIM SALICRUP
Editor-in-Chief

Special thanks to:
JayJay Jackson
Rob Birchall
Yishan Li
James Wills
Paul Gravett
Ceridwen Scott Roberts
Emma Hayes
Dewi Rhys-Jones
Caroline Wajsblum
Delphine Guillemoteau
...and all our family and friends

Hardcover ISBN: 978-1-5458-0721-7
Paperback ISBN: 978-1-5458-0722-4

Printed in China
October 2021

Papercutz books may be purchased for business or promotional use.
For information on bulk purchases please contact Macmillan Corporate and Premium Sales Department at
(800) 221-795 x5442.

Distributed by Macmillan
First printing

PREFACE

WHO WAS QUEEN ELIZABETH I?

Elizabeth Tudor was one of the most important Queens to ever rule England. She was born on September 7th 1533, the daughter of Henry VIII and his second wife, Anne Boleyn. She had a half-brother (Edward) and a half-sister (Mary) who both ruled England before her, but neither of them had any children of their own, and when Mary died in 1558, Elizabeth inherited the throne. Elizabeth was just 25 years old, and would rule for 44 years.

Elizabeth was extremely clever – she could speak five foreign languages, as well as her native English, and was very good at playing politics. She had to be, because being queen was very dangerous! There were many plots to assassinate her, and to put someone else on the throne instead. Also, a lot of people felt it was wrong for a woman to rule alone – but Elizabeth knew that if she married, her husband would become king and take all the power. Because of this, she never married, and never had children. She became known as "the virgin queen." (The state of Virginia is named after her.)

Even today, Elizabeth is remembered as one of the best rulers England has ever had. Under her rule, England grew stronger and more influential, and there was more freedom of worship than there had been before. She wanted to help the poor live a better life. She set up schools, hospitals, and orphanages, and passed laws that made it easier for them to work and for children to learn a trade. Elizabeth's reign became known as England's "Golden Age." But life was still very hard compared to today!

Elizabeth was also the last monarch to rule England and not Scotland. The next monarch would rule both England *and* Scotland as a United Kingdom. But that's another story...

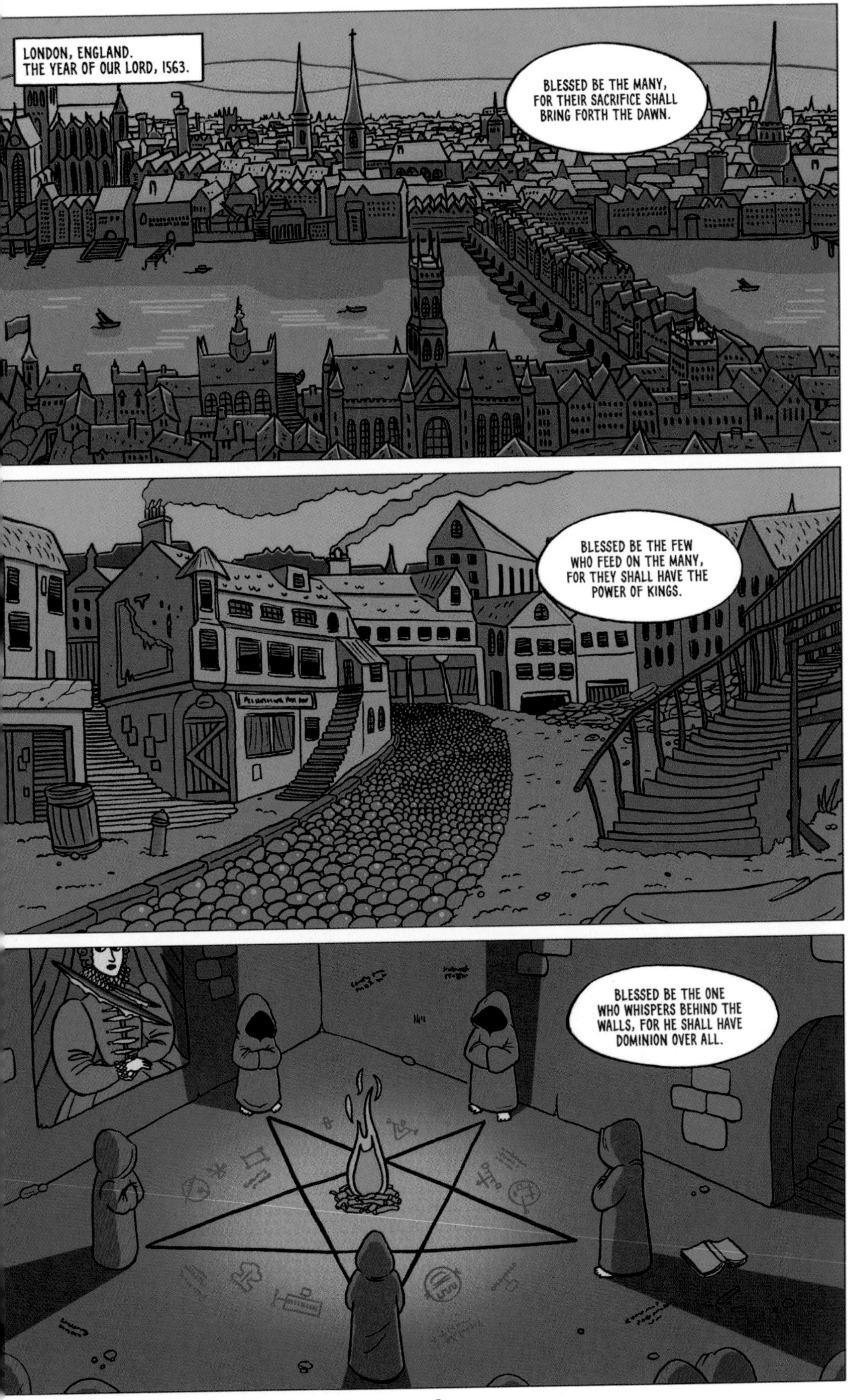
LONDON, ENGLAND.
THE YEAR OF OUR LORD, 1563.
BLESSED BE THE MANY, FOR THEIR SACRIFICE SHALL BRING FORTH THE DAWN.
BLESSED BE THE FEW WHO FEED ON THE MANY, FOR THEY SHALL HAVE THE POWER OF KINGS.
BLESSED BE THE ONE WHO WHISPERS BEHIND THE WALLS, FOR HE SHALL HAVE DOMINION OVER ALL.

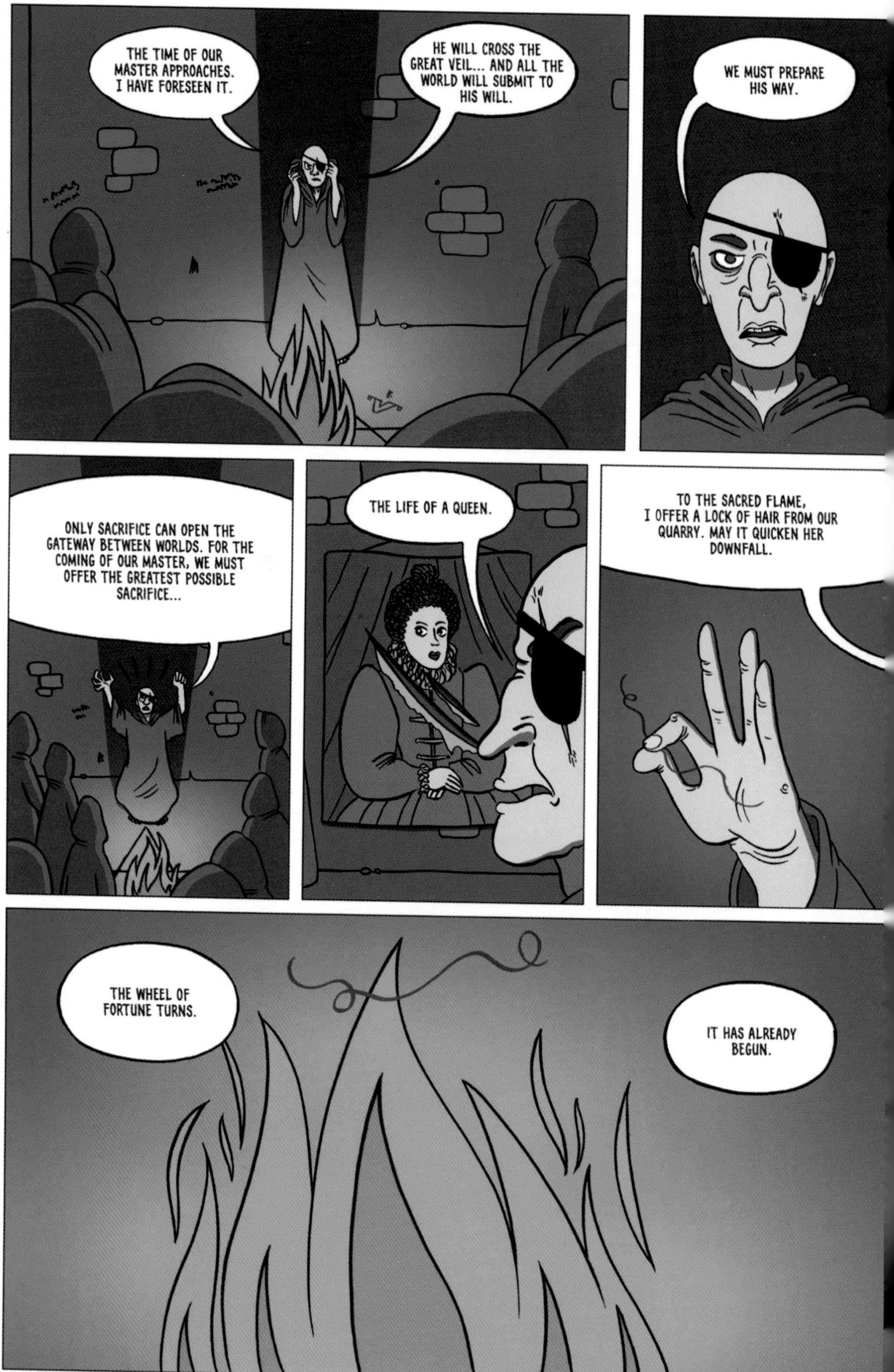
THE TIME OF OUR MASTER APPROACHES. I HAVE FORESEEN IT.
HE WILL CROSS THE GREAT VEIL... AND ALL THE WORLD WILL SUBMIT TO HIS WILL.
WE MUST PREPARE HIS WAY.
ONLY SACRIFICE CAN OPEN THE GATEWAY BETWEEN WORLDS. FOR THE COMING OF OUR MASTER, WE MUST OFFER THE GREATEST POSSIBLE SACRIFICE...
THE LIFE OF A QUEEN.
TO THE SACRED FLAME, I OFFER A LOCK OF HAIR FROM OUR QUARRY. MAY IT QUICKEN HER DOWNFALL.
THE WHEEL OF FORTUNE TURNS.
IT HAS ALREADY BEGUN.

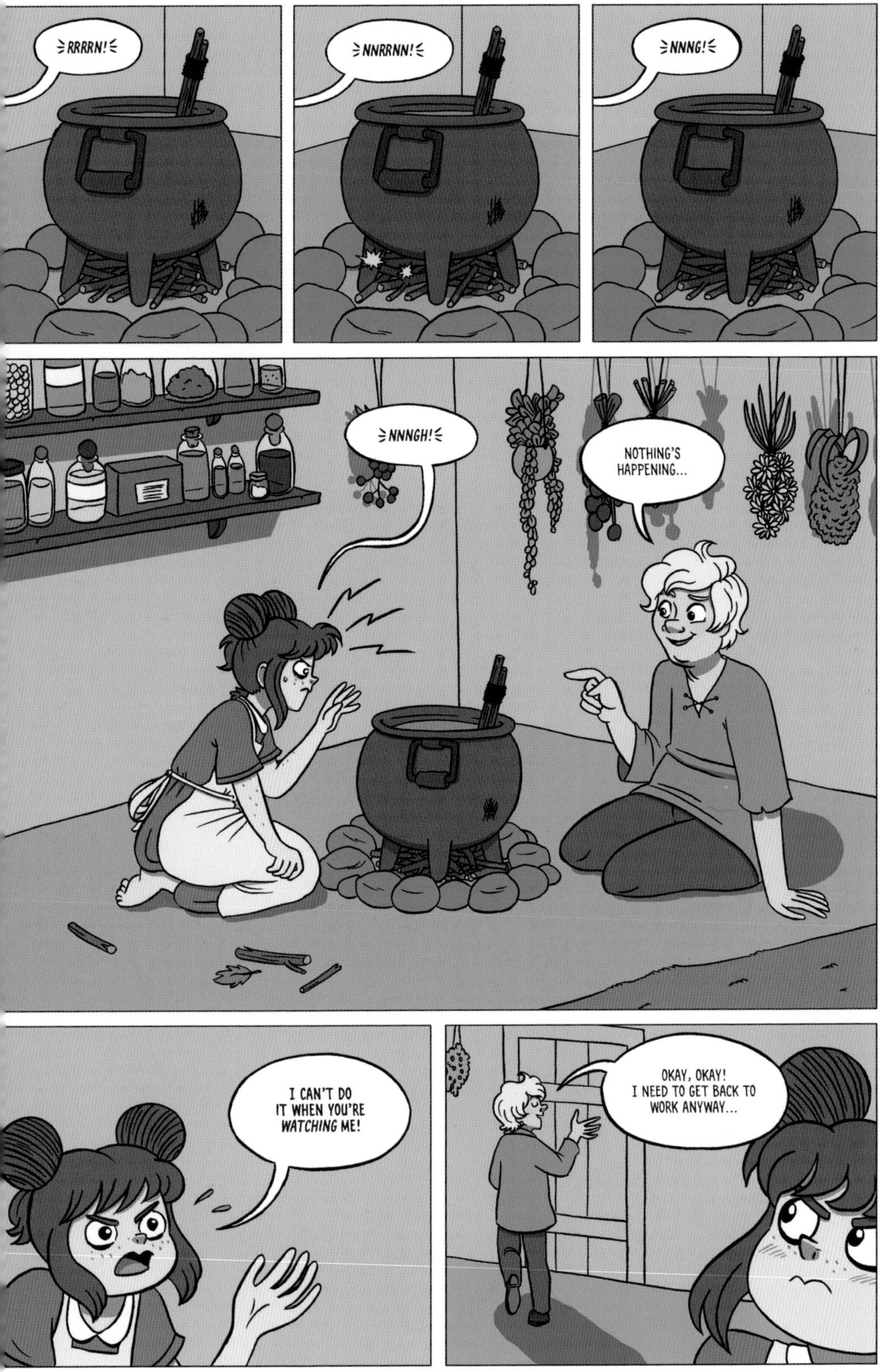
RRRRN!
NNRRNN!
NNNG!
NNNGH!
NOTHING'S HAPPENING...
I CAN'T DO IT WHEN YOU'RE *WATCHING* ME!
OKAY, OKAY! I NEED TO GET BACK TO WORK ANYWAY...

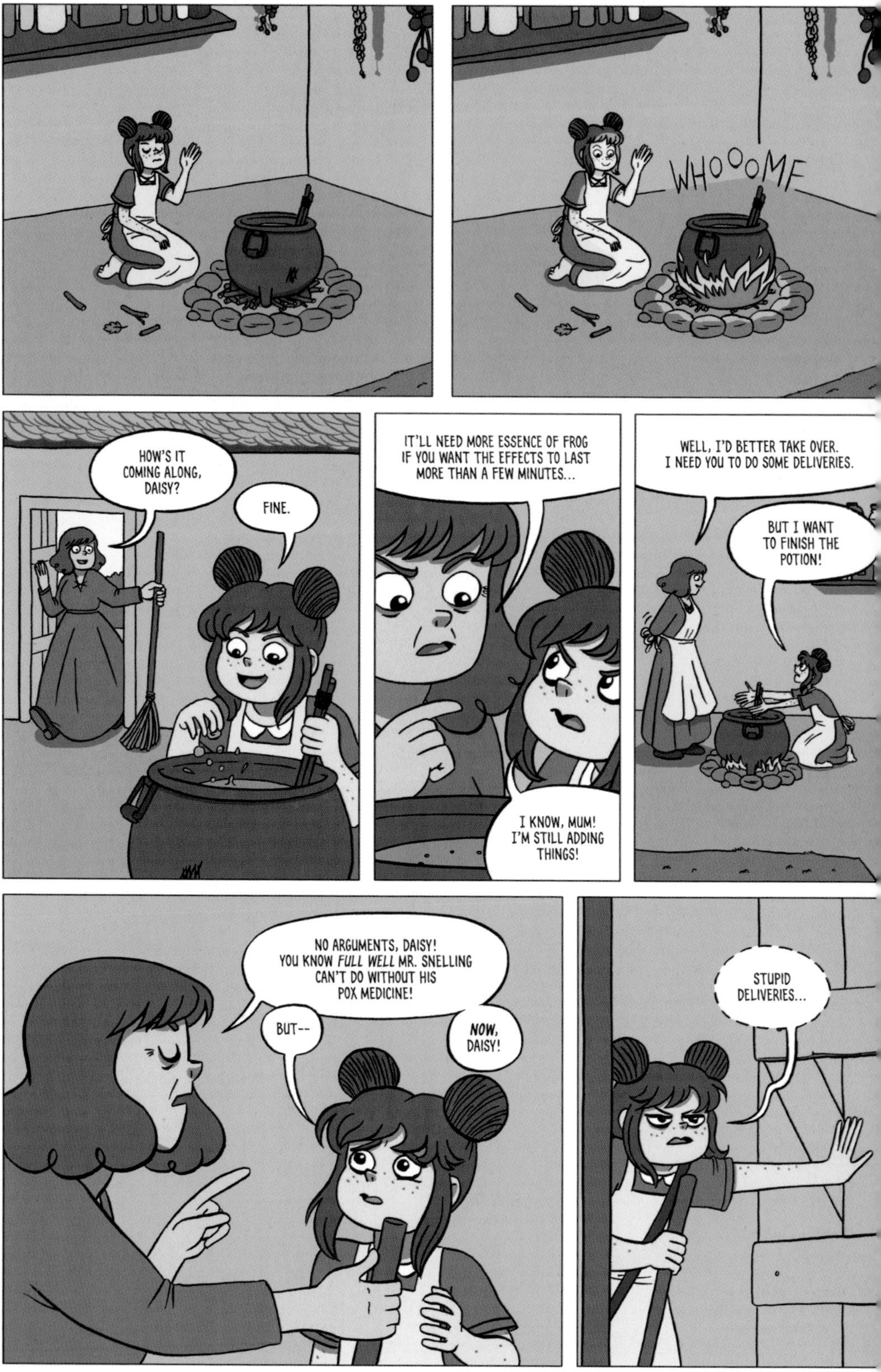
WHOOOMF
HOW'S IT COMING ALONG, DAISY?
FINE.
IT'LL NEED MORE ESSENCE OF FROG IF YOU WANT THE EFFECTS TO LAST MORE THAN A FEW MINUTES...
I KNOW, MUM! I'M STILL ADDING THINGS!
WELL, I'D BETTER TAKE OVER. I NEED YOU TO DO SOME DELIVERIES.
BUT I WANT TO FINISH THE POTION!
NO ARGUMENTS, DAISY! YOU KNOW *FULL WELL* MR. SNELLING CAN'T DO WITHOUT HIS POX MEDICINE!
BUT--
NOW, DAISY!
STUPID DELIVERIES...

"THE WHEEL OF FORTUNE"

BY BENJAMIN DICKSON AND RACHAEL SMITH

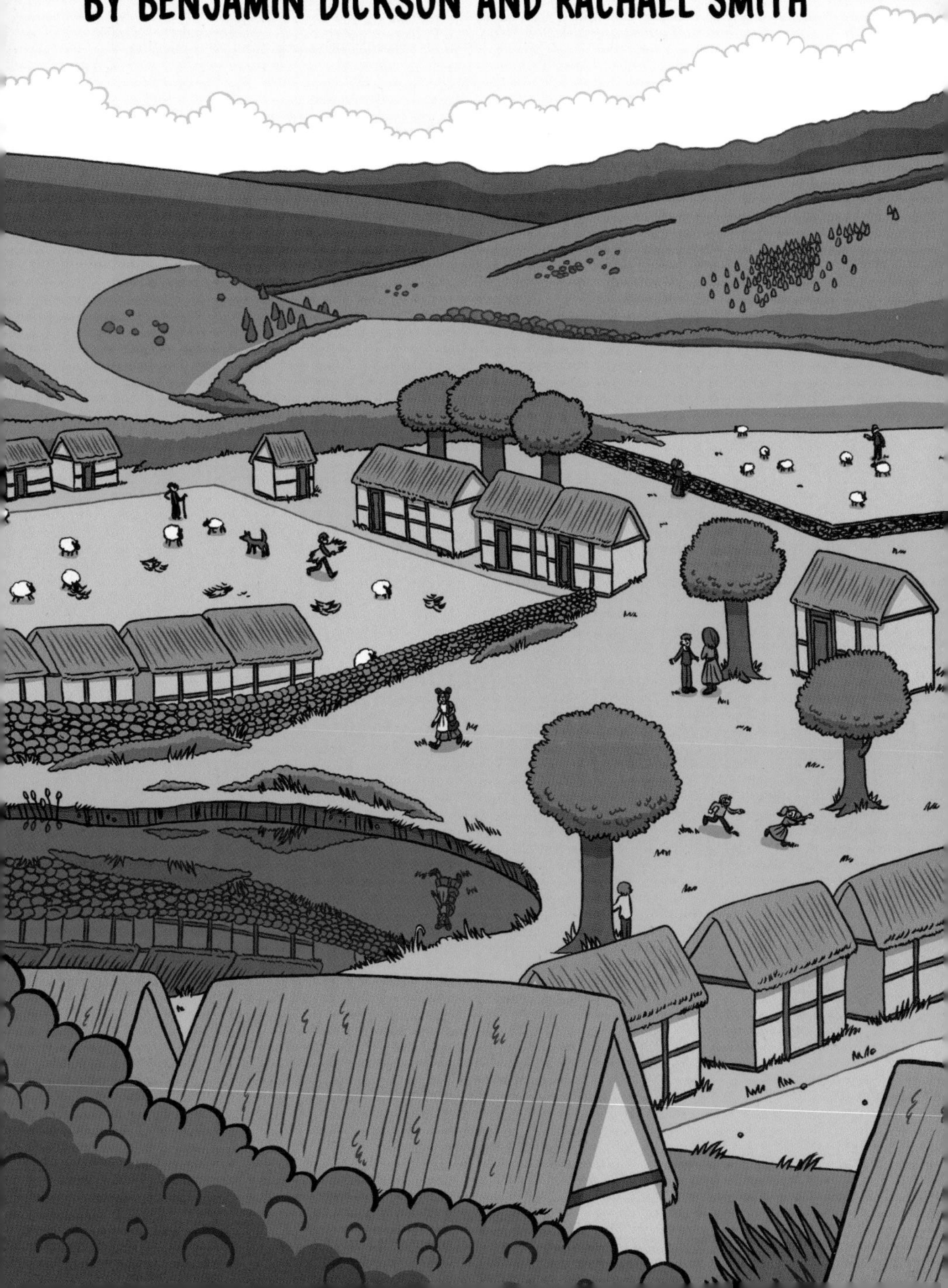

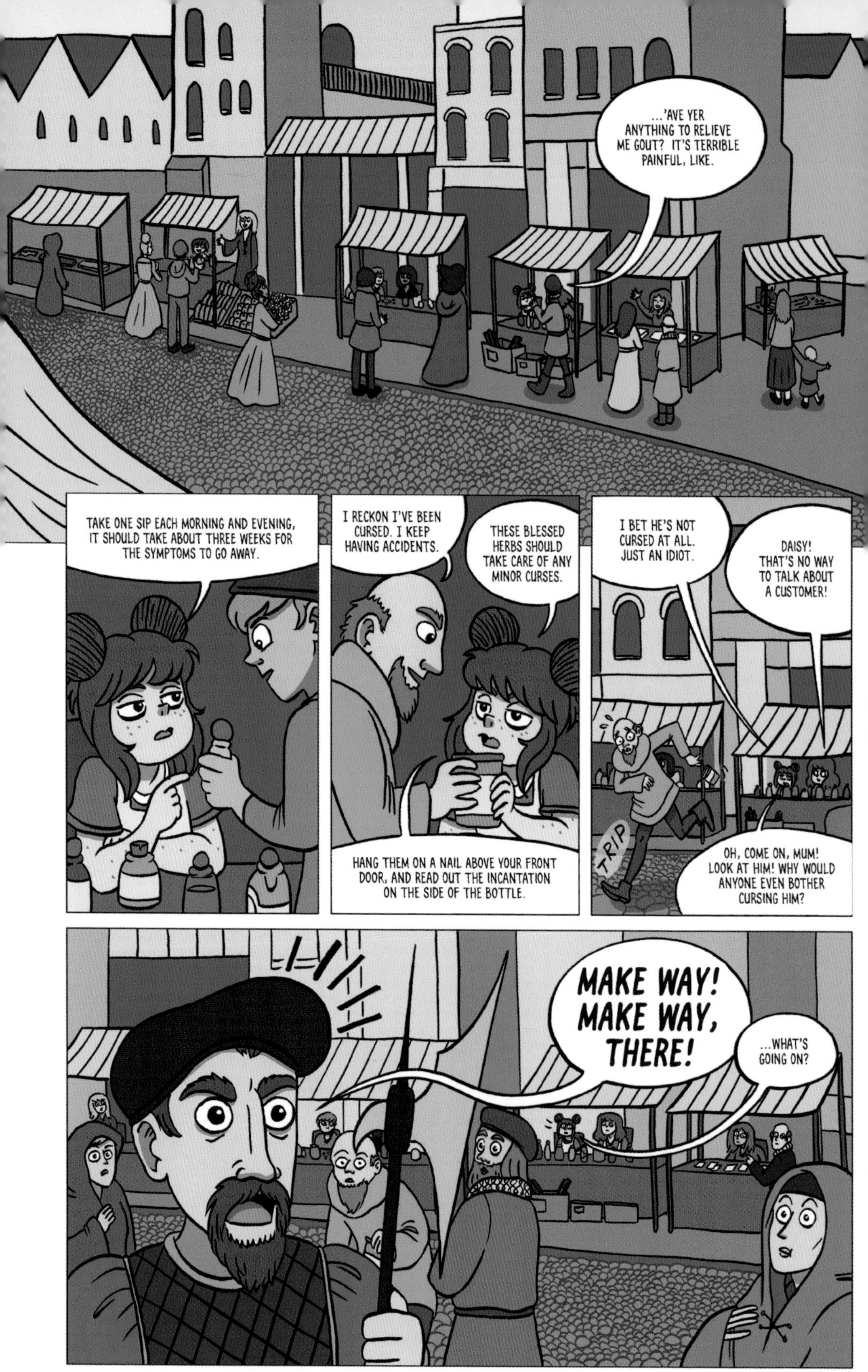
...'AVE YER ANYTHING TO RELIEVE ME GOUT? IT'S TERRIBLE PAINFUL, LIKE.
TAKE ONE SIP EACH MORNING AND EVENING, IT SHOULD TAKE ABOUT THREE WEEKS FOR THE SYMPTOMS TO GO AWAY.
I RECKON I'VE BEEN CURSED. I KEEP HAVING ACCIDENTS.
THESE BLESSED HERBS SHOULD TAKE CARE OF ANY MINOR CURSES.
HANG THEM ON A NAIL ABOVE YOUR FRONT DOOR, AND READ OUT THE INCANTATION ON THE SIDE OF THE BOTTLE.
I BET HE'S NOT CURSED AT ALL. JUST AN IDIOT.
DAISY! THAT'S NO WAY TO TALK ABOUT A CUSTOMER!
TRIP
OH, COME ON, MUM! LOOK AT HIM! WHY WOULD ANYONE EVEN BOTHER CURSING HIM?
MAKE WAY! MAKE WAY, THERE!
...WHAT'S GOING ON?

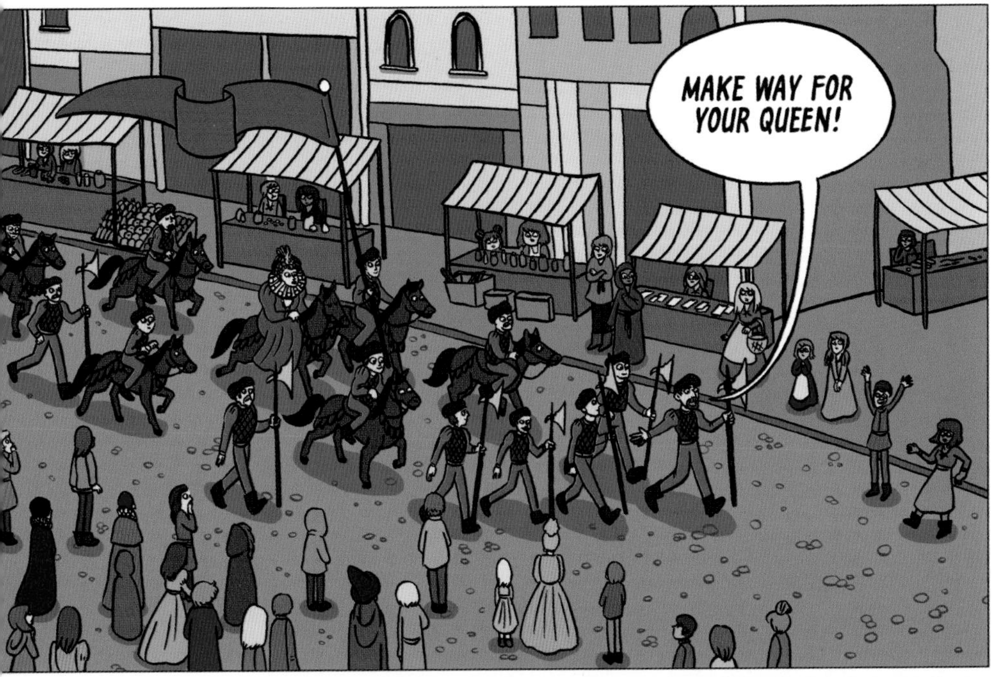
MAKE WAY FOR YOUR QUEEN!

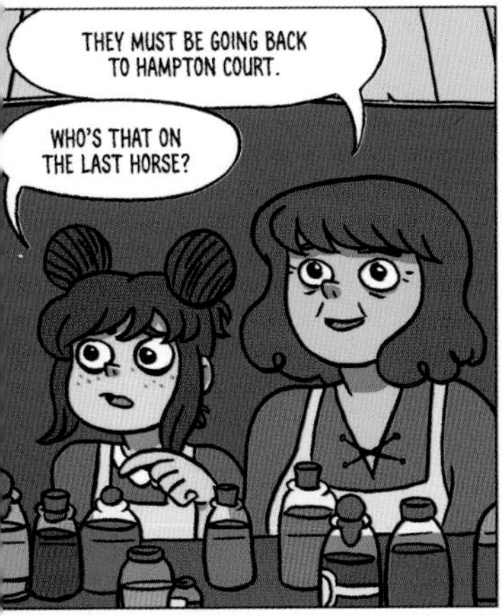
THEY MUST BE GOING BACK TO HAMPTON COURT.
WHO'S THAT ON THE LAST HORSE?

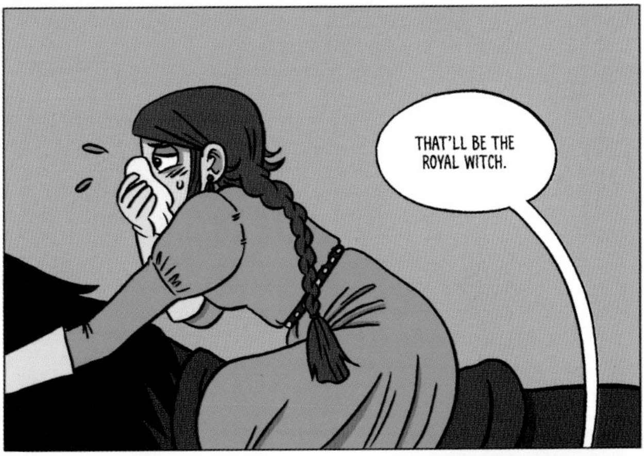
THAT'LL BE THE ROYAL WITCH.

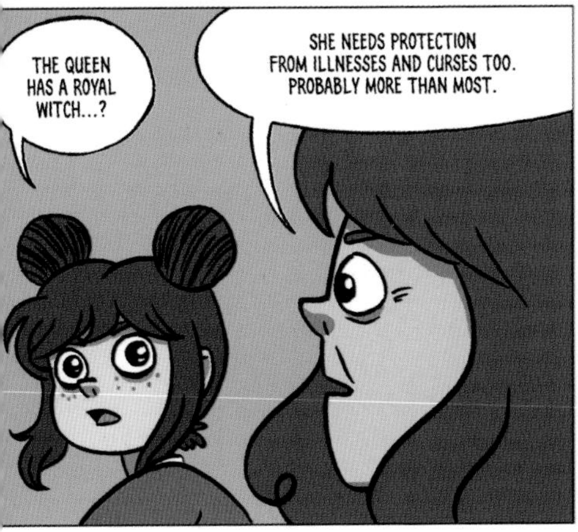
THE QUEEN HAS A ROYAL WITCH...?
SHE NEEDS PROTECTION FROM ILLNESSES AND CURSES TOO. PROBABLY MORE THAN MOST.

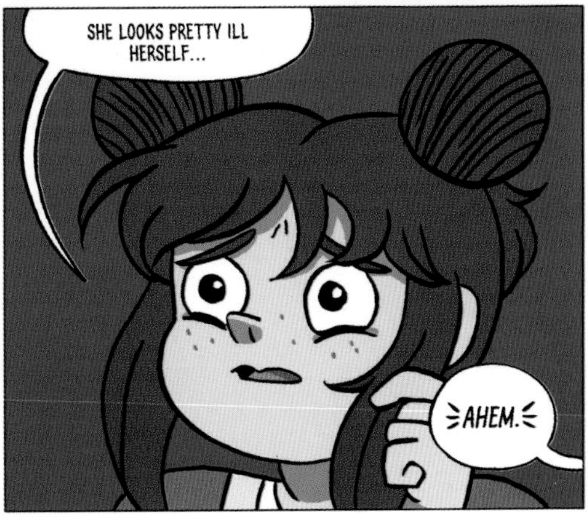
SHE LOOKS PRETTY ILL HERSELF...
AHEM.

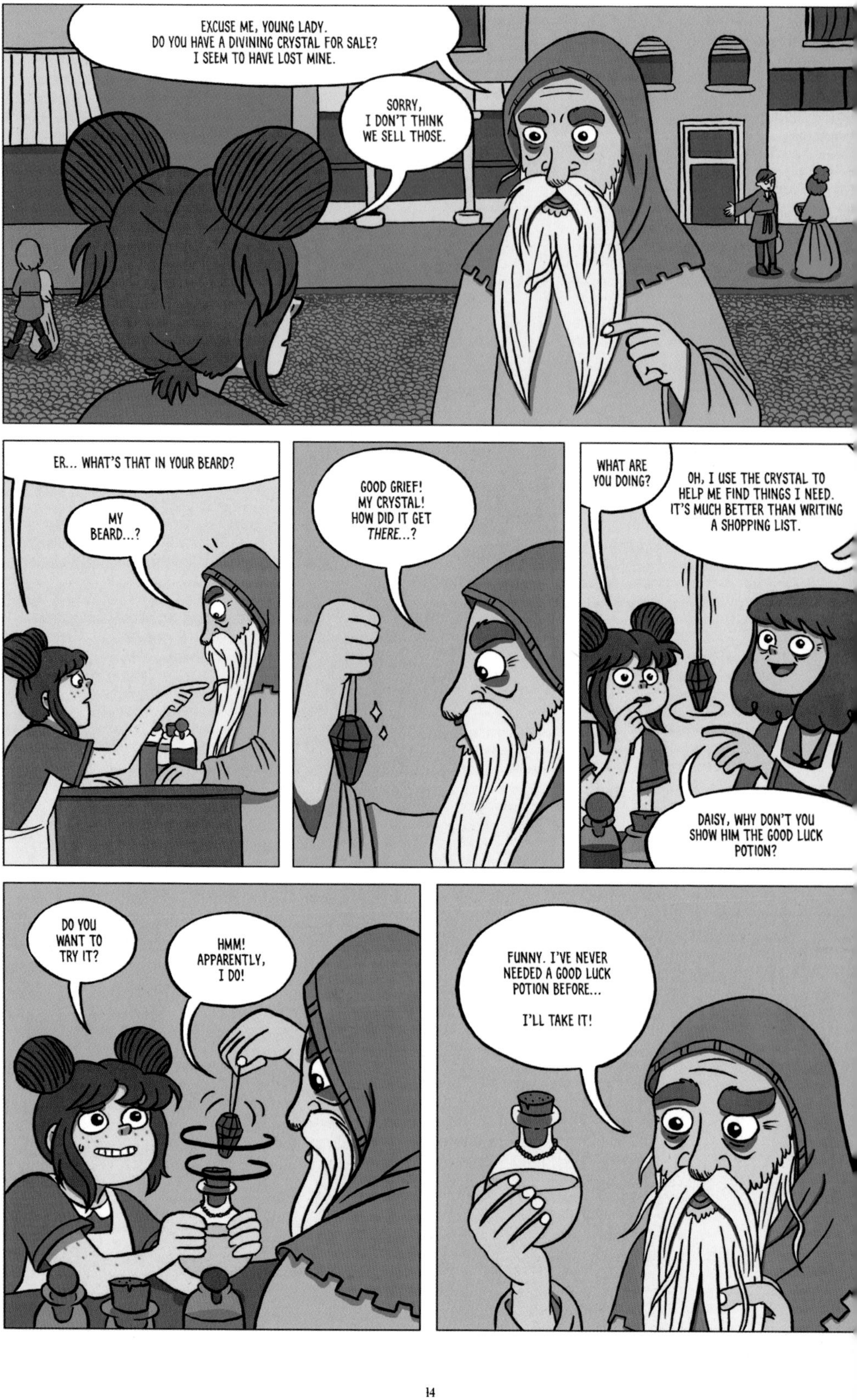
EXCUSE ME, YOUNG LADY. DO YOU HAVE A DIVINING CRYSTAL FOR SALE? I SEEM TO HAVE LOST MINE.
SORRY, I DON'T THINK WE SELL THOSE.
ER... WHAT'S THAT IN YOUR BEARD?
MY BEARD...?
GOOD GRIEF! MY CRYSTAL! HOW DID IT GET *THERE*...?
WHAT ARE YOU DOING?
OH, I USE THE CRYSTAL TO HELP ME FIND THINGS I NEED. IT'S MUCH BETTER THAN WRITING A SHOPPING LIST.
DAISY, WHY DON'T YOU SHOW HIM THE GOOD LUCK POTION?
DO YOU WANT TO TRY IT?
HMM! APPARENTLY, I DO!
FUNNY. I'VE NEVER NEEDED A GOOD LUCK POTION BEFORE...
I'LL TAKE IT!

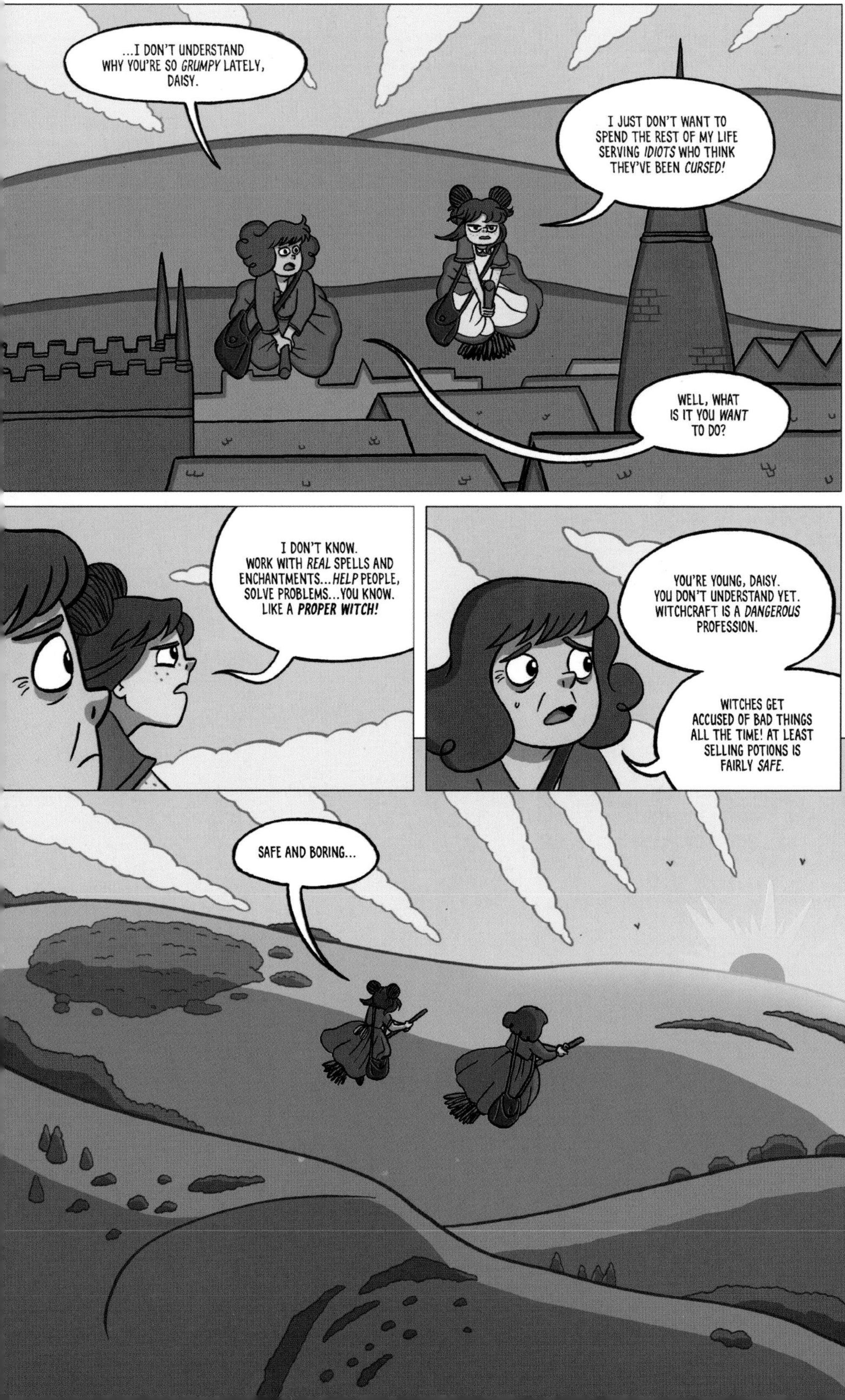
...I DON'T UNDERSTAND WHY YOU'RE SO *GRUMPY* LATELY, DAISY.
I JUST DON'T WANT TO SPEND THE REST OF MY LIFE SERVING *IDIOTS* WHO THINK THEY'VE BEEN *CURSED!*
WELL, WHAT IS IT YOU *WANT* TO DO?
I DON'T KNOW. WORK WITH *REAL* SPELLS AND ENCHANTMENTS...*HELP* PEOPLE, SOLVE PROBLEMS...YOU KNOW. LIKE A ***PROPER WITCH!***
YOU'RE YOUNG, DAISY. YOU DON'T UNDERSTAND YET. WITCHCRAFT IS A *DANGEROUS* PROFESSION.
WITCHES GET ACCUSED OF BAD THINGS ALL THE TIME! AT LEAST SELLING POTIONS IS FAIRLY *SAFE*.
SAFE AND BORING...

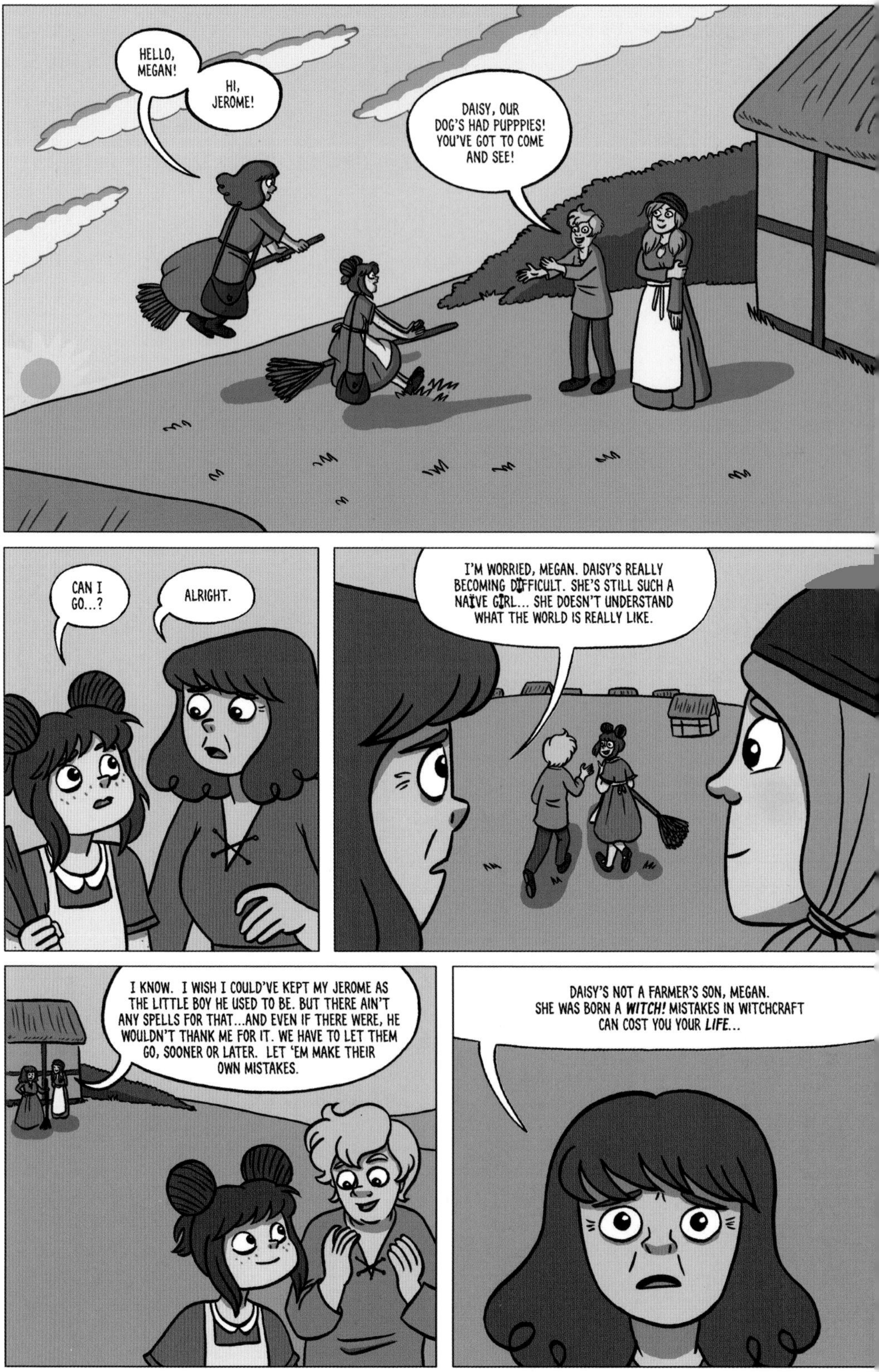

HELLO, MEGAN!
HI, JEROME!
DAISY, OUR DOG'S HAD PUPPPIES! YOU'VE GOT TO COME AND SEE!
CAN I GO...?
ALRIGHT.
I'M WORRIED, MEGAN. DAISY'S REALLY BECOMING DIFFICULT. SHE'S STILL SUCH A NAÏVE GIRL... SHE DOESN'T UNDERSTAND WHAT THE WORLD IS REALLY LIKE.
I KNOW. I WISH I COULD'VE KEPT MY JEROME AS THE LITTLE BOY HE USED TO BE. BUT THERE AIN'T ANY SPELLS FOR THAT...AND EVEN IF THERE WERE, HE WOULDN'T THANK ME FOR IT. WE HAVE TO LET THEM GO, SOONER OR LATER. LET 'EM MAKE THEIR OWN MISTAKES.
DAISY'S NOT A FARMER'S SON, MEGAN. SHE WAS BORN A *WITCH!* MISTAKES IN WITCHCRAFT CAN COST YOU YOUR *LIFE*...

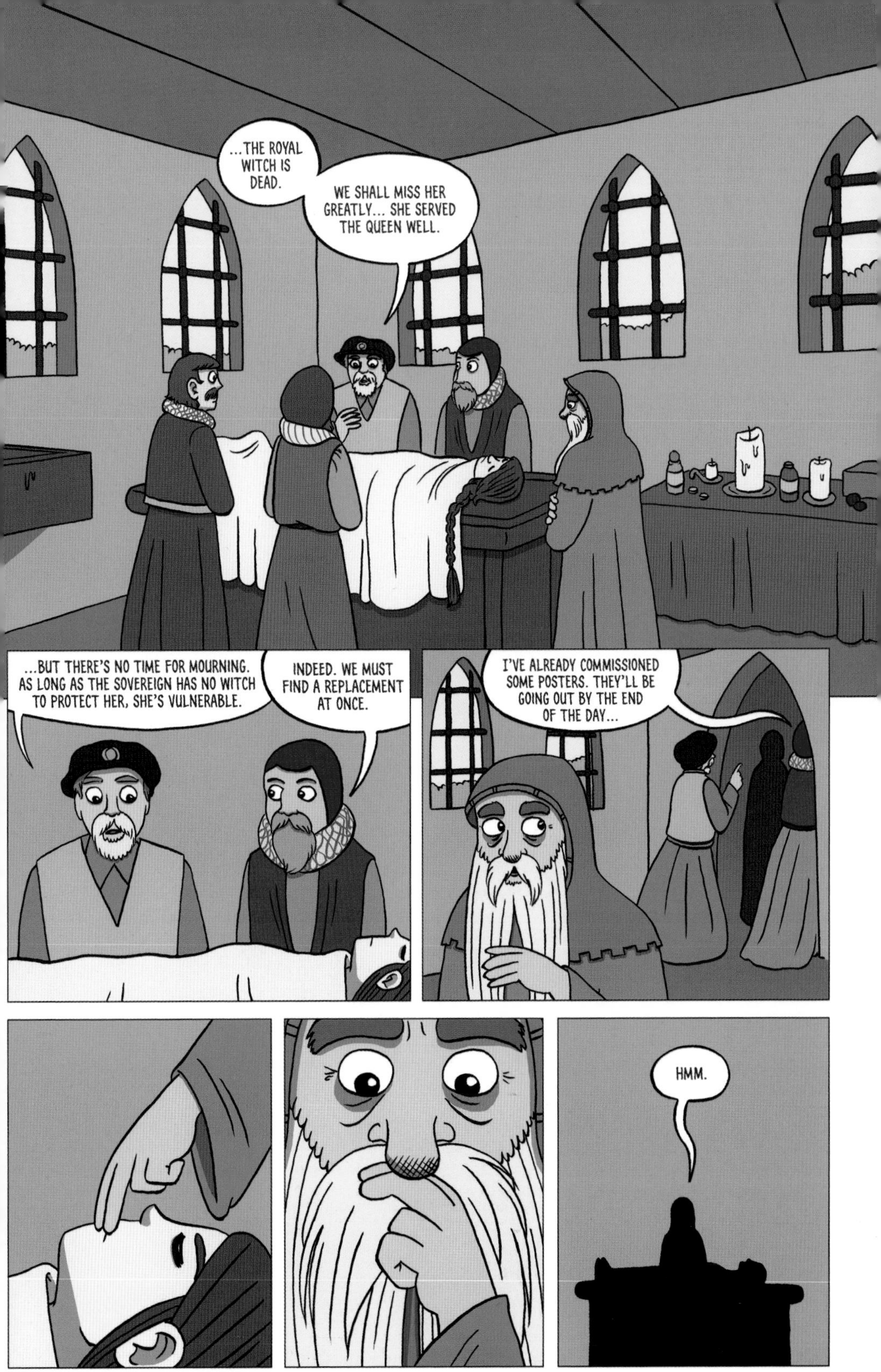
...THE ROYAL WITCH IS DEAD.
WE SHALL MISS HER GREATLY... SHE SERVED THE QUEEN WELL.
...BUT THERE'S NO TIME FOR MOURNING. AS LONG AS THE SOVEREIGN HAS NO WITCH TO PROTECT HER, SHE'S VULNERABLE.
INDEED. WE MUST FIND A REPLACEMENT AT ONCE.
I'VE ALREADY COMMISSIONED SOME POSTERS. THEY'LL BE GOING OUT BY THE END OF THE DAY...
HMM.

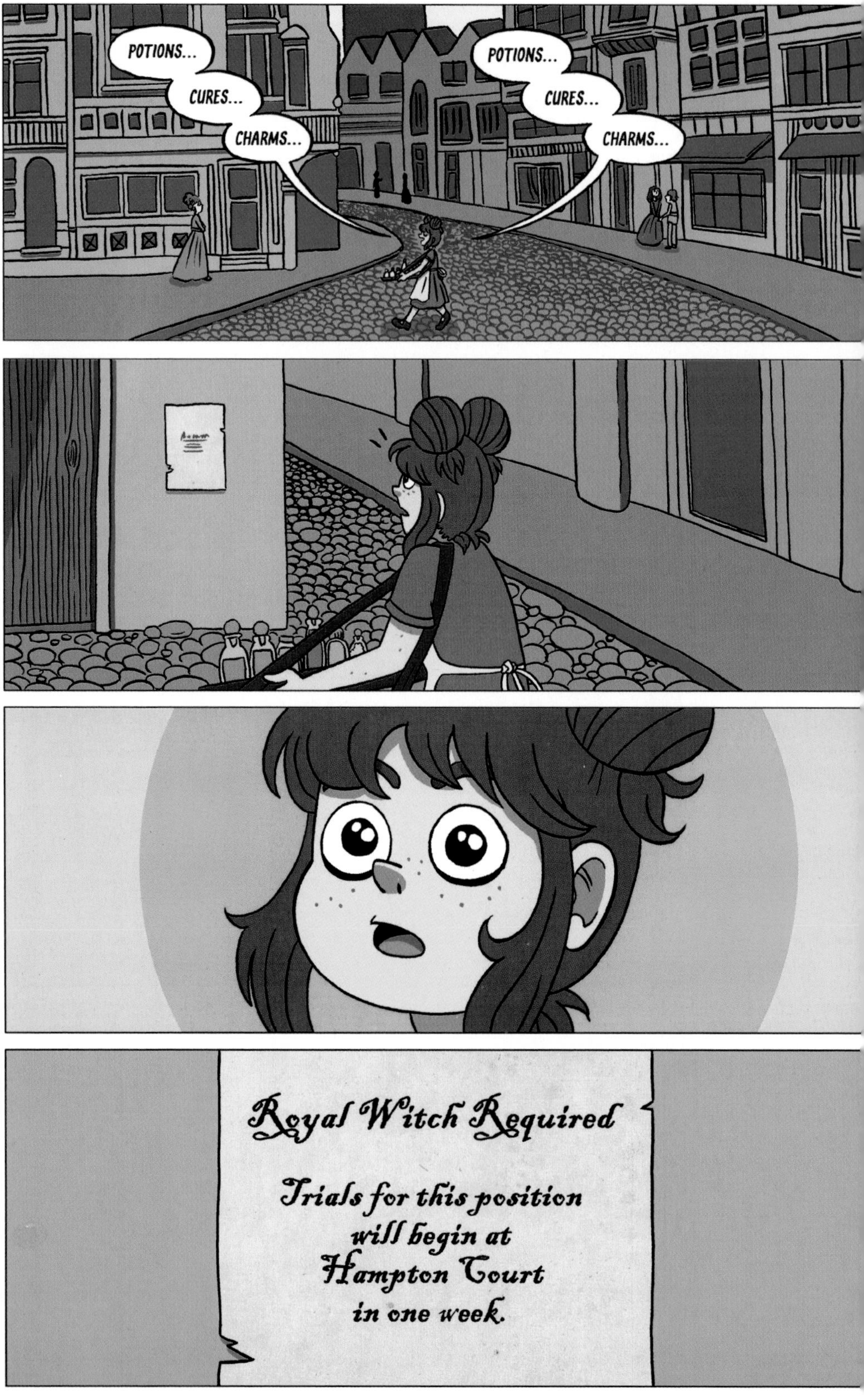
POTIONS...
CURES...
CHARMS...
POTIONS...
CURES...
CHARMS...
Royal Witch Required
Trials for this position will begin at Hampton Court in one week.

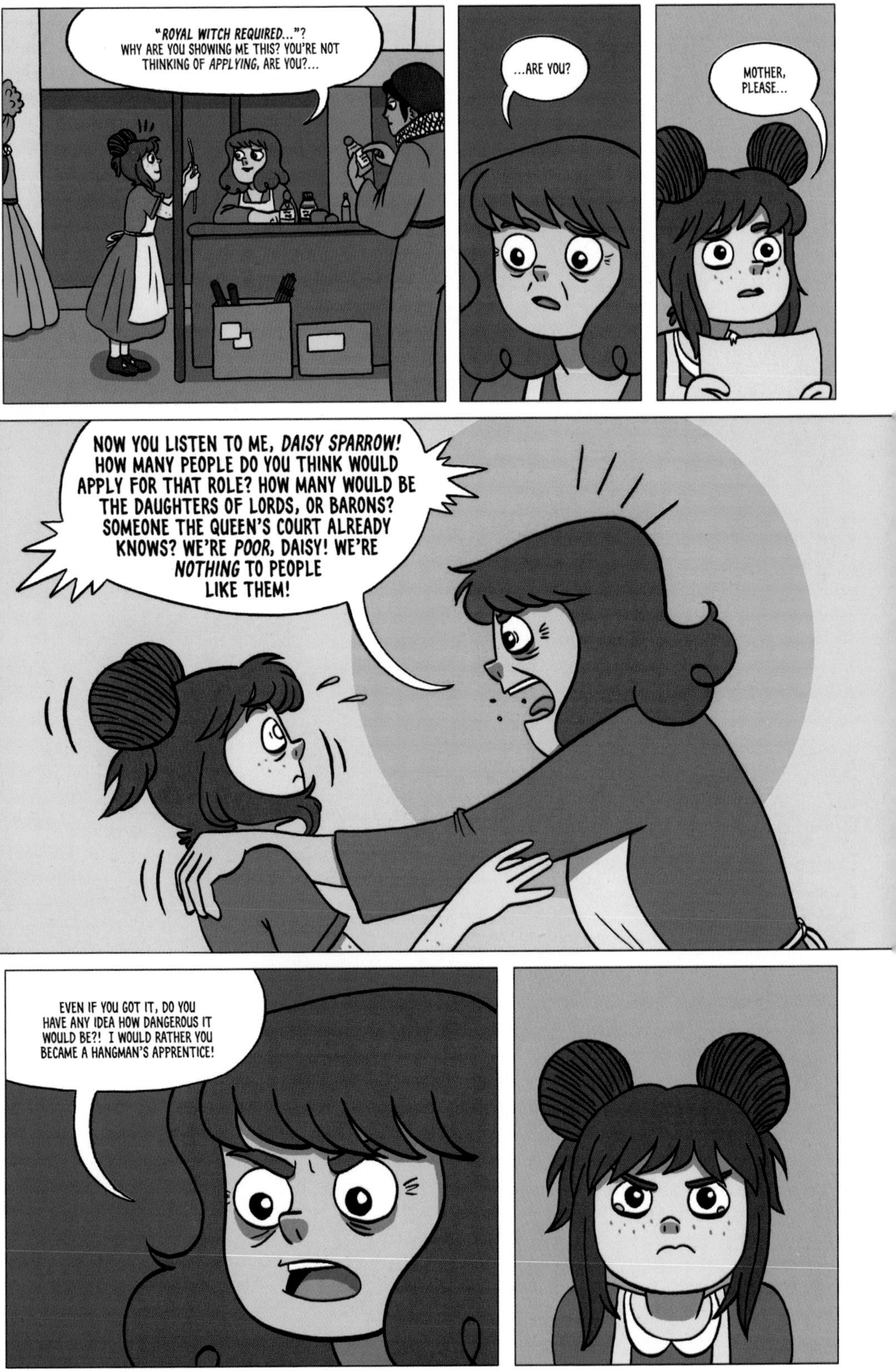
"ROYAL WITCH REQUIRED..."? WHY ARE YOU SHOWING ME THIS? YOU'RE NOT THINKING OF APPLYING, ARE YOU?...
...ARE YOU?
MOTHER, PLEASE...
NOW YOU LISTEN TO ME, DAISY SPARROW! HOW MANY PEOPLE DO YOU THINK WOULD APPLY FOR THAT ROLE? HOW MANY WOULD BE THE DAUGHTERS OF LORDS, OR BARONS? SOMEONE THE QUEEN'S COURT ALREADY KNOWS? WE'RE POOR, DAISY! WE'RE NOTHING TO PEOPLE LIKE THEM!
EVEN IF YOU GOT IT, DO YOU HAVE ANY IDEA HOW DANGEROUS IT WOULD BE?! I WOULD RATHER YOU BECAME A HANGMAN'S APPRENTICE!

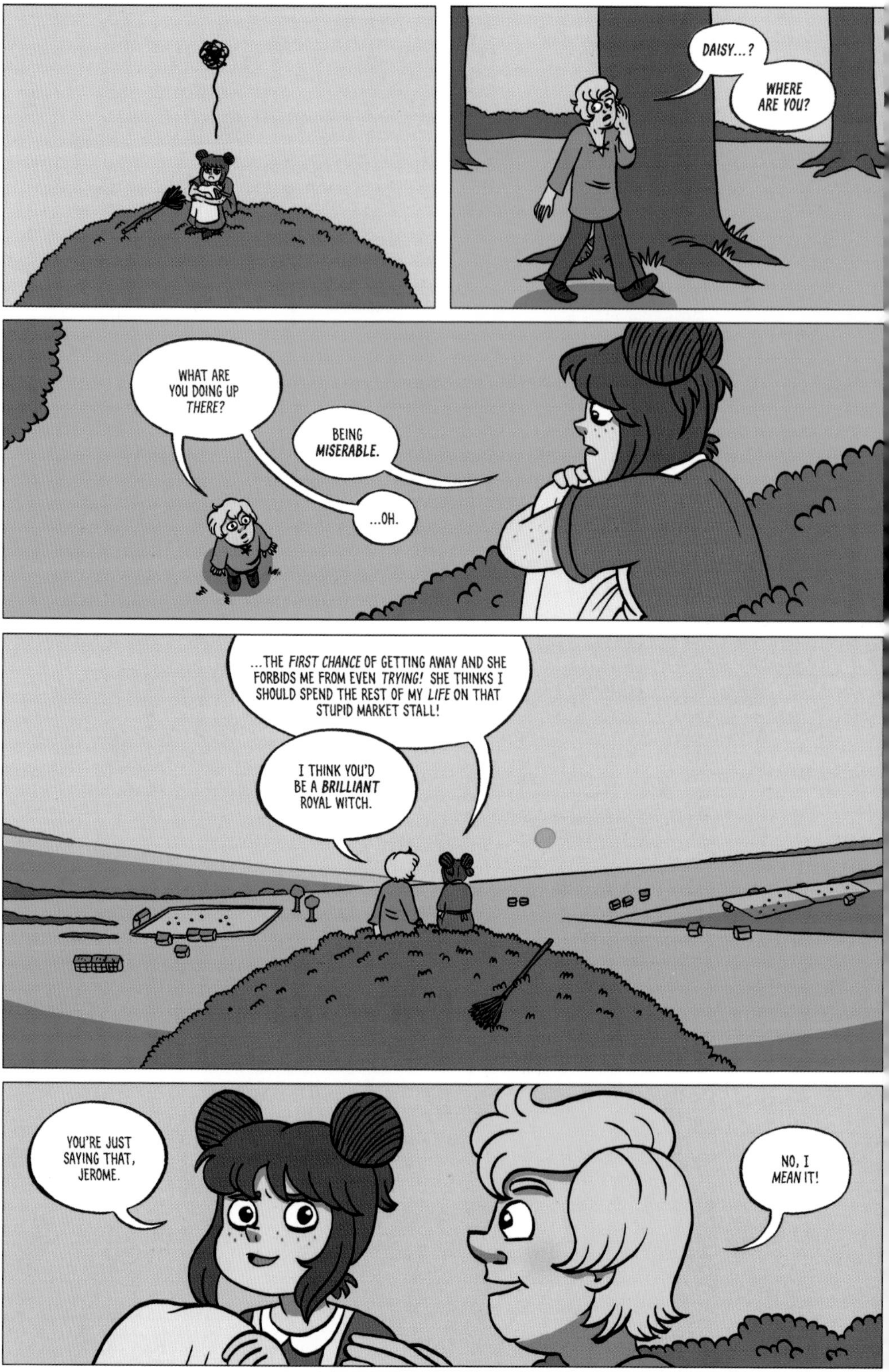
DAISY...?
WHERE ARE YOU?
WHAT ARE YOU DOING UP THERE?
BEING MISERABLE.
...OH.
...THE FIRST CHANCE OF GETTING AWAY AND SHE FORBIDS ME FROM EVEN TRYING! SHE THINKS I SHOULD SPEND THE REST OF MY LIFE ON THAT STUPID MARKET STALL!
I THINK YOU'D BE A BRILLIANT ROYAL WITCH.
YOU'RE JUST SAYING THAT, JEROME.
NO, I MEAN IT!

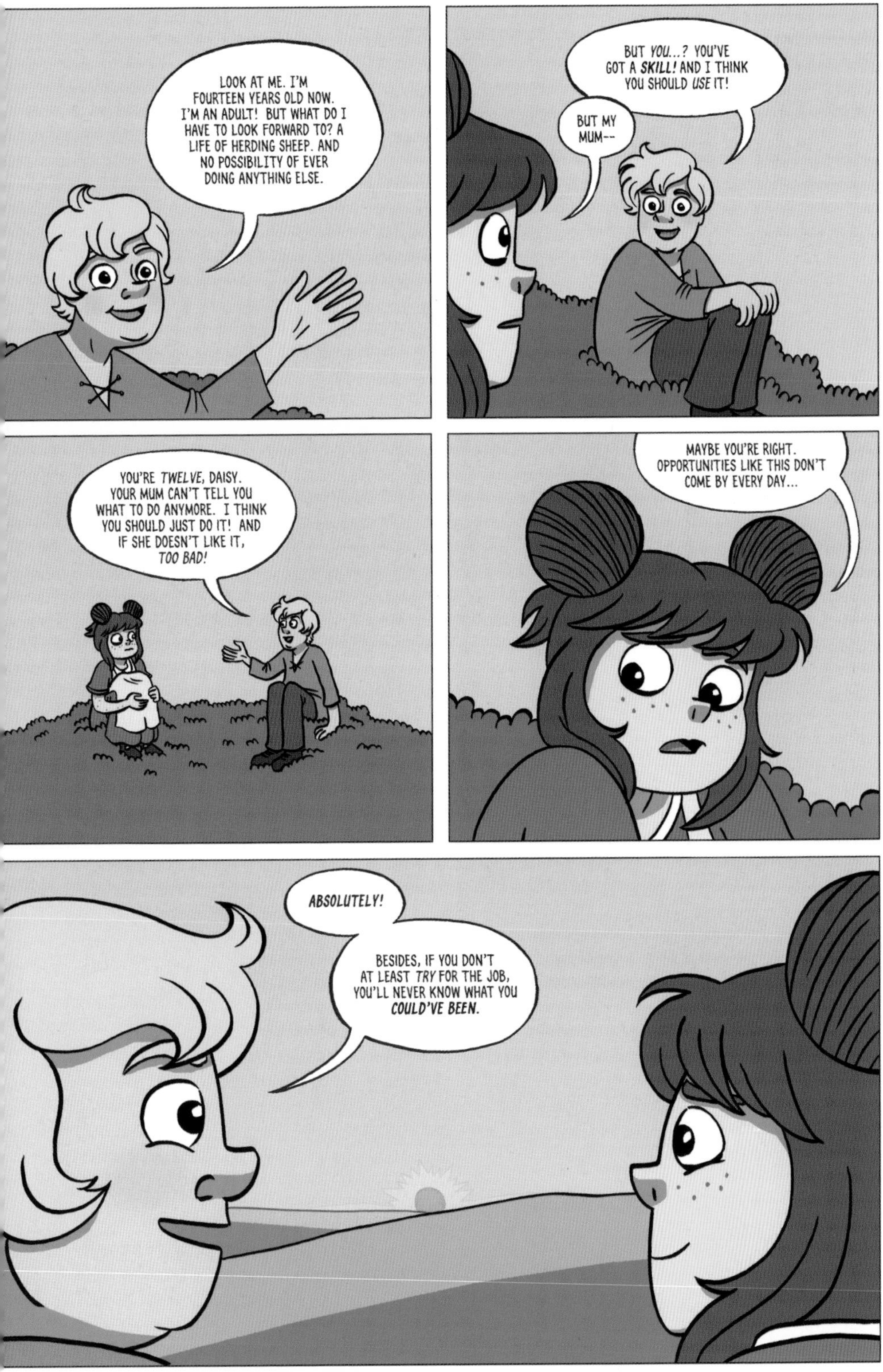
LOOK AT ME. I'M FOURTEEN YEARS OLD NOW. I'M AN ADULT! BUT WHAT DO I HAVE TO LOOK FORWARD TO? A LIFE OF HERDING SHEEP. AND NO POSSIBILITY OF EVER DOING ANYTHING ELSE.
BUT *YOU...?* YOU'VE GOT A ***SKILL!*** AND I THINK YOU SHOULD *USE* IT!
BUT MY MUM--
YOU'RE *TWELVE*, DAISY. YOUR MUM CAN'T TELL YOU WHAT TO DO ANYMORE. I THINK YOU SHOULD JUST DO IT! AND IF SHE DOESN'T LIKE IT, *TOO BAD!*
MAYBE YOU'RE RIGHT. OPPORTUNITIES LIKE THIS DON'T COME BY EVERY DAY...
ABSOLUTELY!
BESIDES, IF YOU DON'T AT LEAST *TRY* FOR THE JOB, YOU'LL NEVER KNOW WHAT YOU ***COULD'VE BEEN.***

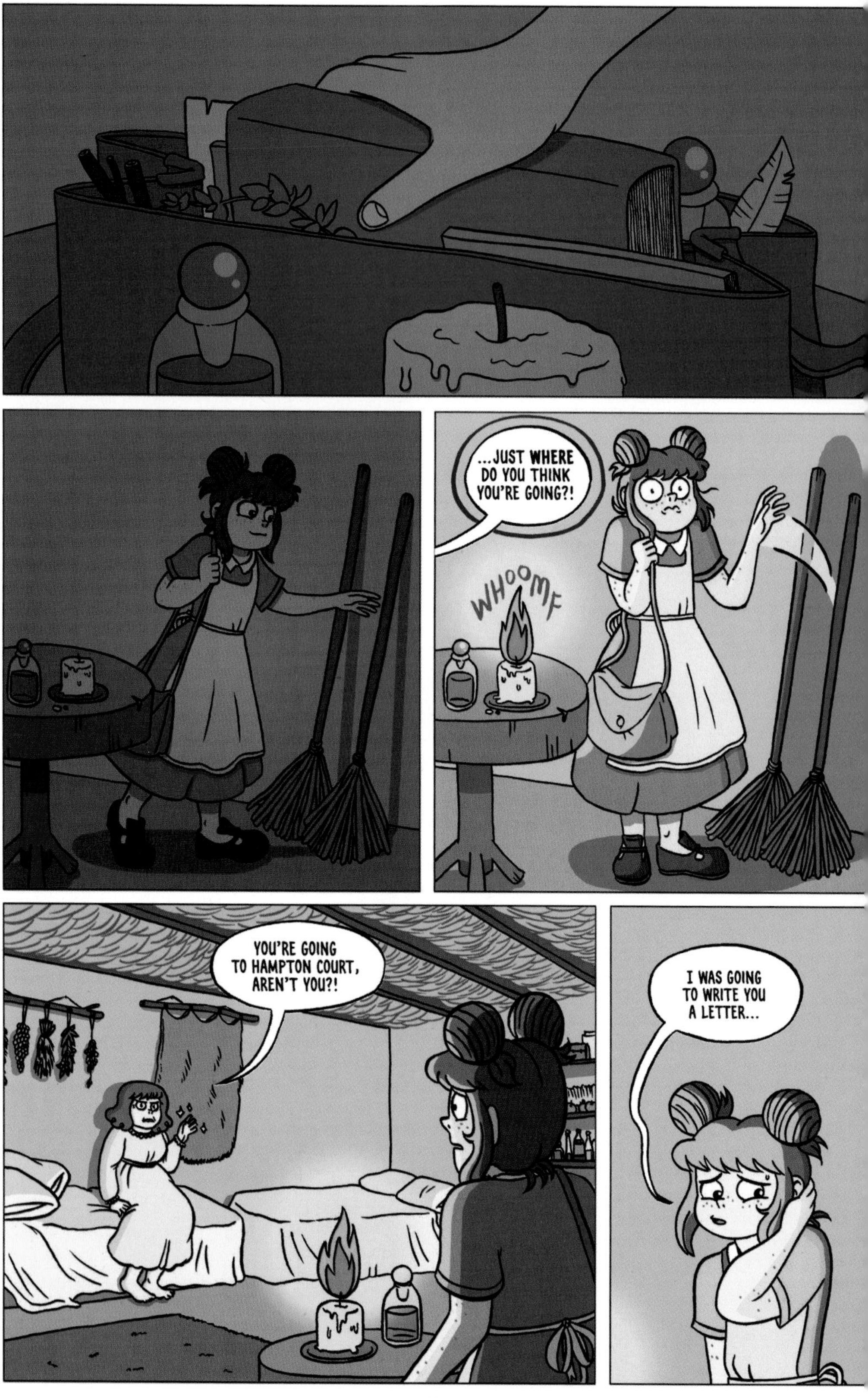
...JUST WHERE DO YOU THINK YOU'RE GOING?!
WHOOMF
YOU'RE GOING TO HAMPTON COURT, AREN'T YOU?!
I WAS GOING TO WRITE YOU A LETTER...

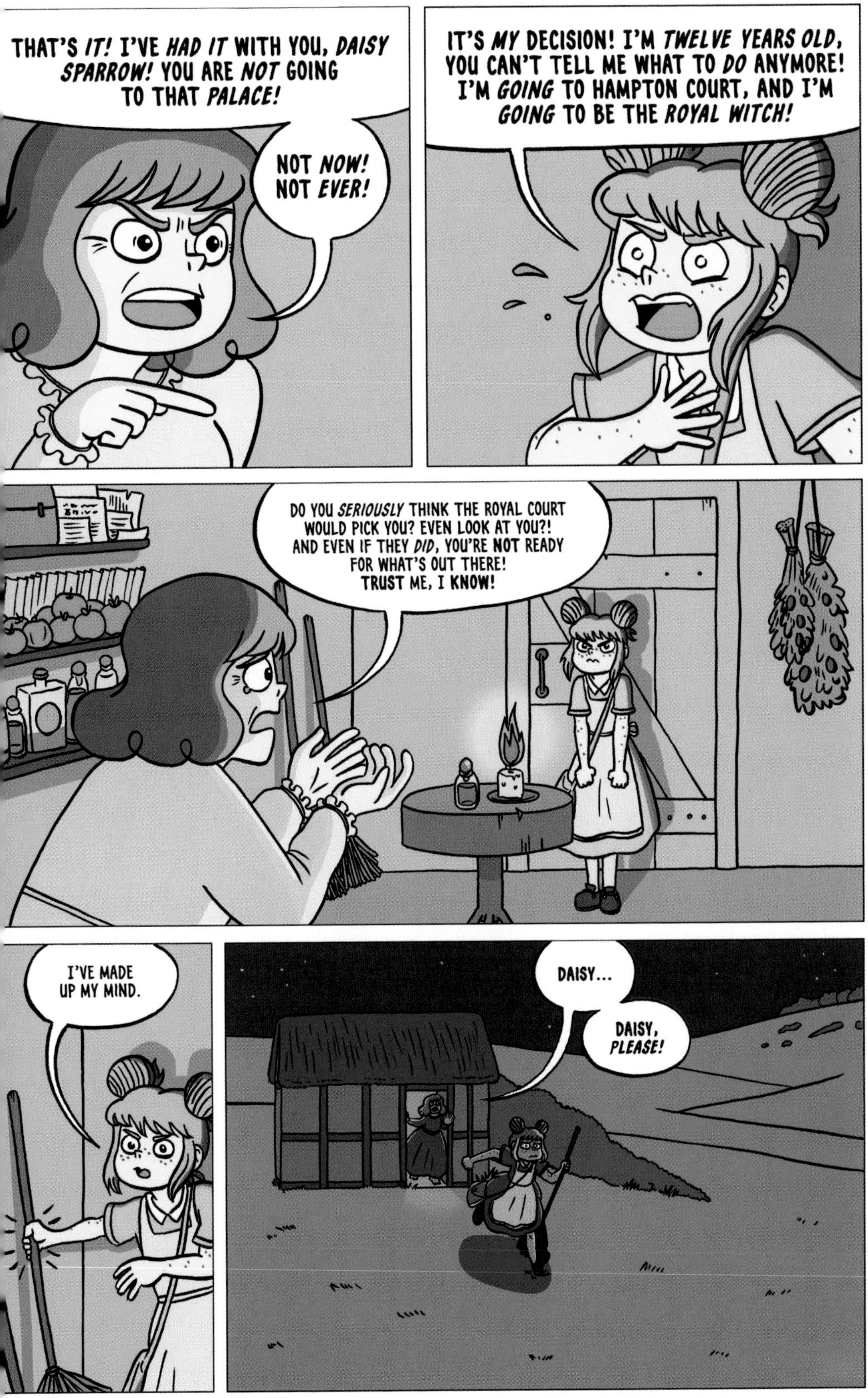
THAT'S *IT!* I'VE *HAD IT* WITH YOU, *DAISY SPARROW!* YOU ARE *NOT* GOING TO THAT *PALACE!*
NOT *NOW!* NOT *EVER!*
IT'S *MY* DECISION! I'M *TWELVE YEARS OLD*, YOU CAN'T TELL ME WHAT TO *DO* ANYMORE! I'M *GOING* TO HAMPTON COURT, AND I'M *GOING* TO BE THE *ROYAL WITCH!*
DO YOU *SERIOUSLY* THINK THE ROYAL COURT WOULD PICK YOU? EVEN LOOK AT YOU?! AND EVEN IF THEY *DID*, YOU'RE **NOT** READY FOR WHAT'S OUT THERE! **TRUST ME, I KNOW!**
I'VE MADE UP MY MIND.
DAISY...
DAISY, *PLEASE!*

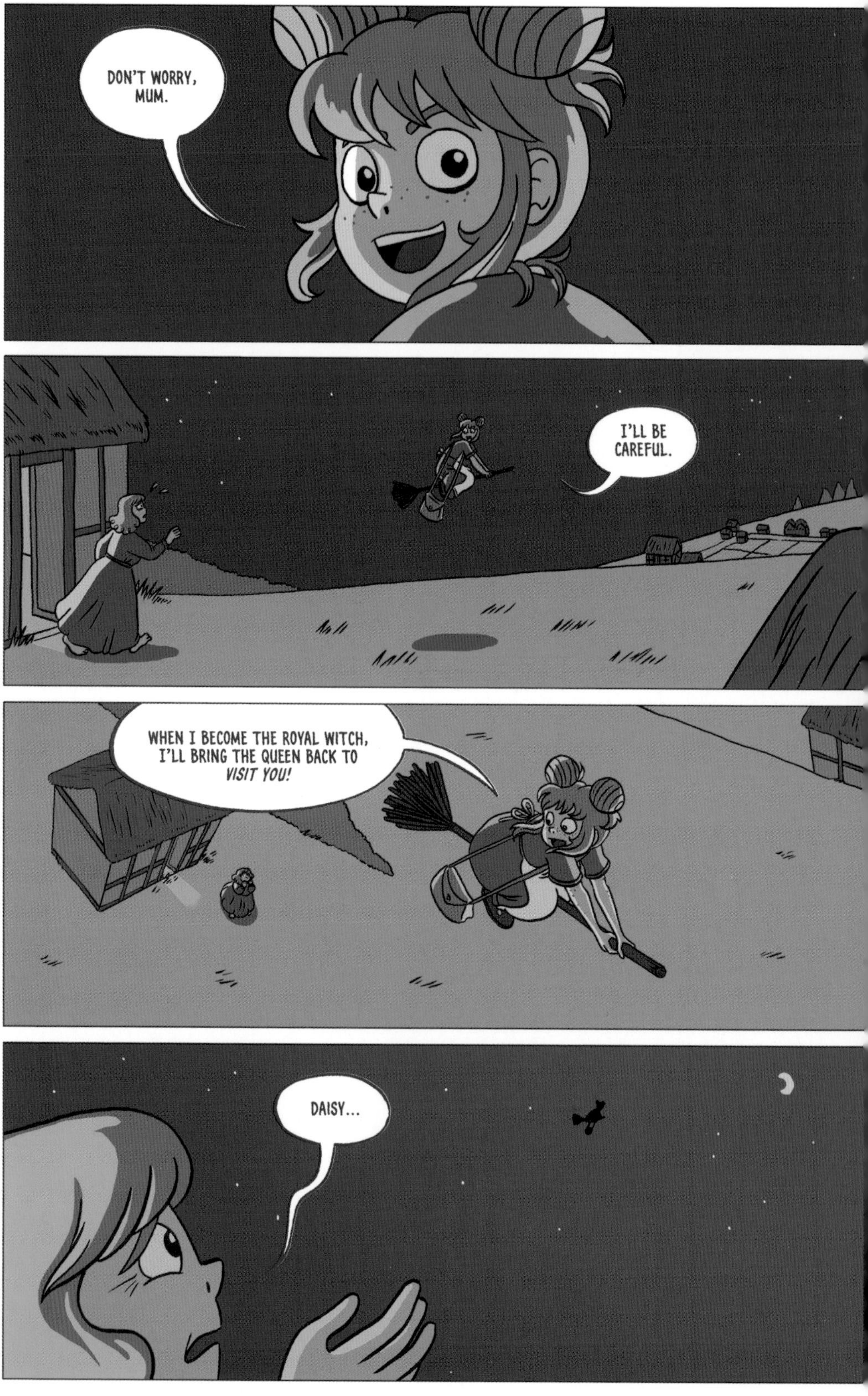
DON'T WORRY, MUM.
I'LL BE CAREFUL.
WHEN I BECOME THE ROYAL WITCH, I'LL BRING THE QUEEN BACK TO *VISIT YOU!*
DAISY...

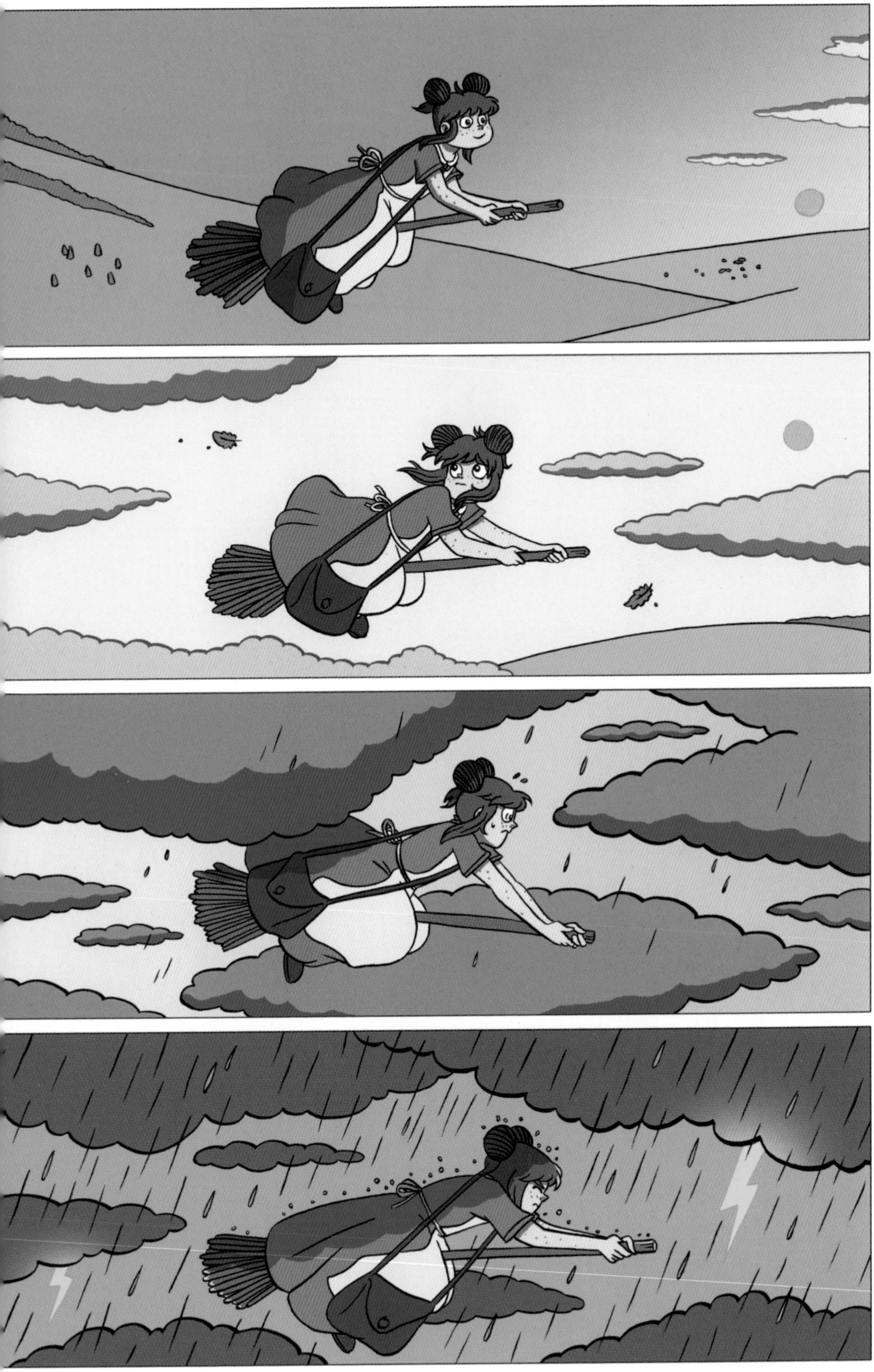

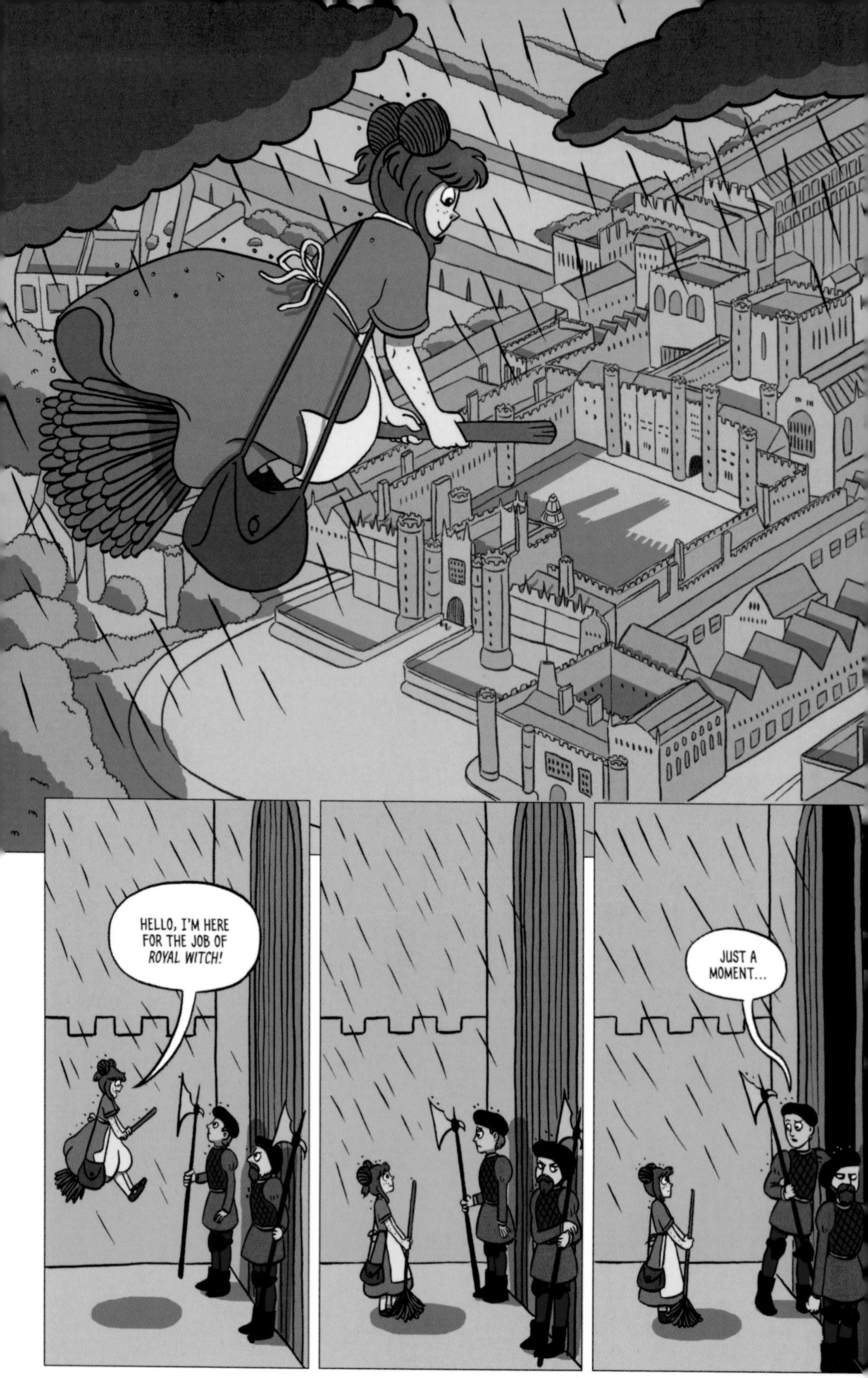
HELLO, I'M HERE FOR THE JOB OF *ROYAL WITCH!*
JUST A MOMENT...

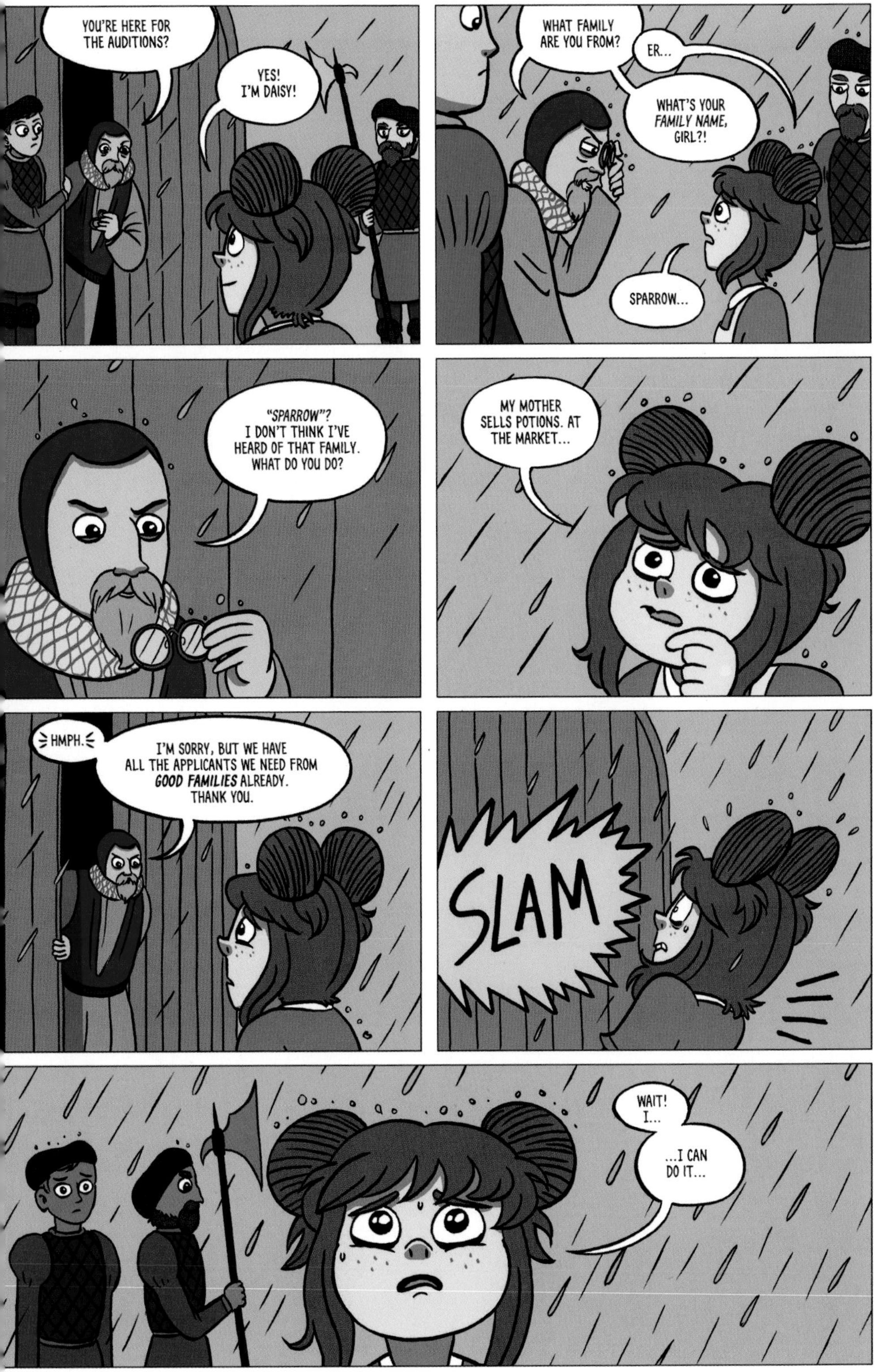
YOU'RE HERE FOR THE AUDITIONS?
YES! I'M DAISY!
WHAT FAMILY ARE YOU FROM?
ER...
WHAT'S YOUR *FAMILY NAME*, GIRL?!
SPARROW...
"SPARROW"? I DON'T THINK I'VE HEARD OF THAT FAMILY. WHAT DO YOU DO?
MY MOTHER SELLS POTIONS. AT THE MARKET...
HMPH.
I'M SORRY, BUT WE HAVE ALL THE APPLICANTS WE NEED FROM ***GOOD FAMILIES*** ALREADY. THANK YOU.
SLAM
WAIT! I...
...I CAN DO IT...

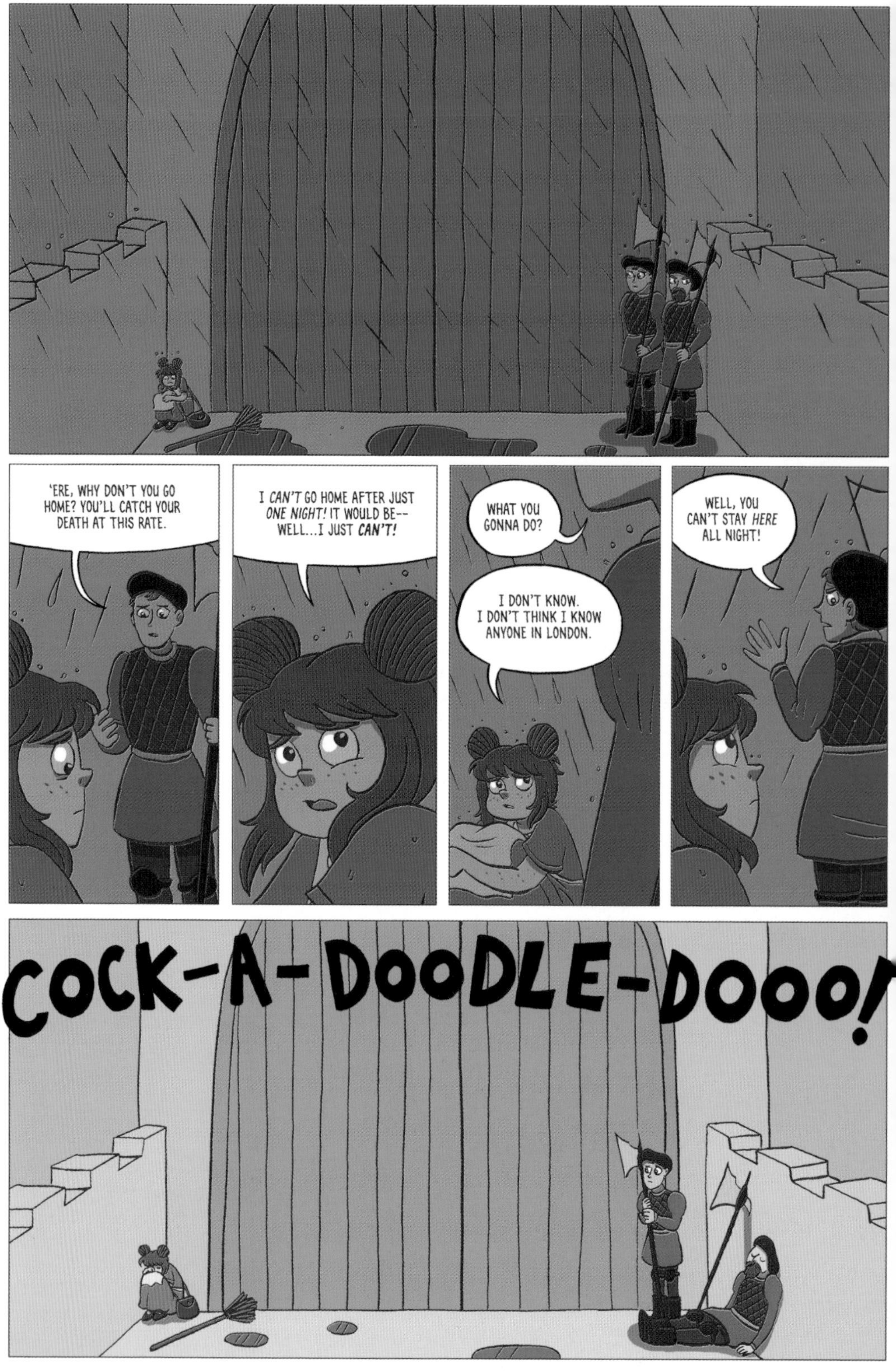
'ERE, WHY DON'T YOU GO HOME? YOU'LL CATCH YOUR DEATH AT THIS RATE.
I CAN'T GO HOME AFTER JUST ONE NIGHT! IT WOULD BE-- WELL...I JUST CAN'T!
WHAT YOU GONNA DO?
I DON'T KNOW. I DON'T THINK I KNOW ANYONE IN LONDON.
WELL, YOU CAN'T STAY HERE ALL NIGHT!
COCK-A-DOODLE-DOOO!

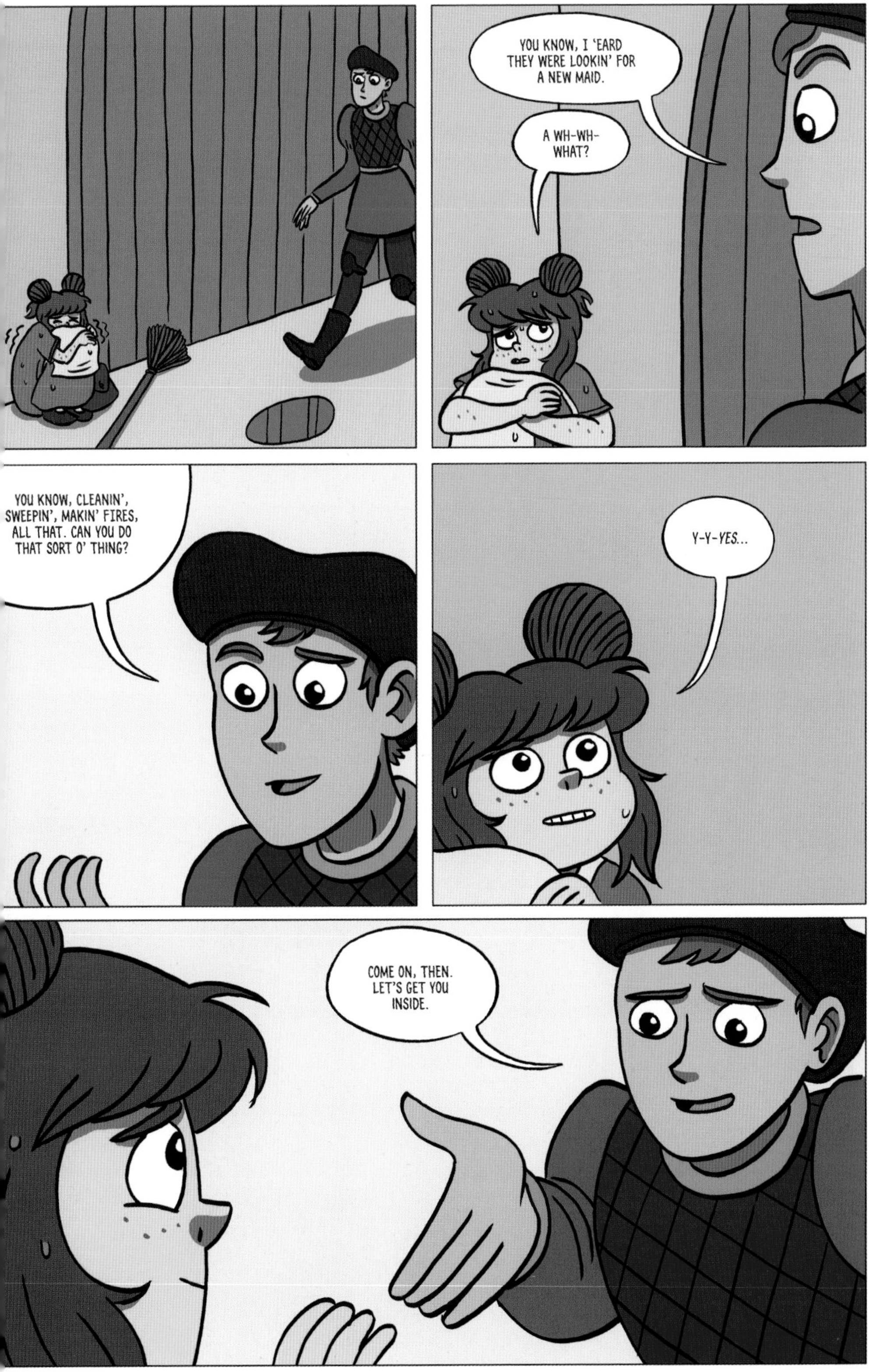
YOU KNOW, I 'EARD THEY WERE LOOKIN' FOR A NEW MAID.
A WH-WH-WHAT?
YOU KNOW, CLEANIN', SWEEPIN', MAKIN' FIRES, ALL THAT. CAN YOU DO THAT SORT O' THING?
Y-Y-*YES*...
COME ON, THEN. LET'S GET YOU INSIDE.

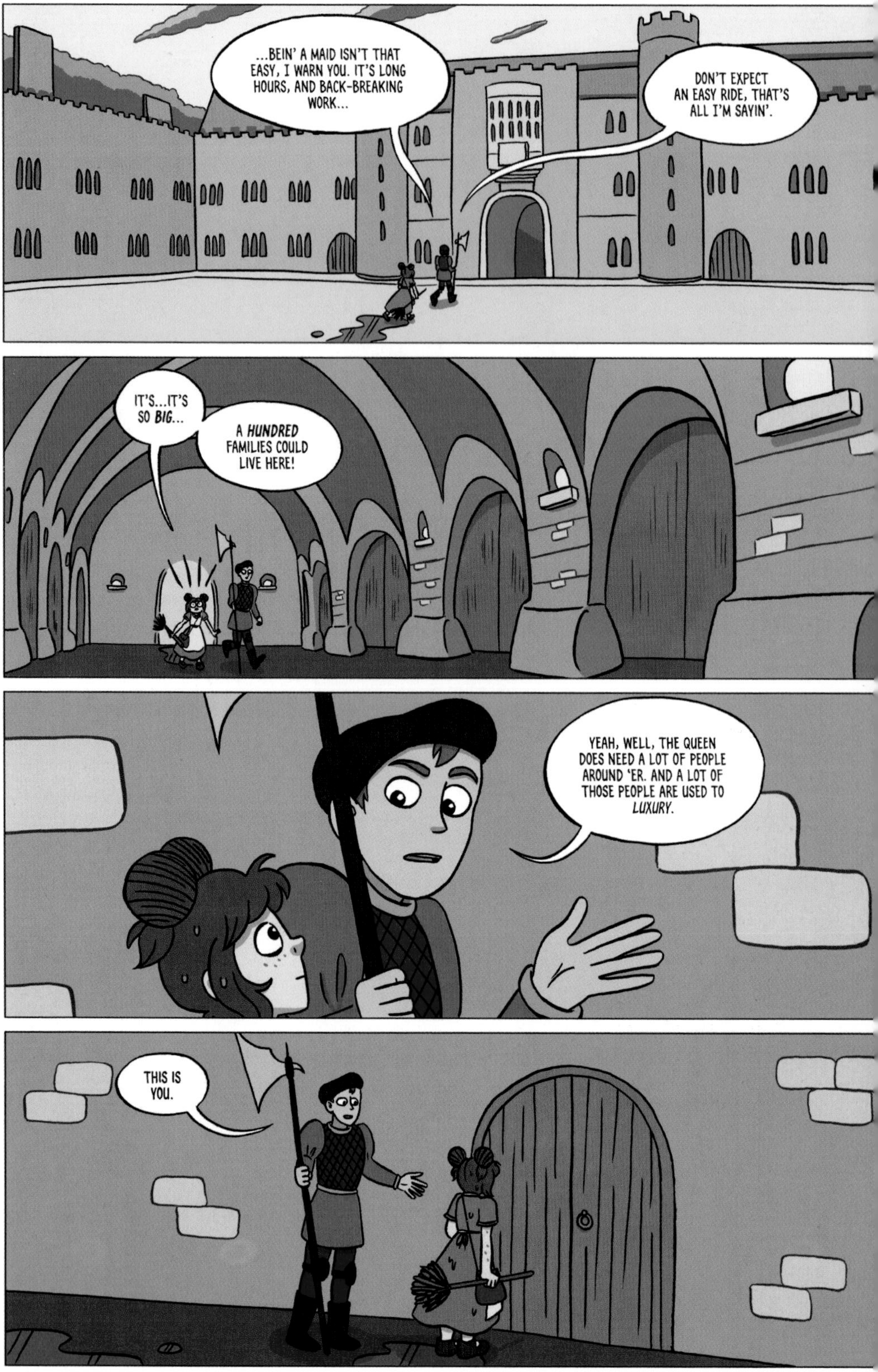
...BEIN' A MAID ISN'T THAT EASY, I WARN YOU. IT'S LONG HOURS, AND BACK-BREAKING WORK...
DON'T EXPECT AN EASY RIDE, THAT'S ALL I'M SAYIN'.
IT'S...IT'S SO *BIG*...
A ***HUNDRED*** FAMILIES COULD LIVE HERE!
YEAH, WELL, THE QUEEN DOES NEED A LOT OF PEOPLE AROUND 'ER. AND A LOT OF THOSE PEOPLE ARE USED TO *LUXURY*.
THIS IS YOU.

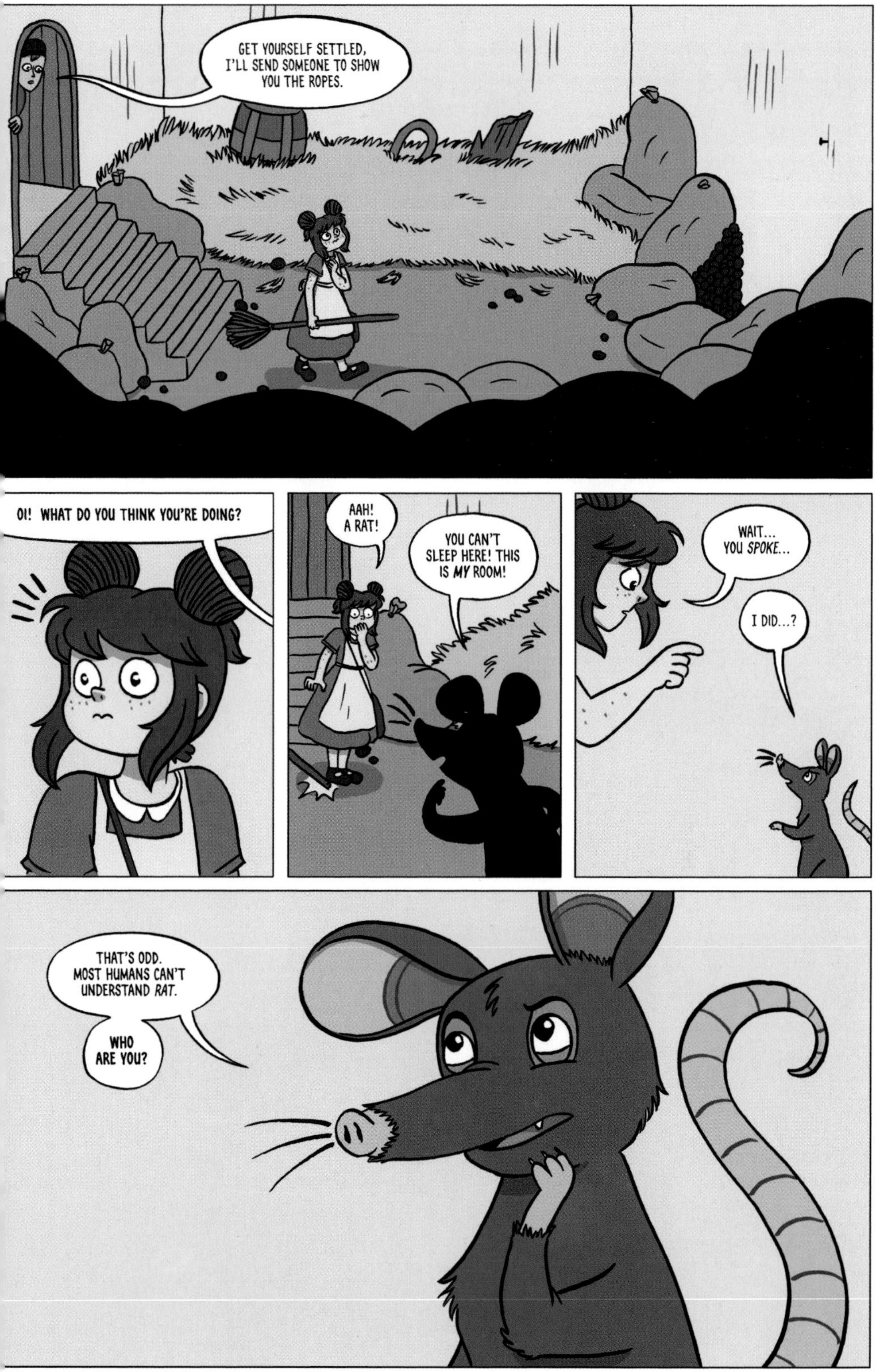
GET YOURSELF SETTLED, I'LL SEND SOMEONE TO SHOW YOU THE ROPES.
OI! WHAT DO YOU THINK YOU'RE DOING?
AAH! A RAT!
YOU CAN'T SLEEP HERE! THIS IS *MY* ROOM!
WAIT... YOU *SPOKE*...
I DID...?
THAT'S ODD. MOST HUMANS CAN'T UNDERSTAND *RAT*.
WHO ARE YOU?

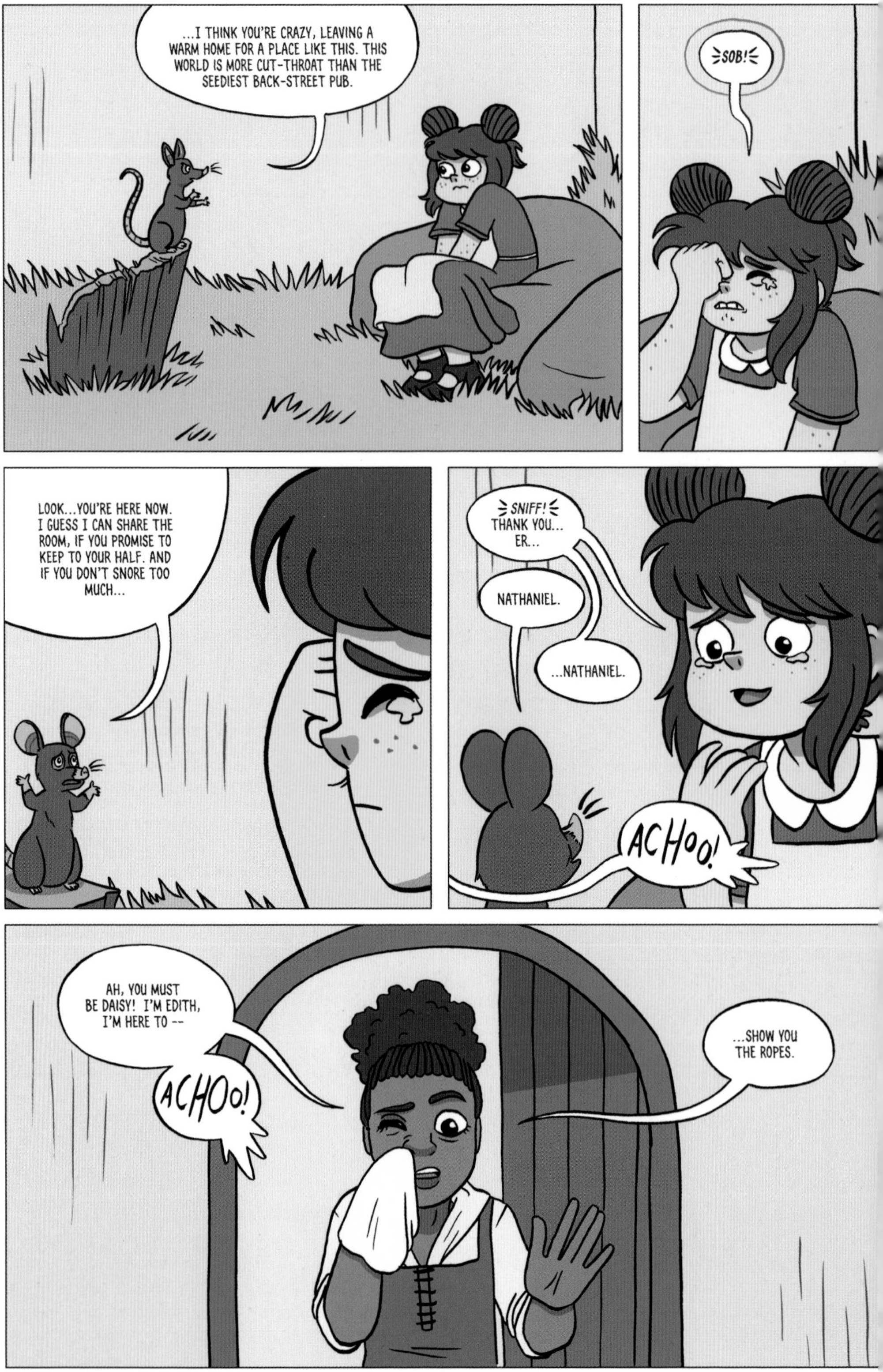
...I THINK YOU'RE CRAZY, LEAVING A WARM HOME FOR A PLACE LIKE THIS. THIS WORLD IS MORE CUT-THROAT THAN THE SEEDIEST BACK-STREET PUB.
SOB!
LOOK...YOU'RE HERE NOW. I GUESS I CAN SHARE THE ROOM, IF YOU PROMISE TO KEEP TO YOUR HALF. AND IF YOU DON'T SNORE TOO MUCH...
SNIFF! THANK YOU... ER...
NATHANIEL.
...NATHANIEL.
ACHOO!
AH, YOU MUST BE DAISY! I'M EDITH, I'M HERE TO --
ACHOO!
...SHOW YOU THE ROPES.

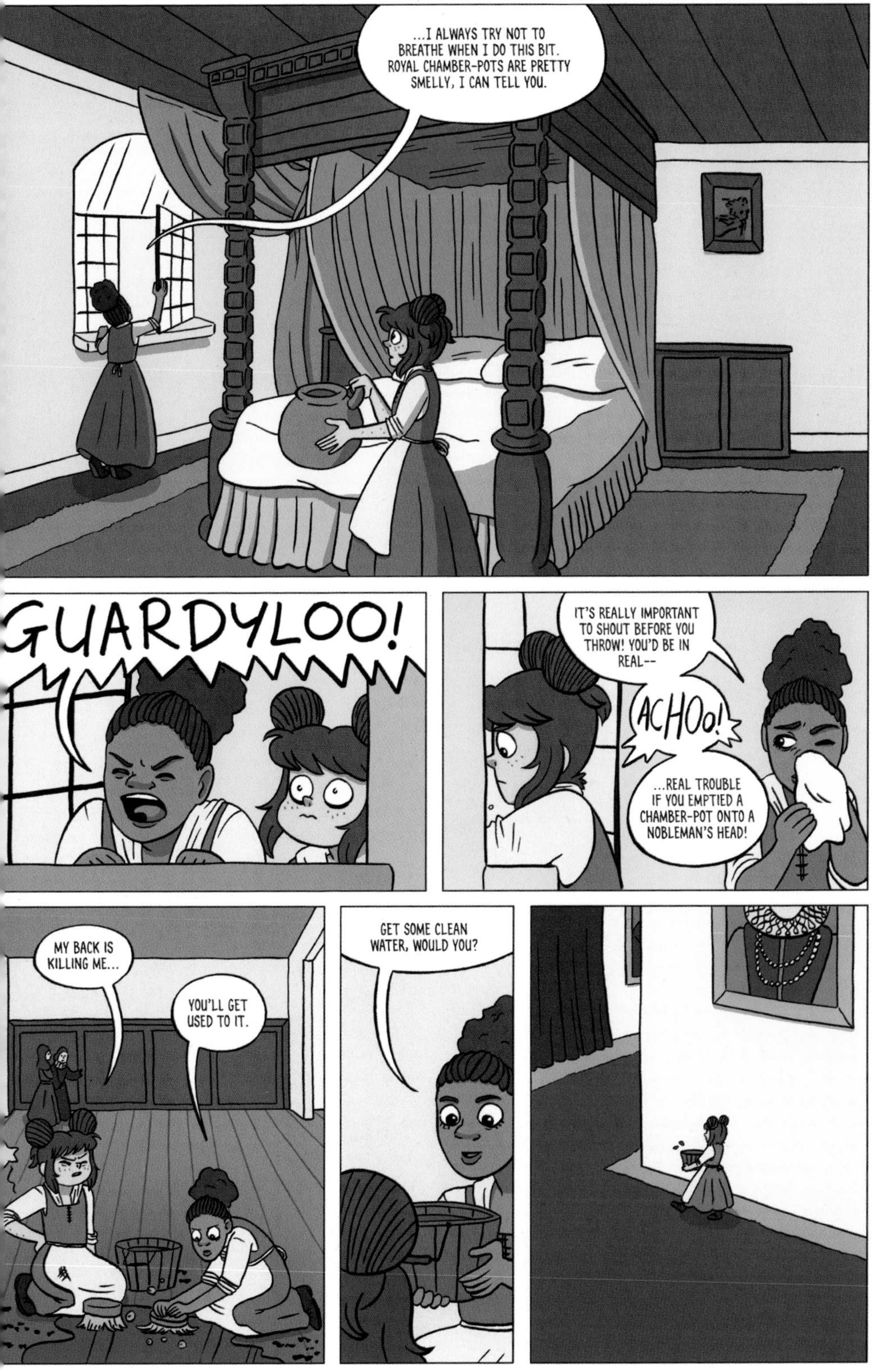
...I ALWAYS TRY NOT TO BREATHE WHEN I DO THIS BIT. ROYAL CHAMBER-POTS ARE PRETTY SMELLY, I CAN TELL YOU.
GUARDYLOO!
IT'S REALLY IMPORTANT TO SHOUT BEFORE YOU THROW! YOU'D BE IN REAL--
ACHOo!
...REAL TROUBLE IF YOU EMPTIED A CHAMBER-POT ONTO A NOBLEMAN'S HEAD!
MY BACK IS KILLING ME...
YOU'LL GET USED TO IT.
GET SOME CLEAN WATER, WOULD YOU?

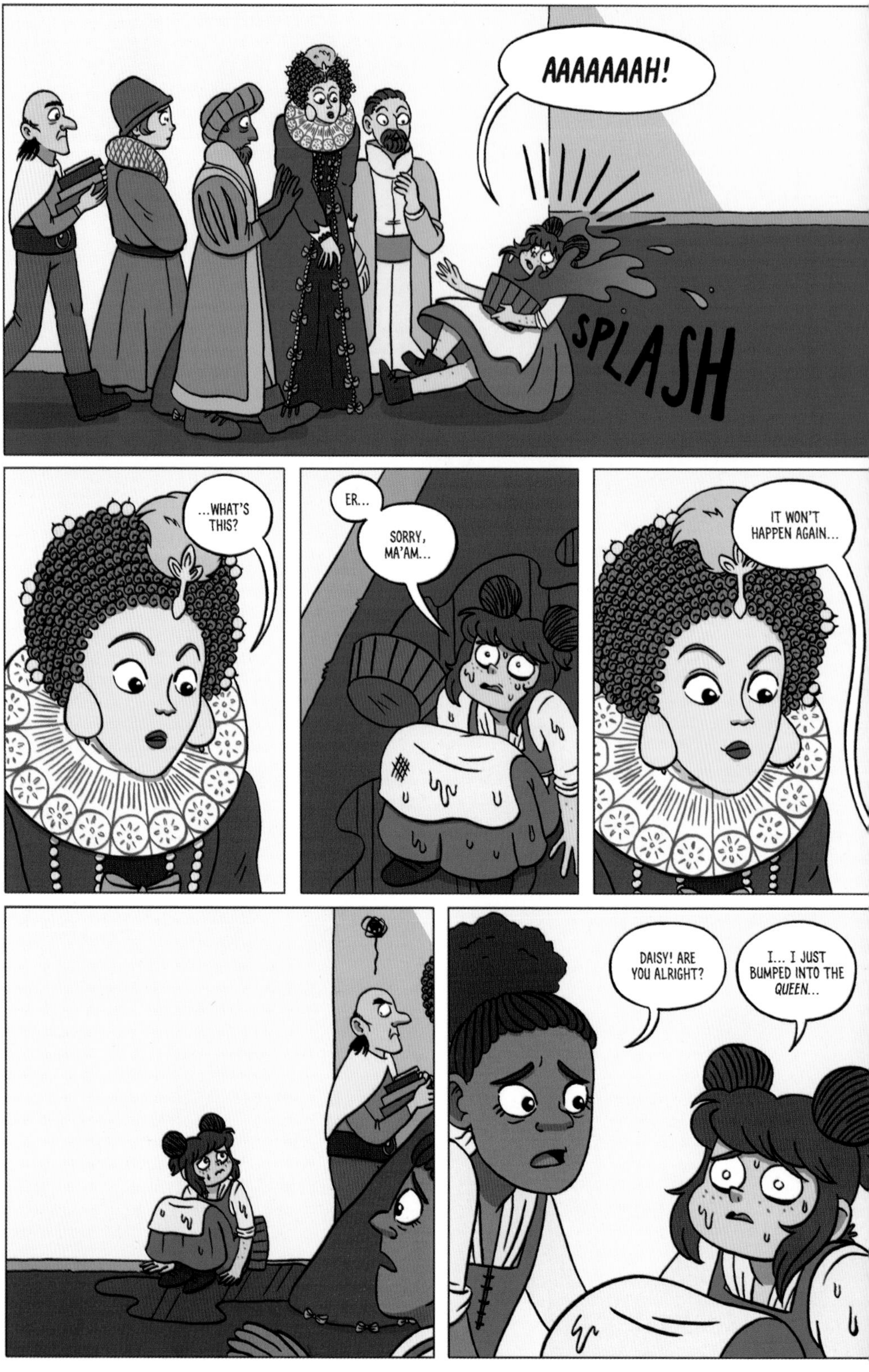
AAAAAAAH!
SPLASH
...WHAT'S THIS?
ER...
SORRY, MA'AM...
IT WON'T HAPPEN AGAIN...
DAISY! ARE YOU ALRIGHT?
I... I JUST BUMPED INTO THE *QUEEN*...

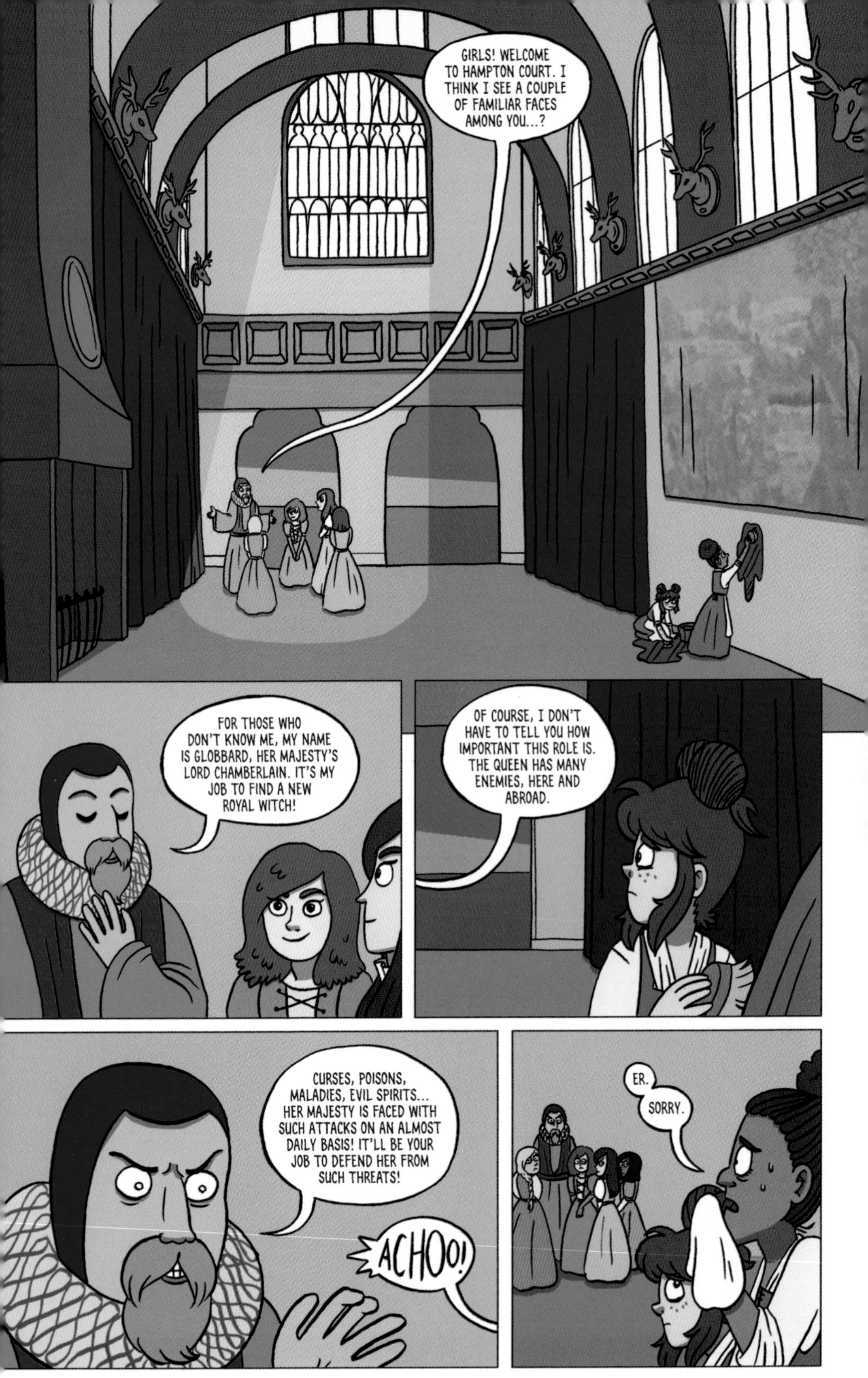
GIRLS! WELCOME TO HAMPTON COURT. I THINK I SEE A COUPLE OF FAMILIAR FACES AMONG YOU...?
FOR THOSE WHO DON'T KNOW ME, MY NAME IS GLOBBARD, HER MAJESTY'S LORD CHAMBERLAIN. IT'S MY JOB TO FIND A NEW ROYAL WITCH!
OF COURSE, I DON'T HAVE TO TELL YOU HOW IMPORTANT THIS ROLE IS. THE QUEEN HAS MANY ENEMIES, HERE AND ABROAD.
CURSES, POISONS, MALADIES, EVIL SPIRITS... HER MAJESTY IS FACED WITH SUCH ATTACKS ON AN ALMOST DAILY BASIS! IT'LL BE YOUR JOB TO DEFEND HER FROM SUCH THREATS!
ACHOO!
ER.
SORRY.

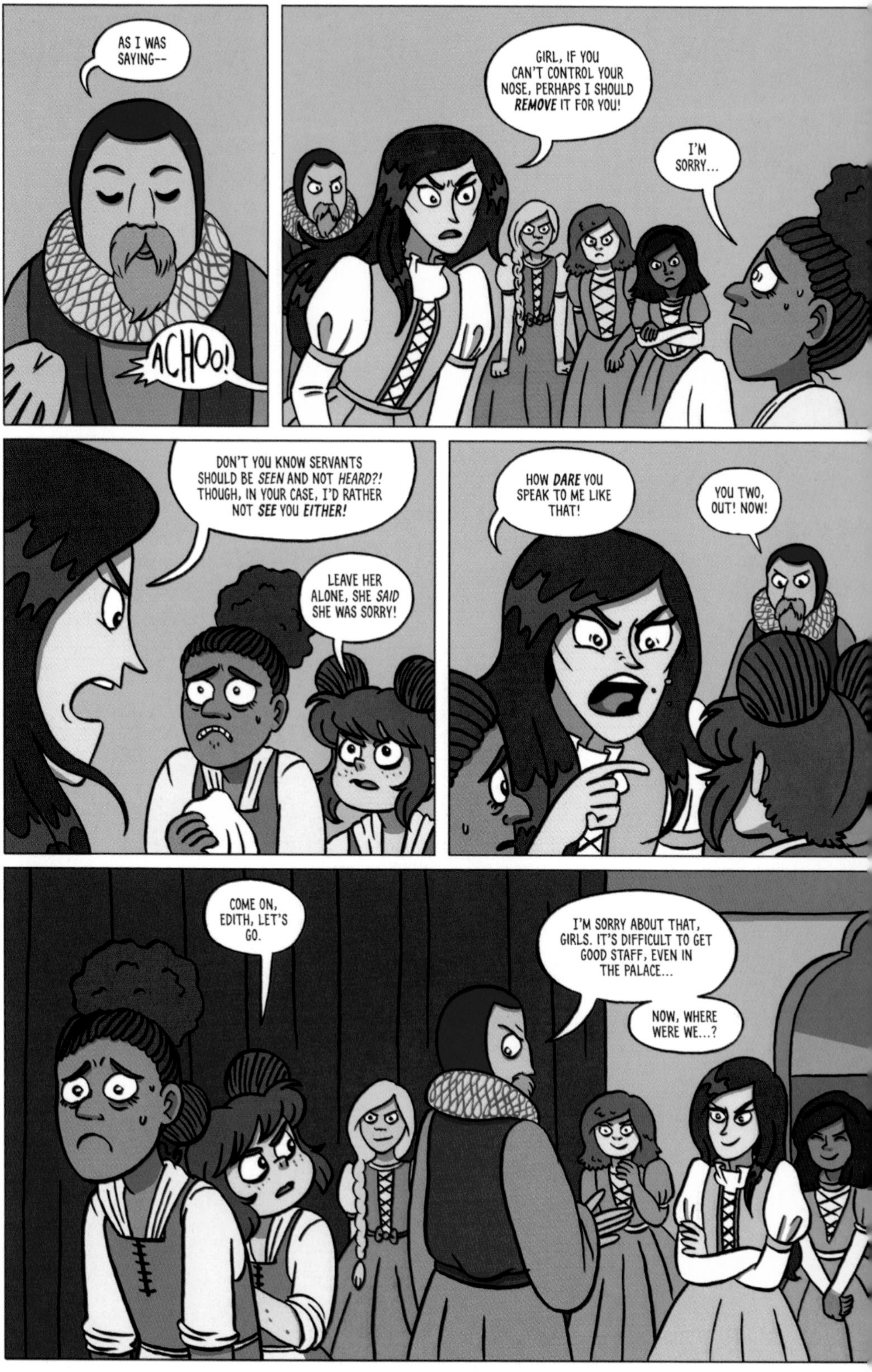
AS I WAS SAYING--
ACHOO!
GIRL, IF YOU CAN'T CONTROL YOUR NOSE, PERHAPS I SHOULD REMOVE IT FOR YOU!
I'M SORRY...
DON'T YOU KNOW SERVANTS SHOULD BE SEEN AND NOT HEARD?! THOUGH, IN YOUR CASE, I'D RATHER NOT SEE YOU EITHER!
LEAVE HER ALONE, SHE SAID SHE WAS SORRY!
HOW DARE YOU SPEAK TO ME LIKE THAT!
YOU TWO, OUT! NOW!
COME ON, EDITH, LET'S GO.
I'M SORRY ABOUT THAT, GIRLS. IT'S DIFFICULT TO GET GOOD STAFF, EVEN IN THE PALACE...
NOW, WHERE WERE WE...?

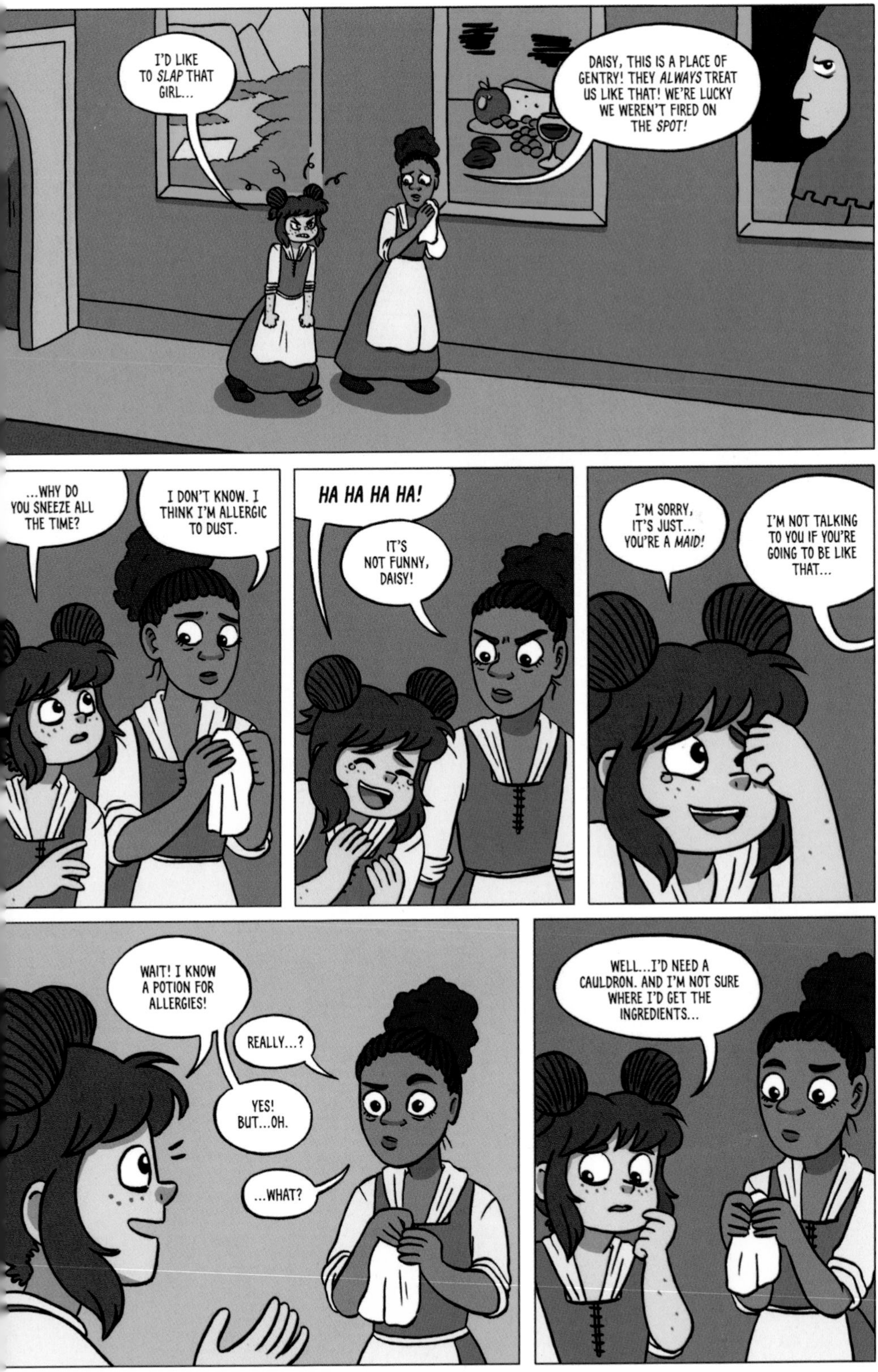
I'D LIKE TO *SLAP* THAT GIRL...
DAISY, THIS IS A PLACE OF GENTRY! THEY *ALWAYS* TREAT US LIKE THAT! WE'RE LUCKY WE WEREN'T FIRED ON THE *SPOT!*
...WHY DO YOU SNEEZE ALL THE TIME?
I DON'T KNOW. I THINK I'M ALLERGIC TO DUST.
HA HA HA HA!
IT'S NOT FUNNY, DAISY!
I'M SORRY, IT'S JUST... YOU'RE A *MAID!*
I'M NOT TALKING TO YOU IF YOU'RE GOING TO BE LIKE THAT...
WAIT! I KNOW A POTION FOR ALLERGIES!
REALLY...?
YES! BUT...OH.
...WHAT?
WELL...I'D NEED A CAULDRON. AND I'M NOT SURE WHERE I'D GET THE INGREDIENTS...

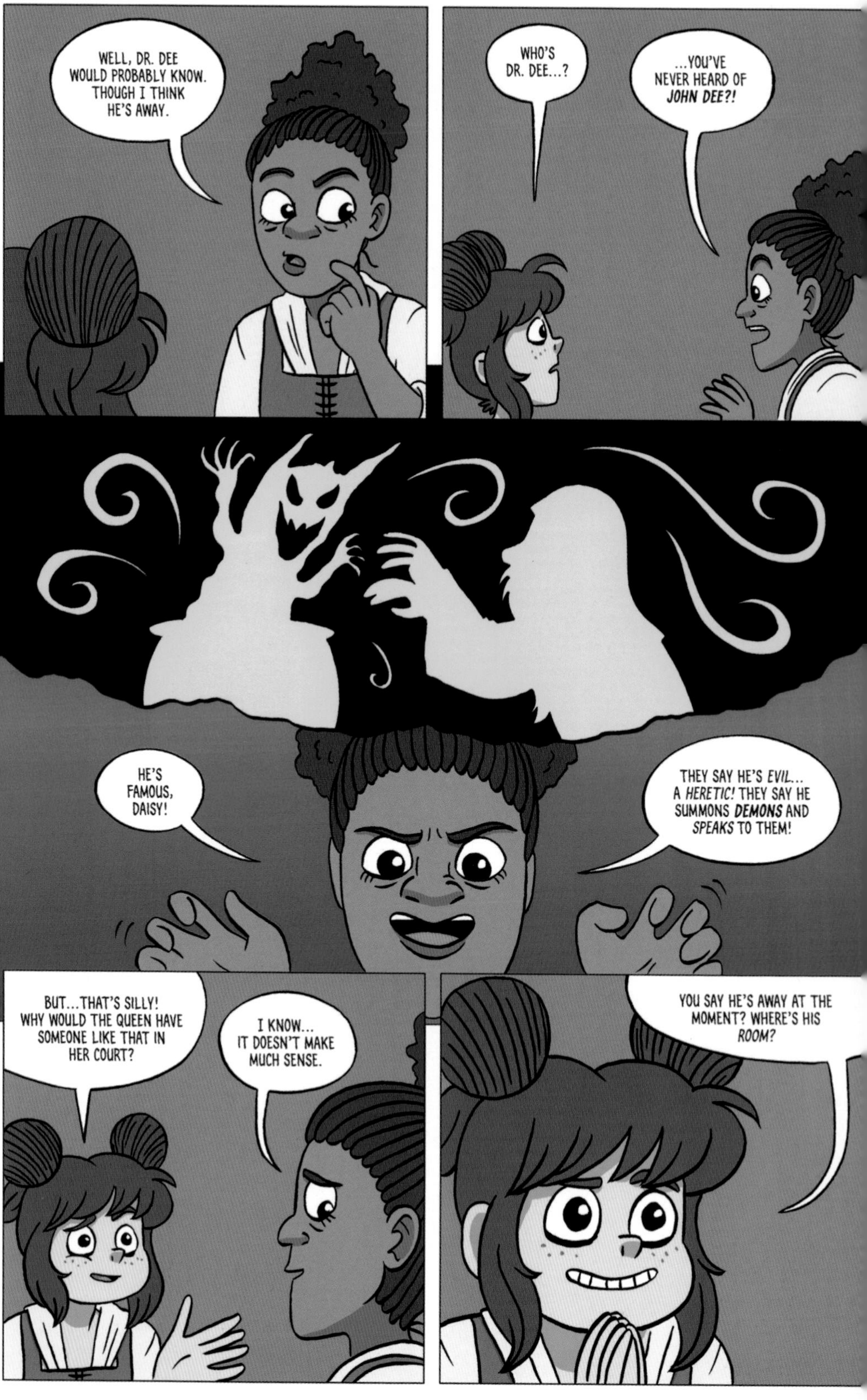
WELL, DR. DEE WOULD PROBABLY KNOW. THOUGH I THINK HE'S AWAY.
WHO'S DR. DEE...?
...YOU'VE NEVER HEARD OF JOHN DEE?!
HE'S FAMOUS, DAISY!
THEY SAY HE'S EVIL... A HERETIC! THEY SAY HE SUMMONS DEMONS AND SPEAKS TO THEM!
BUT...THAT'S SILLY! WHY WOULD THE QUEEN HAVE SOMEONE LIKE THAT IN HER COURT?
I KNOW... IT DOESN'T MAKE MUCH SENSE.
YOU SAY HE'S AWAY AT THE MOMENT? WHERE'S HIS ROOM?

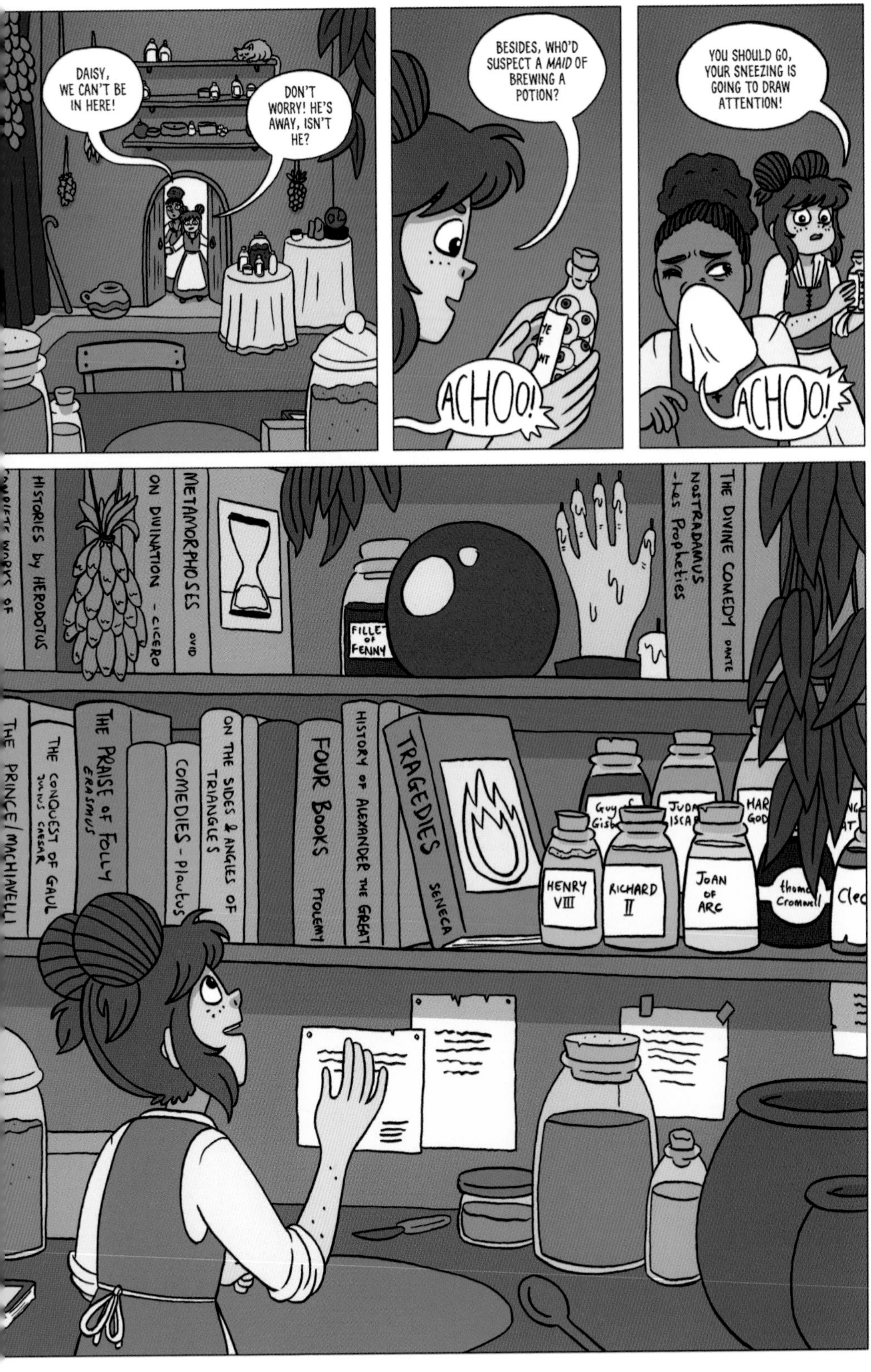
DAISY, WE CAN'T BE IN HERE!
DON'T WORRY! HE'S AWAY, ISN'T HE?
BESIDES, WHO'D SUSPECT A *MAID* OF BREWING A POTION?
ACHOO!
YOU SHOULD GO, YOUR SNEEZING IS GOING TO DRAW ATTENTION!
ACHOO!
HISTORIES by HERODOTUS
ON DIVINATION - CICERO
METAMORPHOSES OVID
FILLET OF FENNY
NOSTRADAMUS -les Propheties
THE DIVINE COMEDY DANTE
THE PRINCE/MACHIAVELLI
THE CONQUEST OF GAUL JULIUS CAESAR
THE PRAISE OF FOLLY ERASMUS
COMEDIES - Plautus
ON THE SIDES & ANGLES OF TRIANGLES
FOUR BOOKS PTOLEMY
HISTORY OF ALEXANDER THE GREAT
TRAGEDIES SENECA
HENRY VIII
RICHARD II
JOAN OF ARC

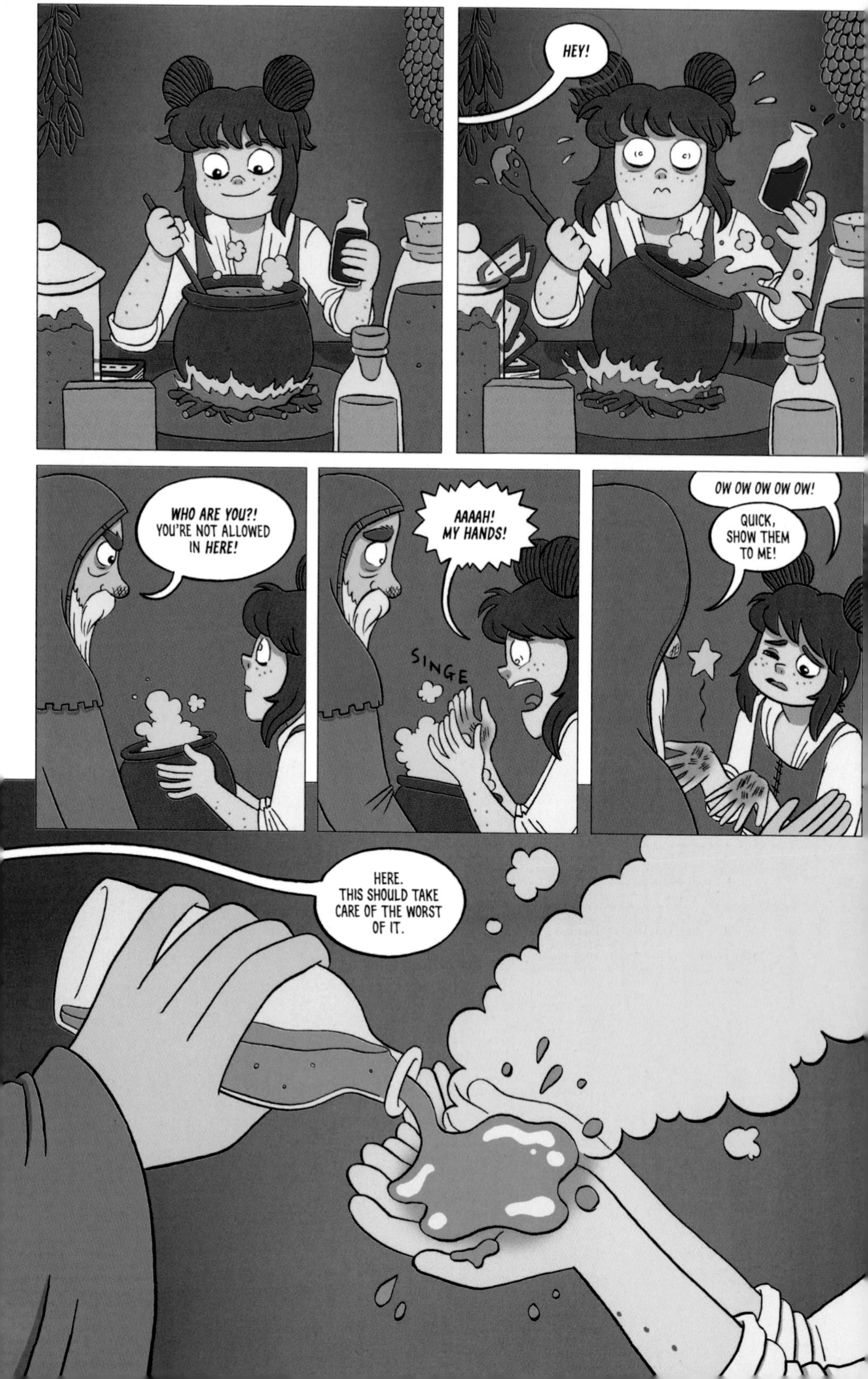
HEY!
WHO ARE YOU?! YOU'RE NOT ALLOWED IN HERE!
AAAAH! MY HANDS!
SINGE
OW OW OW OW OW!
QUICK, SHOW THEM TO ME!
HERE. THIS SHOULD TAKE CARE OF THE WORST OF IT.

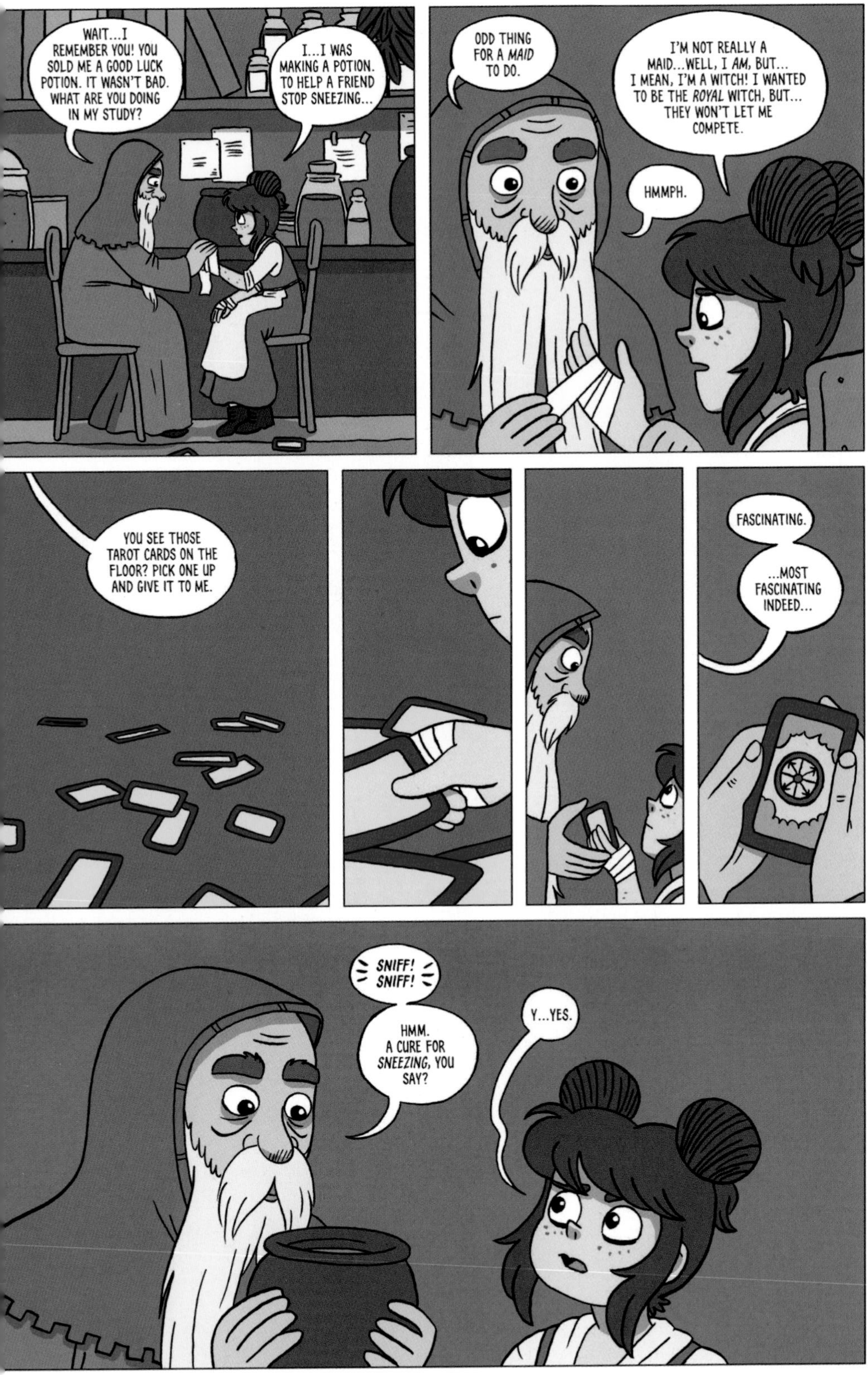
WAIT...I REMEMBER YOU! YOU SOLD ME A GOOD LUCK POTION. IT WASN'T BAD. WHAT ARE YOU DOING IN MY STUDY?
I...I WAS MAKING A POTION. TO HELP A FRIEND STOP SNEEZING...
ODD THING FOR A *MAID* TO DO.
I'M NOT REALLY A MAID...WELL, I *AM*, BUT... I MEAN, I'M A WITCH! I WANTED TO BE THE *ROYAL* WITCH, BUT... THEY WON'T LET ME COMPETE.
HMMPH.
YOU SEE THOSE TAROT CARDS ON THE FLOOR? PICK ONE UP AND GIVE IT TO ME.
FASCINATING.
...MOST FASCINATING INDEED...
SNIFF! SNIFF!
HMM. A CURE FOR *SNEEZING*, YOU SAY?
Y...YES.

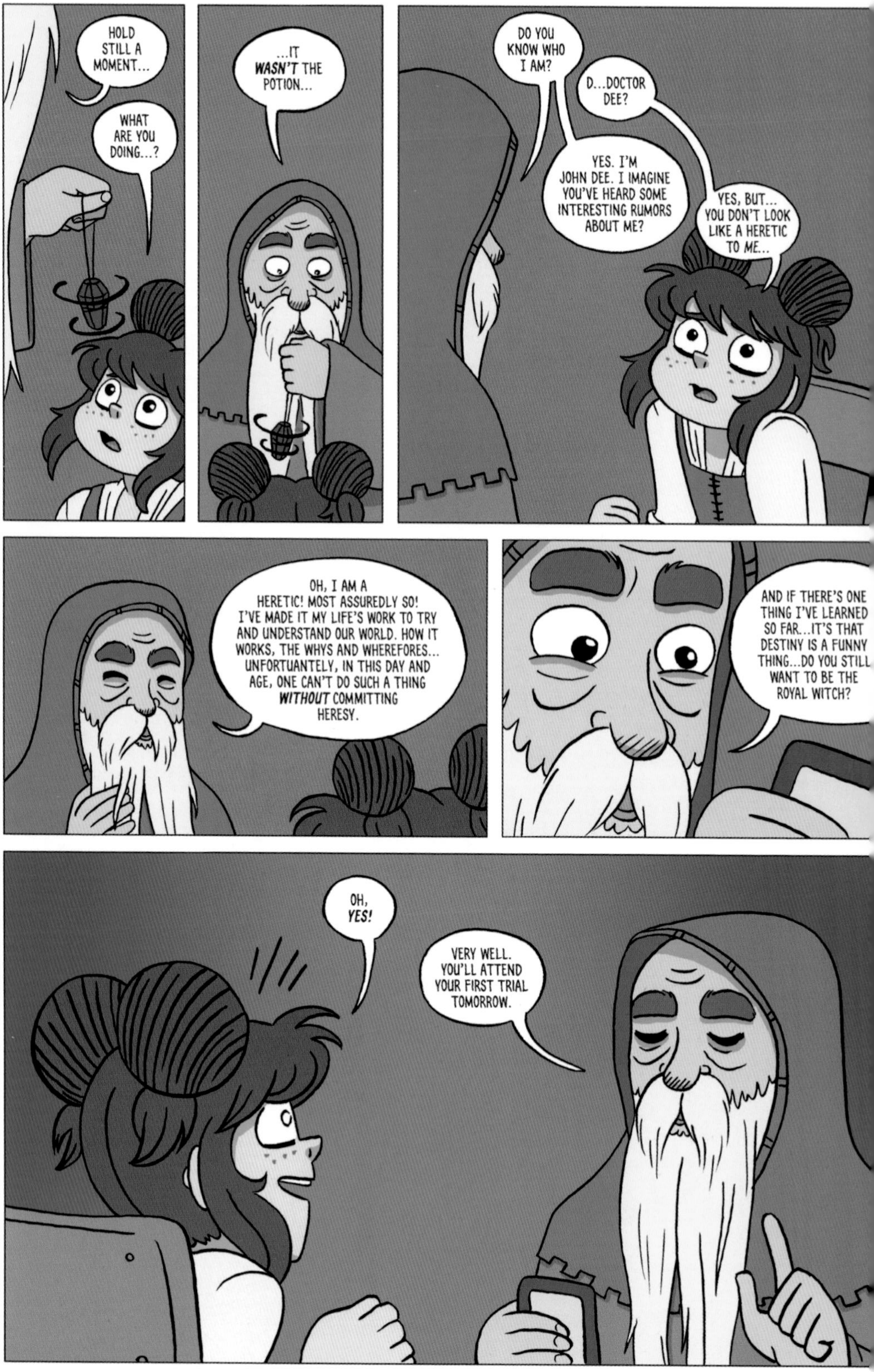

HOLD STILL A MOMENT...
WHAT ARE YOU DOING...?
...IT WASN'T THE POTION...
DO YOU KNOW WHO I AM?
D...DOCTOR DEE?
YES. I'M JOHN DEE. I IMAGINE YOU'VE HEARD SOME INTERESTING RUMORS ABOUT ME?
YES, BUT... YOU DON'T LOOK LIKE A HERETIC TO ME...
OH, I AM A HERETIC! MOST ASSUREDLY SO! I'VE MADE IT MY LIFE'S WORK TO TRY AND UNDERSTAND OUR WORLD. HOW IT WORKS, THE WHYS AND WHEREFORES... UNFORTUANTELY, IN THIS DAY AND AGE, ONE CAN'T DO SUCH A THING WITHOUT COMMITTING HERESY.
AND IF THERE'S ONE THING I'VE LEARNED SO FAR...IT'S THAT DESTINY IS A FUNNY THING...DO YOU STILL WANT TO BE THE ROYAL WITCH?
OH, YES!
VERY WELL. YOU'LL ATTEND YOUR FIRST TRIAL TOMORROW.

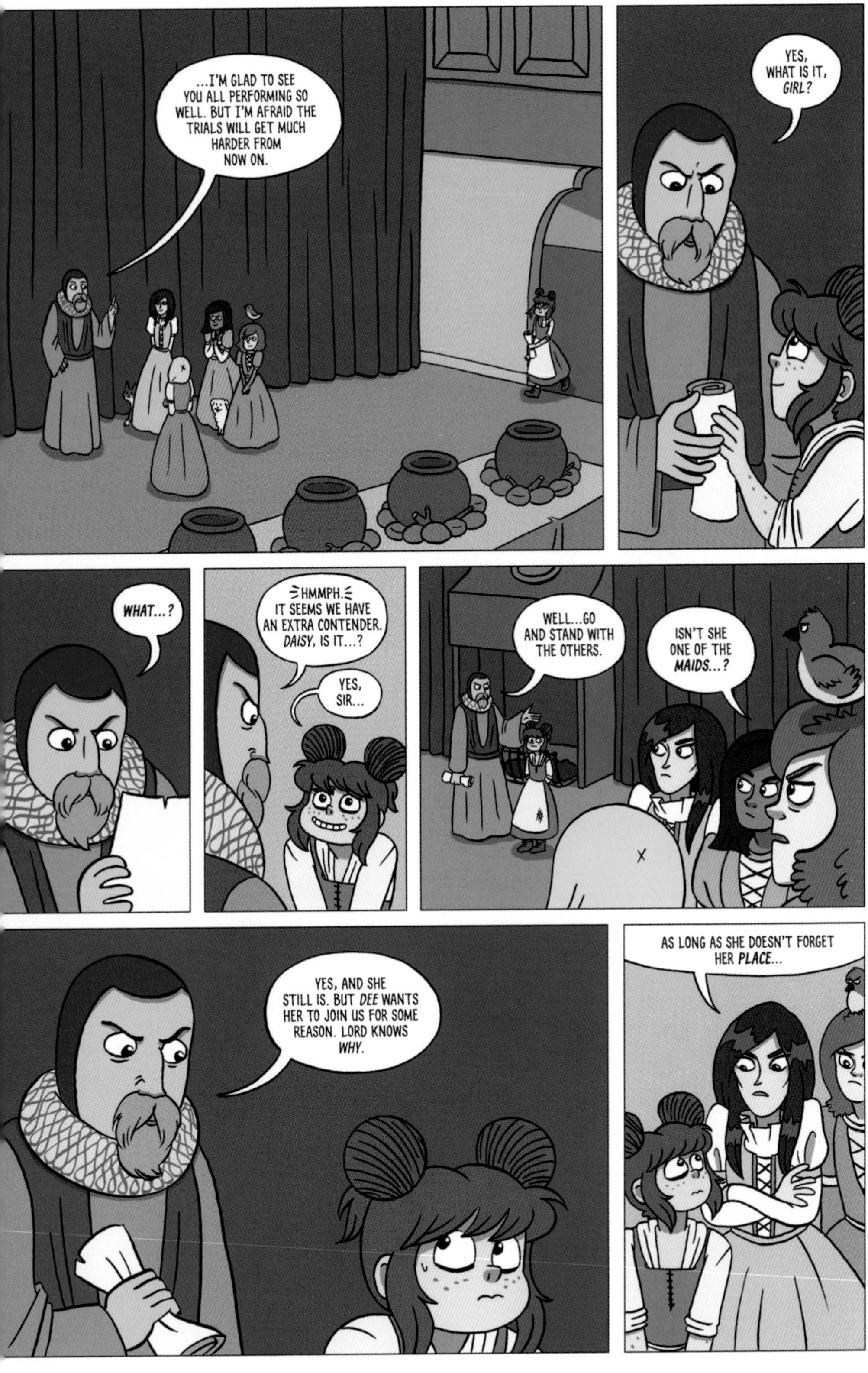
...I'M GLAD TO SEE YOU ALL PERFORMING SO WELL. BUT I'M AFRAID THE TRIALS WILL GET MUCH HARDER FROM NOW ON.
YES, WHAT IS IT, *GIRL?*
WHAT...?
HMMPH. IT SEEMS WE HAVE AN EXTRA CONTENDER. *DAISY,* IS IT...?
YES, SIR...
WELL...GO AND STAND WITH THE OTHERS.
ISN'T SHE ONE OF THE *MAIDS...?*
YES, AND SHE STILL IS. BUT *DEE* WANTS HER TO JOIN US FOR SOME REASON. LORD KNOWS *WHY.*
AS LONG AS SHE DOESN'T FORGET HER *PLACE...*

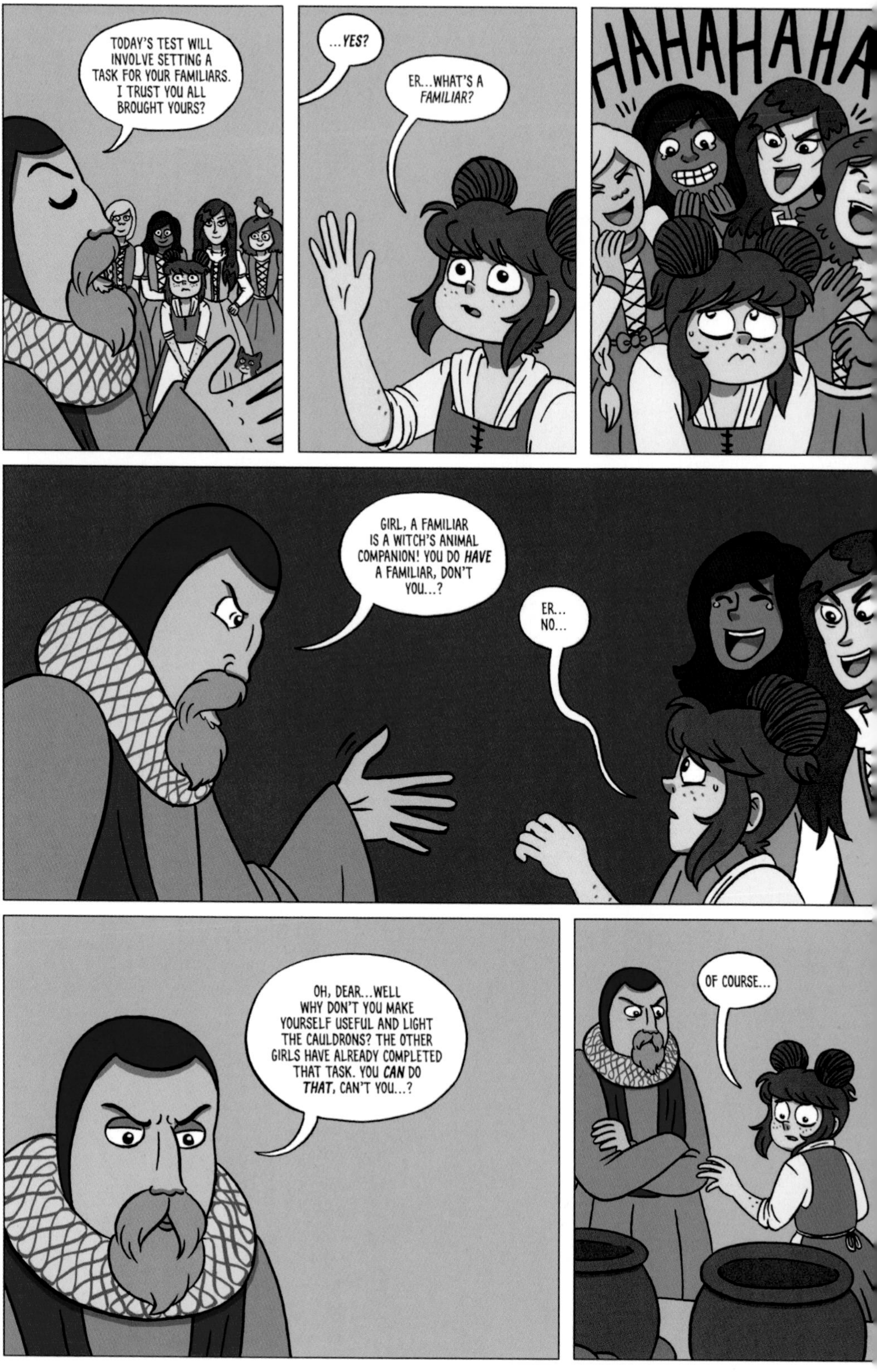
TODAY'S TEST WILL INVOLVE SETTING A TASK FOR YOUR FAMILIARS. I TRUST YOU ALL BROUGHT YOURS?
...YES?
ER...WHAT'S A FAMILIAR?
HAHAHAHAHA
GIRL, A FAMILIAR IS A WITCH'S ANIMAL COMPANION! YOU DO HAVE A FAMILIAR, DON'T YOU...?
ER... NO...
OH, DEAR...WELL WHY DON'T YOU MAKE YOURSELF USEFUL AND LIGHT THE CAULDRONS? THE OTHER GIRLS HAVE ALREADY COMPLETED THAT TASK. YOU CAN DO THAT, CAN'T YOU...?
OF COURSE...

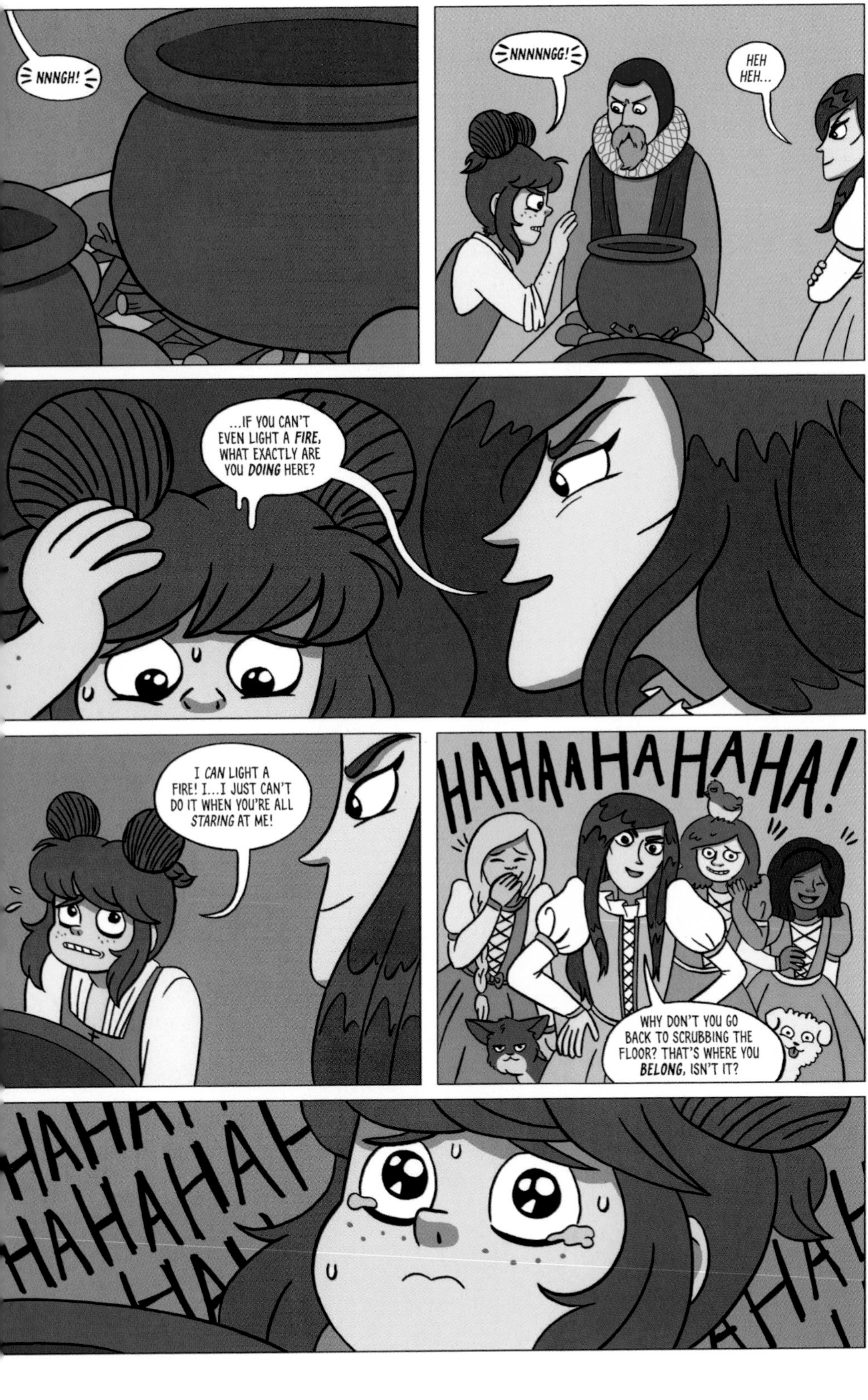
NNNGH!
NNNNNGG!
HEH HEH...
...IF YOU CAN'T EVEN LIGHT A FIRE, WHAT EXACTLY ARE YOU DOING HERE?
I CAN LIGHT A FIRE! I...I JUST CAN'T DO IT WHEN YOU'RE ALL STARING AT ME!
HAHAAHAHAHA!
WHY DON'T YOU GO BACK TO SCRUBBING THE FLOOR? THAT'S WHERE YOU BELONG, ISN'T IT?
HAHAHAHA

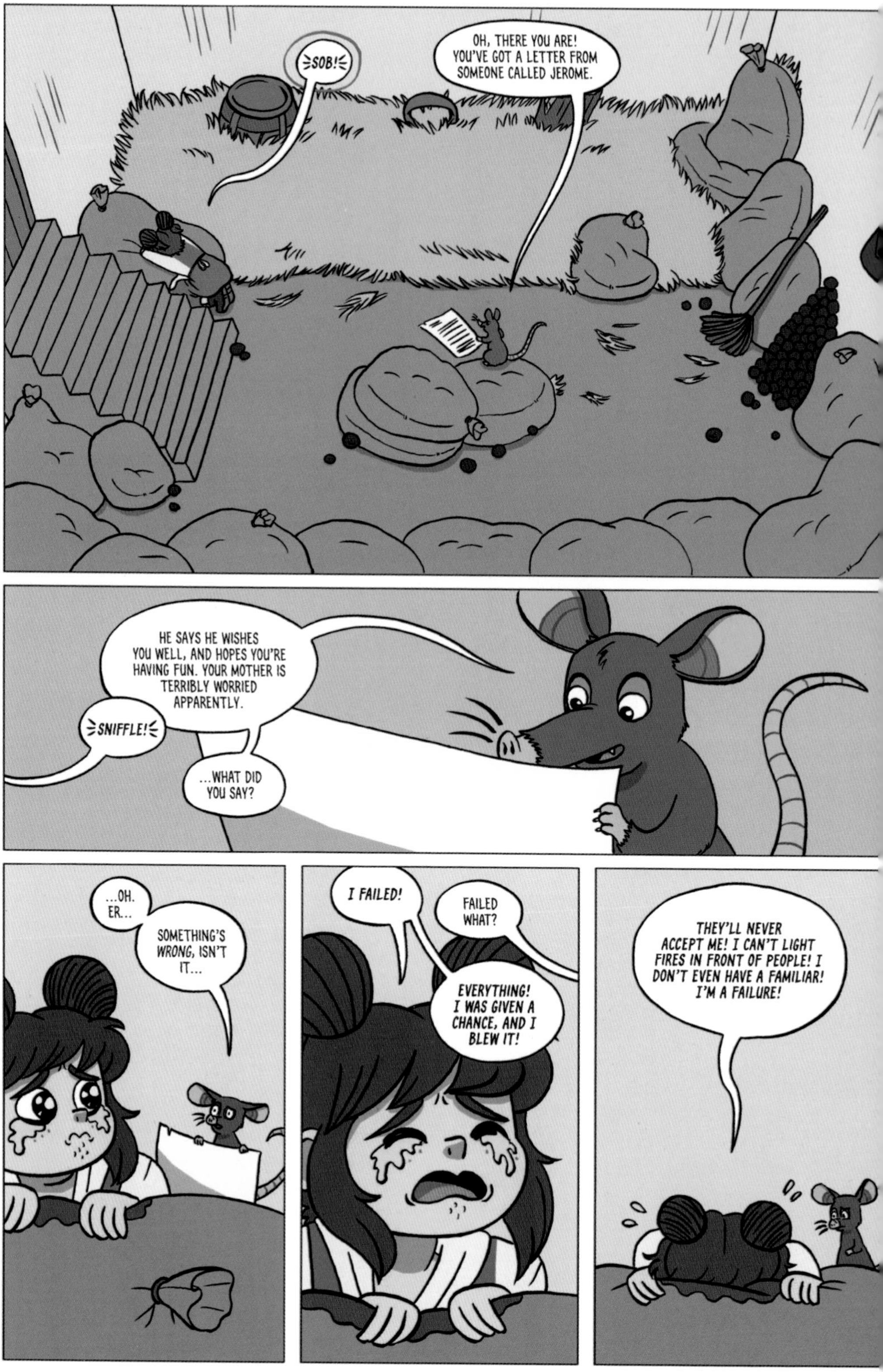
SOB!
OH, THERE YOU ARE! YOU'VE GOT A LETTER FROM SOMEONE CALLED JEROME.
HE SAYS HE WISHES YOU WELL, AND HOPES YOU'RE HAVING FUN. YOUR MOTHER IS TERRIBLY WORRIED APPARENTLY.
SNIFFLE!
...WHAT DID YOU SAY?
...OH. ER...
SOMETHING'S WRONG, ISN'T IT...
I FAILED!
FAILED WHAT?
EVERYTHING! I WAS GIVEN A CHANCE, AND I BLEW IT!
THEY'LL NEVER ACCEPT ME! I CAN'T LIGHT FIRES IN FRONT OF PEOPLE! I DON'T EVEN HAVE A FAMILIAR! I'M A FAILURE!

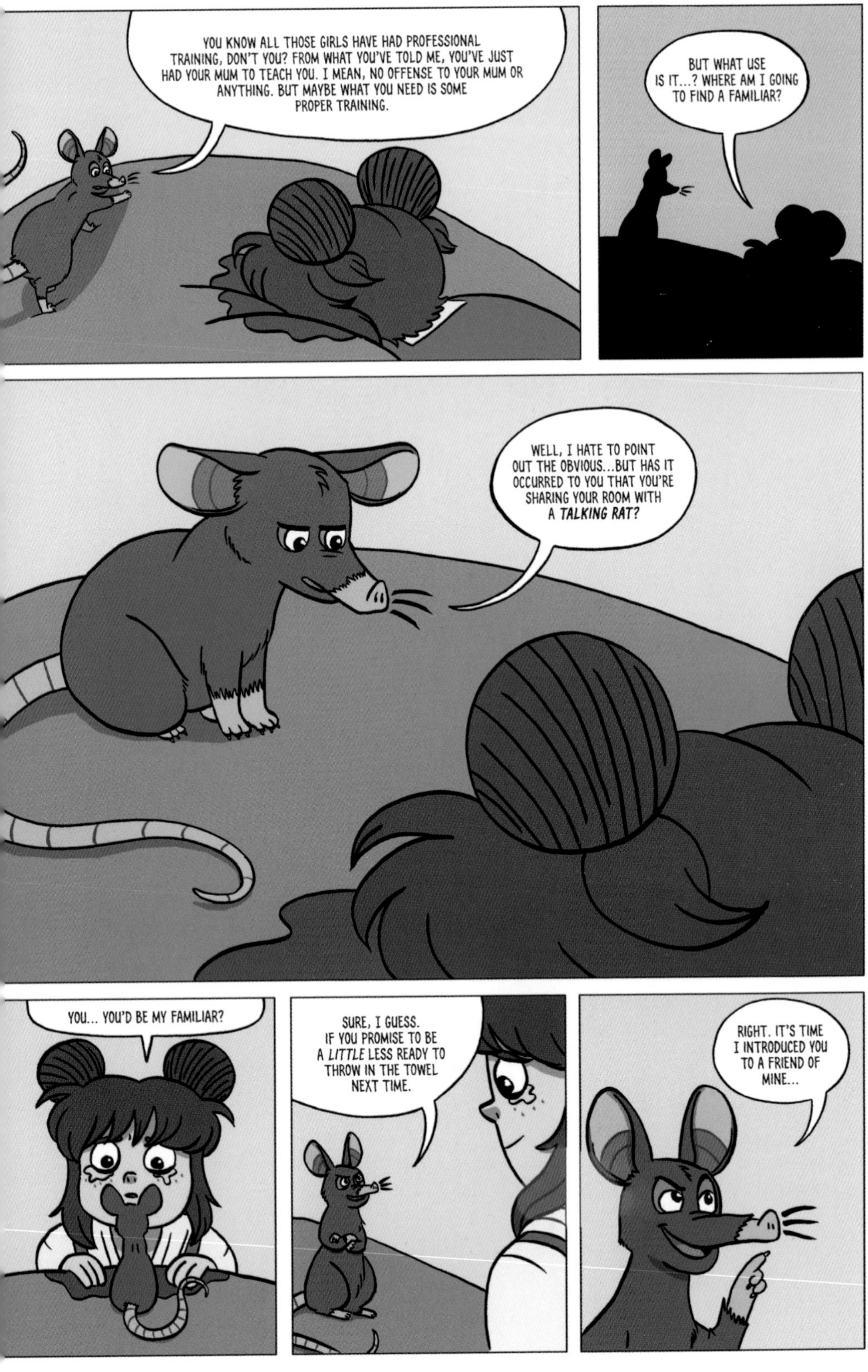
YOU KNOW ALL THOSE GIRLS HAVE HAD PROFESSIONAL TRAINING, DON'T YOU? FROM WHAT YOU'VE TOLD ME, YOU'VE JUST HAD YOUR MUM TO TEACH YOU. I MEAN, NO OFFENSE TO YOUR MUM OR ANYTHING. BUT MAYBE WHAT YOU NEED IS SOME PROPER TRAINING.
BUT WHAT USE IS IT...? WHERE AM I GOING TO FIND A FAMILIAR?
WELL, I HATE TO POINT OUT THE OBVIOUS...BUT HAS IT OCCURRED TO YOU THAT YOU'RE SHARING YOUR ROOM WITH A *TALKING RAT?*
YOU... YOU'D BE MY FAMILIAR?
SURE, I GUESS. IF YOU PROMISE TO BE A *LITTLE* LESS READY TO THROW IN THE TOWEL NEXT TIME.
RIGHT. IT'S TIME I INTRODUCED YOU TO A FRIEND OF MINE...

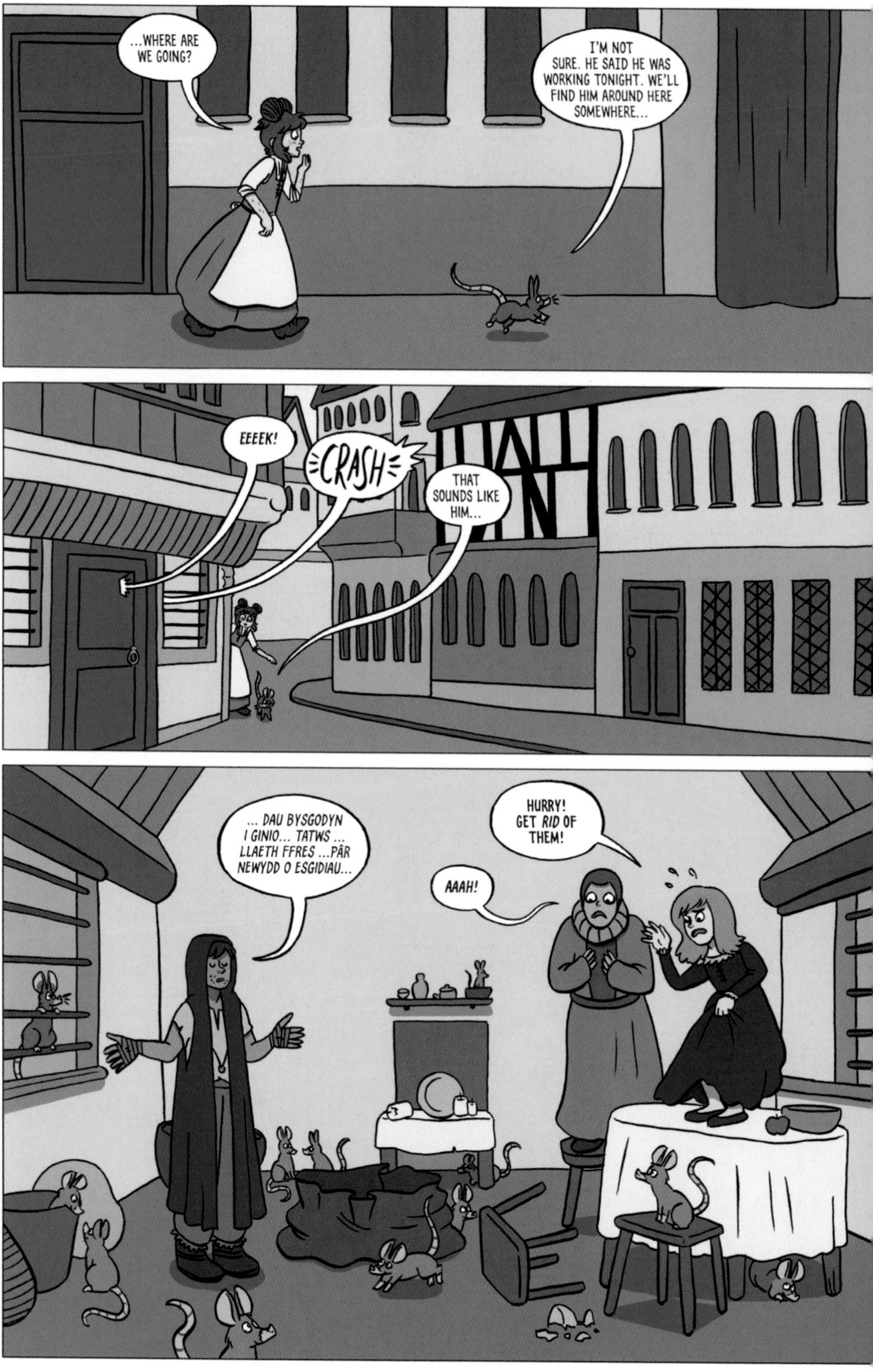
...WHERE ARE WE GOING?
I'M NOT SURE. HE SAID HE WAS WORKING TONIGHT. WE'LL FIND HIM AROUND HERE SOMEWHERE...
EEEEK!
CRASH
THAT SOUNDS LIKE HIM...
... DAU BYSGODYN I GINIO... TATWS ... LLAETH FFRES ...PÂR NEWYDD O ESGIDIAU...
HURRY! GET *RID* OF THEM!
AAAH!

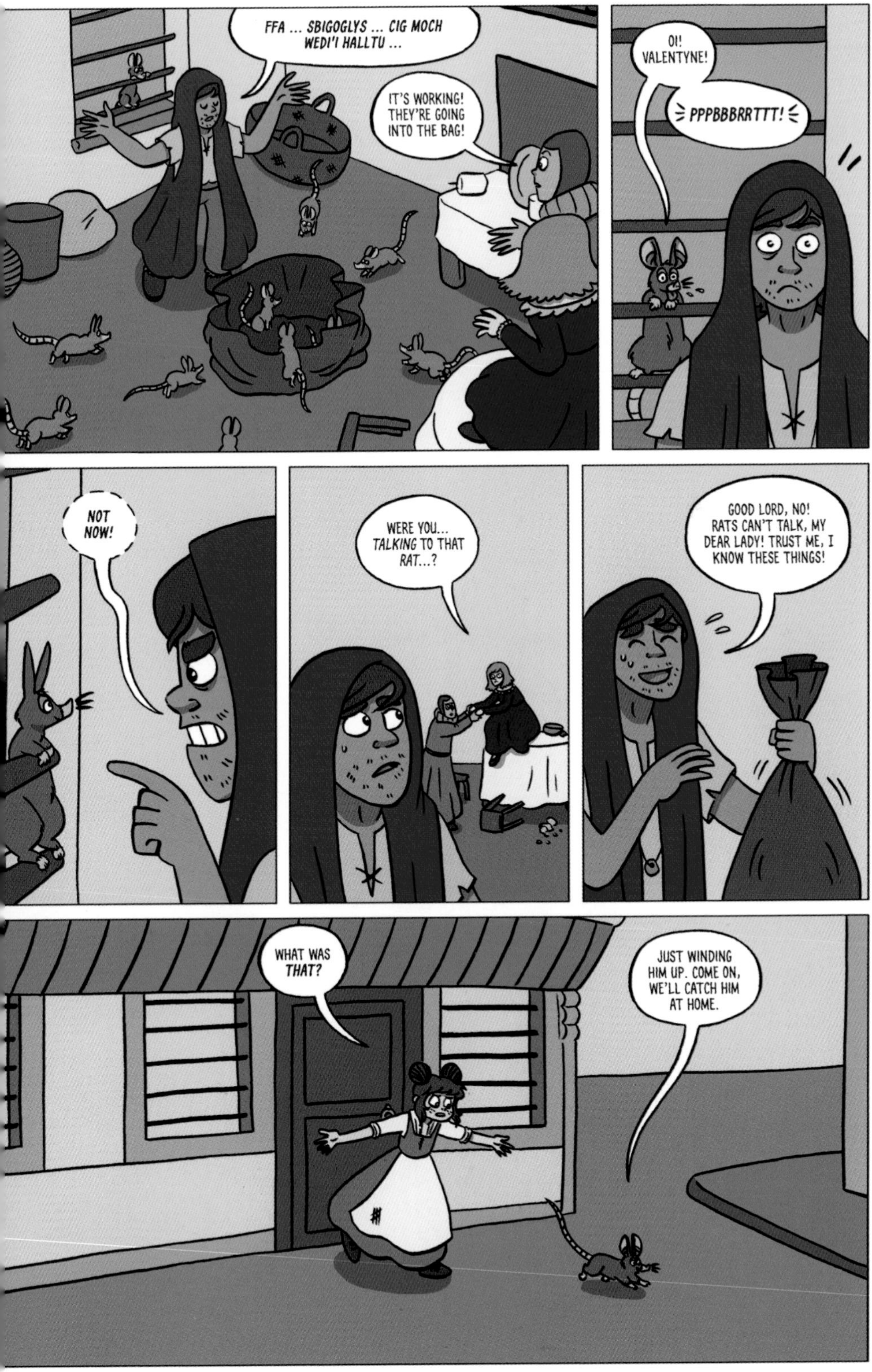
FFA ... SBIGOGLYS ... CIG MOCH WEDI'I HALLTU ...
IT'S WORKING! THEY'RE GOING INTO THE BAG!
OI! VALENTYNE!
PPPBBBRRTTT!
NOT NOW!
WERE YOU... TALKING TO THAT RAT...?
GOOD LORD, NO! RATS CAN'T TALK, MY DEAR LADY! TRUST ME, I KNOW THESE THINGS!
WHAT WAS THAT?
JUST WINDING HIM UP. COME ON, WE'LL CATCH HIM AT HOME.

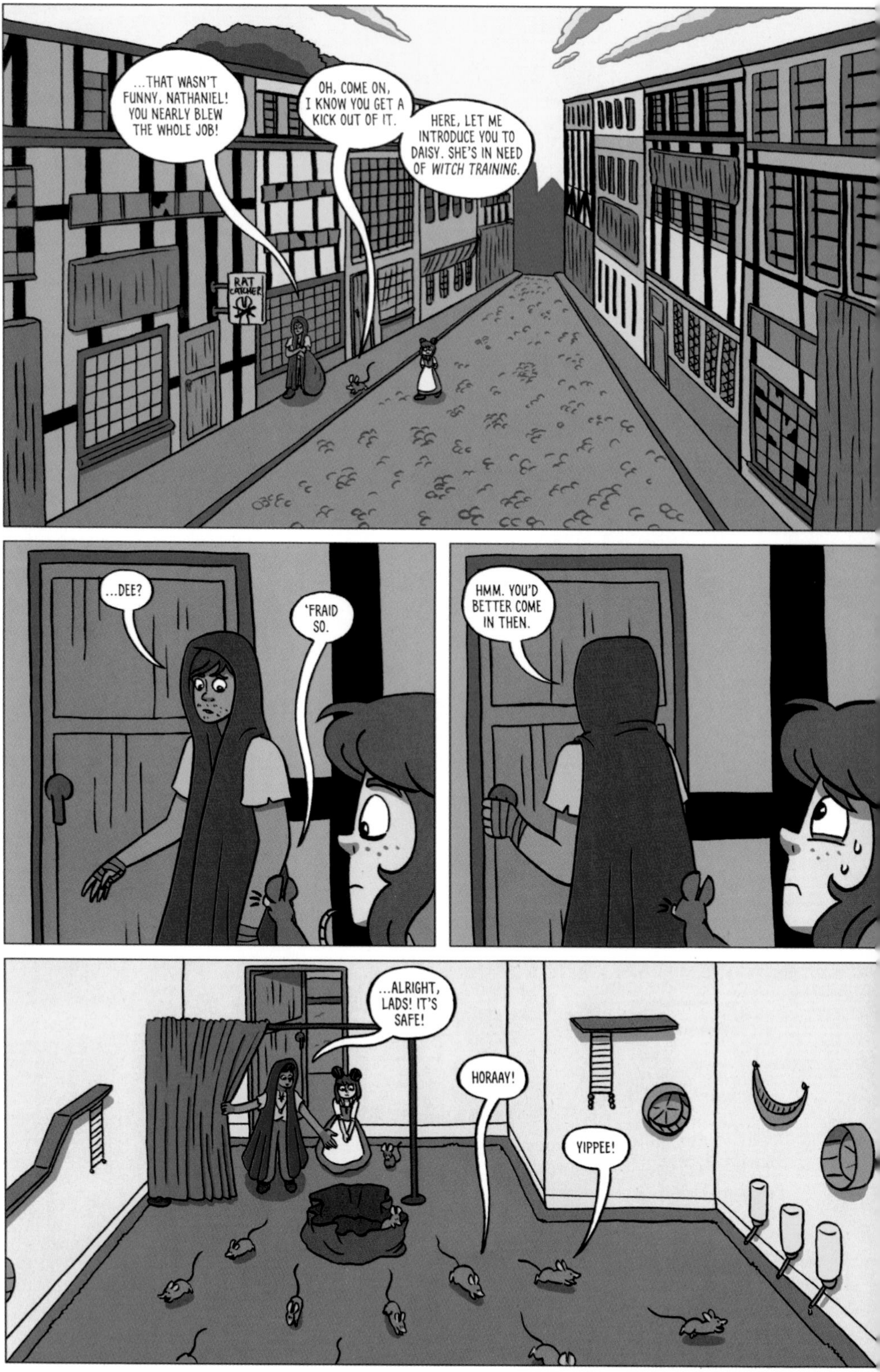
...THAT WASN'T FUNNY, NATHANIEL! YOU NEARLY BLEW THE WHOLE JOB!
OH, COME ON, I KNOW YOU GET A KICK OUT OF IT.
HERE, LET ME INTRODUCE YOU TO DAISY. SHE'S IN NEED OF *WITCH TRAINING*.
RAT CATCHER
...DEE?
'FRAID SO.
HMM. YOU'D BETTER COME IN THEN.
...ALRIGHT, LADS! IT'S SAFE!
HORAAY!
YIPPEE!

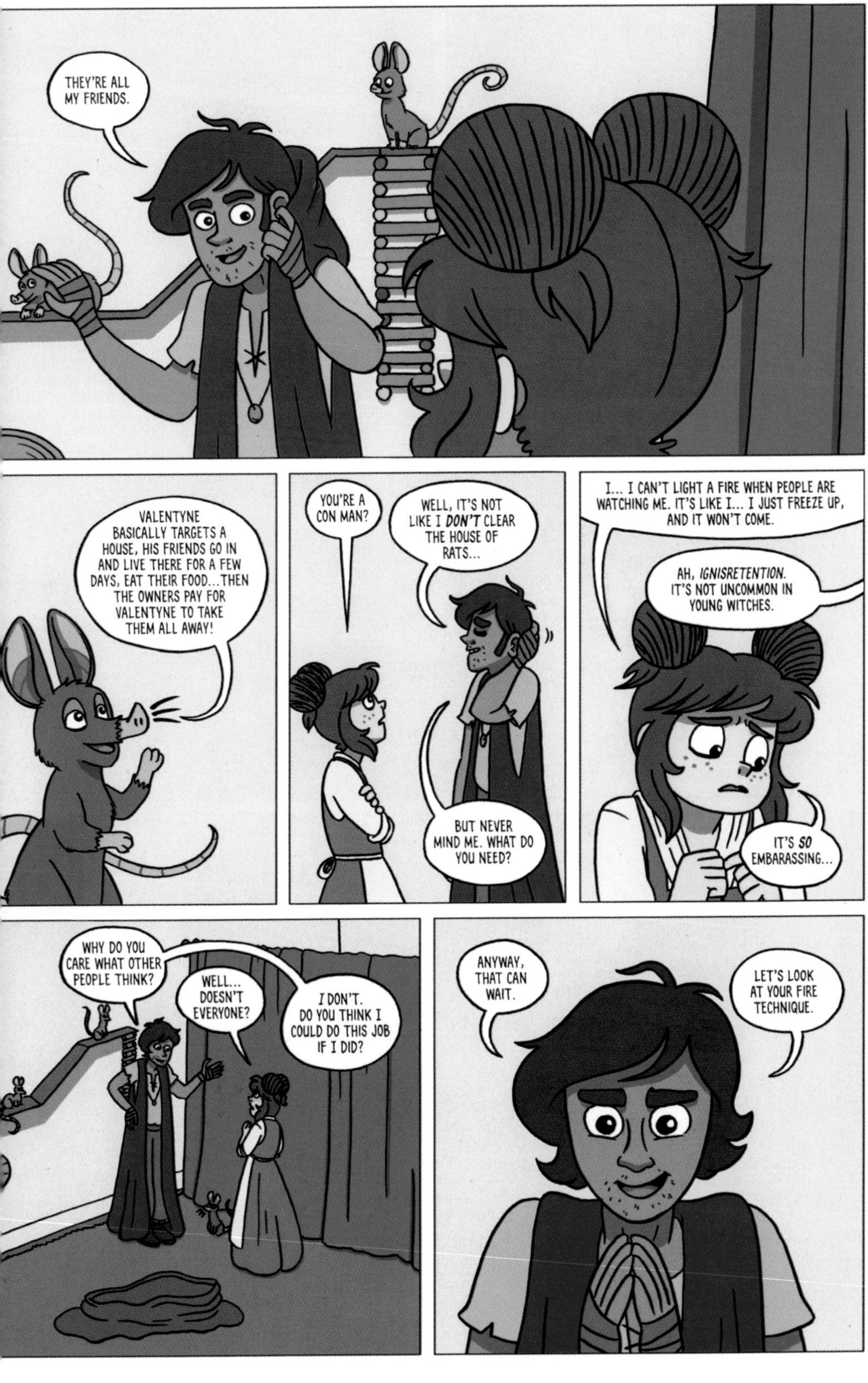
THEY'RE ALL MY FRIENDS.
VALENTYNE BASICALLY TARGETS A HOUSE, HIS FRIENDS GO IN AND LIVE THERE FOR A FEW DAYS, EAT THEIR FOOD...THEN THE OWNERS PAY FOR VALENTYNE TO TAKE THEM ALL AWAY!
YOU'RE A CON MAN?
WELL, IT'S NOT LIKE I DON'T CLEAR THE HOUSE OF RATS...
BUT NEVER MIND ME. WHAT DO YOU NEED?
I... I CAN'T LIGHT A FIRE WHEN PEOPLE ARE WATCHING ME. IT'S LIKE I... I JUST FREEZE UP, AND IT WON'T COME.
AH, IGNISRETENTION. IT'S NOT UNCOMMON IN YOUNG WITCHES.
IT'S SO EMBARASSING...
WHY DO YOU CARE WHAT OTHER PEOPLE THINK?
WELL... DOESN'T EVERYONE?
I DON'T. DO YOU THINK I COULD DO THIS JOB IF I DID?
ANYWAY, THAT CAN WAIT.
LET'S LOOK AT YOUR FIRE TECHNIQUE.

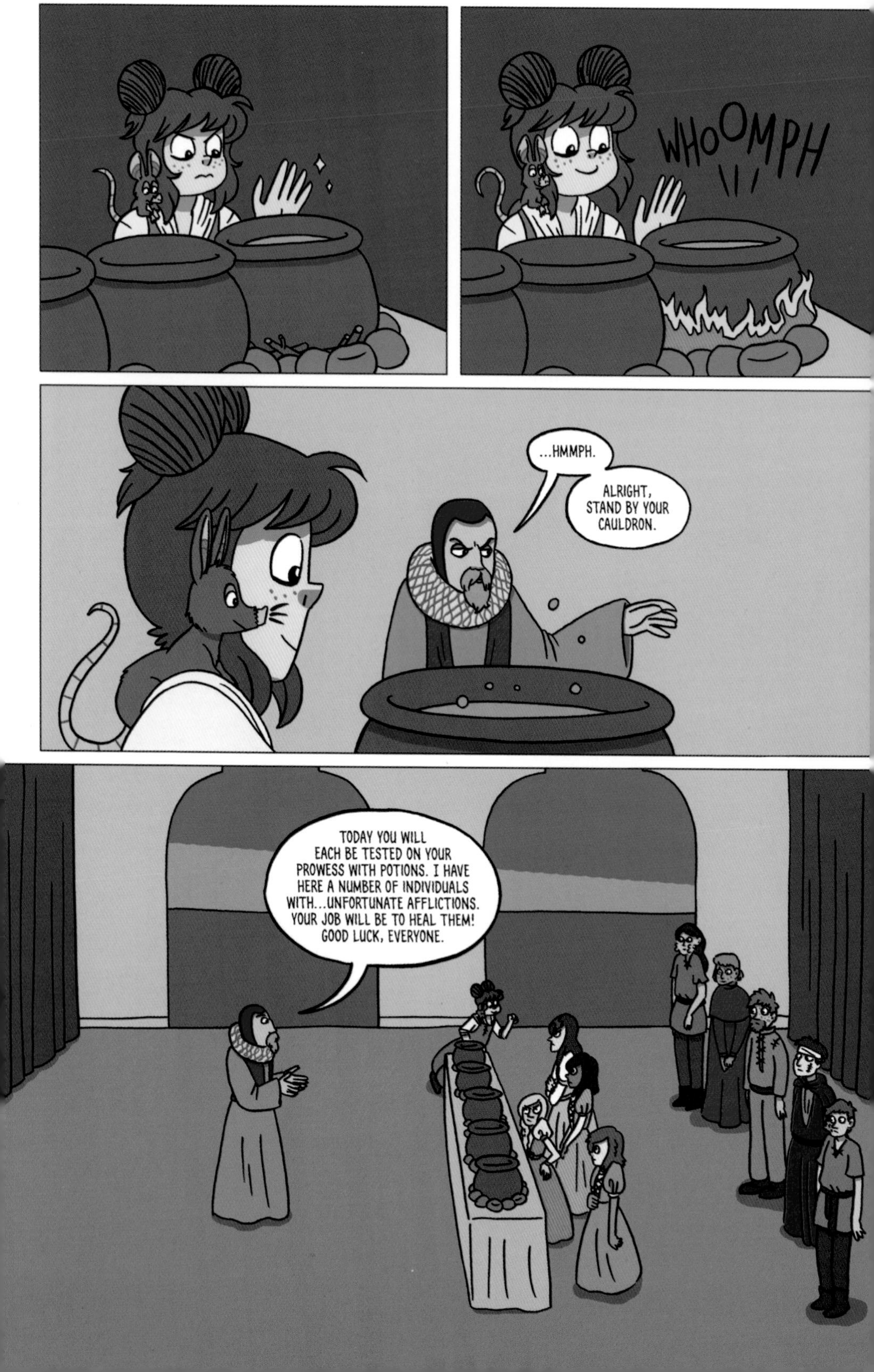
WHOOMPH
...HMMPH.
ALRIGHT, STAND BY YOUR CAULDRON.
TODAY YOU WILL EACH BE TESTED ON YOUR PROWESS WITH POTIONS. I HAVE HERE A NUMBER OF INDIVIDUALS WITH...UNFORTUNATE AFFLICTIONS. YOUR JOB WILL BE TO HEAL THEM! GOOD LUCK, EVERYONE.

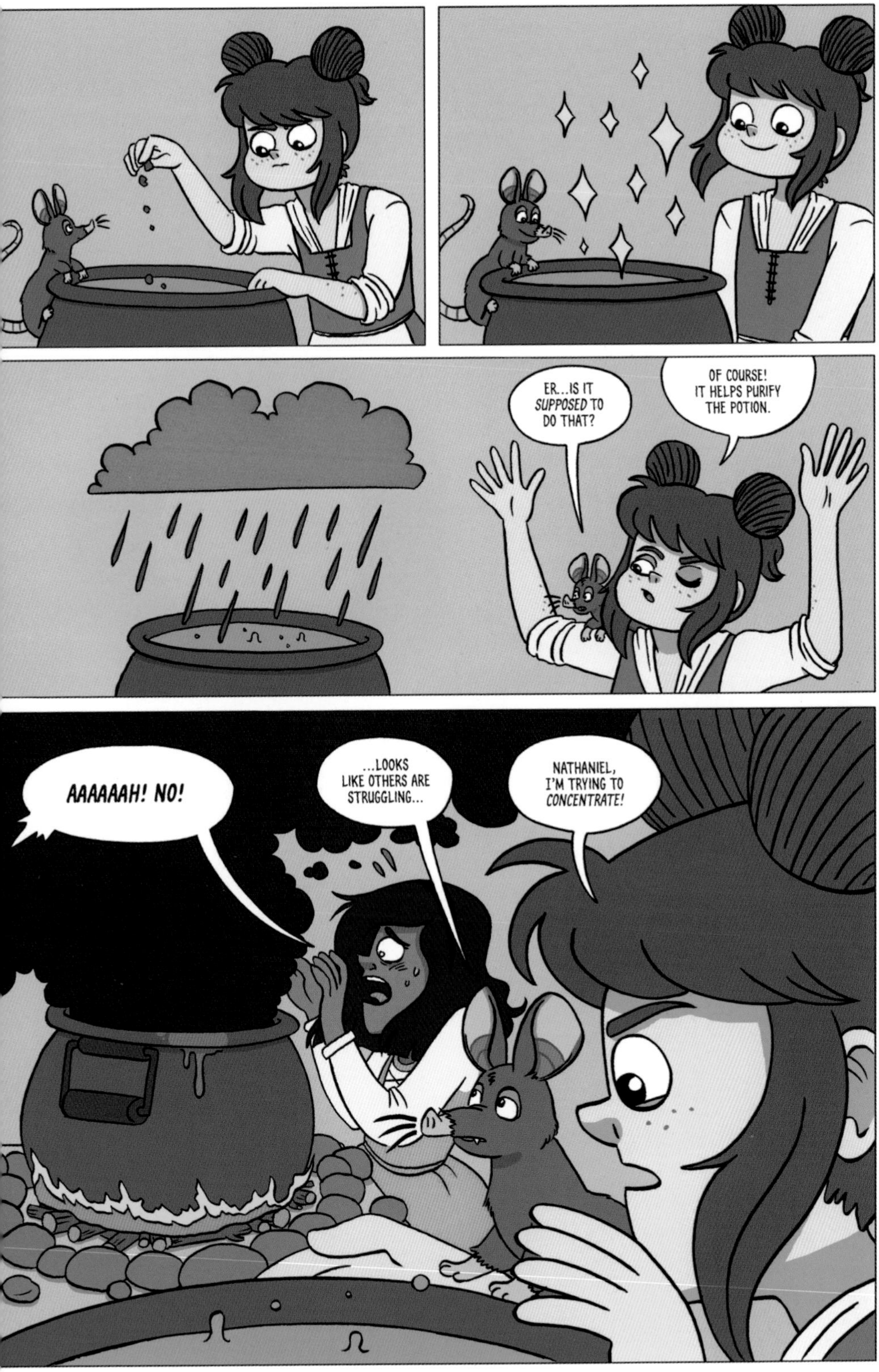
ER...IS IT *SUPPOSED* TO DO THAT?
OF COURSE! IT HELPS PURIFY THE POTION.
AAAAAAH! NO!
...LOOKS LIKE OTHERS ARE STRUGGLING...
NATHANIEL, I'M TRYING TO *CONCENTRATE!*

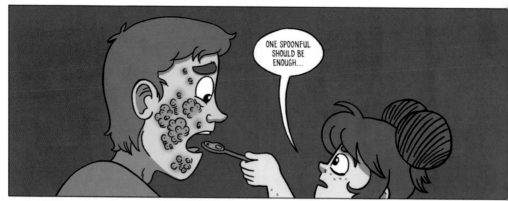

ONE SPOONFUL SHOULD BE ENOUGH...

BLIMEY, MISS! I'M CURED!

I'LL GIVE YOU A VIAL TO TAKE AWAY. YOU'LL NEED TO TAKE ONE SPOONFUL EACH DAY FOR A COUPLE OF WEEKS TO MAKE SURE IT DOESN'T COME BACK.

HEY, CAN YOU CURE ME AS WELL?

AND ME!

WHAT ARE YOU DOING?! YOU'RE MY PATIENT!

BUT HER POTION'S BETTER!

YOU UNGRATEFUL PEASANT...!

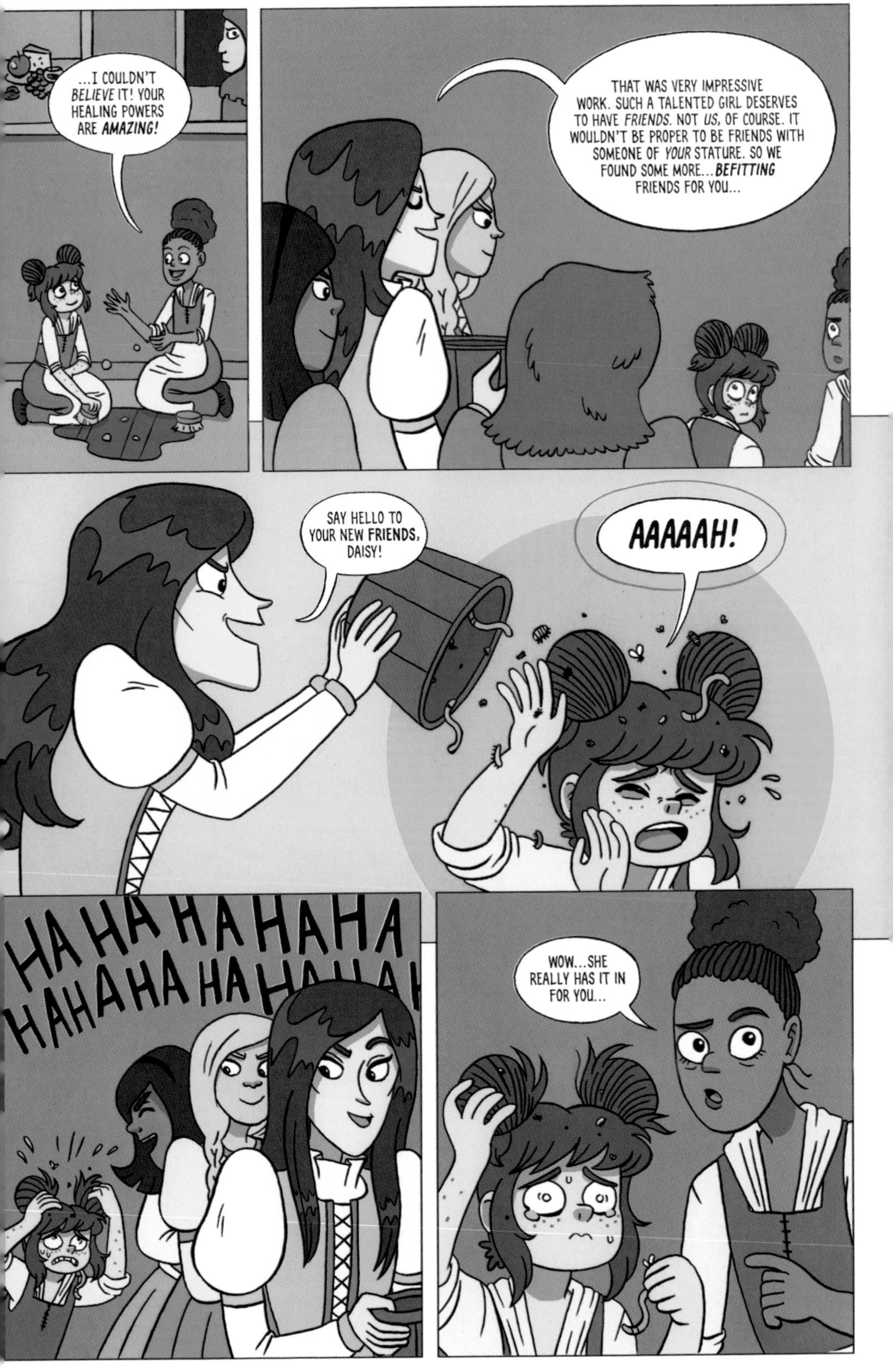

...I COULDN'T BELIEVE IT! YOUR HEALING POWERS ARE AMAZING!
THAT WAS VERY IMPRESSIVE WORK. SUCH A TALENTED GIRL DESERVES TO HAVE FRIENDS. NOT US, OF COURSE. IT WOULDN'T BE PROPER TO BE FRIENDS WITH SOMEONE OF YOUR STATURE. SO WE FOUND SOME MORE...BEFITTING FRIENDS FOR YOU...
SAY HELLO TO YOUR NEW FRIENDS, DAISY!
AAAAAH!
HA HA HA HA HA HA
HA HA HA HA HA
WOW...SHE REALLY HAS IT IN FOR YOU...

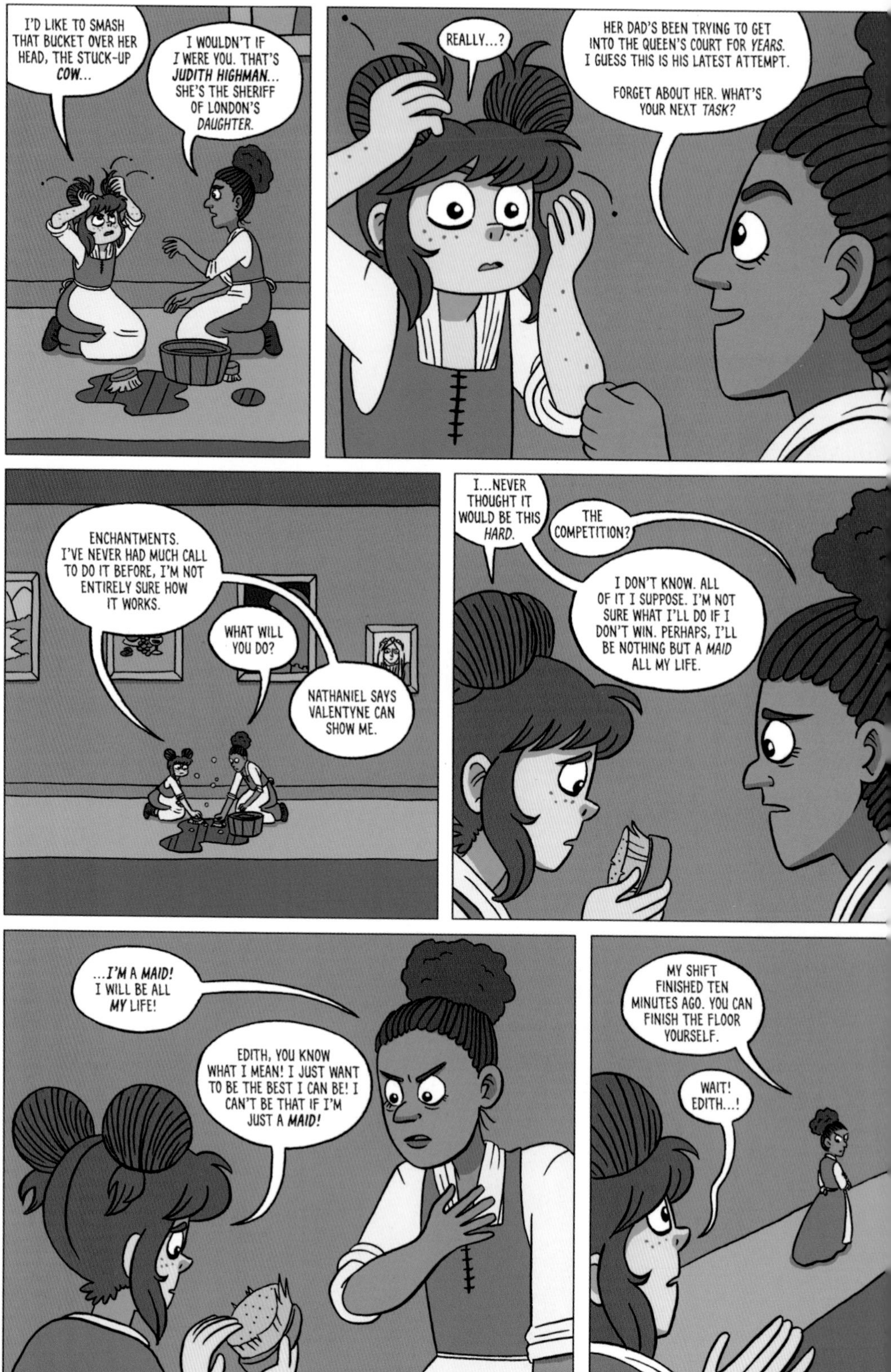
I'D LIKE TO SMASH THAT BUCKET OVER HER HEAD, THE STUCK-UP COW...
I WOULDN'T IF I WERE YOU. THAT'S JUDITH HIGHMAN... SHE'S THE SHERIFF OF LONDON'S DAUGHTER.
REALLY...?
HER DAD'S BEEN TRYING TO GET INTO THE QUEEN'S COURT FOR YEARS. I GUESS THIS IS HIS LATEST ATTEMPT.
FORGET ABOUT HER. WHAT'S YOUR NEXT TASK?
ENCHANTMENTS. I'VE NEVER HAD MUCH CALL TO DO IT BEFORE, I'M NOT ENTIRELY SURE HOW IT WORKS.
WHAT WILL YOU DO?
NATHANIEL SAYS VALENTYNE CAN SHOW ME.
I...NEVER THOUGHT IT WOULD BE THIS HARD.
THE COMPETITION?
I DON'T KNOW. ALL OF IT I SUPPOSE. I'M NOT SURE WHAT I'LL DO IF I DON'T WIN. PERHAPS, I'LL BE NOTHING BUT A MAID ALL MY LIFE.
...I'M A MAID! I WILL BE ALL MY LIFE!
EDITH, YOU KNOW WHAT I MEAN! I JUST WANT TO BE THE BEST I CAN BE! I CAN'T BE THAT IF I'M JUST A MAID!
MY SHIFT FINISHED TEN MINUTES AGO. YOU CAN FINISH THE FLOOR YOURSELF.
WAIT! EDITH...!

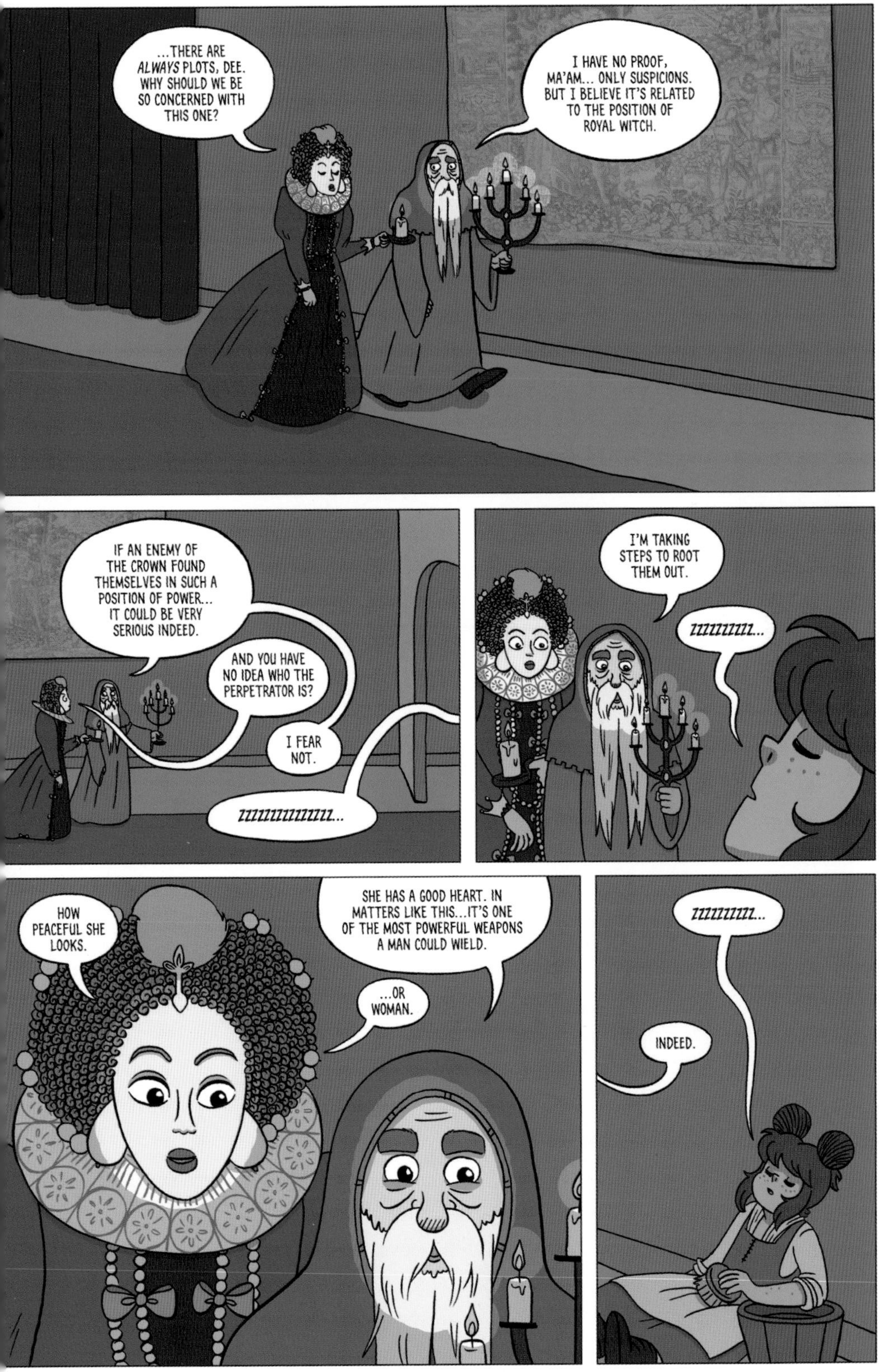
...THERE ARE *ALWAYS* PLOTS, DEE. WHY SHOULD WE BE SO CONCERNED WITH THIS ONE?
I HAVE NO PROOF, MA'AM... ONLY SUSPICIONS. BUT I BELIEVE IT'S RELATED TO THE POSITION OF ROYAL WITCH.
IF AN ENEMY OF THE CROWN FOUND THEMSELVES IN SUCH A POSITION OF POWER... IT COULD BE VERY SERIOUS INDEED.
AND YOU HAVE NO IDEA WHO THE PERPETRATOR IS?
I FEAR NOT.
ZZZZZZZZZZZZZZ...
I'M TAKING STEPS TO ROOT THEM OUT.
ZZZZZZZZZZ...
HOW PEACEFUL SHE LOOKS.
SHE HAS A GOOD HEART. IN MATTERS LIKE THIS...IT'S ONE OF THE MOST POWERFUL WEAPONS A MAN COULD WIELD.
...OR WOMAN.
ZZZZZZZZZZ...
INDEED.

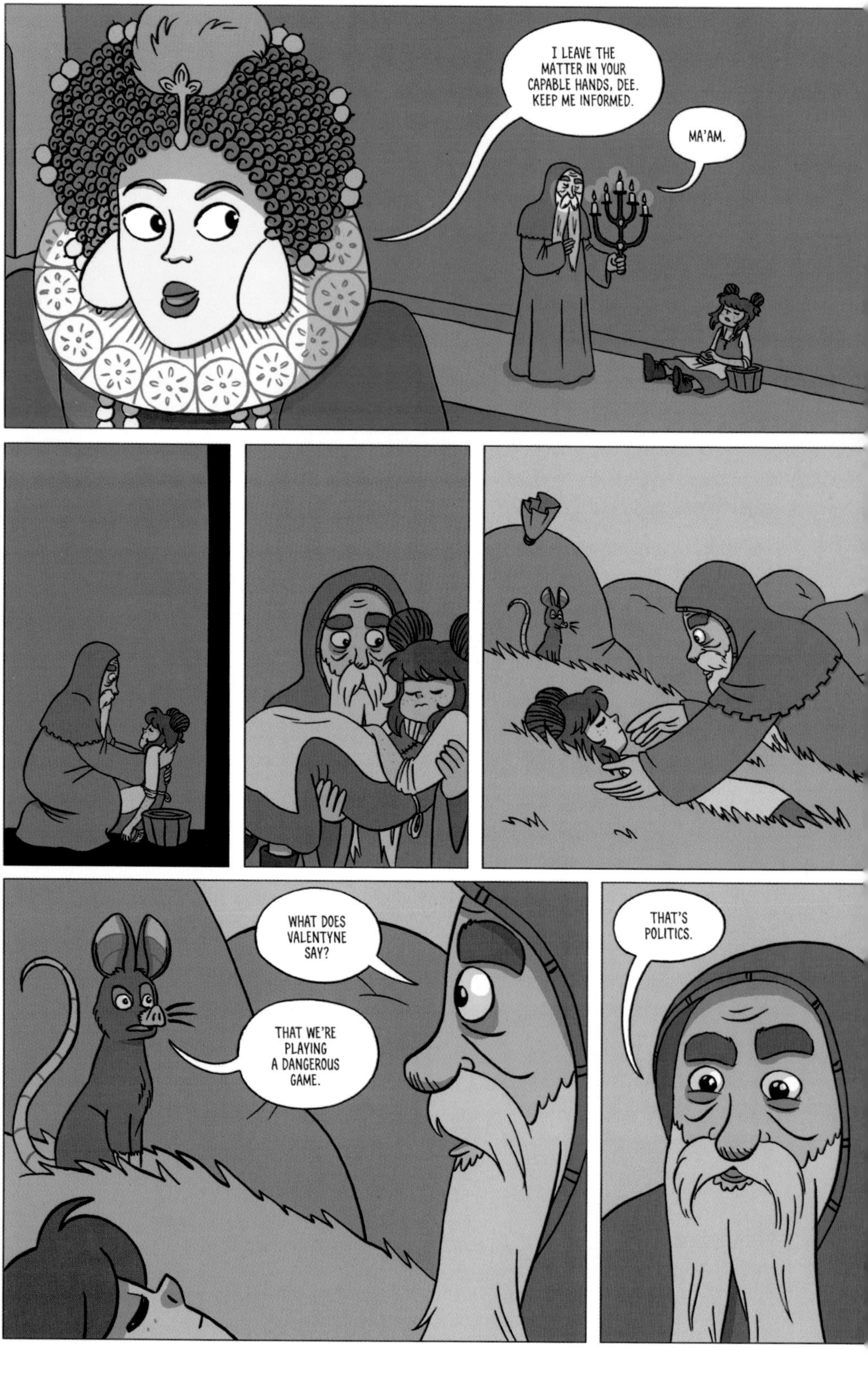
I LEAVE THE MATTER IN YOUR CAPABLE HANDS, DEE. KEEP ME INFORMED.
MA'AM.
WHAT DOES VALENTYNE SAY?
THAT WE'RE PLAYING A DANGEROUS GAME.
THAT'S POLITICS.

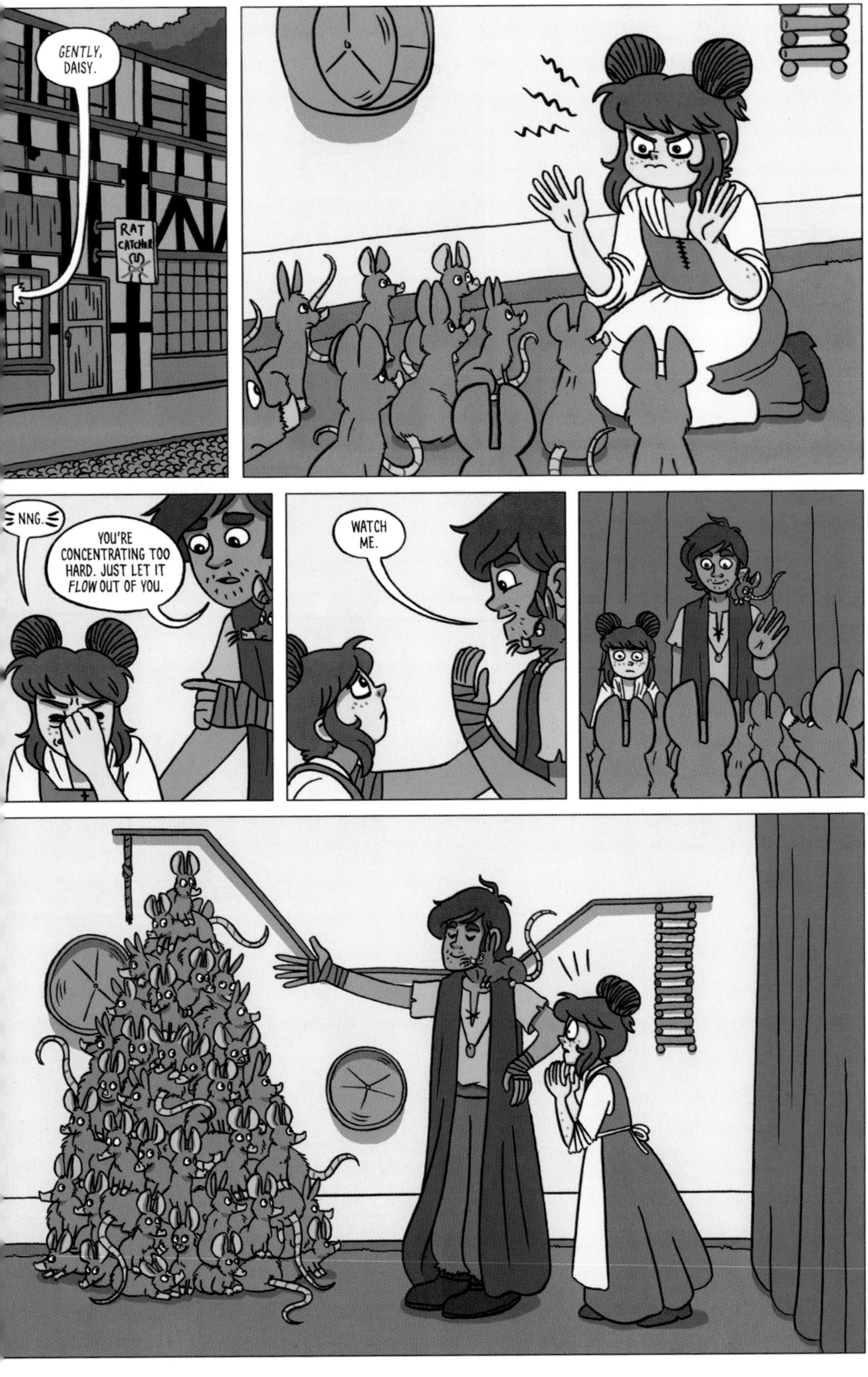

GENTLY, DAISY.
RAT CATCHER
NNG.
YOU'RE CONCENTRATING TOO HARD. JUST LET IT *FLOW* OUT OF YOU.
WATCH ME.

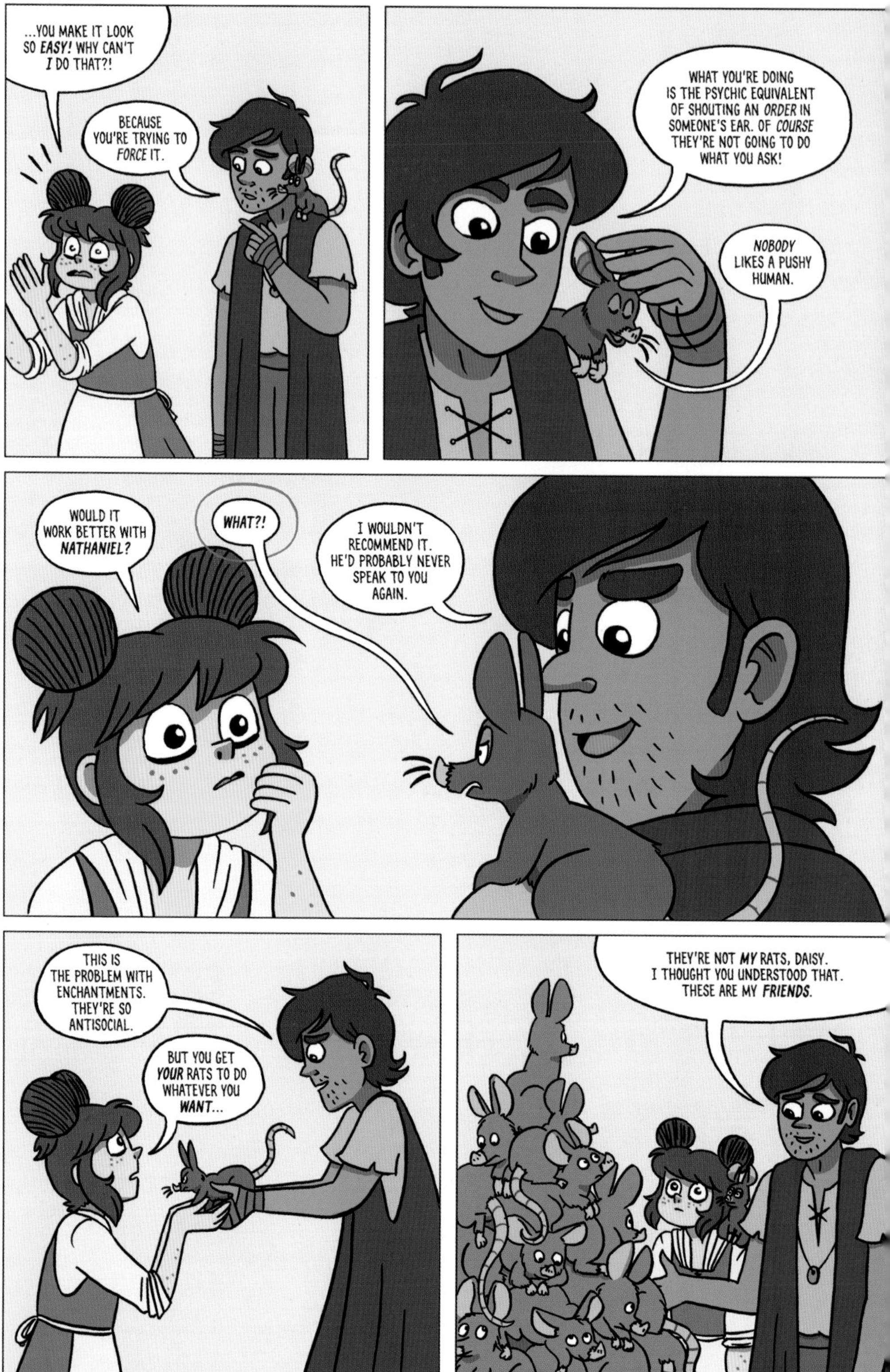
...YOU MAKE IT LOOK SO *EASY!* WHY CAN'T *I* DO THAT?!
BECAUSE YOU'RE TRYING TO *FORCE* IT.
WHAT YOU'RE DOING IS THE PSYCHIC EQUIVALENT OF SHOUTING AN *ORDER* IN SOMEONE'S EAR. OF *COURSE* THEY'RE NOT GOING TO DO WHAT YOU ASK!
NOBODY LIKES A PUSHY HUMAN.
WOULD IT WORK BETTER WITH *NATHANIEL?*
WHAT?!
I WOULDN'T RECOMMEND IT. HE'D PROBABLY NEVER SPEAK TO YOU AGAIN.
THIS IS THE PROBLEM WITH ENCHANTMENTS. THEY'RE SO ANTISOCIAL.
BUT YOU GET *YOUR* RATS TO DO WHATEVER YOU *WANT*...
THEY'RE NOT *MY* RATS, DAISY. I THOUGHT YOU UNDERSTOOD THAT. THESE ARE MY *FRIENDS*.

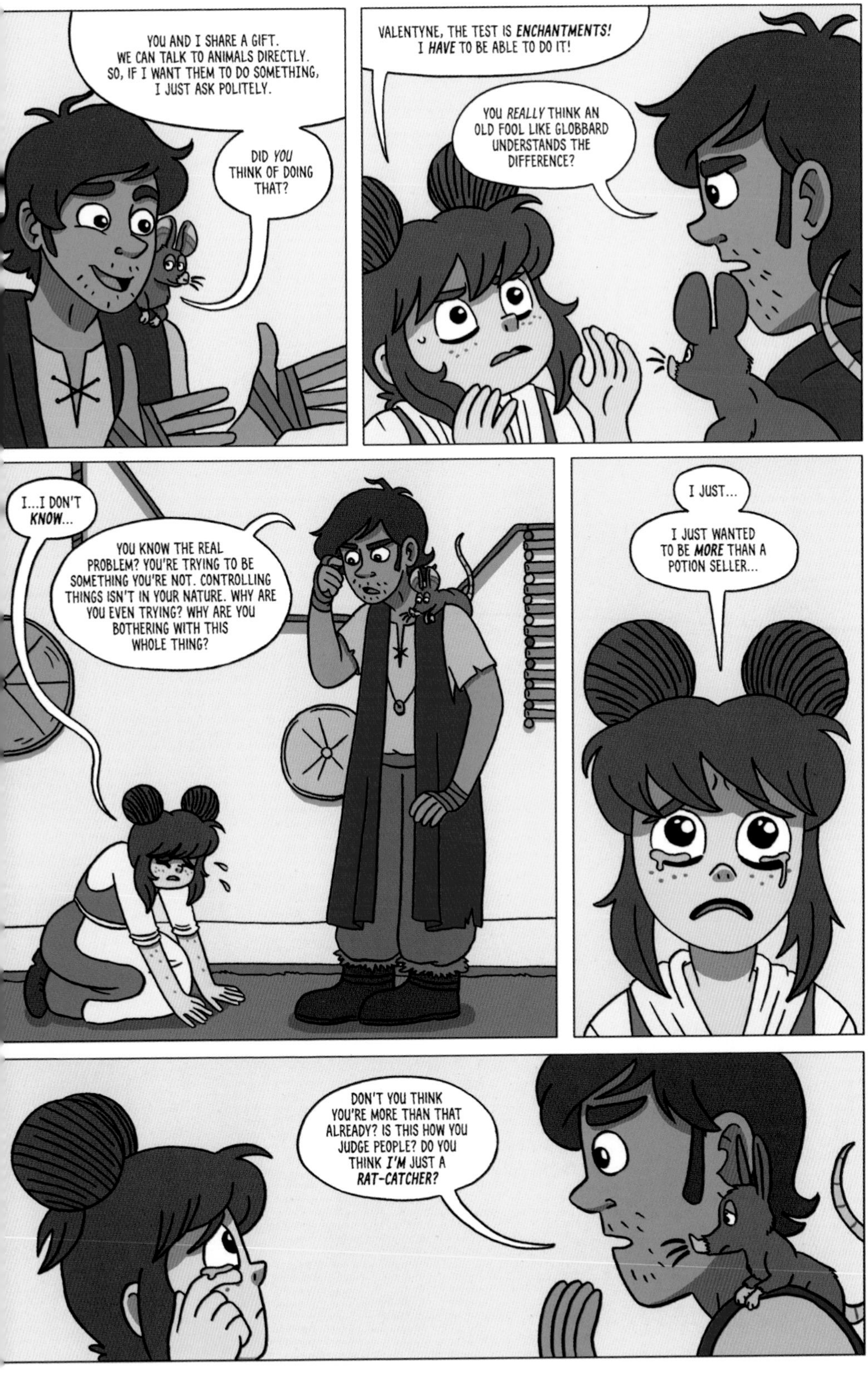

YOU AND I SHARE A GIFT. WE CAN TALK TO ANIMALS DIRECTLY. SO, IF I WANT THEM TO DO SOMETHING, I JUST ASK POLITELY.
DID *YOU* THINK OF DOING THAT?
VALENTYNE, THE TEST IS ***ENCHANTMENTS!*** I ***HAVE*** TO BE ABLE TO DO IT!
YOU *REALLY* THINK AN OLD FOOL LIKE GLOBBARD UNDERSTANDS THE DIFFERENCE?
I...I DON'T ***KNOW***...
YOU KNOW THE REAL PROBLEM? YOU'RE TRYING TO BE SOMETHING YOU'RE NOT. CONTROLLING THINGS ISN'T IN YOUR NATURE. WHY ARE YOU EVEN TRYING? WHY ARE YOU BOTHERING WITH THIS WHOLE THING?
I JUST...
I JUST WANTED TO BE ***MORE*** THAN A POTION SELLER...
DON'T YOU THINK YOU'RE MORE THAN THAT ALREADY? IS THIS HOW YOU JUDGE PEOPLE? DO YOU THINK ***I'M*** JUST A ***RAT-CATCHER?***

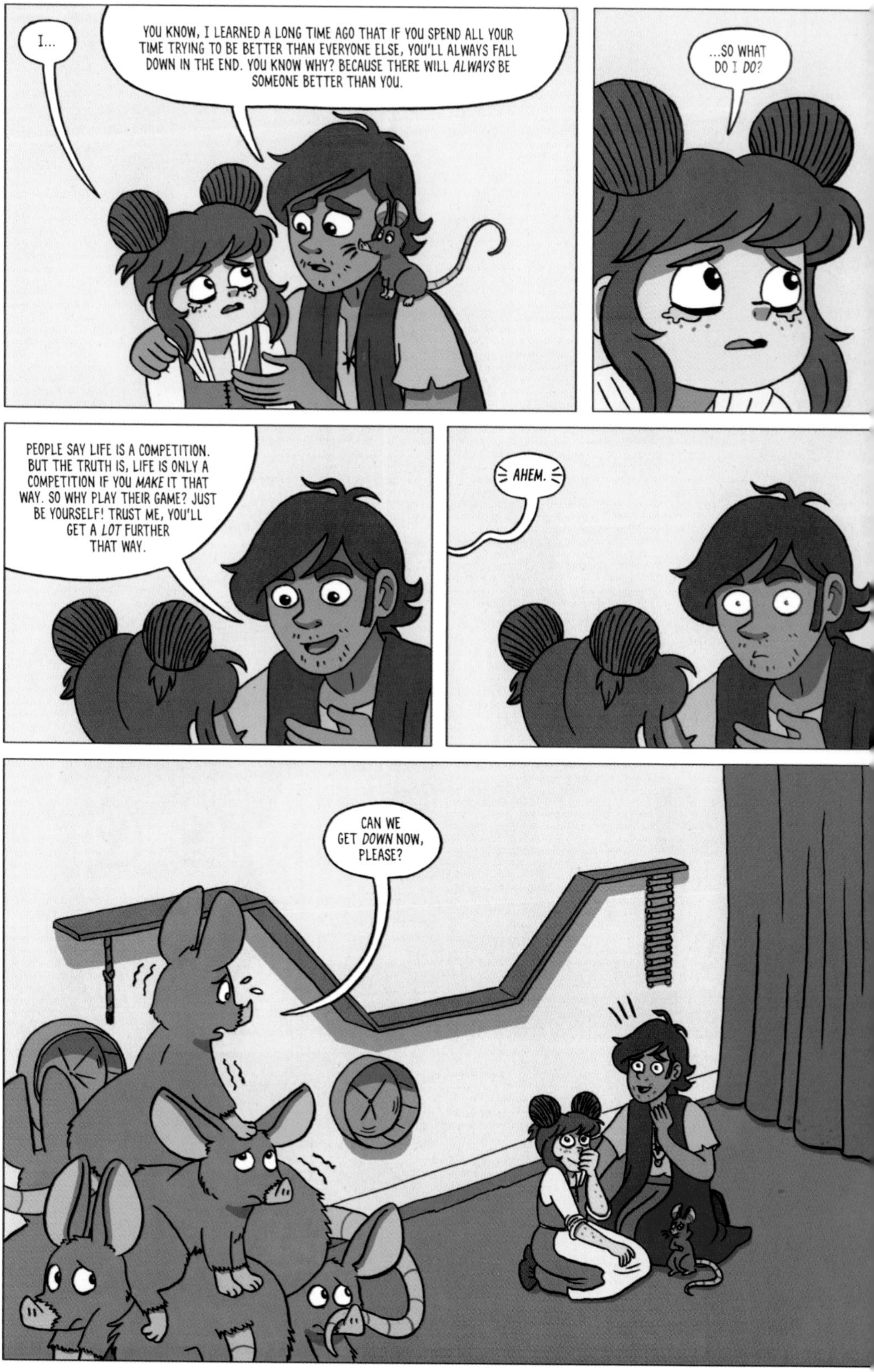
I...
YOU KNOW, I LEARNED A LONG TIME AGO THAT IF YOU SPEND ALL YOUR TIME TRYING TO BE BETTER THAN EVERYONE ELSE, YOU'LL ALWAYS FALL DOWN IN THE END. YOU KNOW WHY? BECAUSE THERE WILL *ALWAYS* BE SOMEONE BETTER THAN YOU.
...SO WHAT DO I *DO?*
PEOPLE SAY LIFE IS A COMPETITION. BUT THE TRUTH IS, LIFE IS ONLY A COMPETITION IF YOU *MAKE* IT THAT WAY. SO WHY PLAY THEIR GAME? JUST BE YOURSELF! TRUST ME, YOU'LL GET A *LOT* FURTHER THAT WAY.
AHEM.
CAN WE GET *DOWN* NOW, PLEASE?

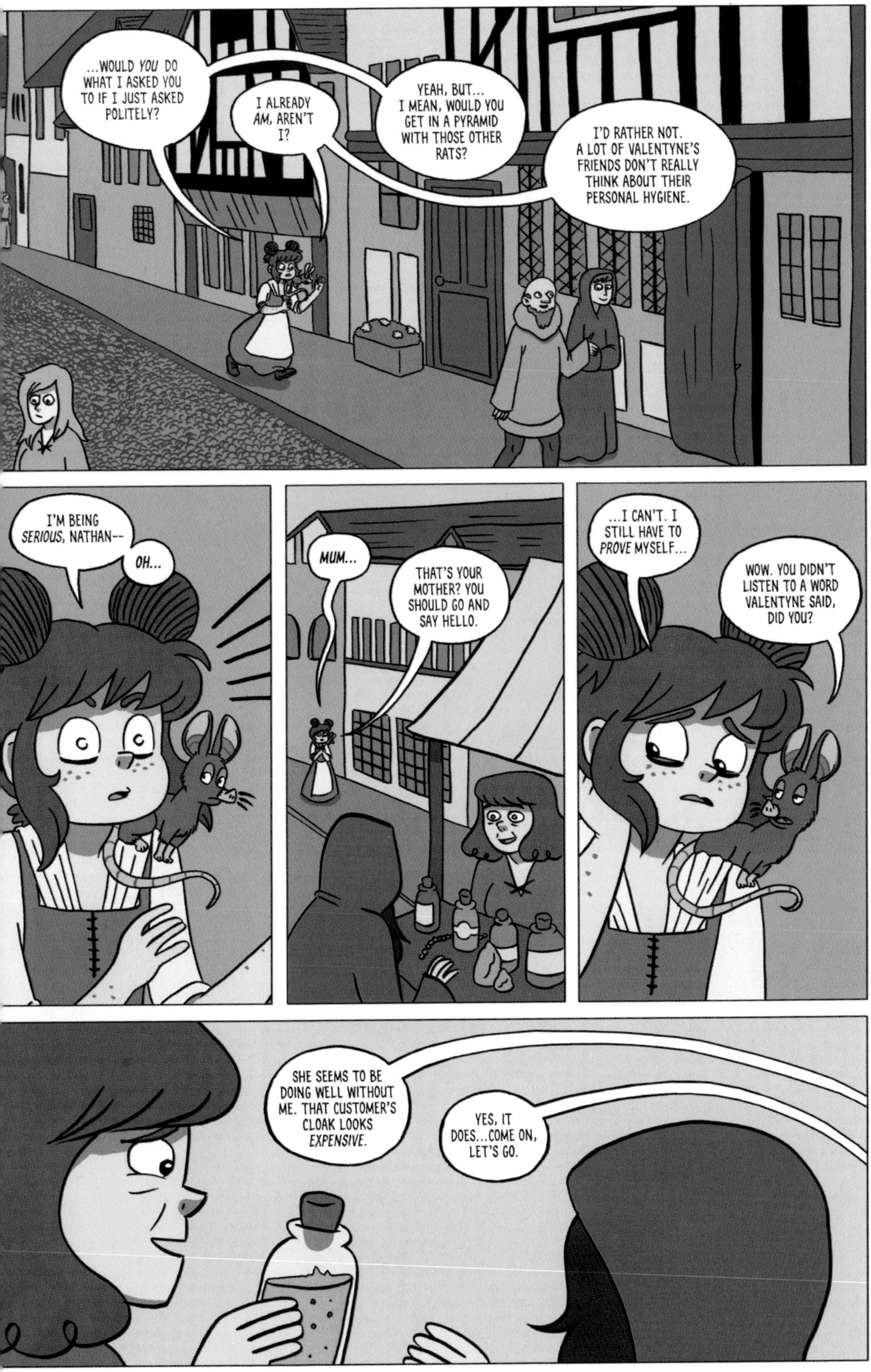
...WOULD *YOU* DO WHAT I ASKED YOU TO IF I JUST ASKED POLITELY?
I ALREADY *AM*, AREN'T I?
YEAH, BUT... I MEAN, WOULD YOU GET IN A PYRAMID WITH THOSE OTHER RATS?
I'D RATHER NOT. A LOT OF VALENTYNE'S FRIENDS DON'T REALLY THINK ABOUT THEIR PERSONAL HYGIENE.
I'M BEING *SERIOUS*, NATHAN--
OH...
MUM...
THAT'S YOUR MOTHER? YOU SHOULD GO AND SAY HELLO.
...I CAN'T. I STILL HAVE TO *PROVE* MYSELF...
WOW. YOU DIDN'T LISTEN TO A WORD VALENTYNE SAID, DID YOU?
SHE SEEMS TO BE DOING WELL WITHOUT ME. THAT CUSTOMER'S CLOAK LOOKS *EXPENSIVE*.
YES, IT DOES...COME ON, LET'S GO.

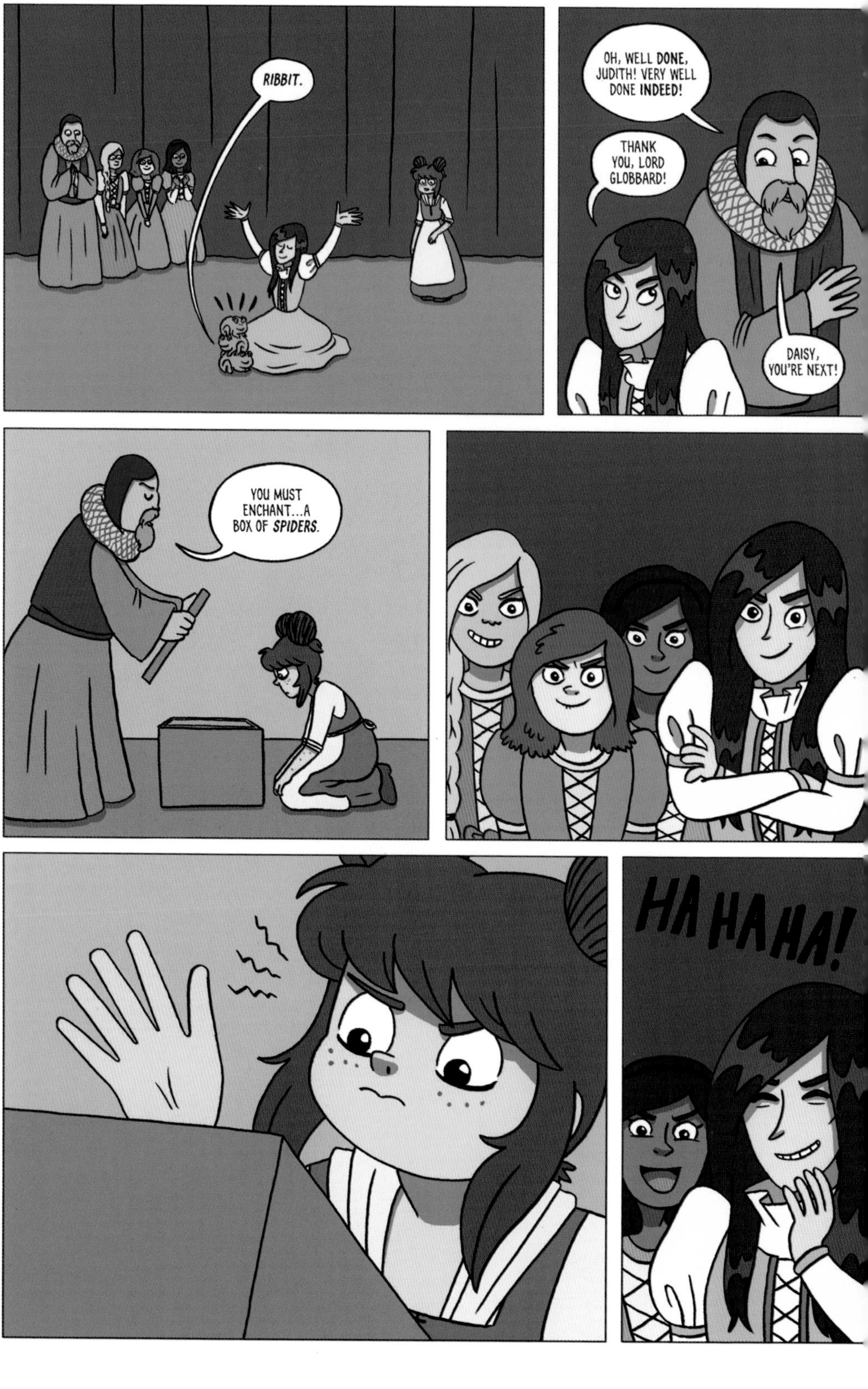
RIBBIT.
OH, WELL DONE, JUDITH! VERY WELL DONE INDEED!
THANK YOU, LORD GLOBBARD!
DAISY, YOU'RE NEXT!
YOU MUST ENCHANT...A BOX OF SPIDERS.
HA HA HA HA!

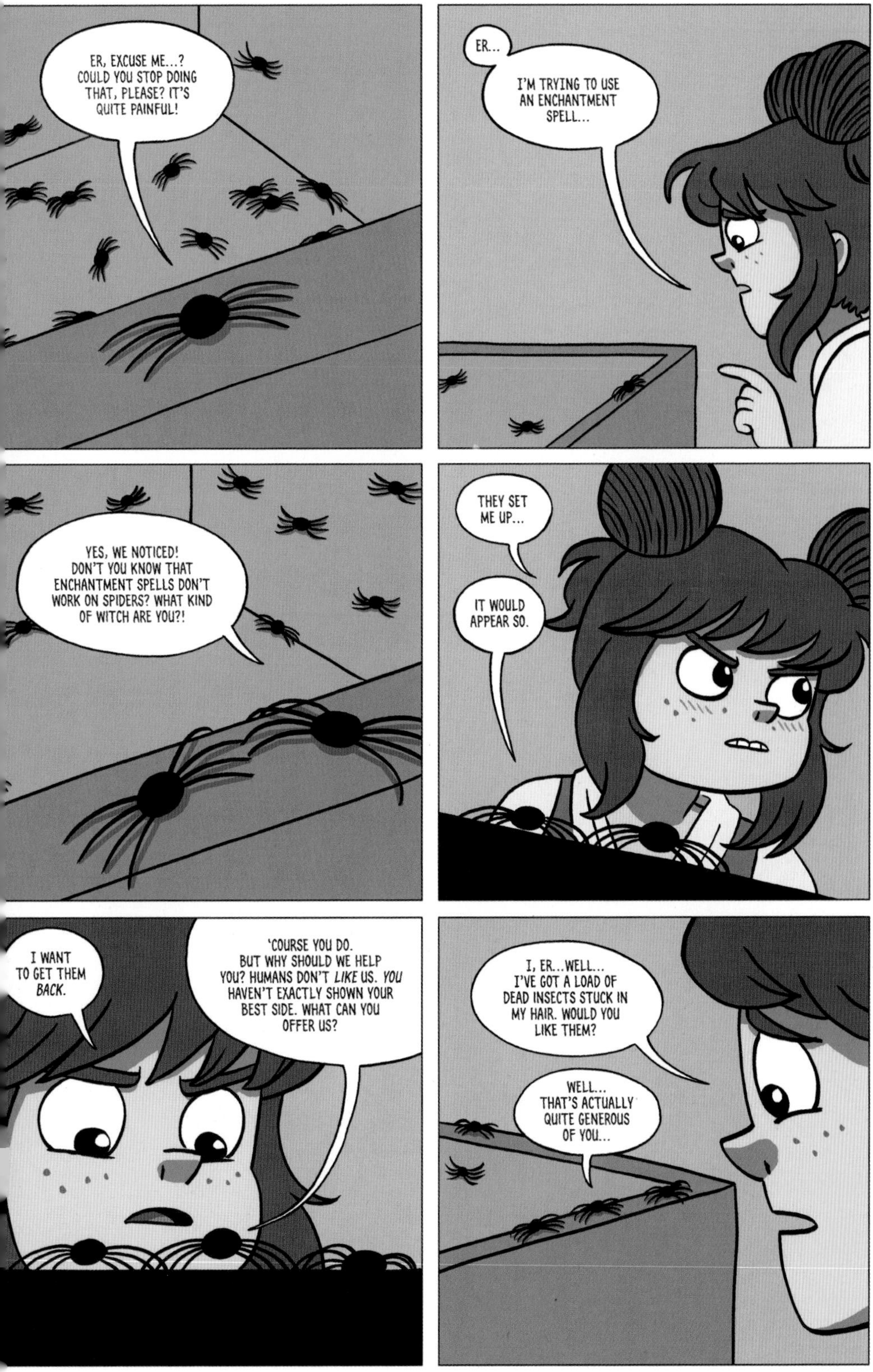
ER, EXCUSE ME...? COULD YOU STOP DOING THAT, PLEASE? IT'S QUITE PAINFUL!
ER...
I'M TRYING TO USE AN ENCHANTMENT SPELL...
YES, WE NOTICED! DON'T YOU KNOW THAT ENCHANTMENT SPELLS DON'T WORK ON SPIDERS? WHAT KIND OF WITCH ARE YOU?!
THEY SET ME UP...
IT WOULD APPEAR SO.
I WANT TO GET THEM *BACK*.
'COURSE YOU DO. BUT WHY SHOULD WE HELP YOU? HUMANS DON'T *LIKE* US. *YOU* HAVEN'T EXACTLY SHOWN YOUR BEST SIDE. WHAT CAN YOU OFFER US?
I, ER...WELL... I'VE GOT A LOAD OF DEAD INSECTS STUCK IN MY HAIR. WOULD YOU LIKE THEM?
WELL... THAT'S ACTUALLY QUITE GENEROUS OF YOU...

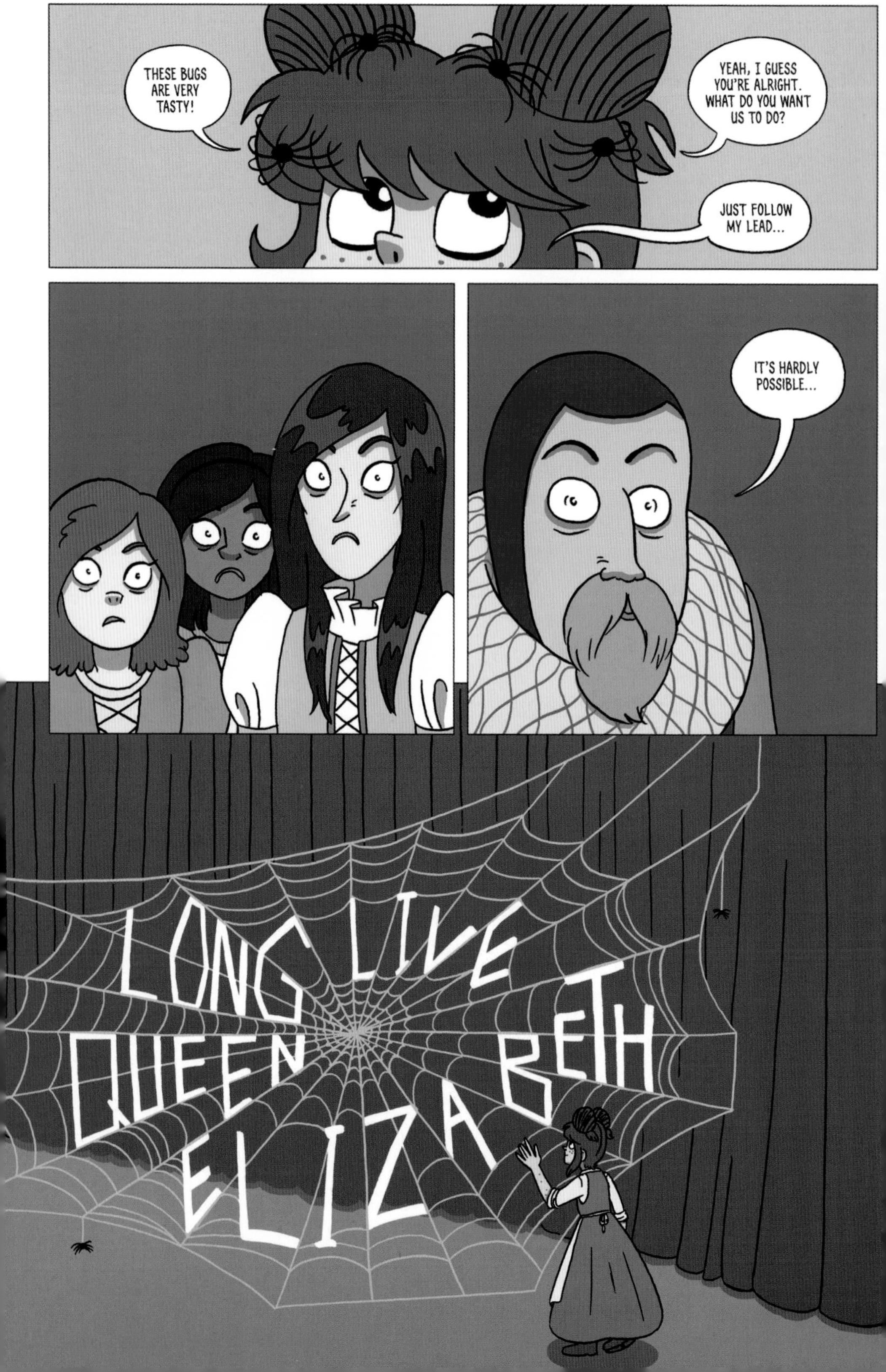
THESE BUGS ARE VERY TASTY!
YEAH, I GUESS YOU'RE ALRIGHT. WHAT DO YOU WANT US TO DO?
JUST FOLLOW MY LEAD...
IT'S HARDLY POSSIBLE...
LONG LIVE QUEEN ELIZABETH

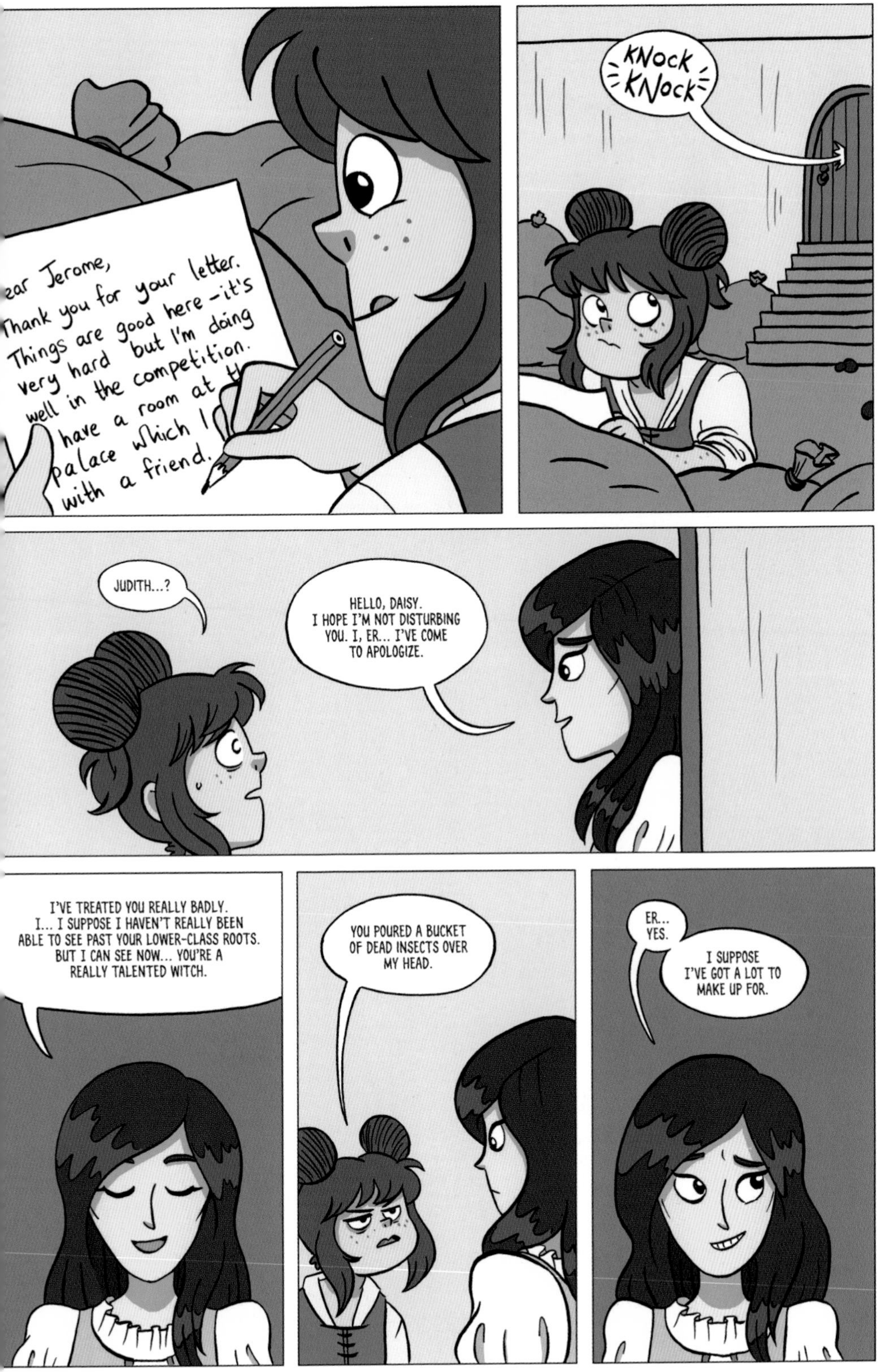

ear Jerome,
Thank you for your letter.
Things are good here - it's
very hard but I'm doing
well in the competition.
have a room at th
palace which I
with a friend.
KNOCK KNOCK
JUDITH...?
HELLO, DAISY. I HOPE I'M NOT DISTURBING YOU. I, ER... I'VE COME TO APOLOGIZE.
I'VE TREATED YOU REALLY BADLY. I... I SUPPOSE I HAVEN'T REALLY BEEN ABLE TO SEE PAST YOUR LOWER-CLASS ROOTS. BUT I CAN SEE NOW... YOU'RE A REALLY TALENTED WITCH.
YOU POURED A BUCKET OF DEAD INSECTS OVER MY HEAD.
ER... YES.
I SUPPOSE I'VE GOT A LOT TO MAKE UP FOR.

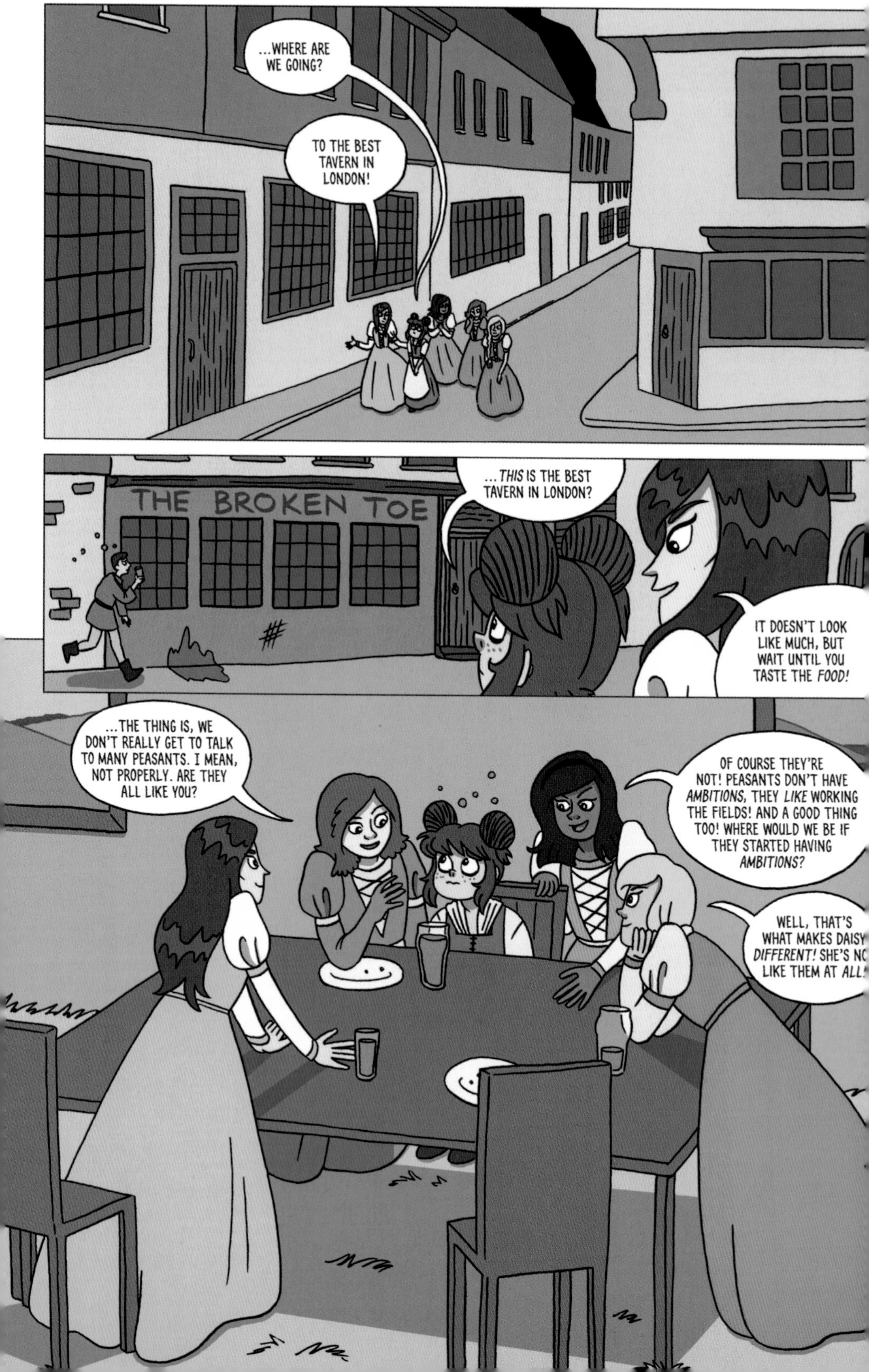
...WHERE ARE WE GOING?
TO THE BEST TAVERN IN LONDON!
THE BROKEN TOE
...*THIS* IS THE BEST TAVERN IN LONDON?
IT DOESN'T LOOK LIKE MUCH, BUT WAIT UNTIL YOU TASTE THE *FOOD!*
...THE THING IS, WE DON'T REALLY GET TO TALK TO MANY PEASANTS. I MEAN, NOT PROPERLY. ARE THEY ALL LIKE YOU?
OF COURSE THEY'RE NOT! PEASANTS DON'T HAVE *AMBITIONS*, THEY *LIKE* WORKING THE FIELDS! AND A GOOD THING TOO! WHERE WOULD WE BE IF THEY STARTED HAVING *AMBITIONS?*
WELL, THAT'S WHAT MAKES DAISY *DIFFERENT!* SHE'S NO LIKE THEM AT *ALL!*

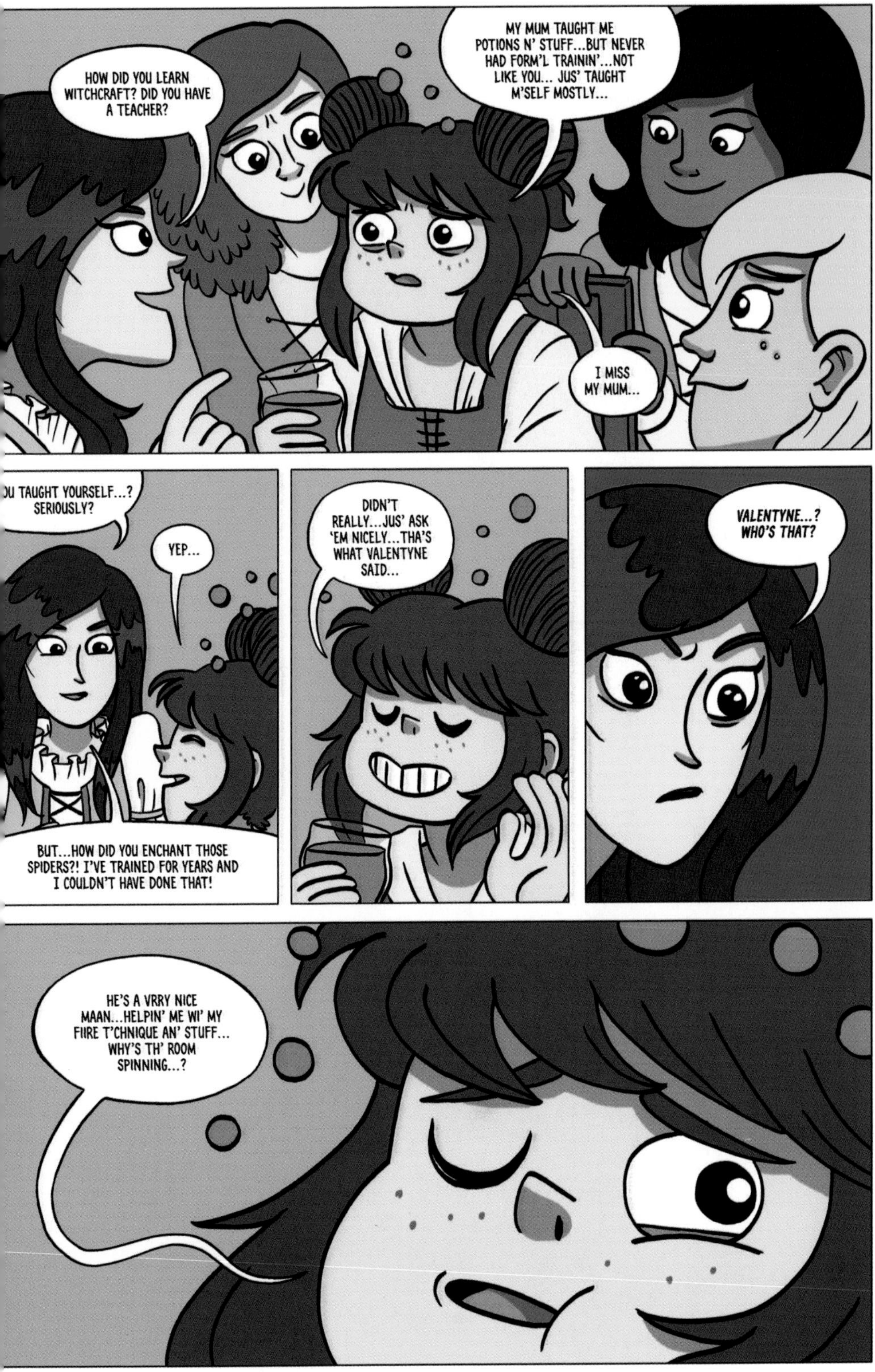
HOW DID YOU LEARN WITCHCRAFT? DID YOU HAVE A TEACHER?
MY MUM TAUGHT ME POTIONS N' STUFF...BUT NEVER HAD FORM'L TRAININ'...NOT LIKE YOU... JUS' TAUGHT M'SELF MOSTLY...
I MISS MY MUM...
OU TAUGHT YOURSELF...? SERIOUSLY?
YEP...
BUT...HOW DID YOU ENCHANT THOSE SPIDERS?! I'VE TRAINED FOR YEARS AND I COULDN'T HAVE DONE THAT!
DIDN'T REALLY...JUS' ASK 'EM NICELY...THA'S WHAT VALENTYNE SAID...
VALENTYNE...? WHO'S THAT?
HE'S A VRRY NICE MAAN...HELPIN' ME WI' MY FIIRE T'CHNIQUE AN' STUFF... WHY'S TH' ROOM SPINNING...?

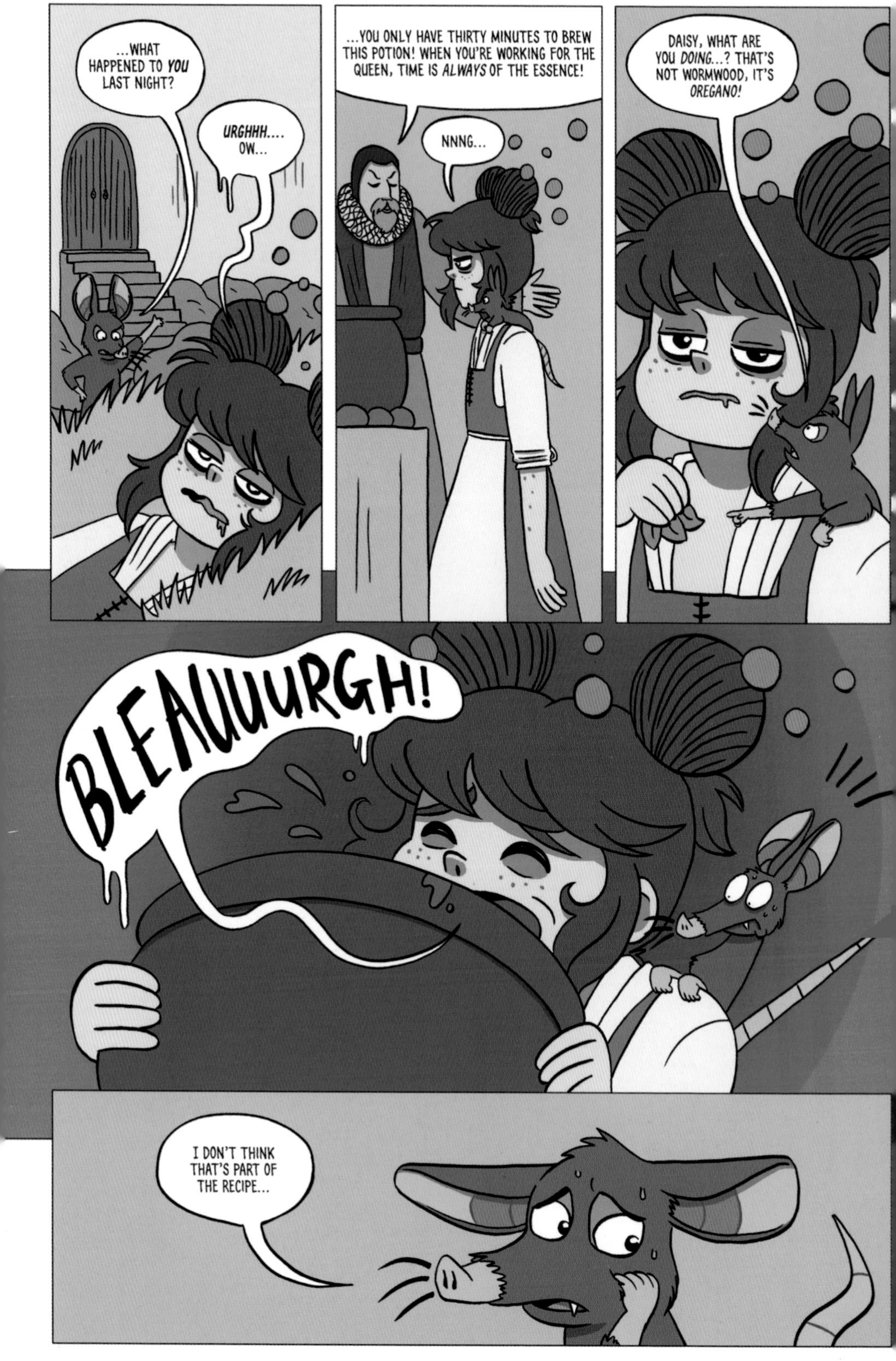
...WHAT HAPPENED TO YOU LAST NIGHT?
URGHHH.... OW...
...YOU ONLY HAVE THIRTY MINUTES TO BREW THIS POTION! WHEN YOU'RE WORKING FOR THE QUEEN, TIME IS ALWAYS OF THE ESSENCE!
NNNG...
DAISY, WHAT ARE YOU DOING...? THAT'S NOT WORMWOOD, IT'S OREGANO!
BLEAUUURGH!
I DON'T THINK THAT'S PART OF THE RECIPE...

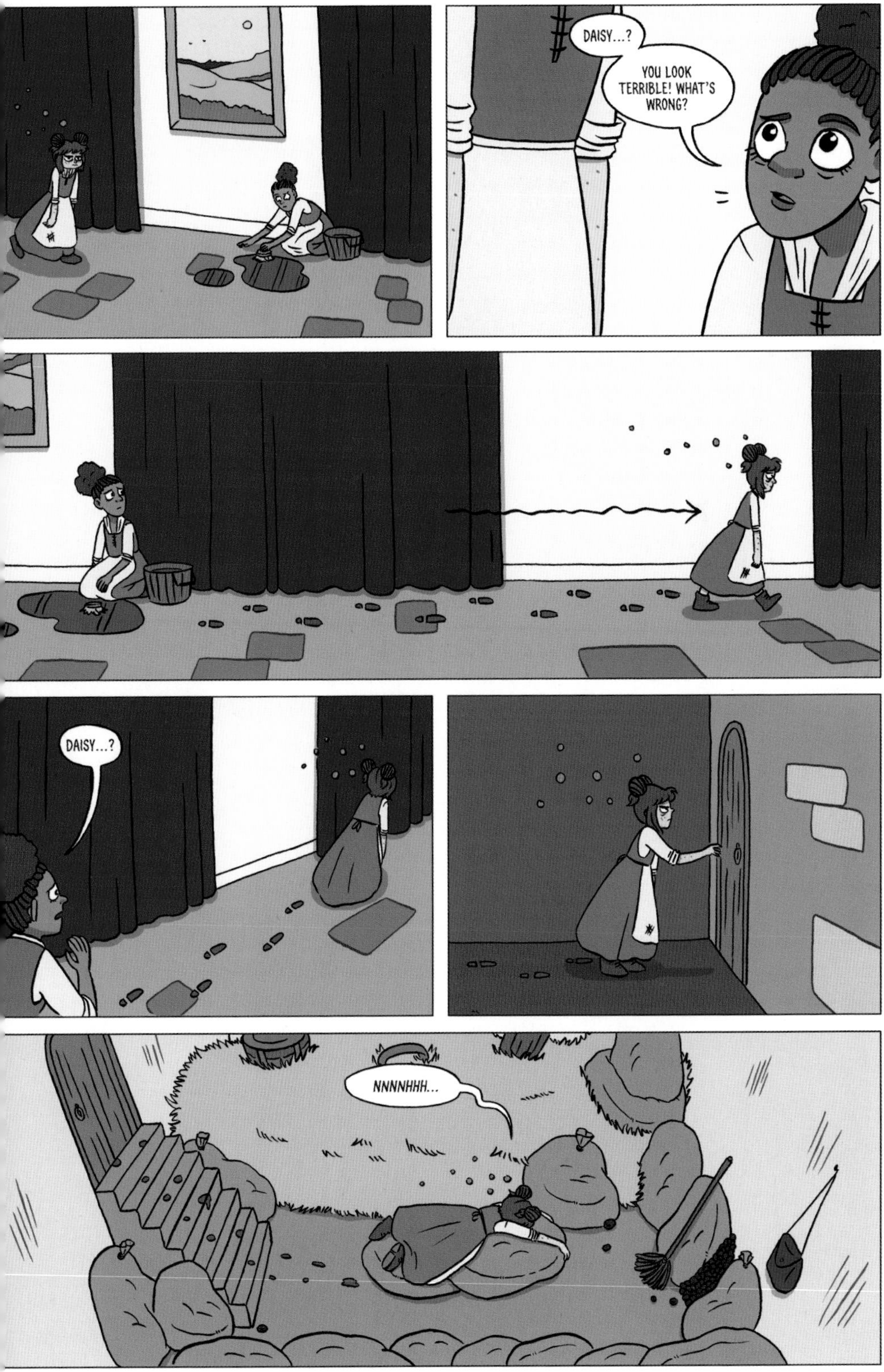
DAISY...?
YOU LOOK TERRIBLE! WHAT'S WRONG?
DAISY...?
NNNNHHH...

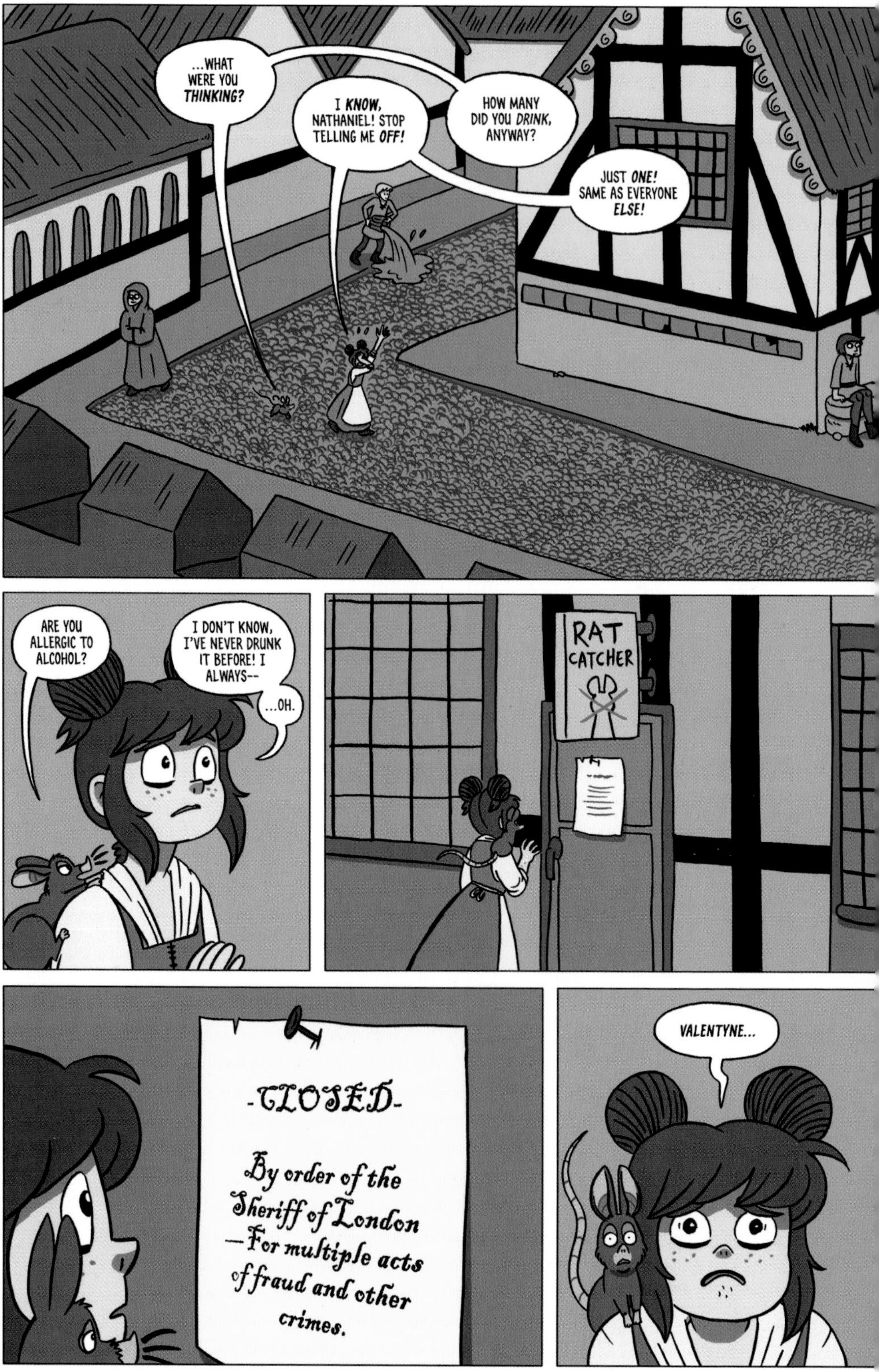
...WHAT WERE YOU THINKING?
I KNOW, NATHANIEL! STOP TELLING ME OFF!
HOW MANY DID YOU DRINK, ANYWAY?
JUST ONE! SAME AS EVERYONE ELSE!
ARE YOU ALLERGIC TO ALCOHOL?
I DON'T KNOW, I'VE NEVER DRUNK IT BEFORE! I ALWAYS--
...OH.
RAT CATCHER
-CLOSED-
By order of the Sheriff of London —For multiple acts of fraud and other crimes.
VALENTYNE...

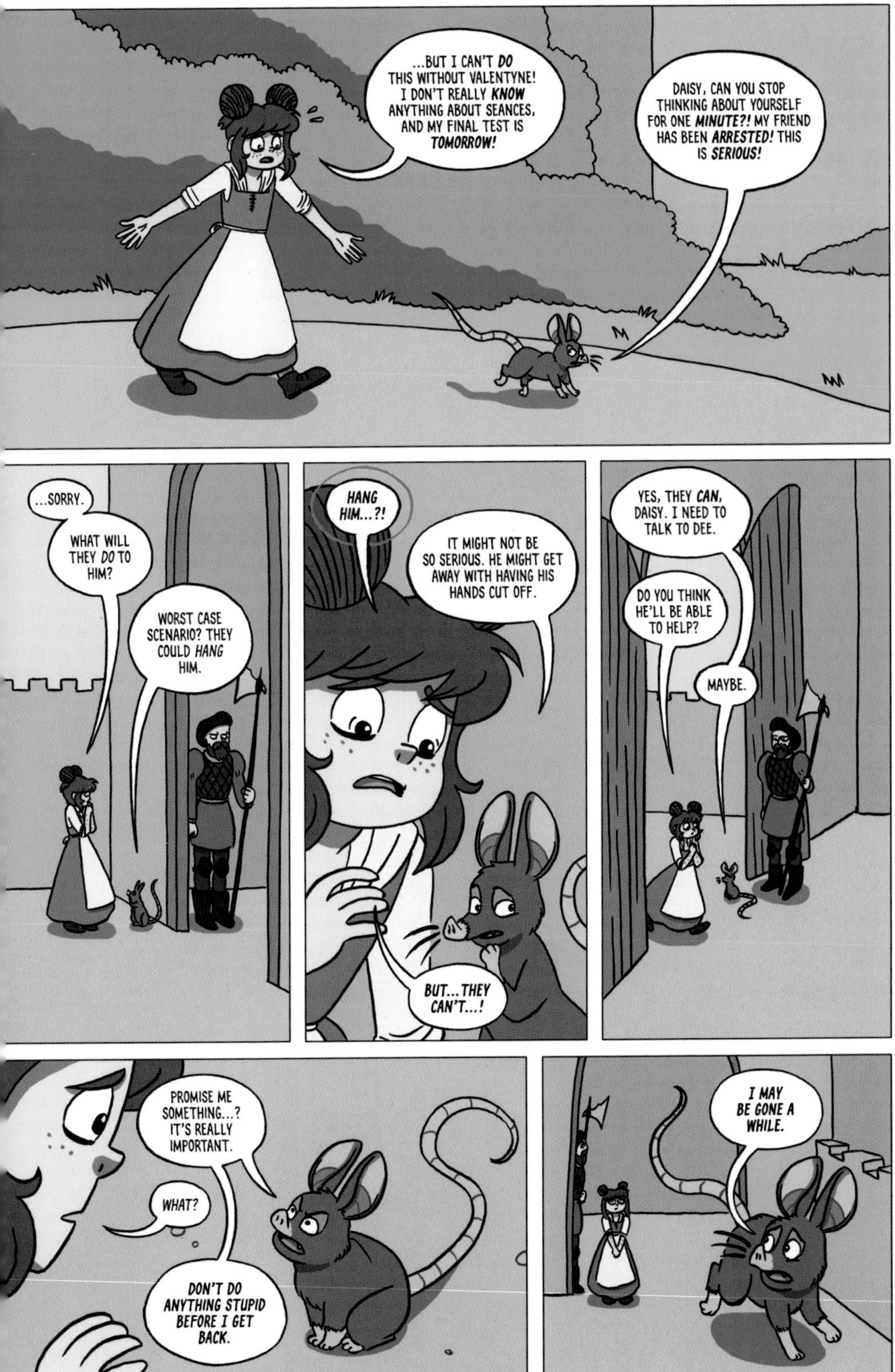
...BUT I CAN'T DO THIS WITHOUT VALENTYNE! I DON'T REALLY KNOW ANYTHING ABOUT SEANCES, AND MY FINAL TEST IS TOMORROW!
DAISY, CAN YOU STOP THINKING ABOUT YOURSELF FOR ONE MINUTE?! MY FRIEND HAS BEEN ARRESTED! THIS IS SERIOUS!
...SORRY.
WHAT WILL THEY DO TO HIM?
WORST CASE SCENARIO? THEY COULD HANG HIM.
HANG HIM...?!
IT MIGHT NOT BE SO SERIOUS. HE MIGHT GET AWAY WITH HAVING HIS HANDS CUT OFF.
BUT...THEY CAN'T...!
YES, THEY CAN, DAISY. I NEED TO TALK TO DEE.
DO YOU THINK HE'LL BE ABLE TO HELP?
MAYBE.
PROMISE ME SOMETHING...? IT'S REALLY IMPORTANT.
WHAT?
DON'T DO ANYTHING STUPID BEFORE I GET BACK.
I MAY BE GONE A WHILE.

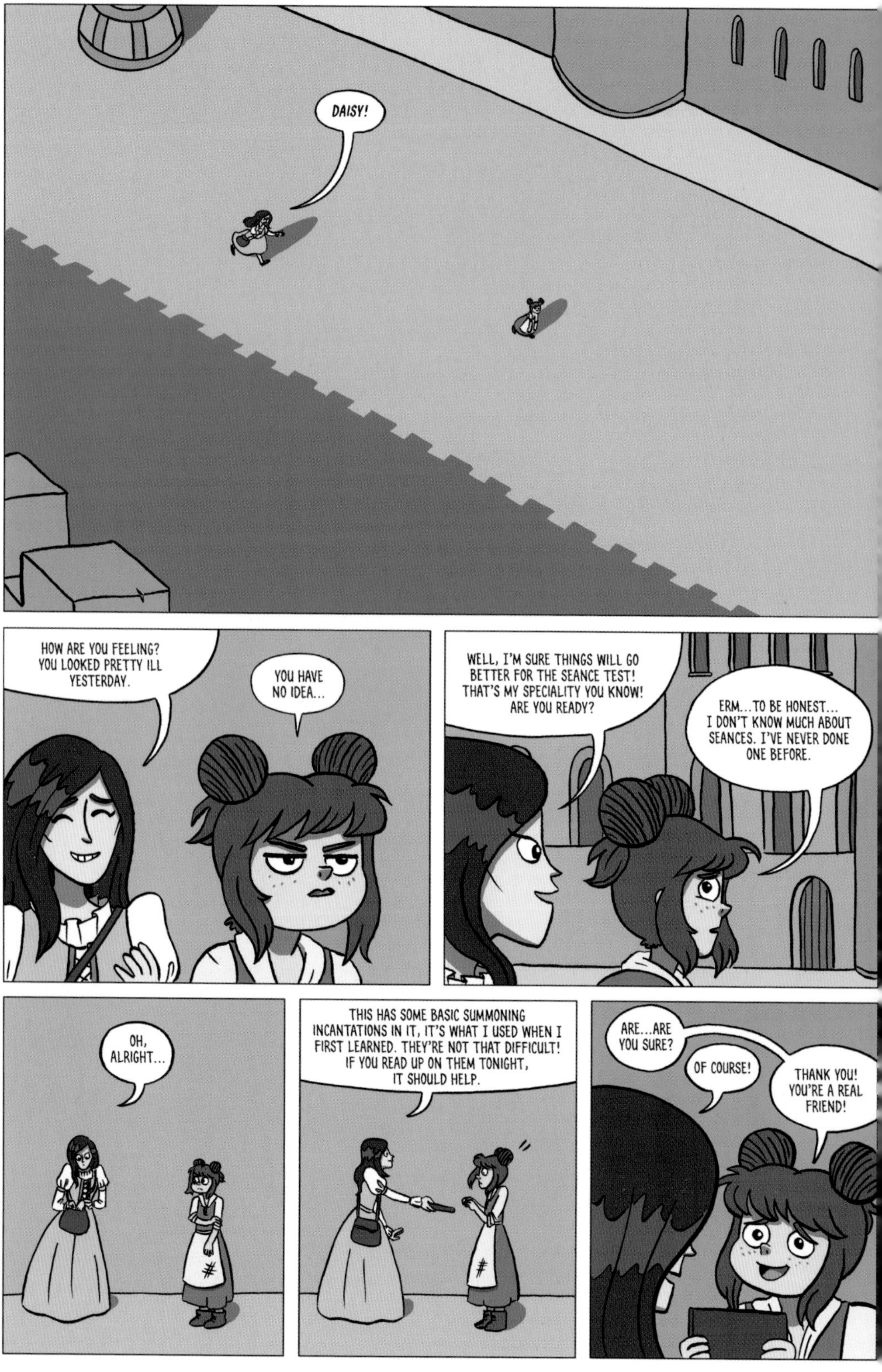
DAISY!
HOW ARE YOU FEELING? YOU LOOKED PRETTY ILL YESTERDAY.
YOU HAVE NO IDEA...
WELL, I'M SURE THINGS WILL GO BETTER FOR THE SEANCE TEST! THAT'S MY SPECIALITY YOU KNOW! ARE YOU READY?
ERM...TO BE HONEST... I DON'T KNOW MUCH ABOUT SEANCES. I'VE NEVER DONE ONE BEFORE.
OH, ALRIGHT...
THIS HAS SOME BASIC SUMMONING INCANTATIONS IN IT, IT'S WHAT I USED WHEN I FIRST LEARNED. THEY'RE NOT THAT DIFFICULT! IF YOU READ UP ON THEM TONIGHT, IT SHOULD HELP.
ARE...ARE YOU SURE?
OF COURSE!
THANK YOU! YOU'RE A REAL FRIEND!

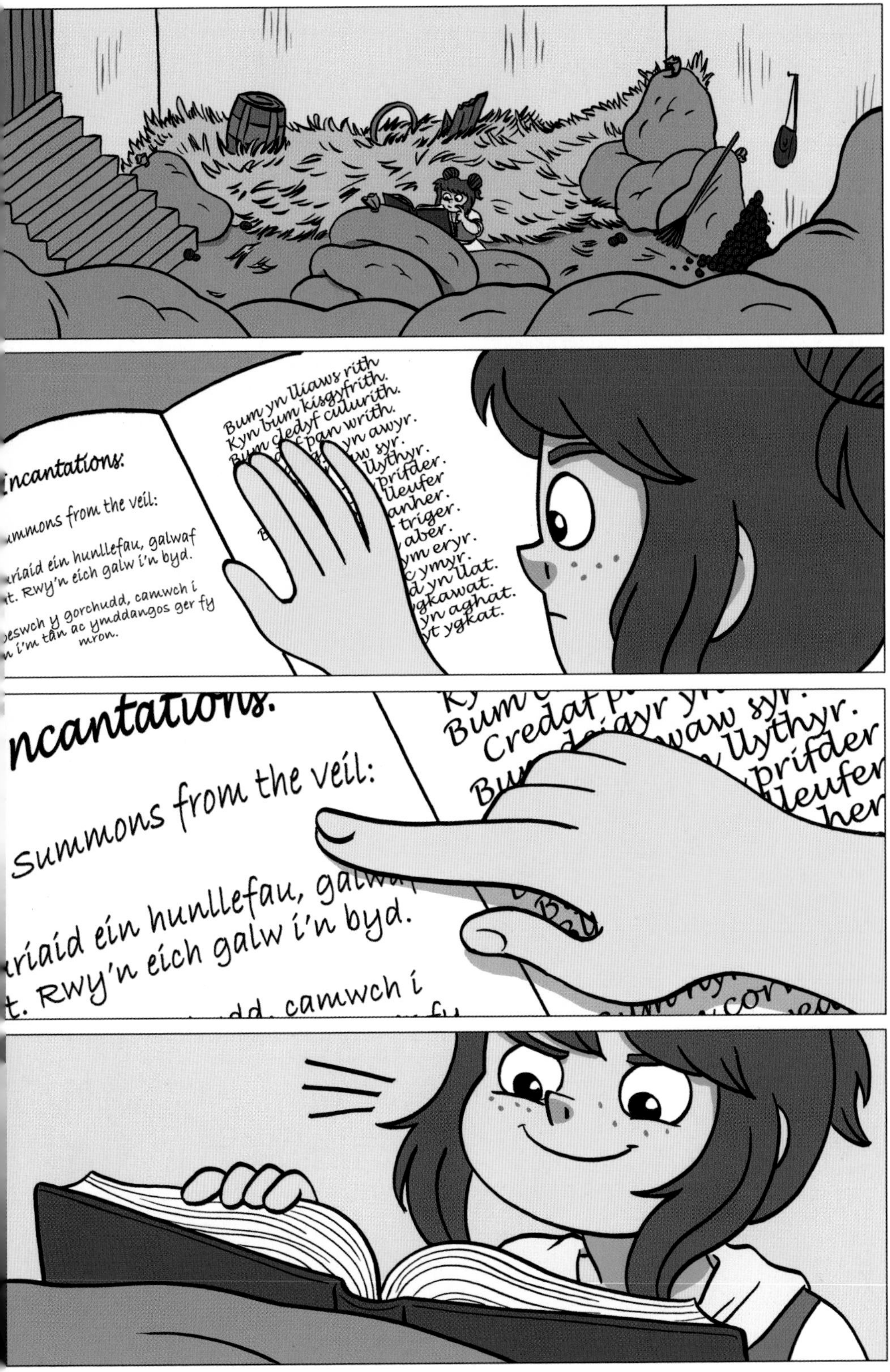

Bum yn lliaws rith
Kyn bum kisgyfrith.
Bum cledyf culurith.
Summons from the veil:
t. Rwy'n eich galw i'n byd.
Summons from the veil:
t. Rwy'n eich galw i'n byd.

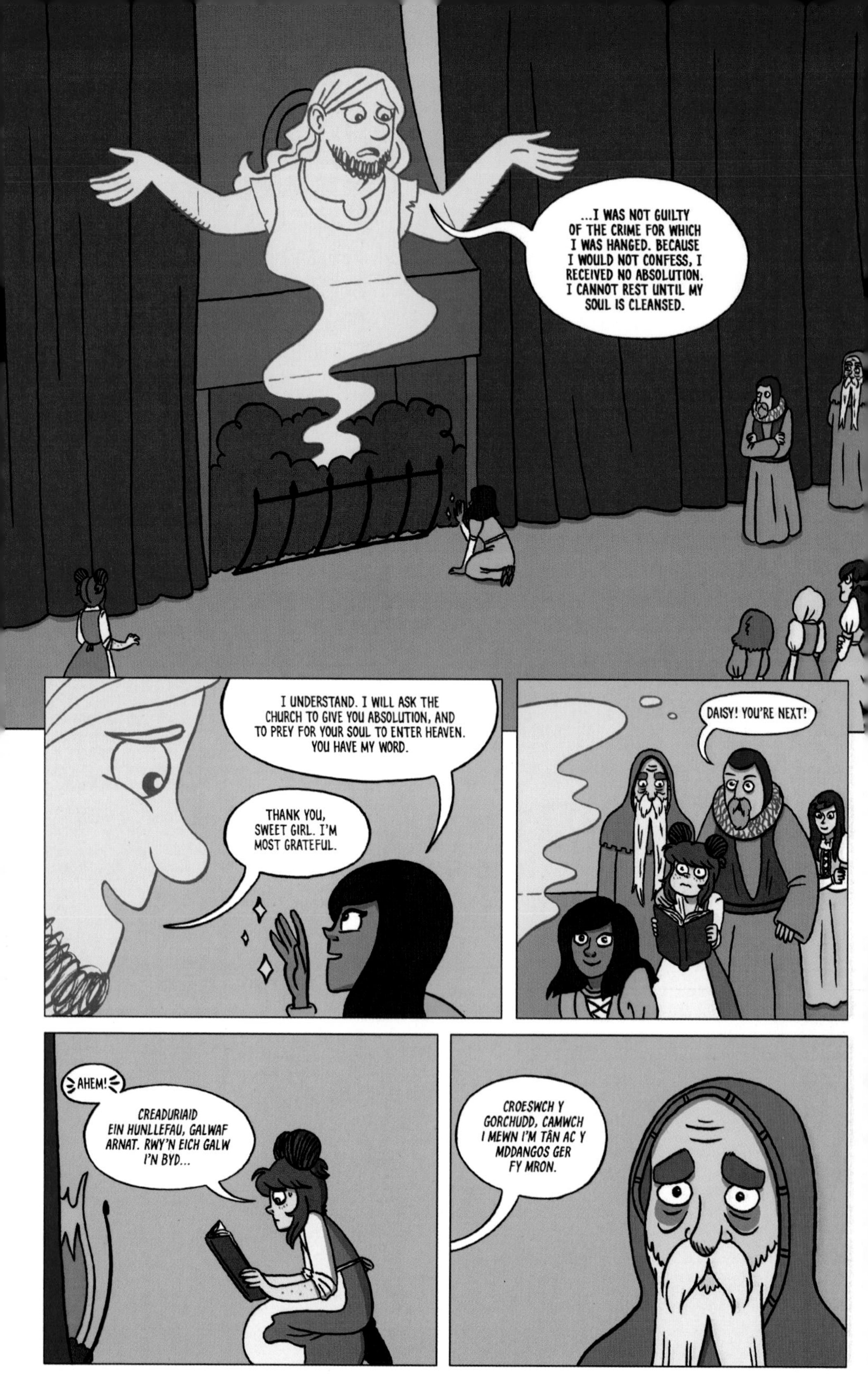

...I WAS NOT GUILTY OF THE CRIME FOR WHICH I WAS HANGED. BECAUSE I WOULD NOT CONFESS, I RECEIVED NO ABSOLUTION. I CANNOT REST UNTIL MY SOUL IS CLEANSED.
I UNDERSTAND. I WILL ASK THE CHURCH TO GIVE YOU ABSOLUTION, AND TO PREY FOR YOUR SOUL TO ENTER HEAVEN. YOU HAVE MY WORD.
THANK YOU, SWEET GIRL. I'M MOST GRATEFUL.
DAISY! YOU'RE NEXT!
AHEM!
CREADURIAID EIN HUNLLEFAU, GALWAF ARNAT. RWY'N EICH GALW I'N BYD...
CROESWCH Y GORCHUDD, CAMWCH I MEWN I'M TÂN AC Y MDDANGOS GER FY MRON.

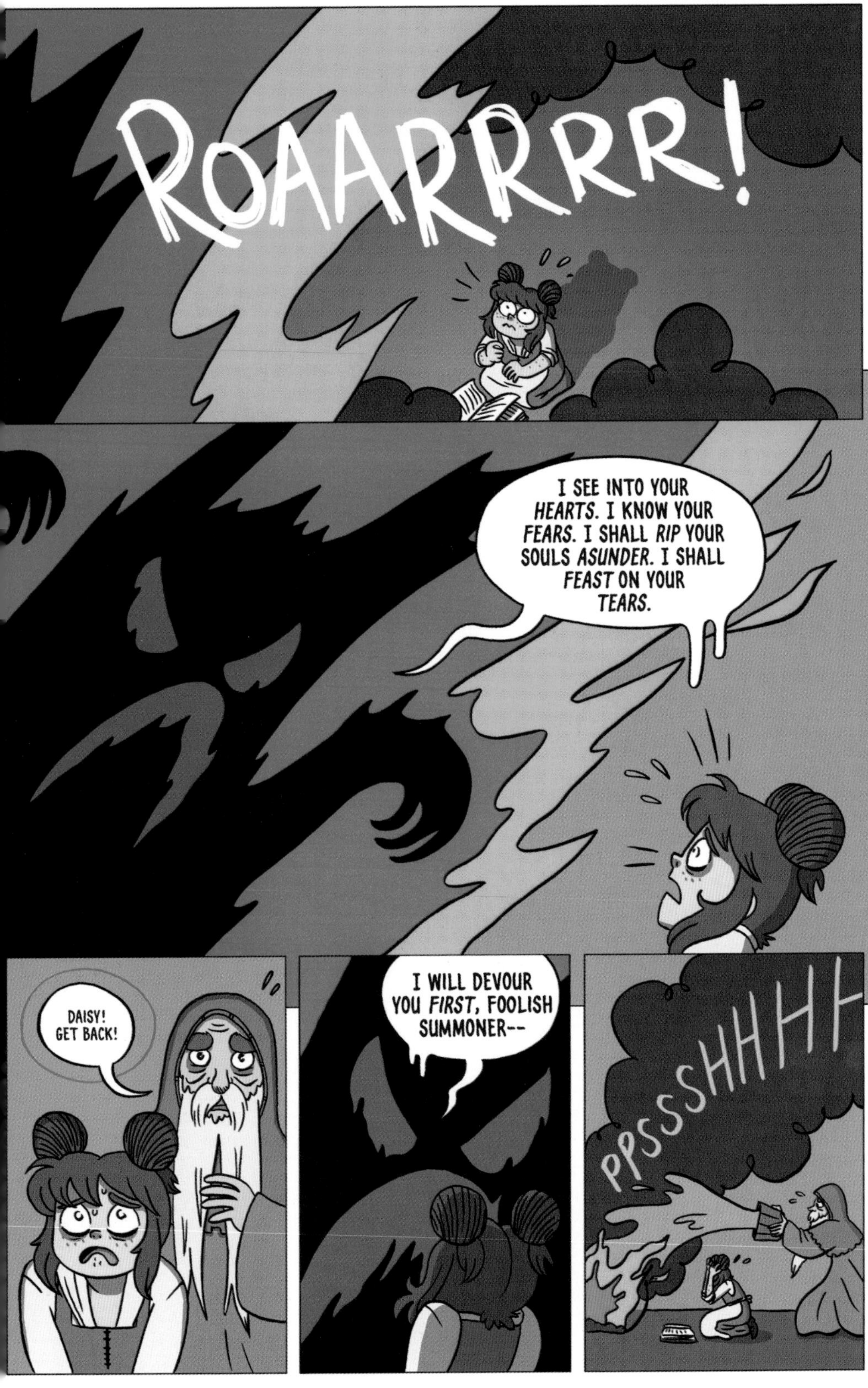
ROAARRRRR!
I SEE INTO YOUR HEARTS. I KNOW YOUR FEARS. I SHALL RIP YOUR SOULS ASUNDER. I SHALL FEAST ON YOUR TEARS.
DAISY! GET BACK!
I WILL DEVOUR YOU FIRST, FOOLISH SUMMONER--
PPSSSHHHHH

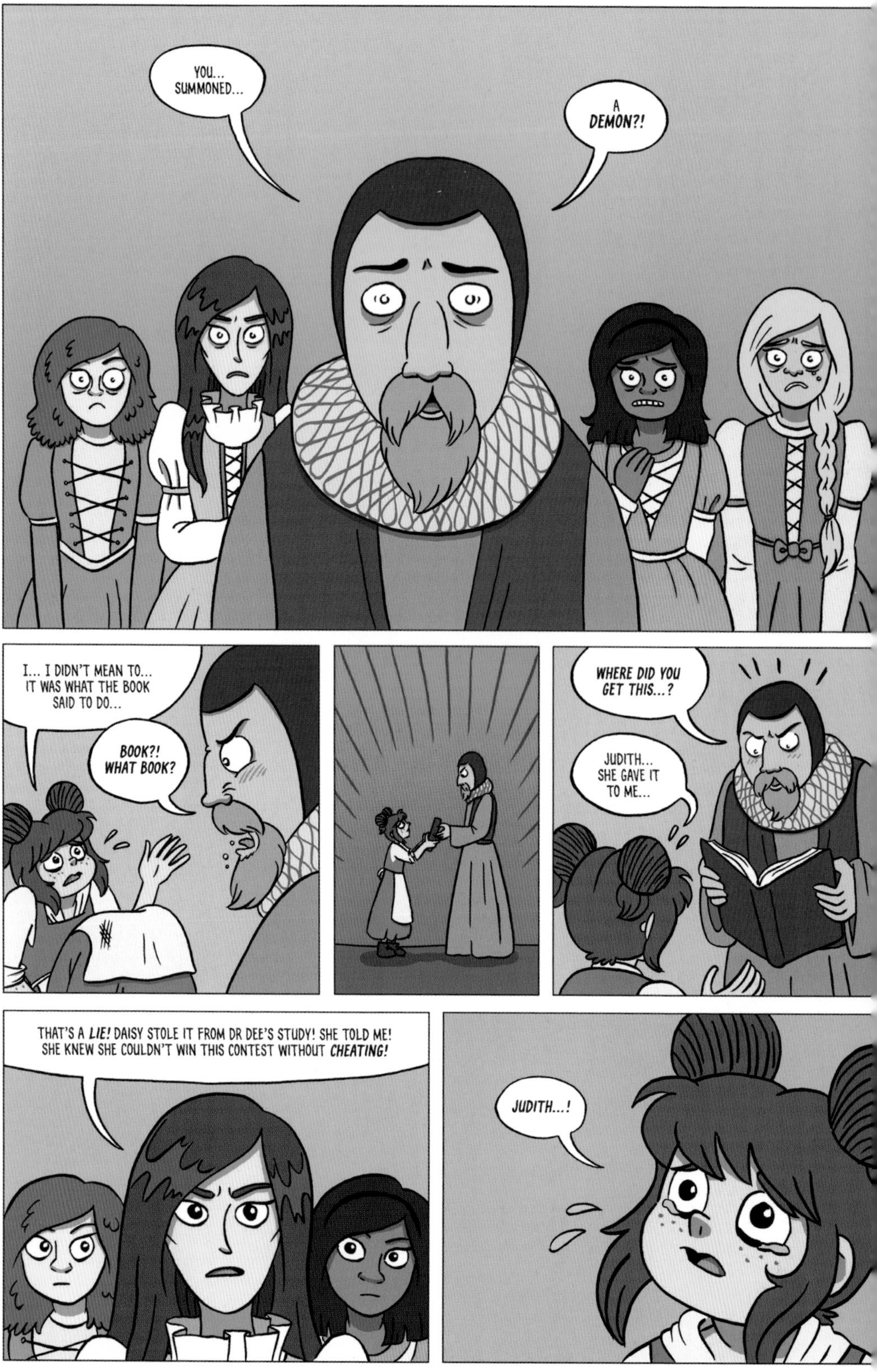
YOU... SUMMONED...
A DEMON?!
I... I DIDN'T MEAN TO... IT WAS WHAT THE BOOK SAID TO DO...
BOOK?! WHAT BOOK?
WHERE DID YOU GET THIS...?
JUDITH... SHE GAVE IT TO ME...
THAT'S A LIE! DAISY STOLE IT FROM DR DEE'S STUDY! SHE TOLD ME! SHE KNEW SHE COULDN'T WIN THIS CONTEST WITHOUT CHEATING!
JUDITH...!

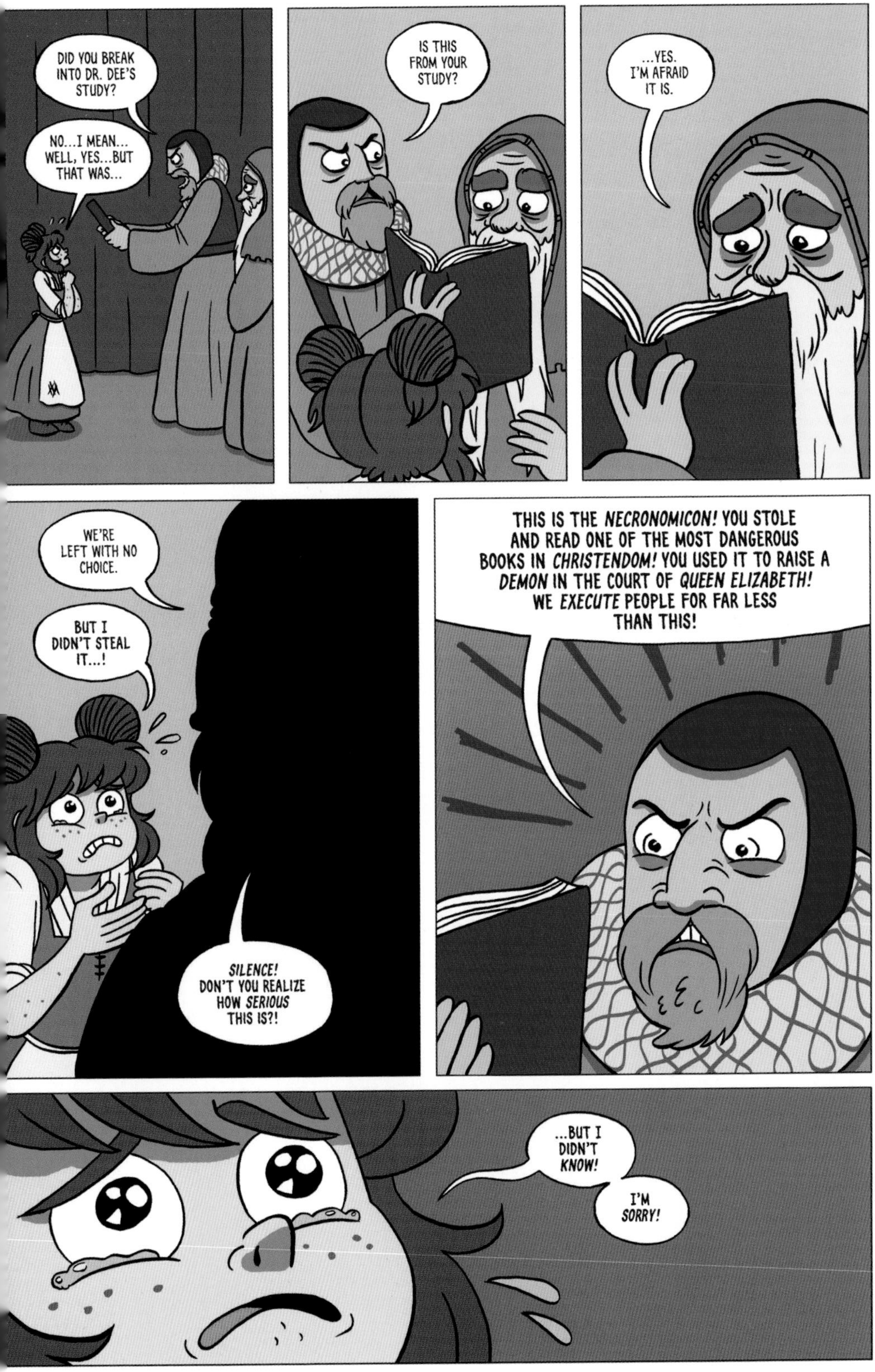
DID YOU BREAK INTO DR. DEE'S STUDY?
NO...I MEAN... WELL, YES...BUT THAT WAS...
IS THIS FROM YOUR STUDY?
...YES. I'M AFRAID IT IS.
WE'RE LEFT WITH NO CHOICE.
BUT I DIDN'T STEAL IT...!
SILENCE! DON'T YOU REALIZE HOW SERIOUS THIS IS?!
THIS IS THE NECRONOMICON! YOU STOLE AND READ ONE OF THE MOST DANGEROUS BOOKS IN CHRISTENDOM! YOU USED IT TO RAISE A DEMON IN THE COURT OF QUEEN ELIZABETH! WE EXECUTE PEOPLE FOR FAR LESS THAN THIS!
...BUT I DIDN'T KNOW!
I'M SORRY!

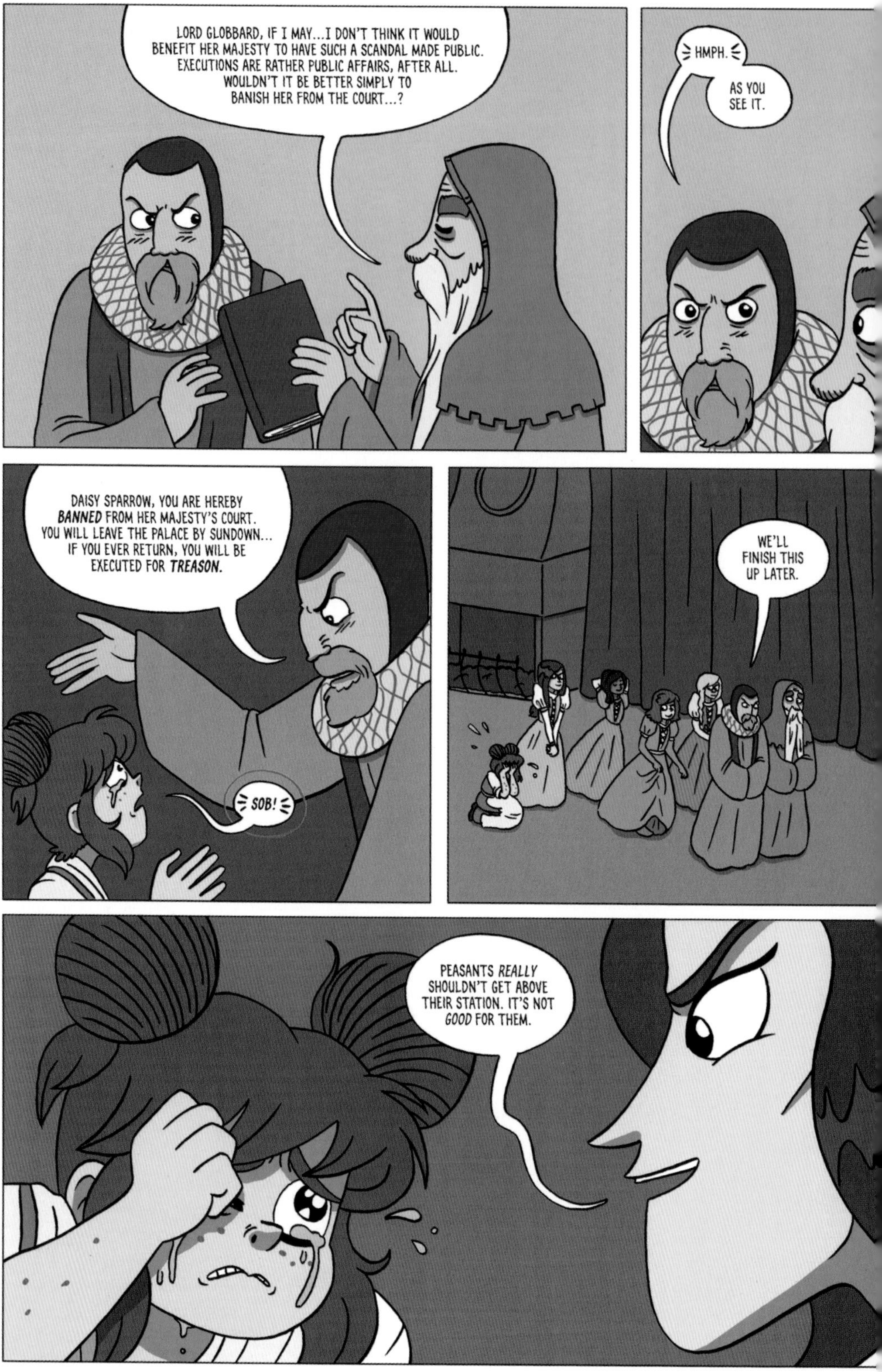
LORD GLOBBARD, IF I MAY...I DON'T THINK IT WOULD BENEFIT HER MAJESTY TO HAVE SUCH A SCANDAL MADE PUBLIC. EXECUTIONS ARE RATHER PUBLIC AFFAIRS, AFTER ALL. WOULDN'T IT BE BETTER SIMPLY TO BANISH HER FROM THE COURT...?
HMPH.
AS YOU SEE IT.
DAISY SPARROW, YOU ARE HEREBY *BANNED* FROM HER MAJESTY'S COURT. YOU WILL LEAVE THE PALACE BY SUNDOWN... IF YOU EVER RETURN, YOU WILL BE EXECUTED FOR *TREASON.*
SOB!
WE'LL FINISH THIS UP LATER.
PEASANTS *REALLY* SHOULDN'T GET ABOVE THEIR STATION. IT'S NOT *GOOD* FOR THEM.

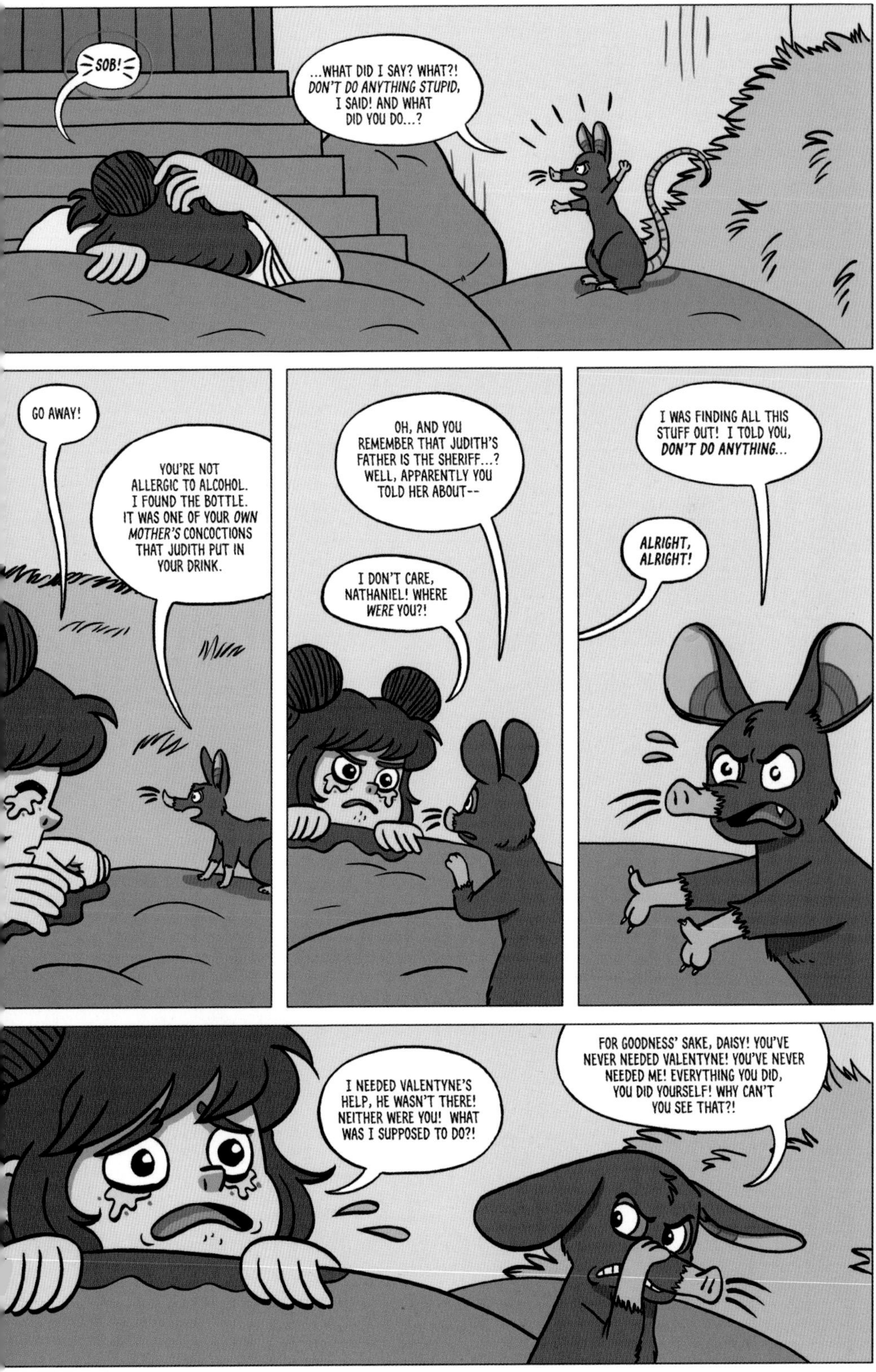
SOB!
...WHAT DID I SAY? WHAT?! DON'T DO ANYTHING STUPID, I SAID! AND WHAT DID YOU DO...?
GO AWAY!
YOU'RE NOT ALLERGIC TO ALCOHOL. I FOUND THE BOTTLE. IT WAS ONE OF YOUR OWN MOTHER'S CONCOCTIONS THAT JUDITH PUT IN YOUR DRINK.
OH, AND YOU REMEMBER THAT JUDITH'S FATHER IS THE SHERIFF...? WELL, APPARENTLY YOU TOLD HER ABOUT--
I DON'T CARE, NATHANIEL! WHERE WERE YOU?!
I WAS FINDING ALL THIS STUFF OUT! I TOLD YOU, DON'T DO ANYTHING...
ALRIGHT, ALRIGHT!
I NEEDED VALENTYNE'S HELP, HE WASN'T THERE! NEITHER WERE YOU! WHAT WAS I SUPPOSED TO DO?!
FOR GOODNESS' SAKE, DAISY! YOU'VE NEVER NEEDED VALENTYNE! YOU'VE NEVER NEEDED ME! EVERYTHING YOU DID, YOU DID YOURSELF! WHY CAN'T YOU SEE THAT?!

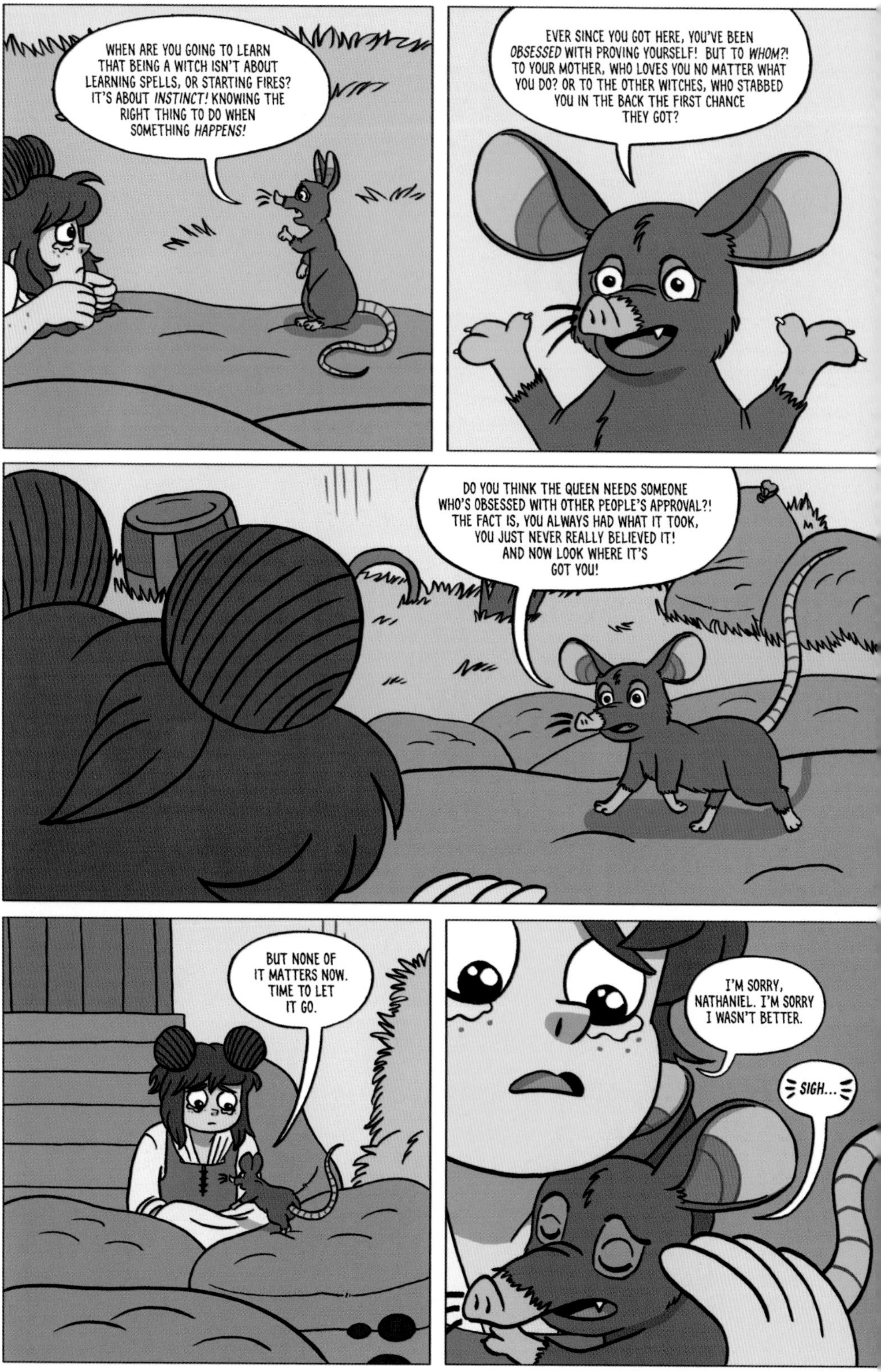
WHEN ARE YOU GOING TO LEARN THAT BEING A WITCH ISN'T ABOUT LEARNING SPELLS, OR STARTING FIRES? IT'S ABOUT *INSTINCT!* KNOWING THE RIGHT THING TO DO WHEN SOMETHING *HAPPENS!*
EVER SINCE YOU GOT HERE, YOU'VE BEEN *OBSESSED* WITH PROVING YOURSELF! BUT TO *WHOM?!* TO YOUR MOTHER, WHO LOVES YOU NO MATTER WHAT YOU DO? OR TO THE OTHER WITCHES, WHO STABBED YOU IN THE BACK THE FIRST CHANCE THEY GOT?
DO YOU THINK THE QUEEN NEEDS SOMEONE WHO'S OBSESSED WITH OTHER PEOPLE'S APPROVAL?! THE FACT IS, YOU ALWAYS HAD WHAT IT TOOK, YOU JUST NEVER REALLY BELIEVED IT! AND NOW LOOK WHERE IT'S GOT YOU!
BUT NONE OF IT MATTERS NOW. TIME TO LET IT GO.
I'M SORRY, NATHANIEL. I'M SORRY I WASN'T BETTER.
SIGH...

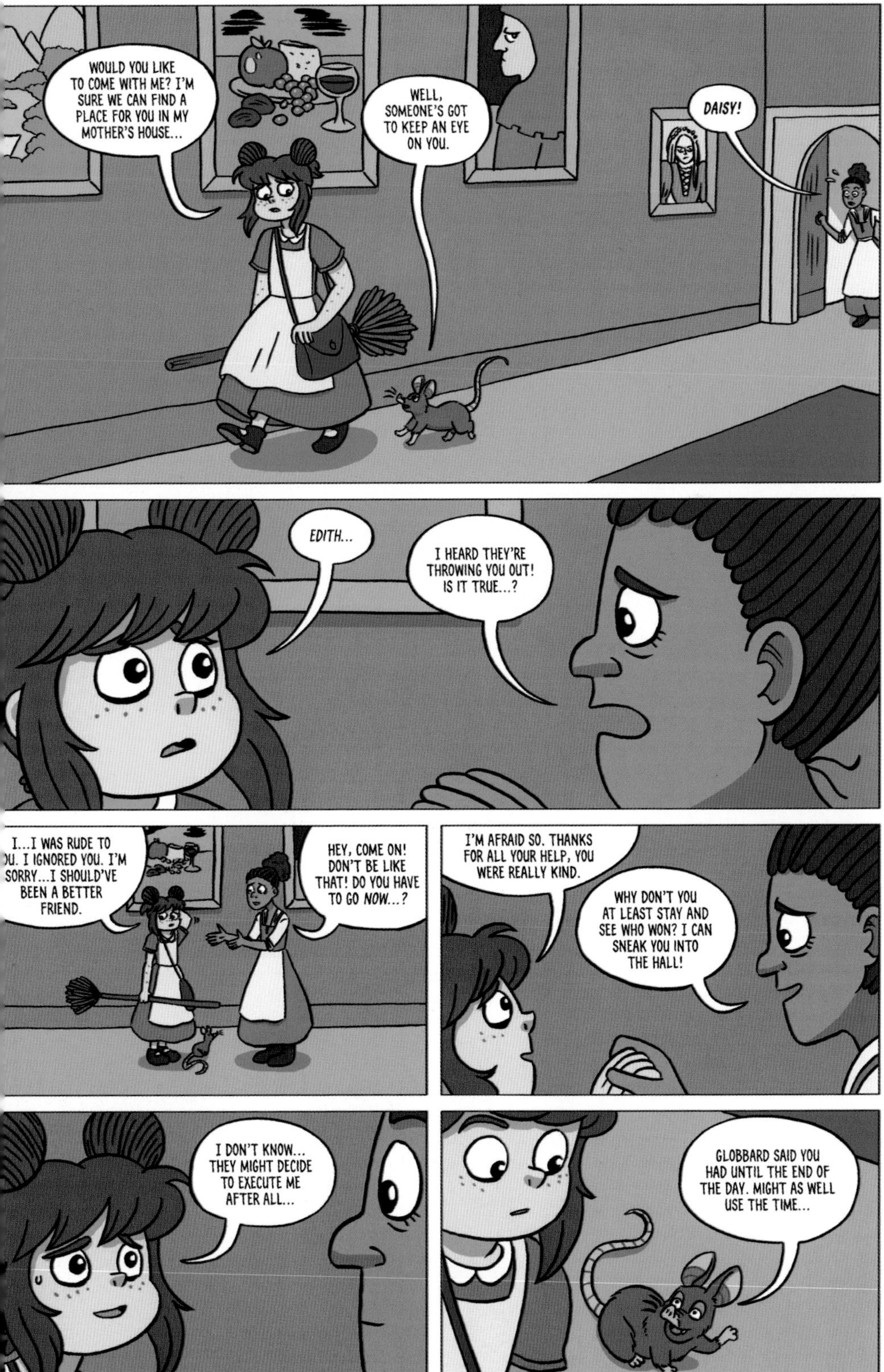
WOULD YOU LIKE TO COME WITH ME? I'M SURE WE CAN FIND A PLACE FOR YOU IN MY MOTHER'S HOUSE...
WELL, SOMEONE'S GOT TO KEEP AN EYE ON YOU.
DAISY!
EDITH...
I HEARD THEY'RE THROWING YOU OUT! IS IT TRUE...?
I...I WAS RUDE TO YOU. I IGNORED YOU. I'M SORRY...I SHOULD'VE BEEN A BETTER FRIEND.
HEY, COME ON! DON'T BE LIKE THAT! DO YOU HAVE TO GO NOW...?
I'M AFRAID SO. THANKS FOR ALL YOUR HELP, YOU WERE REALLY KIND.
WHY DON'T YOU AT LEAST STAY AND SEE WHO WON? I CAN SNEAK YOU INTO THE HALL!
I DON'T KNOW... THEY MIGHT DECIDE TO EXECUTE ME AFTER ALL...
GLOBBARD SAID YOU HAD UNTIL THE END OF THE DAY. MIGHT AS WELL USE THE TIME...

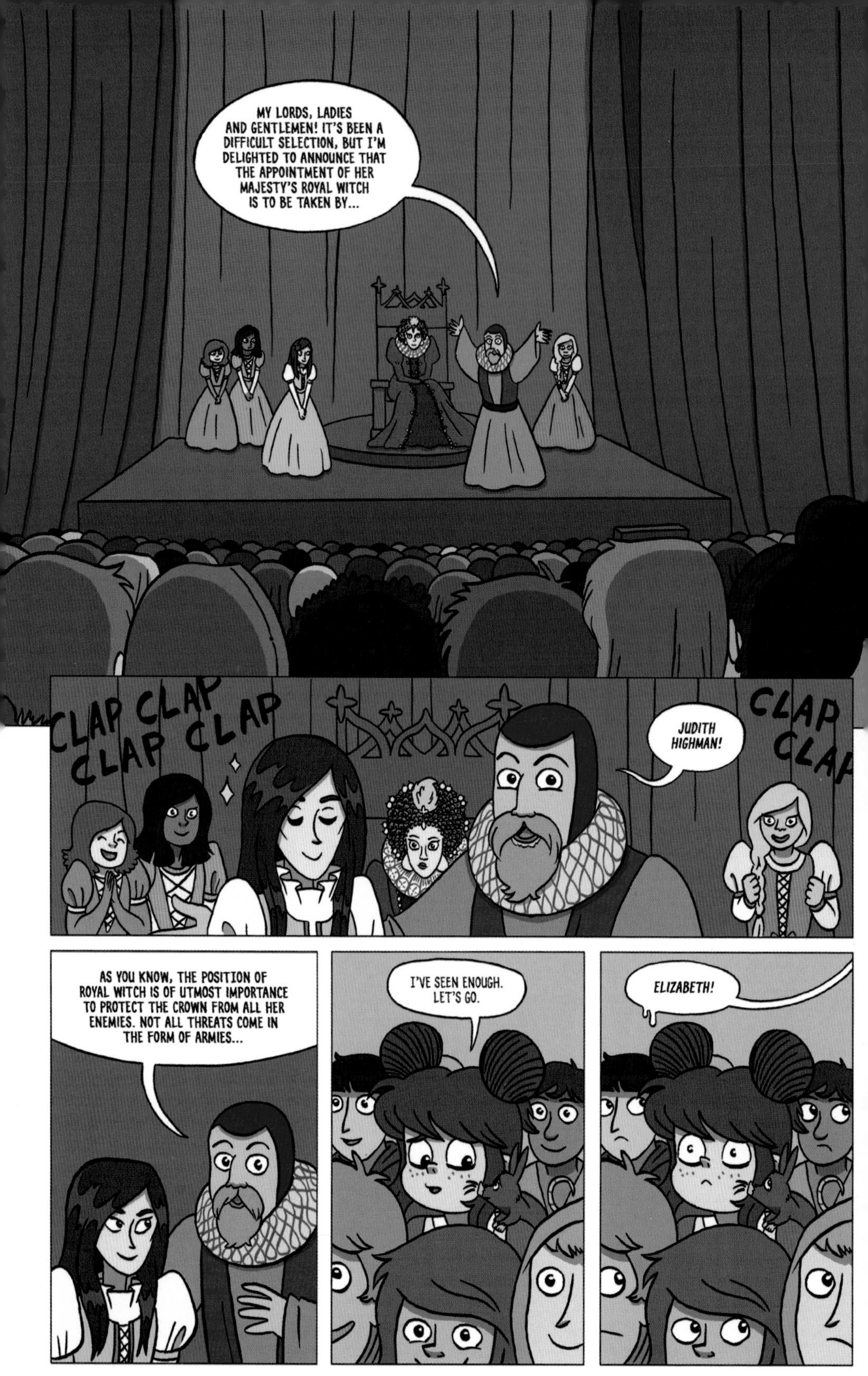
MY LORDS, LADIES AND GENTLEMEN! IT'S BEEN A DIFFICULT SELECTION, BUT I'M DELIGHTED TO ANNOUNCE THAT THE APPOINTMENT OF HER MAJESTY'S ROYAL WITCH IS TO BE TAKEN BY...
CLAP CLAP CLAP CLAP
JUDITH HIGHMAN!
CLAP CLAP
AS YOU KNOW, THE POSITION OF ROYAL WITCH IS OF UTMOST IMPORTANCE TO PROTECT THE CROWN FROM ALL HER ENEMIES. NOT ALL THREATS COME IN THE FORM OF ARMIES...
I'VE SEEN ENOUGH. LET'S GO.
ELIZABETH!

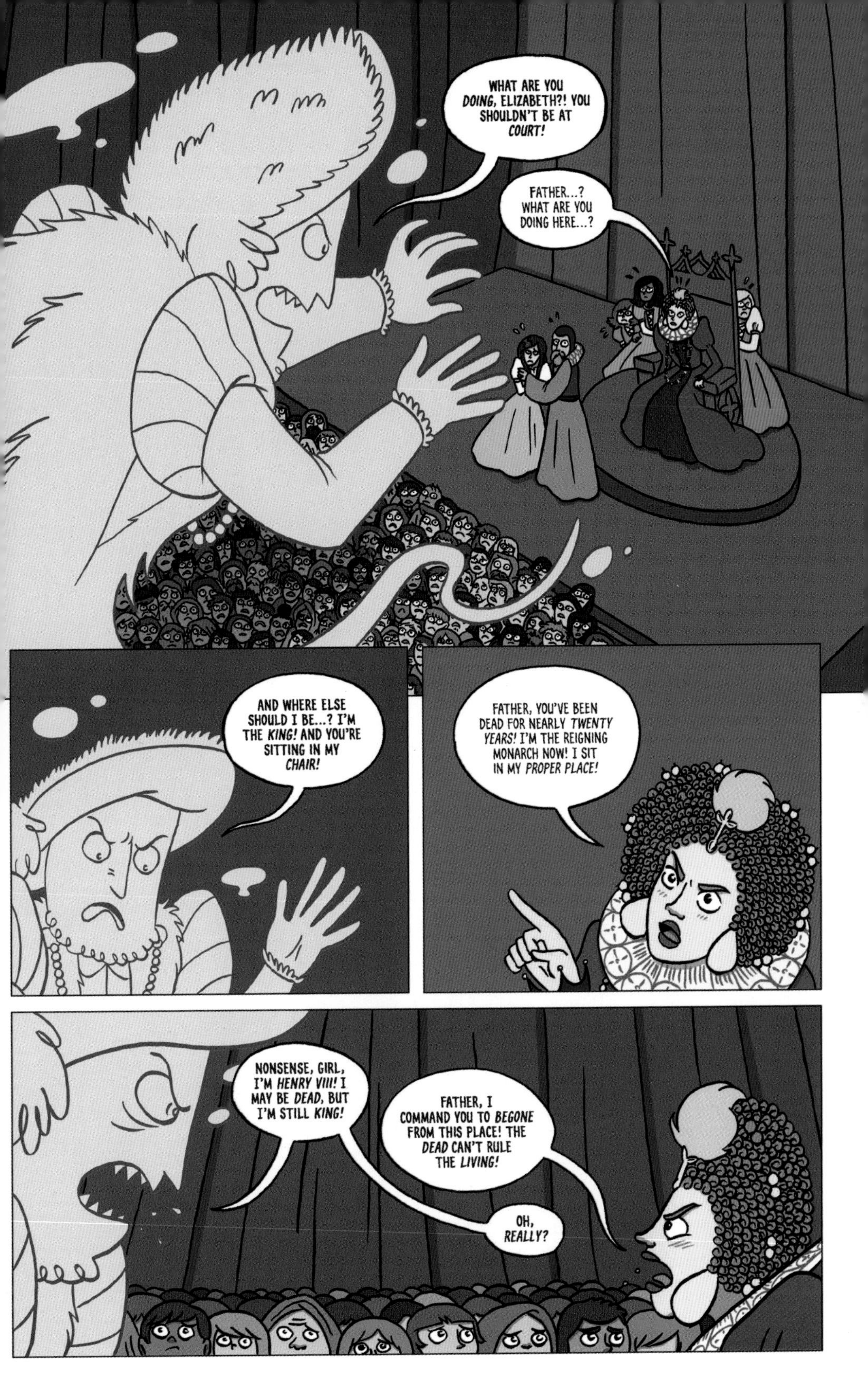
WHAT ARE YOU DOING, ELIZABETH?! YOU SHOULDN'T BE AT COURT!
FATHER...? WHAT ARE YOU DOING HERE...?
AND WHERE ELSE SHOULD I BE...? I'M THE KING! AND YOU'RE SITTING IN MY CHAIR!
FATHER, YOU'VE BEEN DEAD FOR NEARLY TWENTY YEARS! I'M THE REIGNING MONARCH NOW! I SIT IN MY PROPER PLACE!
NONSENSE, GIRL, I'M HENRY VIII! I MAY BE DEAD, BUT I'M STILL KING!
FATHER, I COMMAND YOU TO BEGONE FROM THIS PLACE! THE DEAD CAN'T RULE THE LIVING!
OH, REALLY?

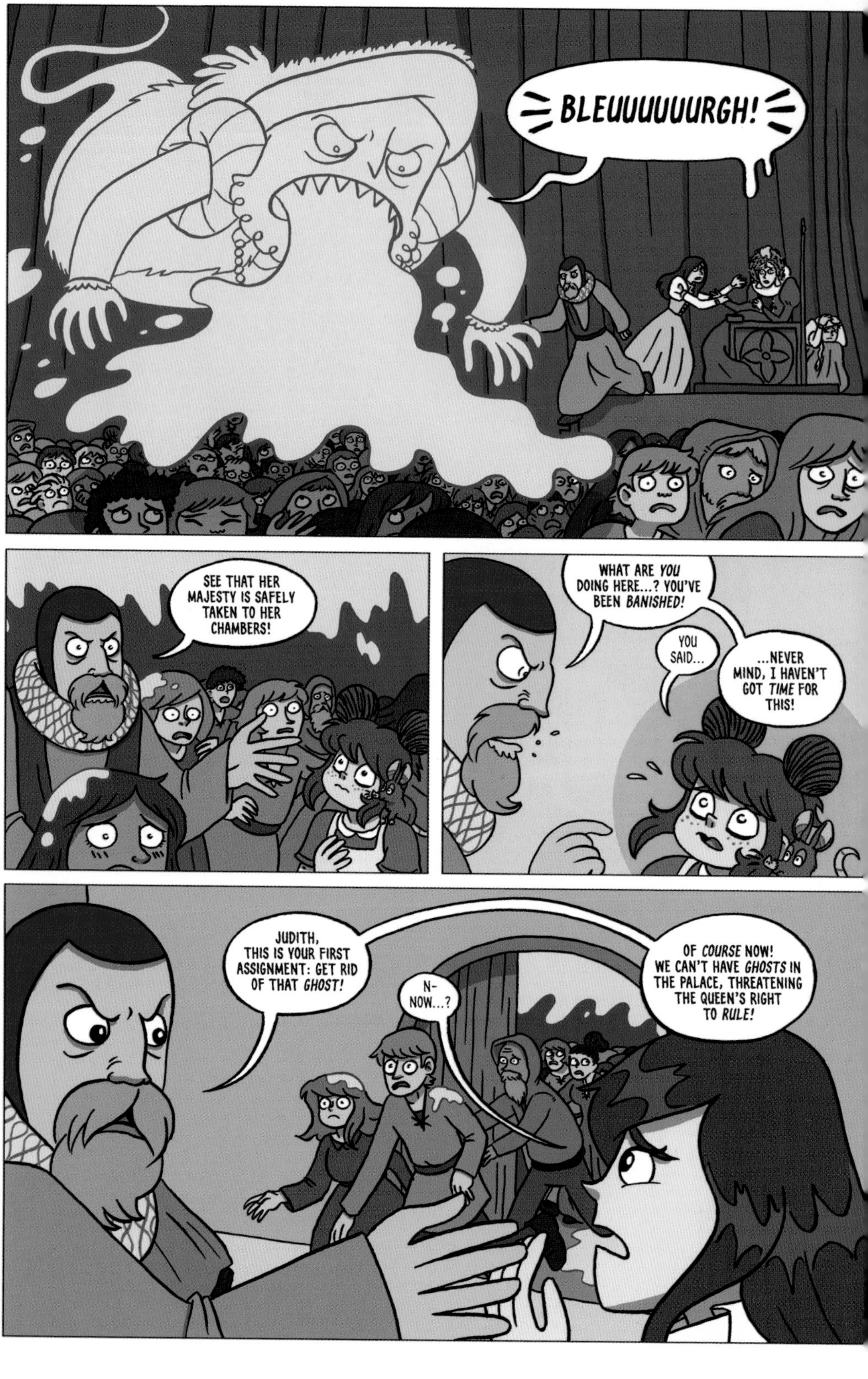
BLEUUUUUURGH!
SEE THAT HER MAJESTY IS SAFELY TAKEN TO HER CHAMBERS!
WHAT ARE *YOU* DOING HERE...? YOU'VE BEEN *BANISHED!*
YOU SAID...
...NEVER MIND, I HAVEN'T GOT *TIME* FOR THIS!
JUDITH, THIS IS YOUR FIRST ASSIGNMENT: GET RID OF THAT *GHOST!*
N-NOW...?
OF *COURSE* NOW! WE CAN'T HAVE *GHOSTS* IN THE PALACE, THREATENING THE QUEEN'S RIGHT TO *RULE!*

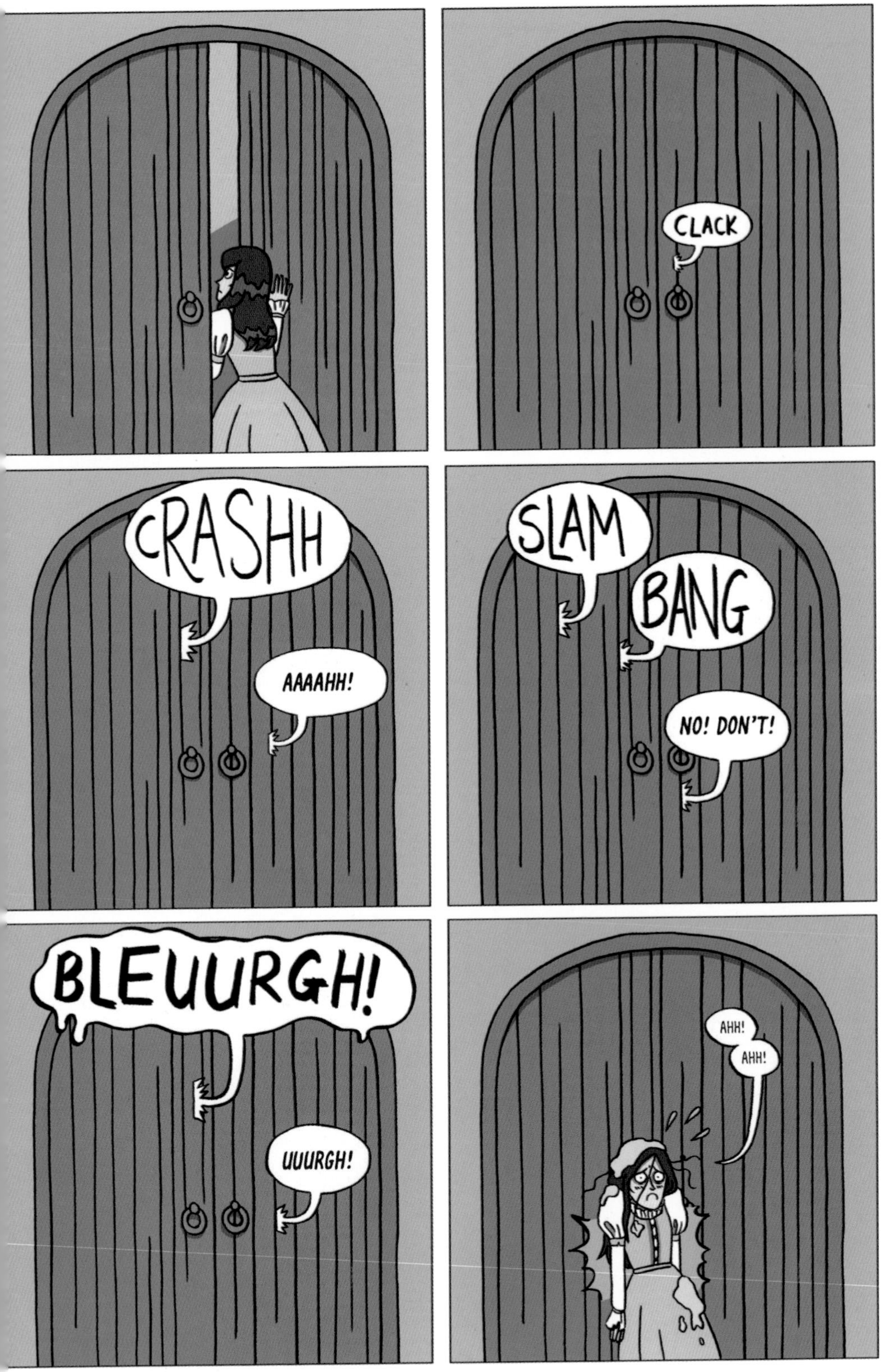
CLACK
CRASHH
AAAAHH!
SLAM
BANG
NO! DON'T!
BLEUURGH!
UUURGH!
AHH!
AHH!

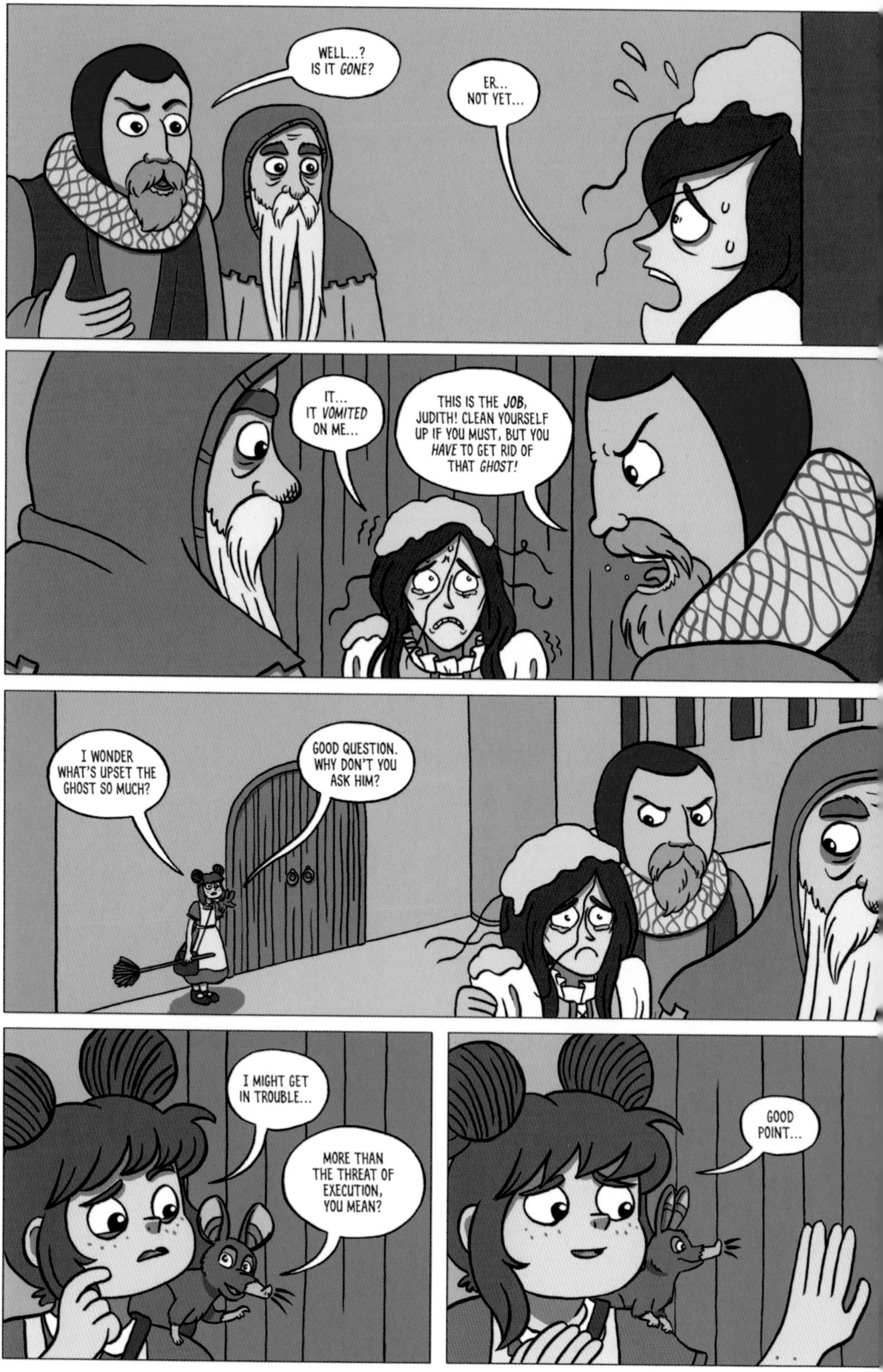
WELL...? IS IT *GONE?*
ER... NOT YET...
IT... IT *VOMITED* ON ME...
THIS IS THE *JOB*, JUDITH! CLEAN YOURSELF UP IF YOU MUST, BUT YOU *HAVE* TO GET RID OF THAT *GHOST!*
I WONDER WHAT'S UPSET THE GHOST SO MUCH?
GOOD QUESTION. WHY DON'T YOU ASK HIM?
I MIGHT GET IN TROUBLE...
MORE THAN THE THREAT OF EXECUTION, YOU MEAN?
GOOD POINT...

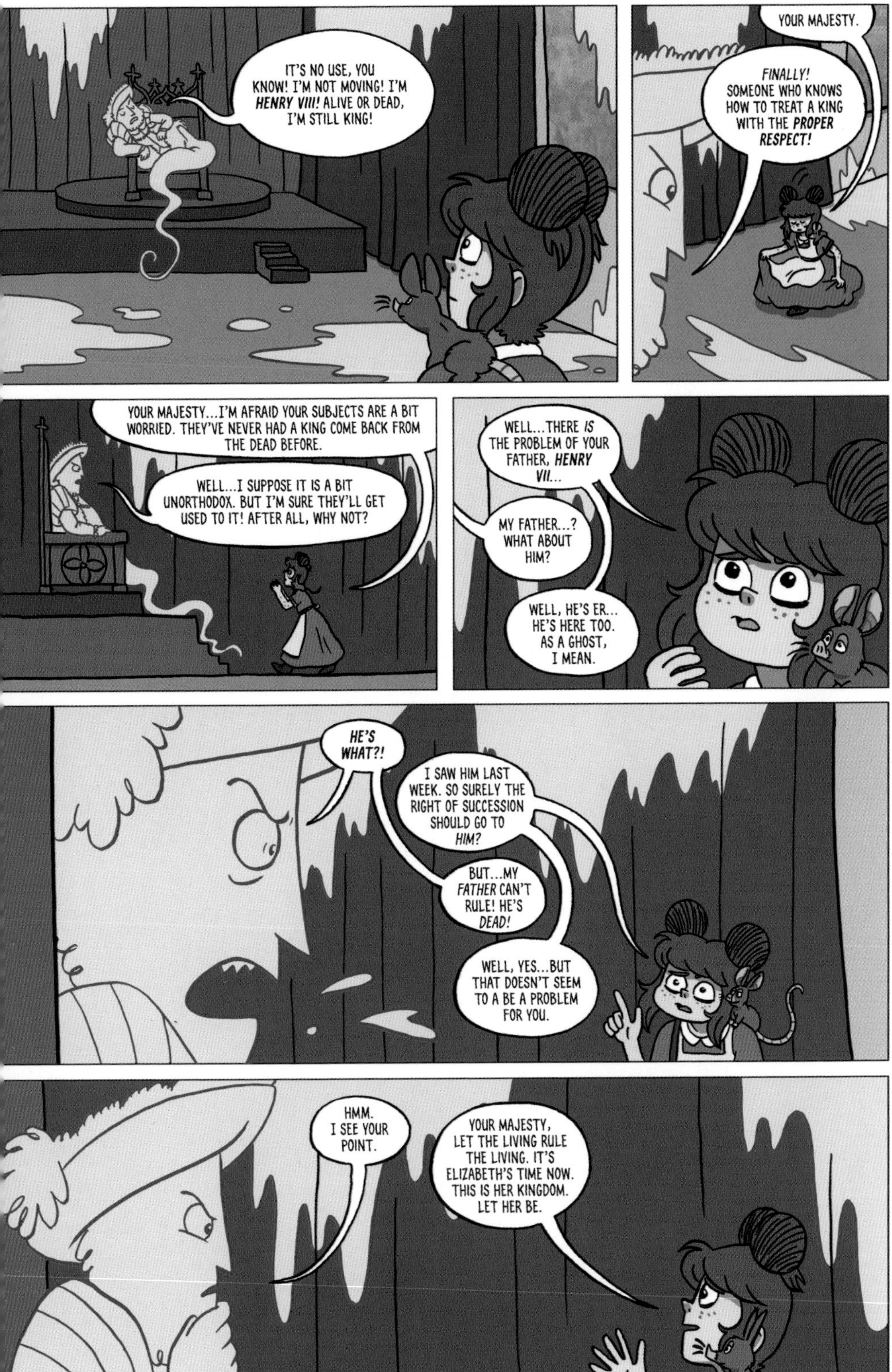

IT'S NO USE, YOU KNOW! I'M NOT MOVING! I'M HENRY VIII! ALIVE OR DEAD, I'M STILL KING!
YOUR MAJESTY.
FINALLY! SOMEONE WHO KNOWS HOW TO TREAT A KING WITH THE PROPER RESPECT!
YOUR MAJESTY...I'M AFRAID YOUR SUBJECTS ARE A BIT WORRIED. THEY'VE NEVER HAD A KING COME BACK FROM THE DEAD BEFORE.
WELL...I SUPPOSE IT IS A BIT UNORTHODOX. BUT I'M SURE THEY'LL GET USED TO IT! AFTER ALL, WHY NOT?
WELL...THERE IS THE PROBLEM OF YOUR FATHER, HENRY VII...
MY FATHER...? WHAT ABOUT HIM?
WELL, HE'S ER... HE'S HERE TOO. AS A GHOST, I MEAN.
HE'S WHAT?!
I SAW HIM LAST WEEK. SO SURELY THE RIGHT OF SUCCESSION SHOULD GO TO HIM?
BUT...MY FATHER CAN'T RULE! HE'S DEAD!
WELL, YES...BUT THAT DOESN'T SEEM TO A BE A PROBLEM FOR YOU.
HMM. I SEE YOUR POINT.
YOUR MAJESTY, LET THE LIVING RULE THE LIVING. IT'S ELIZABETH'S TIME NOW. THIS IS HER KINGDOM. LET HER BE.

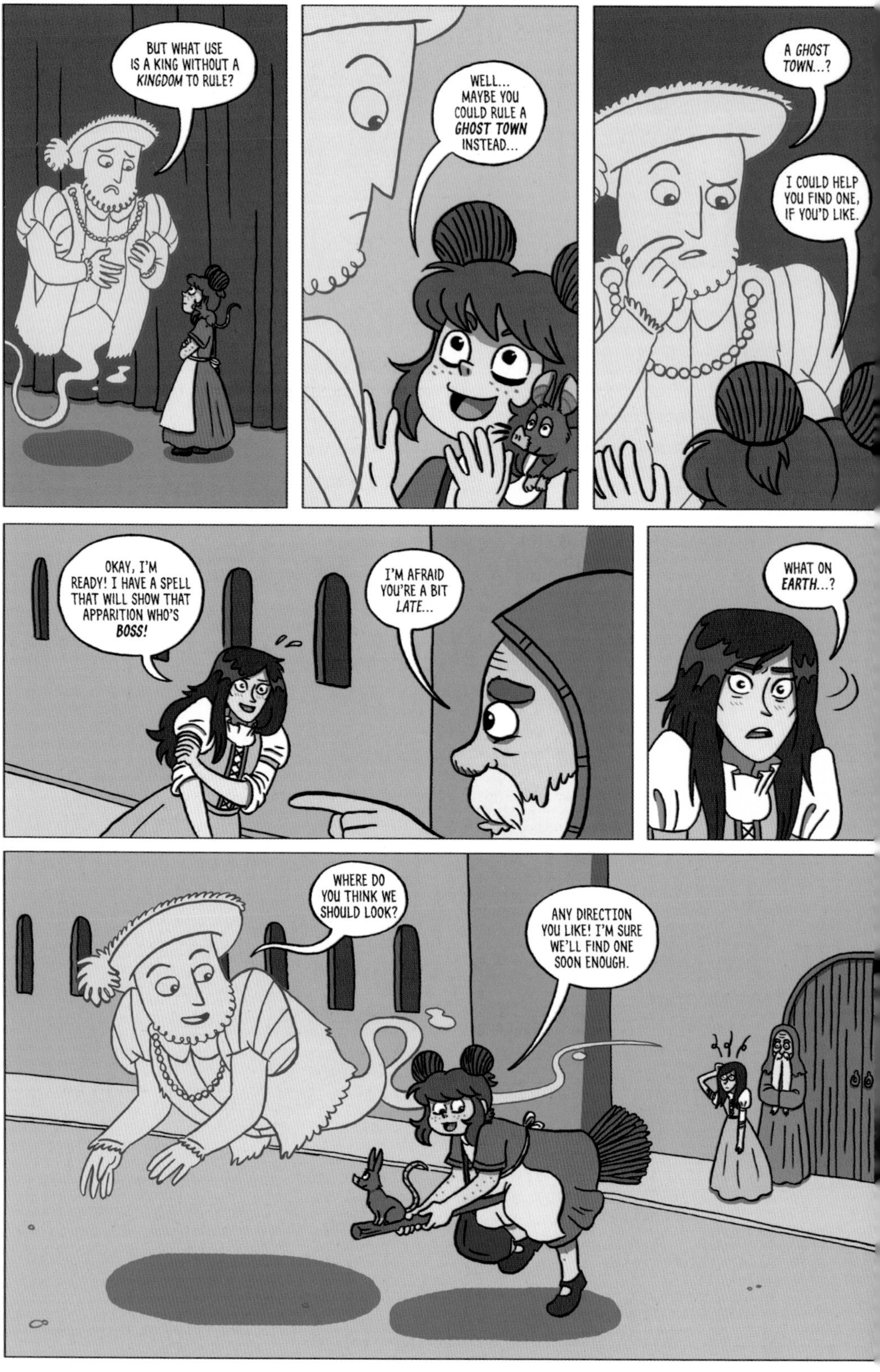
BUT WHAT USE IS A KING WITHOUT A *KINGDOM* TO RULE?
WELL... MAYBE YOU COULD RULE A **GHOST TOWN** INSTEAD...
A *GHOST TOWN*...?
I COULD HELP YOU FIND ONE, IF YOU'D LIKE.
OKAY, I'M READY! I HAVE A SPELL THAT WILL SHOW THAT APPARITION WHO'S **BOSS!**
I'M AFRAID YOU'RE A BIT *LATE*...
WHAT ON **EARTH**...?
WHERE DO YOU THINK WE SHOULD LOOK?
ANY DIRECTION YOU LIKE! I'M SURE WE'LL FIND ONE SOON ENOUGH.

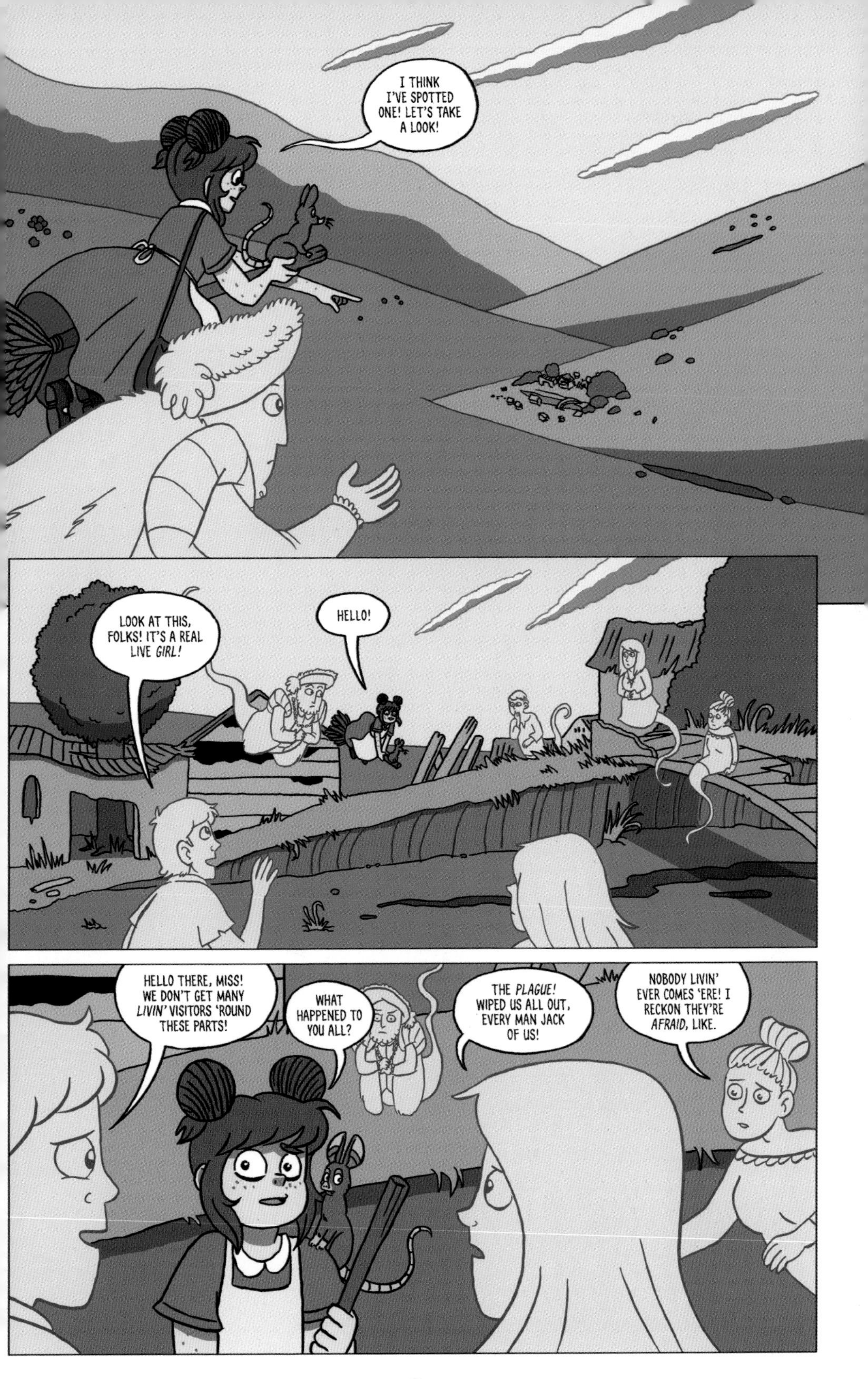
I THINK I'VE SPOTTED ONE! LET'S TAKE A LOOK!
LOOK AT THIS, FOLKS! IT'S A REAL LIVE *GIRL!*
HELLO!
HELLO THERE, MISS! WE DON'T GET MANY *LIVIN'* VISITORS 'ROUND THESE PARTS!
WHAT HAPPENED TO YOU ALL?
THE *PLAGUE!* WIPED US ALL OUT, EVERY MAN JACK OF US!
NOBODY LIVIN' EVER COMES 'ERE! I RECKON THEY'RE *AFRAID*, LIKE.

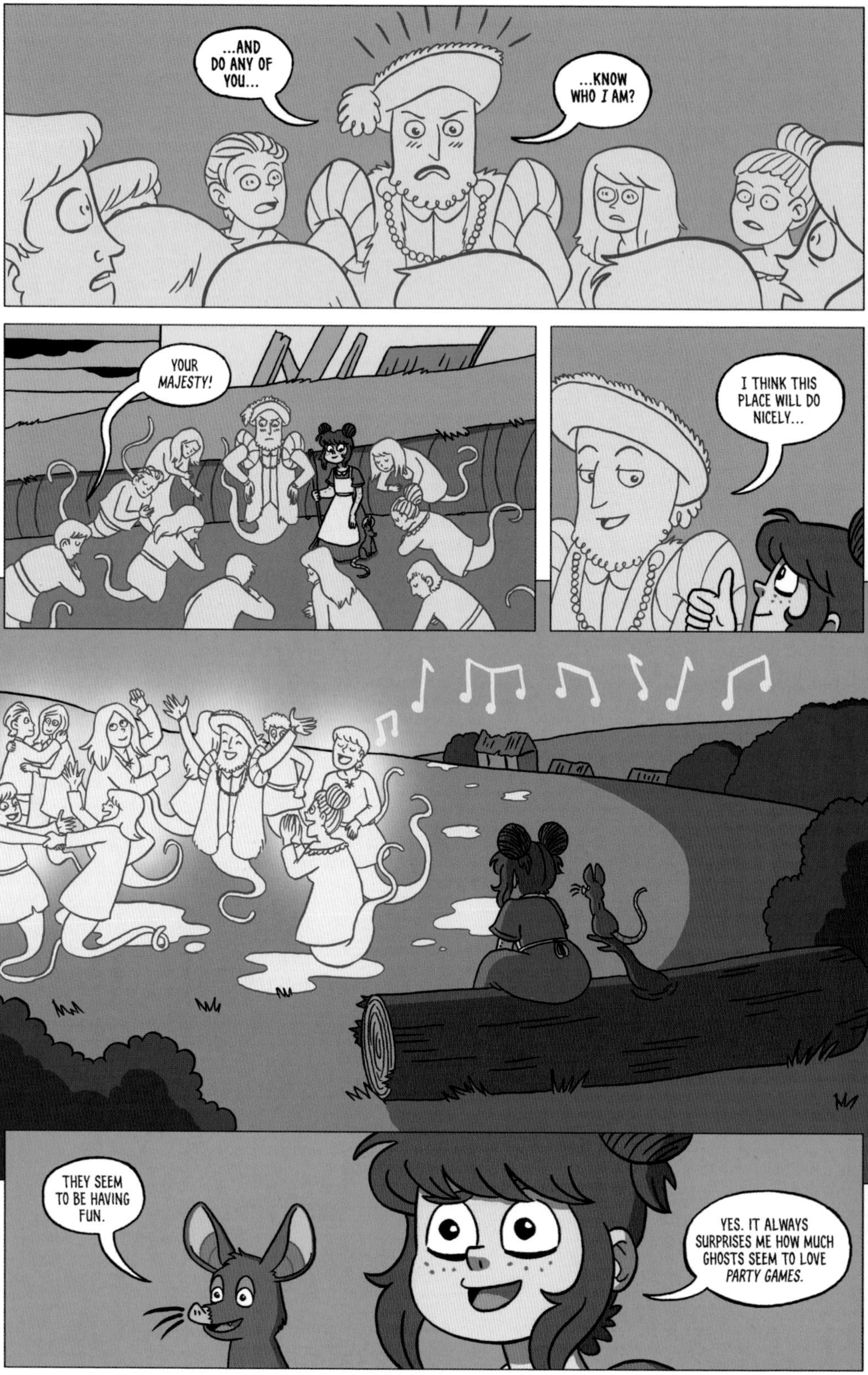
...AND DO ANY OF YOU...
...KNOW WHO *I* AM?
YOUR *MAJESTY!*
I THINK THIS PLACE WILL DO NICELY...
THEY SEEM TO BE HAVING FUN.
YES. IT ALWAYS SURPRISES ME HOW MUCH GHOSTS SEEM TO LOVE *PARTY GAMES.*

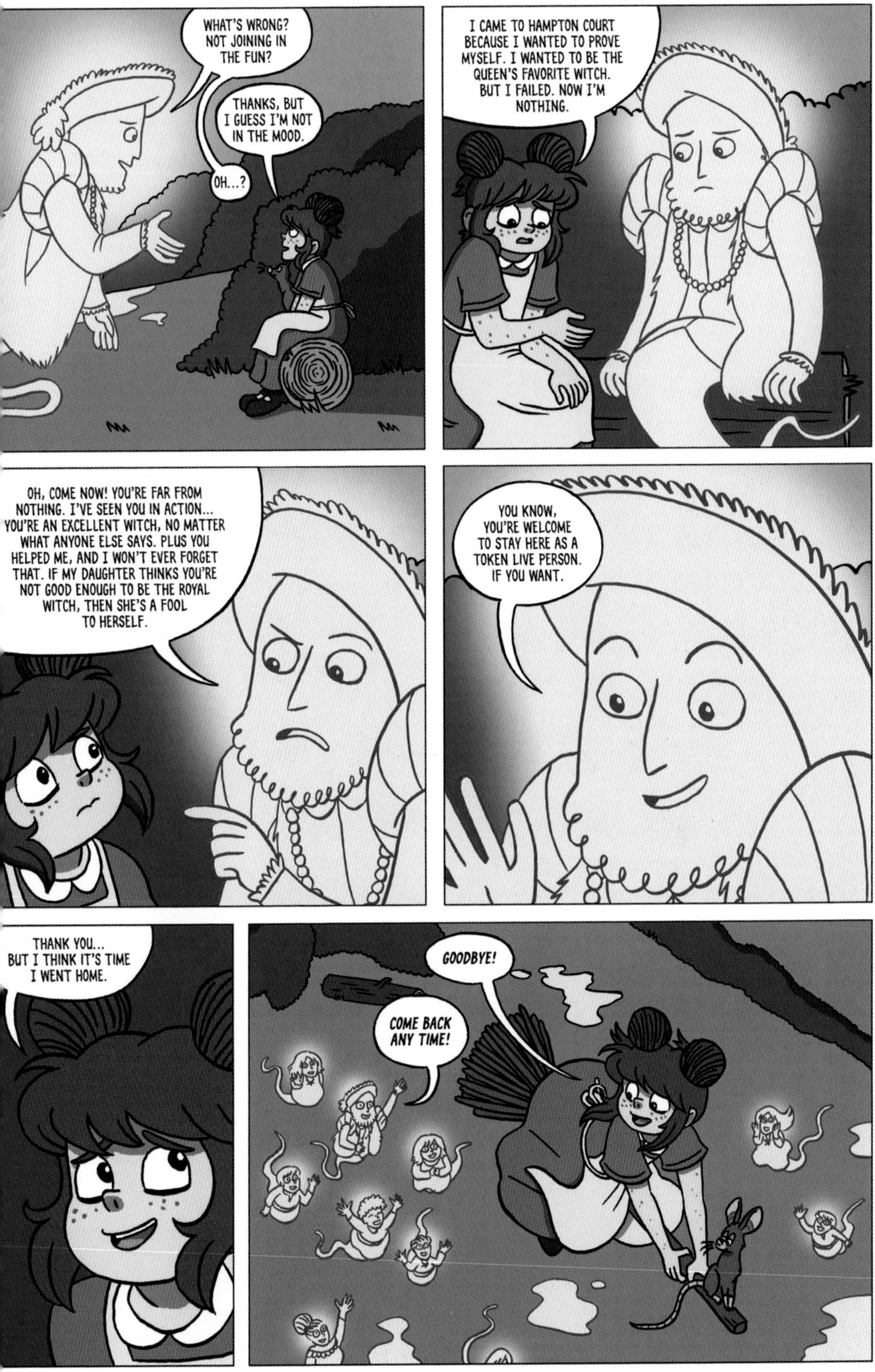
WHAT'S WRONG? NOT JOINING IN THE FUN?
THANKS, BUT I GUESS I'M NOT IN THE MOOD.
OH...?
I CAME TO HAMPTON COURT BECAUSE I WANTED TO PROVE MYSELF. I WANTED TO BE THE QUEEN'S FAVORITE WITCH. BUT I FAILED. NOW I'M NOTHING.
OH, COME NOW! YOU'RE FAR FROM NOTHING. I'VE SEEN YOU IN ACTION... YOU'RE AN EXCELLENT WITCH, NO MATTER WHAT ANYONE ELSE SAYS. PLUS YOU HELPED ME, AND I WON'T EVER FORGET THAT. IF MY DAUGHTER THINKS YOU'RE NOT GOOD ENOUGH TO BE THE ROYAL WITCH, THEN SHE'S A FOOL TO HERSELF.
YOU KNOW, YOU'RE WELCOME TO STAY HERE AS A TOKEN LIVE PERSON. IF YOU WANT.
THANK YOU... BUT I THINK IT'S TIME I WENT HOME.
GOODBYE!
COME BACK ANY TIME!

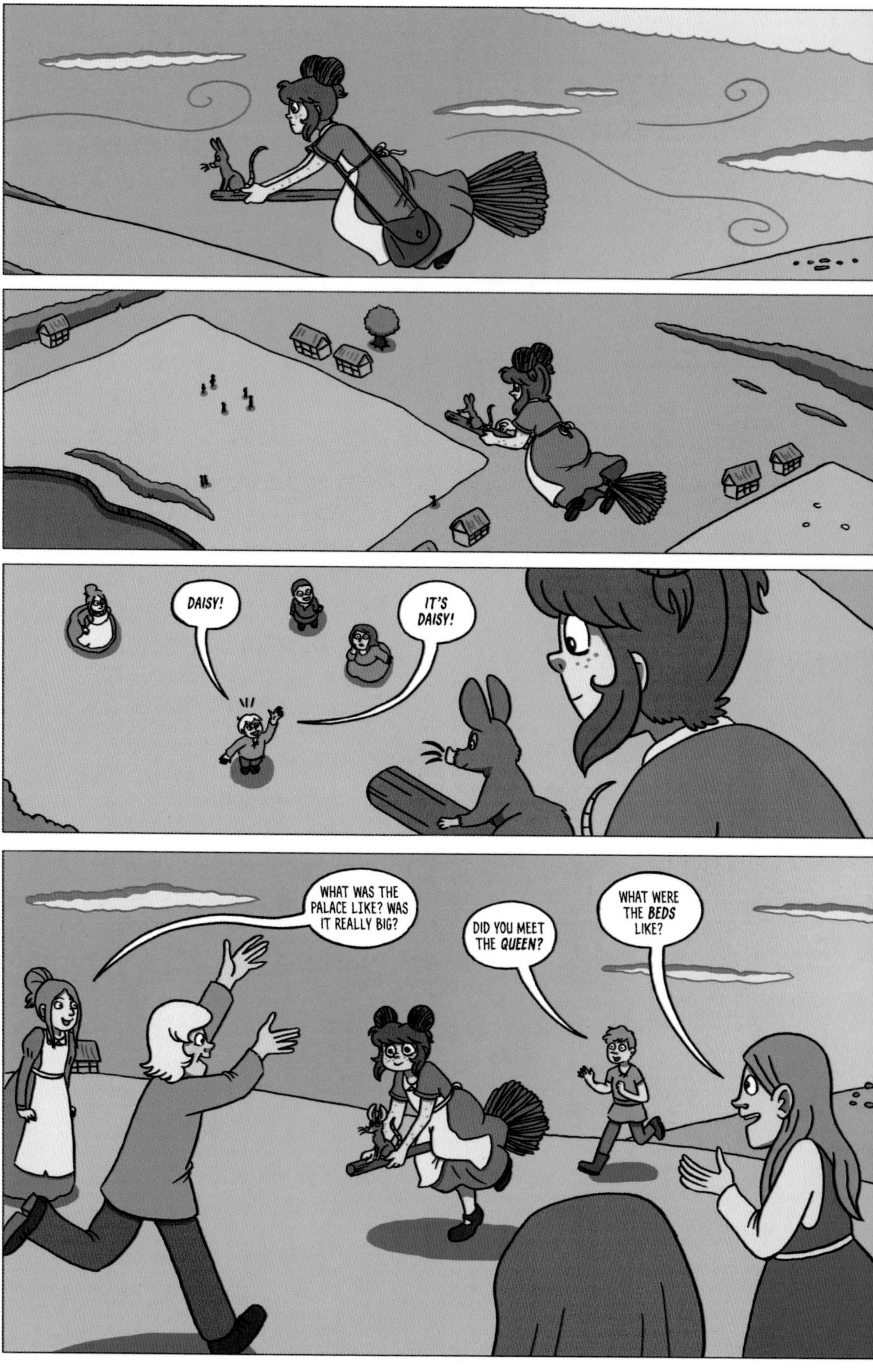
DAISY!
IT'S DAISY!
WHAT WAS THE PALACE LIKE? WAS IT REALLY BIG?
DID YOU MEET THE *QUEEN*?
WHAT WERE THE *BEDS* LIKE?

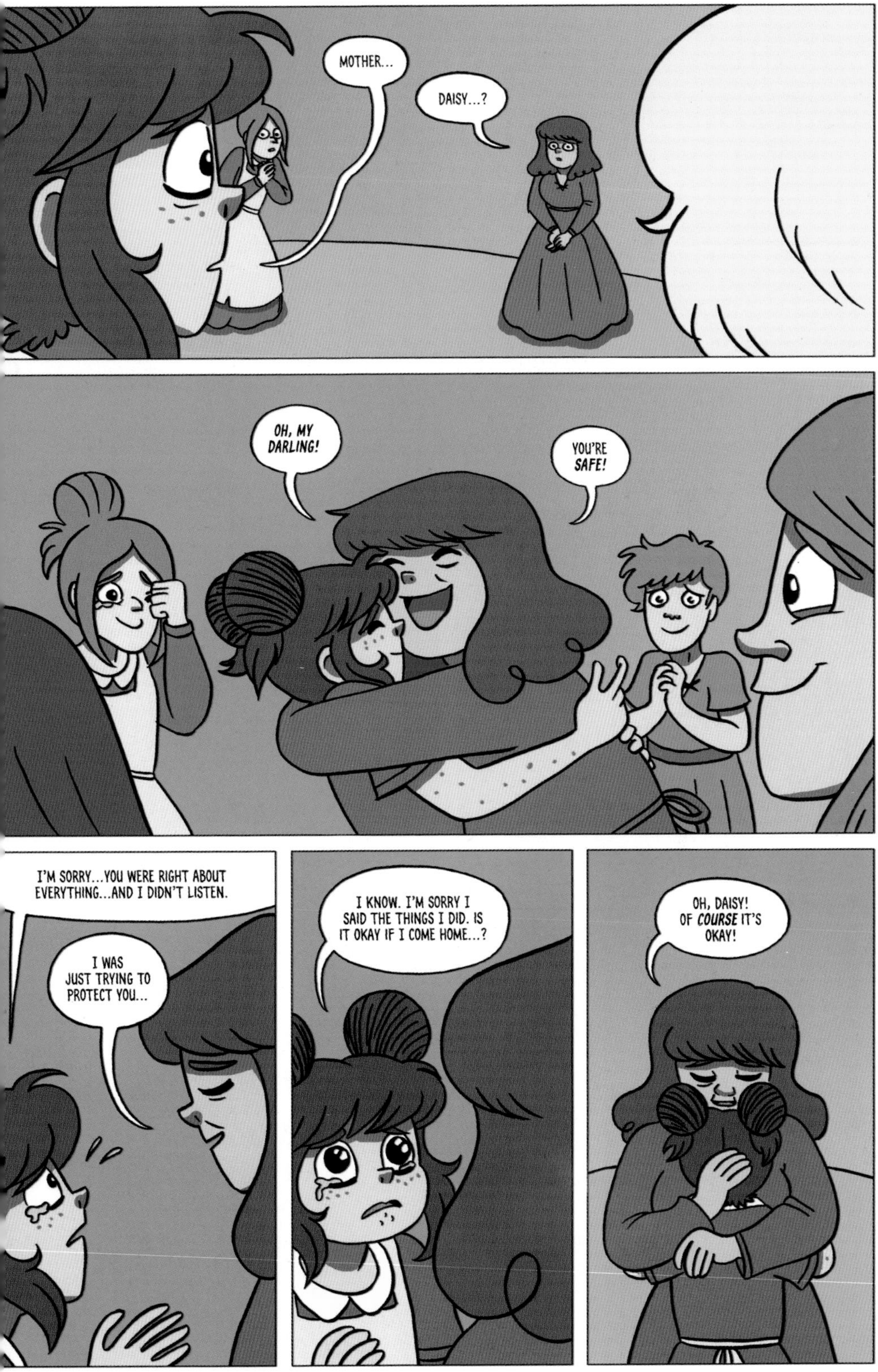

MOTHER...
DAISY...?
OH, MY DARLING!
YOU'RE SAFE!
I'M SORRY...YOU WERE RIGHT ABOUT EVERYTHING...AND I DIDN'T LISTEN.
I WAS JUST TRYING TO PROTECT YOU...
I KNOW. I'M SORRY I SAID THE THINGS I DID. IS IT OKAY IF I COME HOME...?
OH, DAISY! OF COURSE IT'S OKAY!

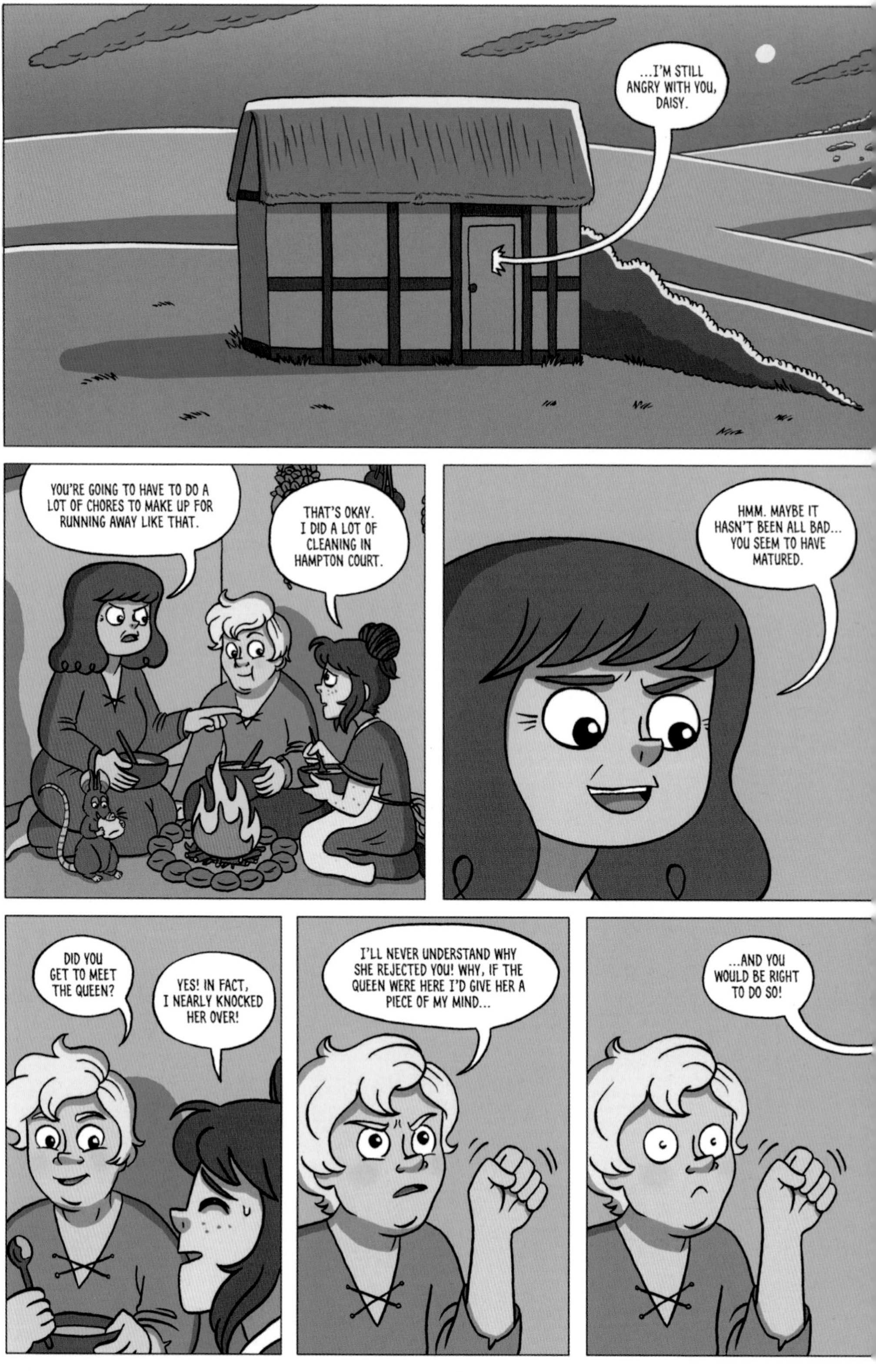
...I'M STILL ANGRY WITH YOU, DAISY.
YOU'RE GOING TO HAVE TO DO A LOT OF CHORES TO MAKE UP FOR RUNNING AWAY LIKE THAT.
THAT'S OKAY. I DID A LOT OF CLEANING IN HAMPTON COURT.
HMM. MAYBE IT HASN'T BEEN ALL BAD... YOU SEEM TO HAVE MATURED.
DID YOU GET TO MEET THE QUEEN?
YES! IN FACT, I NEARLY KNOCKED HER OVER!
I'LL NEVER UNDERSTAND WHY SHE REJECTED YOU! WHY, IF THE QUEEN WERE HERE I'D GIVE HER A PIECE OF MY MIND...
...AND YOU WOULD BE RIGHT TO DO SO!

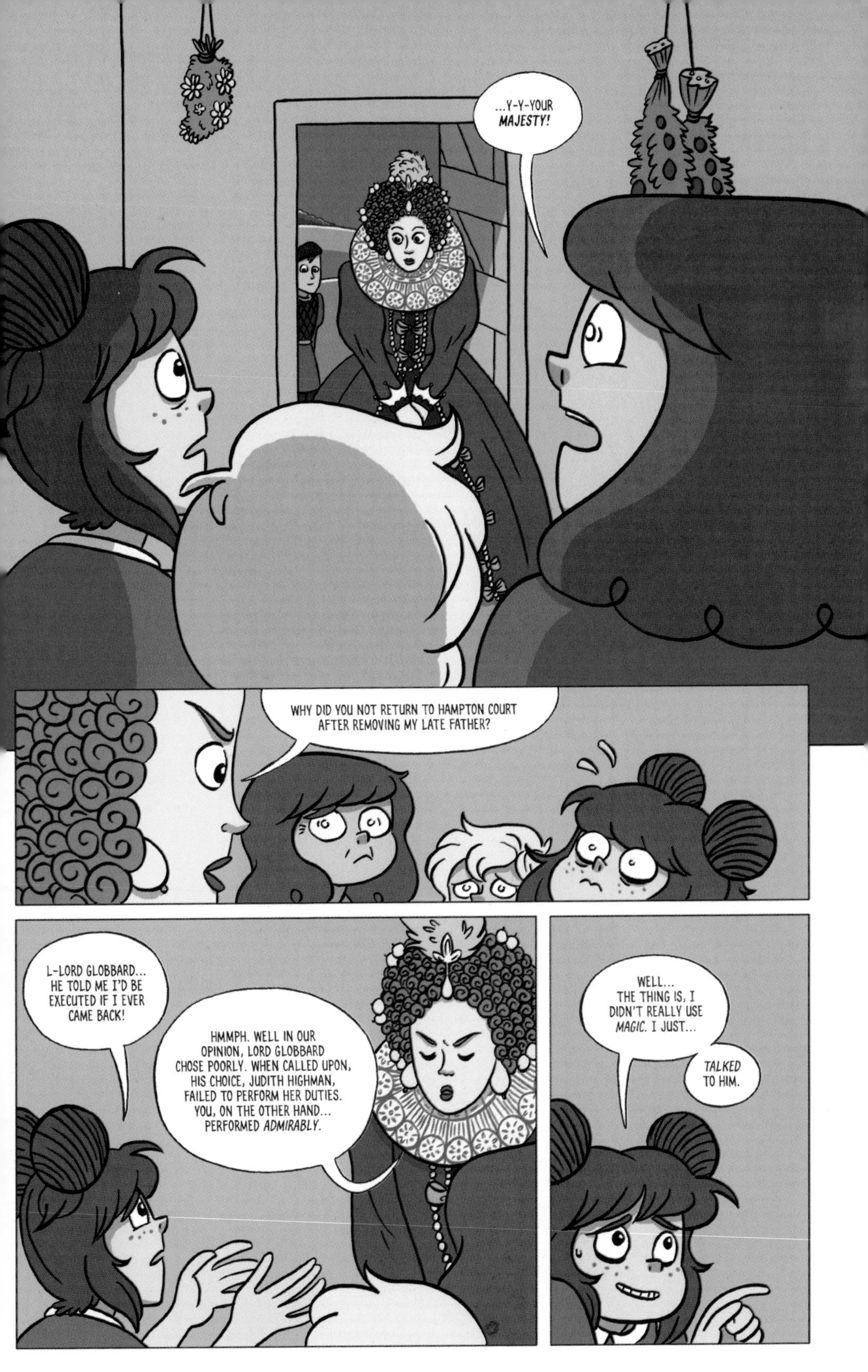
...Y-Y-YOUR MAJESTY!
WHY DID YOU NOT RETURN TO HAMPTON COURT AFTER REMOVING MY LATE FATHER?
L-LORD GLOBBARD... HE TOLD ME I'D BE EXECUTED IF I EVER CAME BACK!
HMMPH. WELL IN OUR OPINION, LORD GLOBBARD CHOSE POORLY. WHEN CALLED UPON, HIS CHOICE, JUDITH HIGHMAN, FAILED TO PERFORM HER DUTIES. YOU, ON THE OTHER HAND... PERFORMED *ADMIRABLY*.
WELL... THE THING IS, I DIDN'T REALLY USE *MAGIC*. I JUST...
TALKED TO HIM.

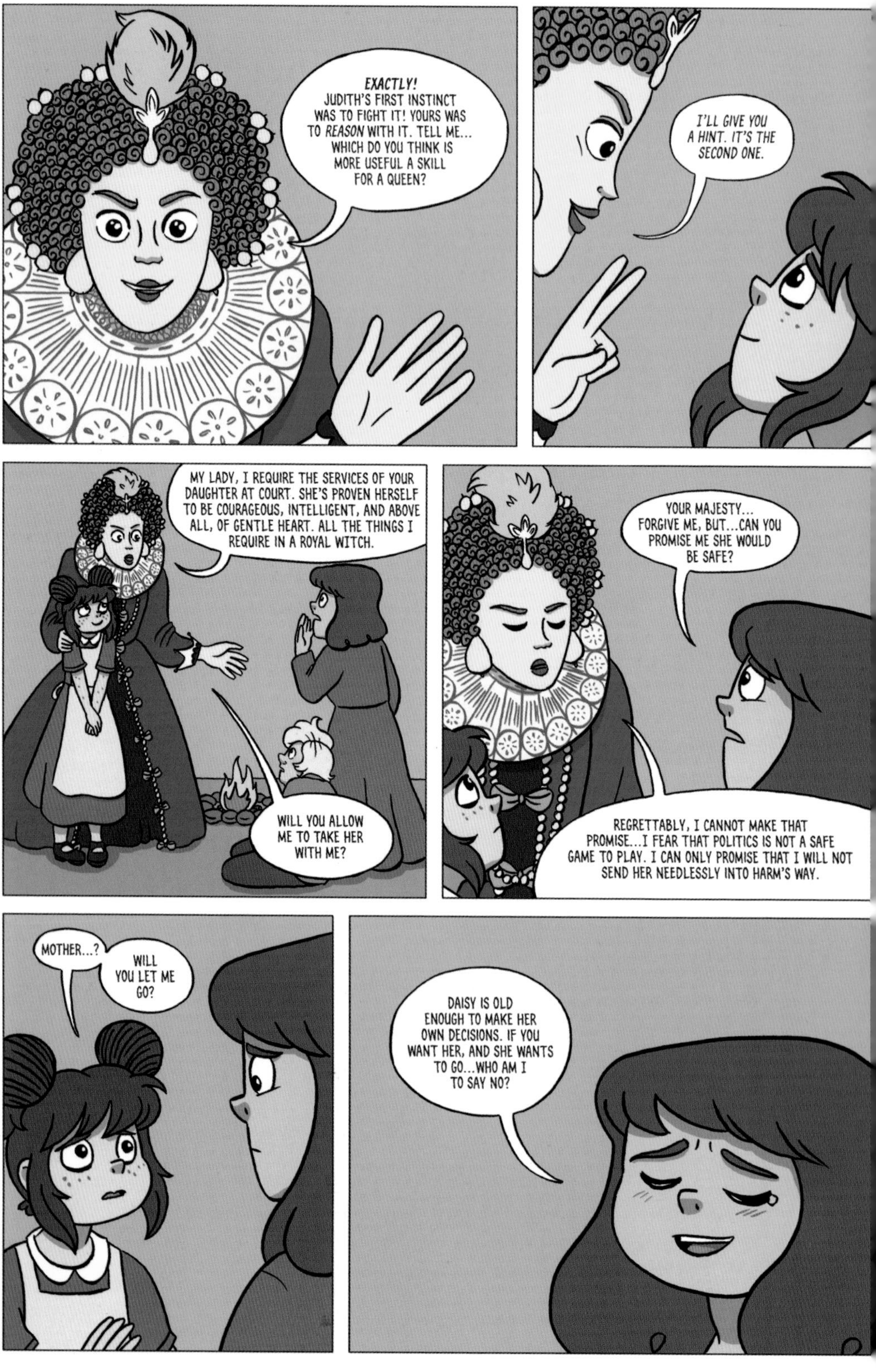

EXACTLY! JUDITH'S FIRST INSTINCT WAS TO FIGHT IT! YOURS WAS TO *REASON* WITH IT. TELL ME... WHICH DO YOU THINK IS MORE USEFUL A SKILL FOR A QUEEN?
I'LL GIVE YOU A HINT. IT'S THE SECOND ONE.
MY LADY, I REQUIRE THE SERVICES OF YOUR DAUGHTER AT COURT. SHE'S PROVEN HERSELF TO BE COURAGEOUS, INTELLIGENT, AND ABOVE ALL, OF GENTLE HEART. ALL THE THINGS I REQUIRE IN A ROYAL WITCH.
WILL YOU ALLOW ME TO TAKE HER WITH ME?
YOUR MAJESTY... FORGIVE ME, BUT...CAN YOU PROMISE ME SHE WOULD BE SAFE?
REGRETTABLY, I CANNOT MAKE THAT PROMISE...I FEAR THAT POLITICS IS NOT A SAFE GAME TO PLAY. I CAN ONLY PROMISE THAT I WILL NOT SEND HER NEEDLESSLY INTO HARM'S WAY.
MOTHER...?
WILL YOU LET ME GO?
DAISY IS OLD ENOUGH TO MAKE HER OWN DECISIONS. IF YOU WANT HER, AND SHE WANTS TO GO...WHO AM I TO SAY NO?

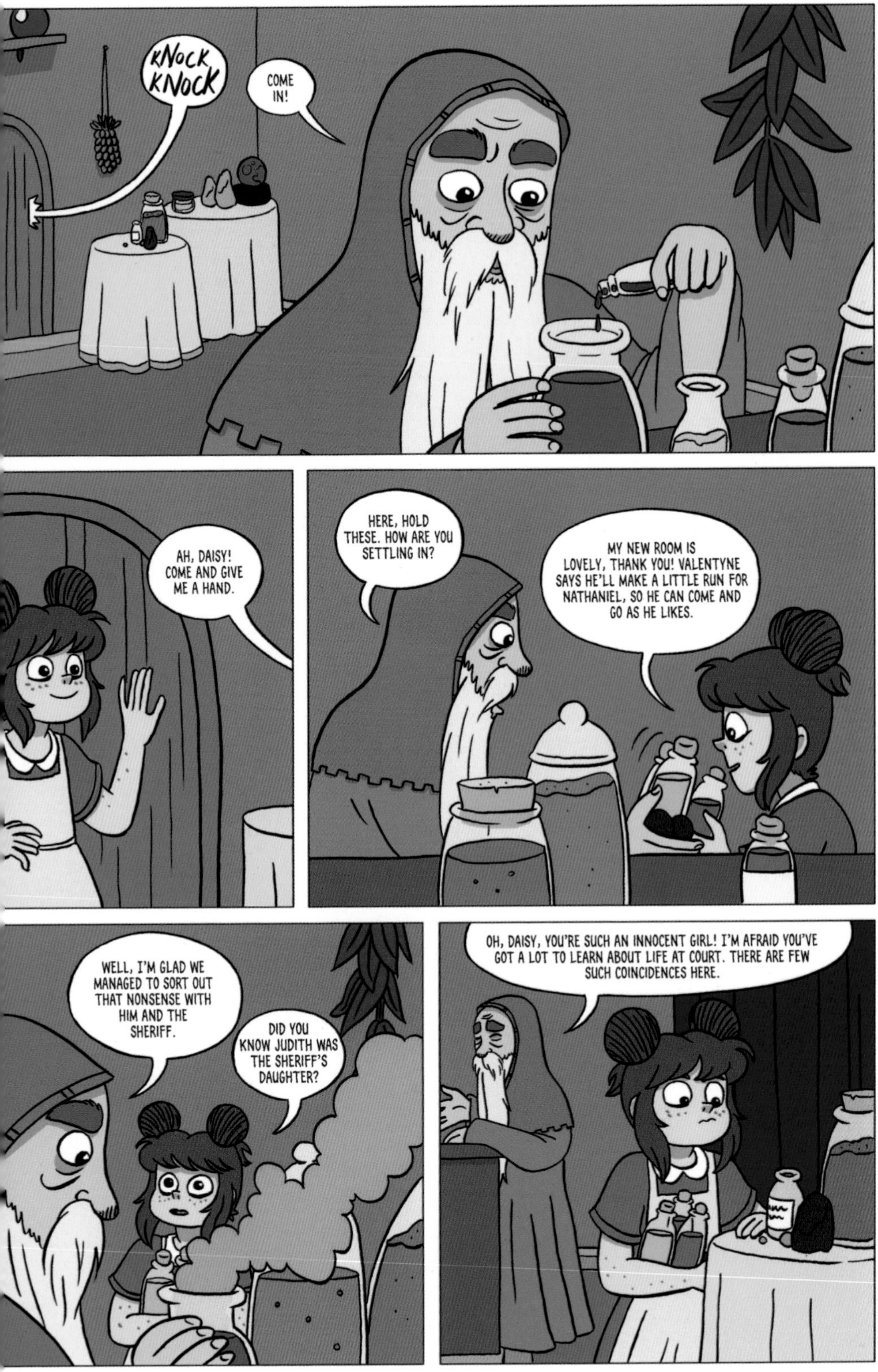
KNOCK KNOCK
COME IN!
AH, DAISY! COME AND GIVE ME A HAND.
HERE, HOLD THESE. HOW ARE YOU SETTLING IN?
MY NEW ROOM IS LOVELY, THANK YOU! VALENTYNE SAYS HE'LL MAKE A LITTLE RUN FOR NATHANIEL, SO HE CAN COME AND GO AS HE LIKES.
WELL, I'M GLAD WE MANAGED TO SORT OUT THAT NONSENSE WITH HIM AND THE SHERIFF.
DID YOU KNOW JUDITH WAS THE SHERIFF'S DAUGHTER?
OH, DAISY, YOU'RE SUCH AN INNOCENT GIRL! I'M AFRAID YOU'VE GOT A LOT TO LEARN ABOUT LIFE AT COURT. THERE ARE FEW SUCH COINCIDENCES HERE.

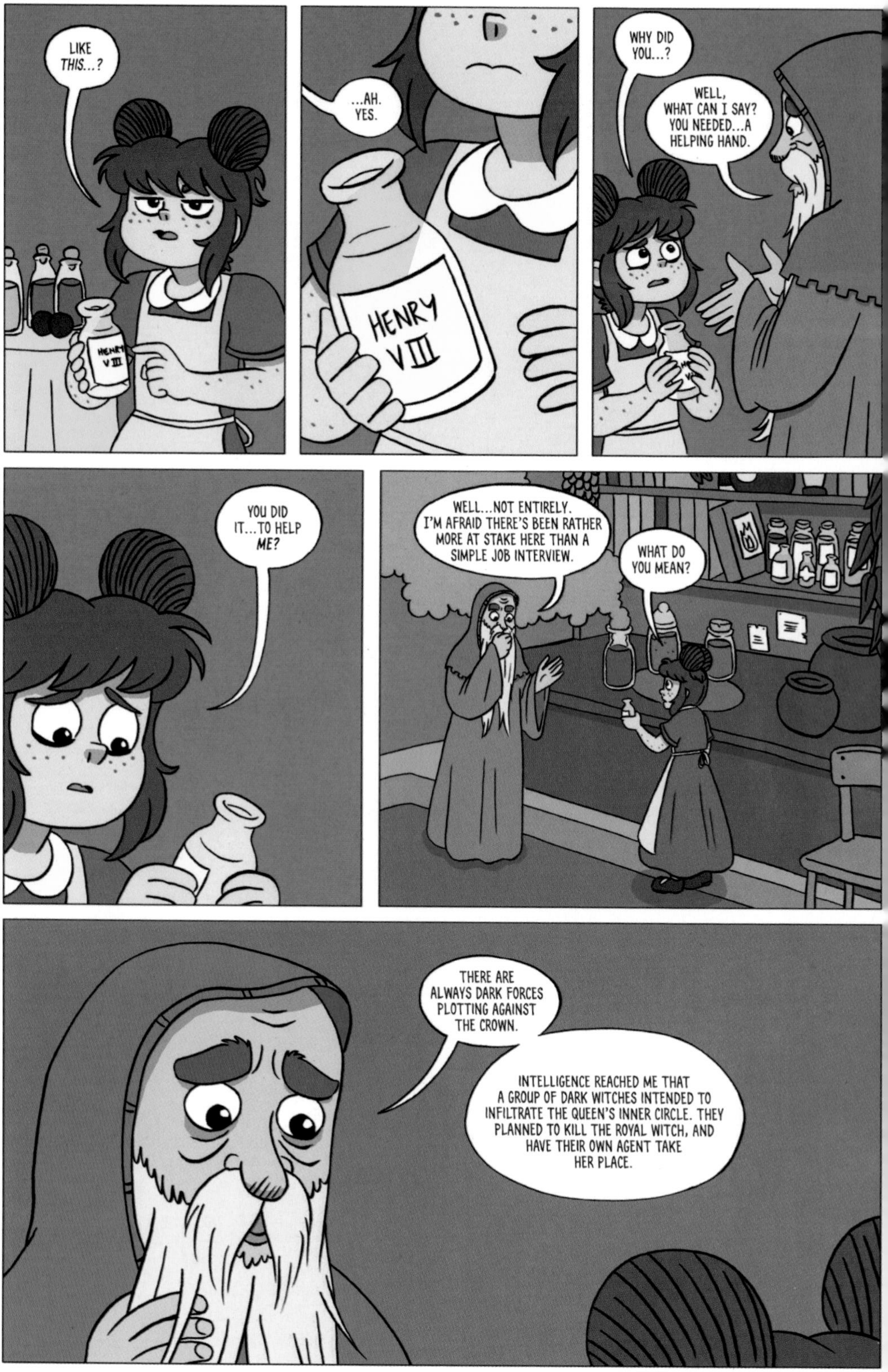
LIKE THIS...?
HENRY VIII
...AH. YES.
HENRY VIII
WHY DID YOU...?
WELL, WHAT CAN I SAY? YOU NEEDED...A HELPING HAND.
YOU DID IT...TO HELP ME?
WELL...NOT ENTIRELY. I'M AFRAID THERE'S BEEN RATHER MORE AT STAKE HERE THAN A SIMPLE JOB INTERVIEW.
WHAT DO YOU MEAN?
THERE ARE ALWAYS DARK FORCES PLOTTING AGAINST THE CROWN.
INTELLIGENCE REACHED ME THAT A GROUP OF DARK WITCHES INTENDED TO INFILTRATE THE QUEEN'S INNER CIRCLE. THEY PLANNED TO KILL THE ROYAL WITCH, AND HAVE THEIR OWN AGENT TAKE HER PLACE.

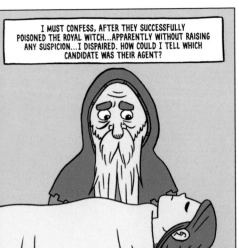

I MUST CONFESS, AFTER THEY SUCCESSFULLY POISONED THE ROYAL WITCH...APPARENTLY WITHOUT RAISING ANY SUSPICION...I DISPAIRED. HOW COULD I TELL WHICH CANDIDATE WAS THEIR AGENT?

THEN, YOU CAME TO ME THAT NIGHT. YOU MADE ME REALIZE THAT I DIDN'T HAVE TO KNOW WHO IT WAS. I ONLY HAD TO KNOW WHO IT WASN'T!

YOU WERE MY WILD CARD, DAISY. I KNEW THAT IF I COULD CARRY YOU THROUGH, YOU'D EXPOSE THE DARK WITCH FOR ME.

THE ONE WHO WAS WILLING TO DO *ANYTHING* TO WIN...EVEN RISK EXPOSING A *DEMON* TO COURT.

SO...JUDITH DIDN'T STEAL THAT BOOK?

NOT EXACTLY. I ARRANGED FOR HER TO FIND IT.

ACTUALLY, I RATHER EXPECTED HER TO USE IT HERSELF. IT WAS A BRILLIANT MOVE OF HERS TO GIVE IT TO *YOU*.

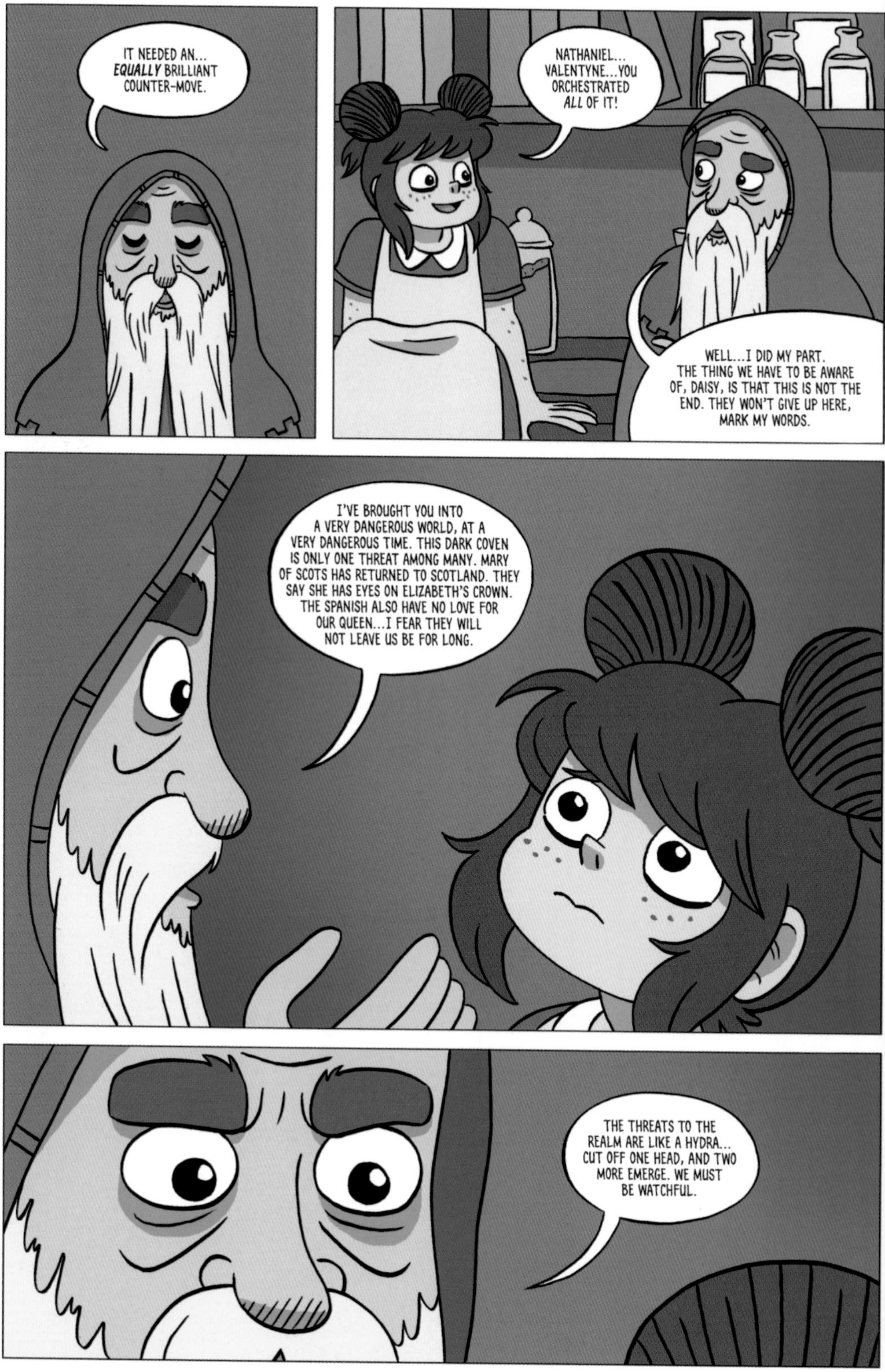
IT NEEDED AN... *EQUALLY* BRILLIANT COUNTER-MOVE.
NATHANIEL... VALENTYNE...YOU ORCHESTRATED *ALL* OF IT!
WELL...I DID MY PART. THE THING WE HAVE TO BE AWARE OF, DAISY, IS THAT THIS IS NOT THE END. THEY WON'T GIVE UP HERE, MARK MY WORDS.
I'VE BROUGHT YOU INTO A VERY DANGEROUS WORLD, AT A VERY DANGEROUS TIME. THIS DARK COVEN IS ONLY ONE THREAT AMONG MANY. MARY OF SCOTS HAS RETURNED TO SCOTLAND. THEY SAY SHE HAS EYES ON ELIZABETH'S CROWN. THE SPANISH ALSO HAVE NO LOVE FOR OUR QUEEN...I FEAR THEY WILL NOT LEAVE US BE FOR LONG.
THE THREATS TO THE REALM ARE LIKE A HYDRA... CUT OFF ONE HEAD, AND TWO MORE EMERGE. WE MUST BE WATCHFUL.

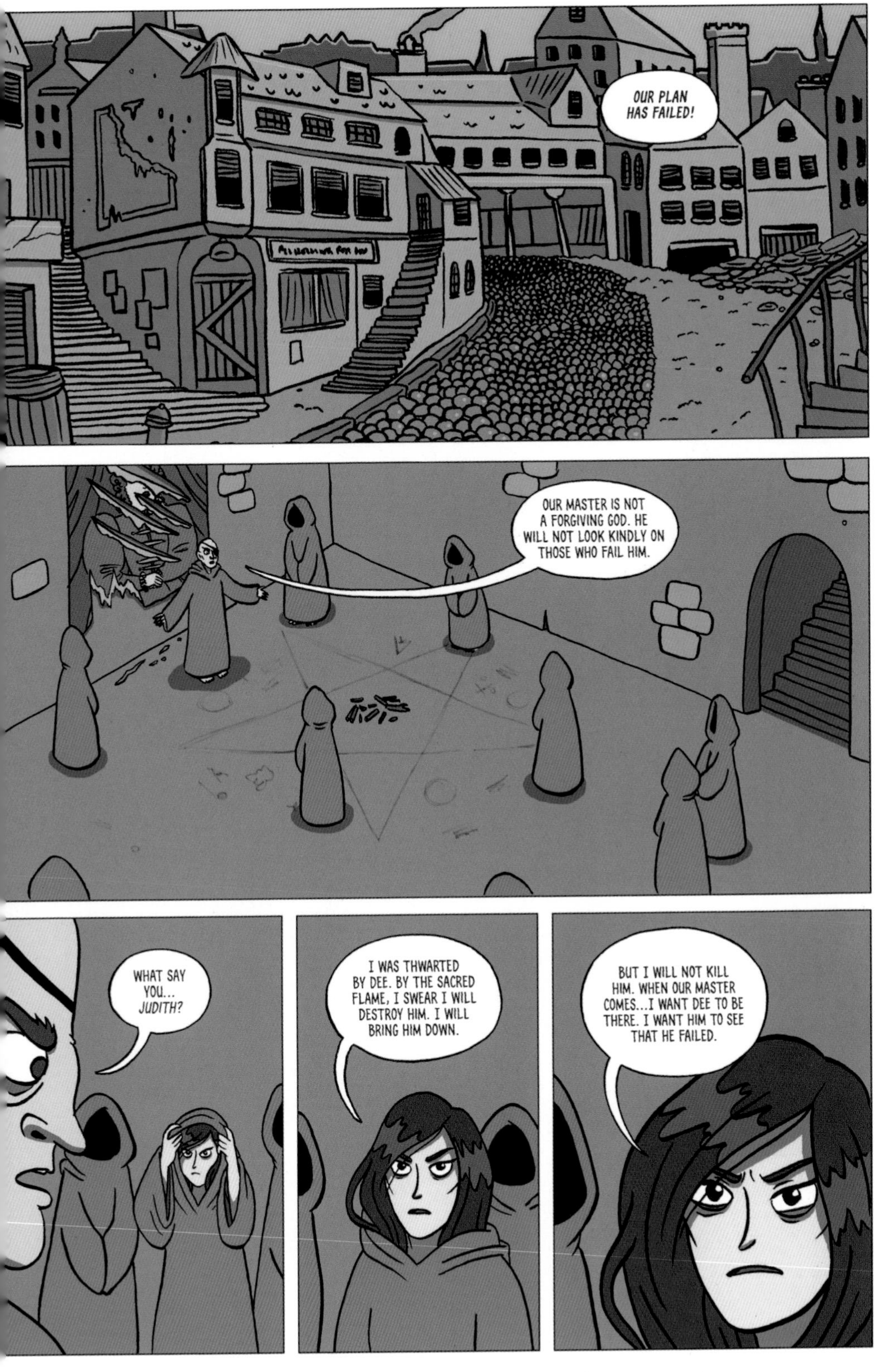

OUR PLAN HAS FAILED!
OUR MASTER IS NOT A FORGIVING GOD. HE WILL NOT LOOK KINDLY ON THOSE WHO FAIL HIM.
WHAT SAY YOU... JUDITH?
I WAS THWARTED BY DEE. BY THE SACRED FLAME, I SWEAR I WILL DESTROY HIM. I WILL BRING HIM DOWN.
BUT I WILL NOT KILL HIM. WHEN OUR MASTER COMES...I WANT DEE TO BE THERE. I WANT HIM TO SEE THAT HE FAILED.

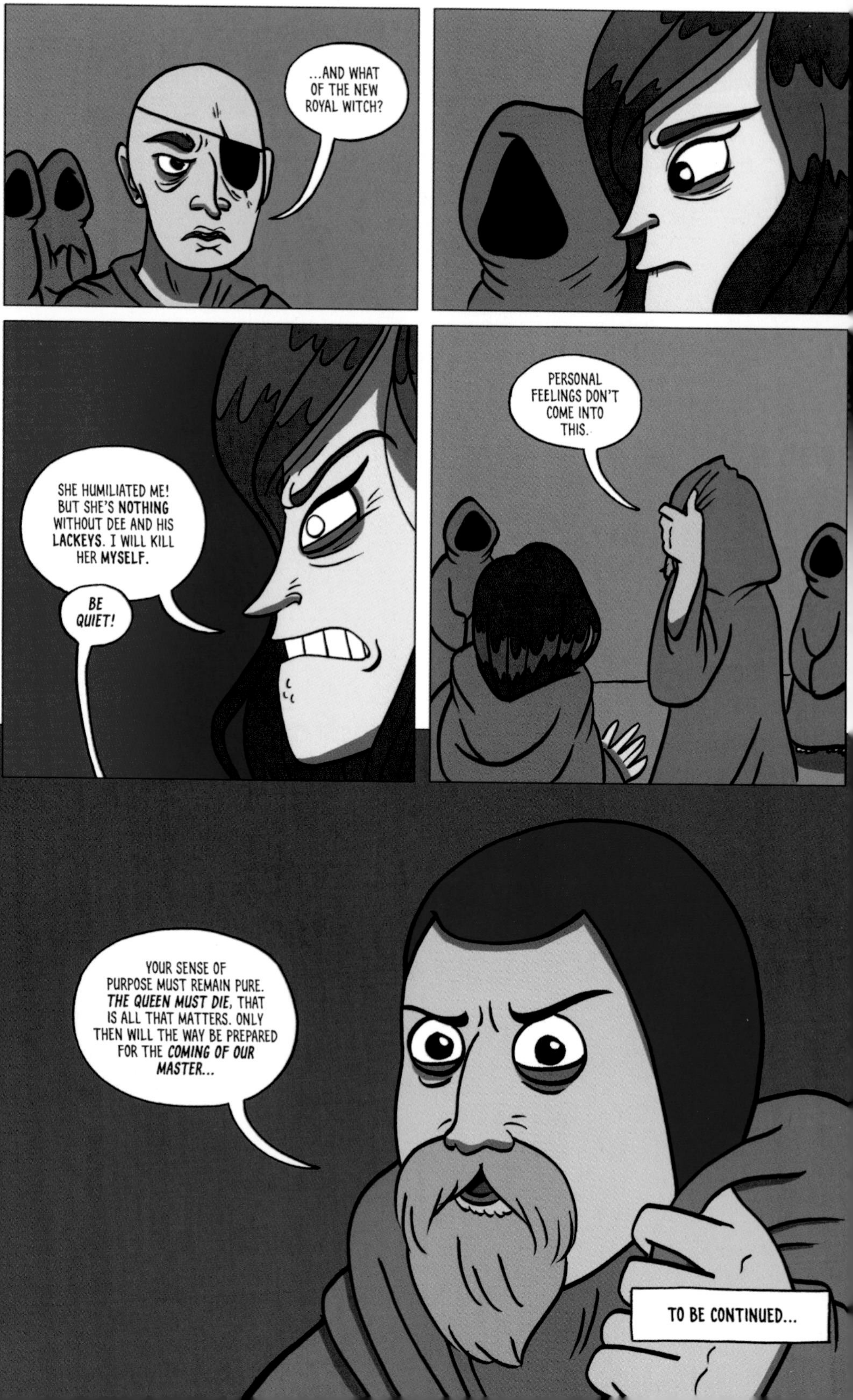
...AND WHAT OF THE NEW ROYAL WITCH?
SHE HUMILIATED ME! BUT SHE'S **NOTHING** WITHOUT DEE AND HIS **LACKEYS**. I WILL KILL HER **MYSELF**.
BE QUIET!
PERSONAL FEELINGS DON'T COME INTO THIS.
YOUR SENSE OF PURPOSE MUST REMAIN PURE. ***THE QUEEN MUST DIE***, THAT IS ALL THAT MATTERS. ONLY THEN WILL THE WAY BE PREPARED FOR THE ***COMING OF OUR MASTER...***
TO BE CONTINUED...

$\mathcal{B}$enjamin Dickson is a writer, artist and lecturer whose previous works include the critically acclaimed *A New Jerusalem* and the very silly *Santa Claus vs the Nazis*. He has published several short stories in Britain, America, and Germany, and has also collaborated on a number of freely available graphic novels on the subject of climate change. He lives and works in Bristol, UK.

More information at: www.bendickson.co.uk

RACHAEL ♥

$\mathcal{R}$achael Smith is an award-winning comic artist and writer. She has created many critically acclaimed graphic novels including *Quarantine Comix, Wired Up Wrong, Stand in Your Power, Artificial Flowers,* and *The Rabbit*. Rachael has worked on Titan's *Doctor Who* comic series and is currently drawing her new book Isabella & Blodwen.

More information at: www.rachaelsmith.org

WATCH OUT FOR PAPERCUTZ

Welcome to the graphic novel, THE QUEEN'S FAVORITE WITCH #1 "The Wheel of Fortune" by Benjamin Dickson, writer, and Rachael Smith, artist, from Papercutz, that bewitched coven of commoners dedicated to publishing great graphic novels for all ages. I'm Jim Salicrup, the Editor-in-Chief and Wicked (male) Witch of East Ninth Street, here to talk about queens throughout the graphic novels proudly published by Papercutz.

Let's start with real-life queen, Queen Elizabeth I, shall we? As we discovered in the informative Preface on page 5 she had quite an interesting life. Yet if you've done just a little bit of research on her, such as checking out her Wikipedia page, you've found no mention of there being a Royal Witch among her advisers. So, is the story presented in this graphic novel pure fiction? Perhaps. But then again, what if there really was a Royal Witch? Would that be something that everyone would know about or would it have been kept secret? We'll leave that for you to decide.

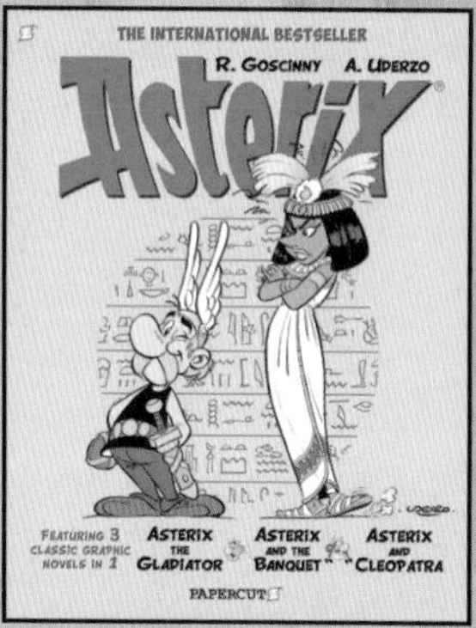
THE INTERNATIONAL BESTSELLER
R. GOSCINNY A. UDERZO
ASTERIX
FEATURING 3 CLASSIC GRAPHIC NOVELS IN 1
ASTERIX THE GLADIATOR
ASTERIX AND THE BANQUET
ASTERIX AND CLEOPATRA
PAPERCUTZ

Another real-life queen was Queen Cleopatra who appeared in ASTERIX Volume Two. ASTERIX to those who may not be familiar with this graphic novel series, one of the most popular in the world... well, not all of it. For sundry reasons not worth going into here, ASTERIX isn't as well-known here in the United States as he is almost everywhere else. Ever-optimistic Papercutz hopes to change that and has become the new North American ASTERIX publisher in 2019. This classic comics series, created by René Goscinny, writer, and Albert Uderzo, over sixty years ago, is about a shrewd little warrior with keen intelligence, who gets his superhuman strength from the druid Panoramix's magic potion. Set in the year 50 BC, Asterix's village in Gaul is surrounded by the forces of the Roman Empire. The Romans have taken over all of Gaul except for this one village due to Asterix's and his friend Obelix's super-powered resistance. And if that wasn't enough to infuriate Rome's emperor, Julius Caesar, when he makes a bet with Cleopatra, Asterix, Obelix, and Panoramix are there to help Cleopatra win.

Uh-oh, it looks like I may not have enough room to talk about the queens found in GILLBERT by Art Baltazar and BLUEBEARD by Metaphrog, perhaps we can get to that in THE QUEEN'S FAVORITE WITCH Volume Two? In the meantime, I wanted to mention yet another Papercutz graphic novel that has a potential queen lurking about somewhere in its pages. To say anymore might be a spoiler. Instead, let's have a short preview of this series, about a young woman, Tara Smith, who finds out her life isn't all she thought it was, and eventually finds herself enrolled in the SCHOOL FOR EXTRATERRESTRIAL GIRLS. The series is by Jeremy Whitley, writer, and Jamie Noguchi, artist, and the preview begins on the next page...

We all hope you enjoyed THE QUEEN'S FAVORITE WITCH. In fact, we're hoping you've fallen under this book's spell and will pick up the next volume to see what happens to Daisy next. We'll be waiting for you!

Thanks,

Jim

STAY IN TOUCH!

EMAIL:	salicrup@papercutz.com
WEB:	papercutz.com
TWITTER:	@papercutzgn
INSTAGRAM:	@papercutzgn
FACEBOOK:	PAPERCUTZGRAPHICNOVELS
REGULAR MAIL:	Papercutz, 160 Broadway, Suite 700, East Wing, New York, NY 10038

Go to papercutz.com and sign up for the free Papercutz e-newsletter!

Special Preview of
THE SCHOOL FOR EXTRATERRESTRIAL GIRLS #2
"Girls Take Flight"

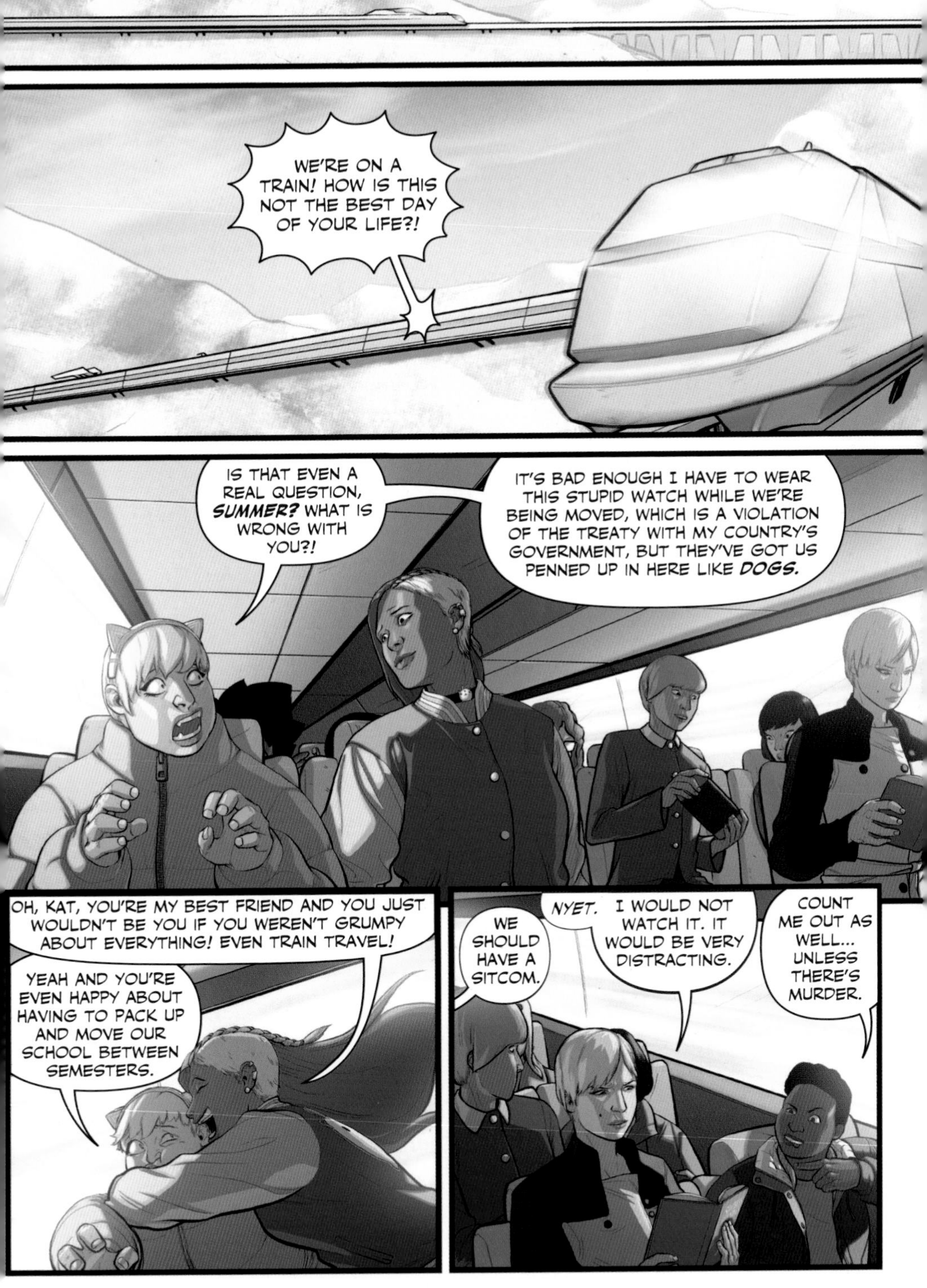
WE'RE ON A TRAIN! HOW IS THIS NOT THE BEST DAY OF YOUR LIFE?!
IS THAT EVEN A REAL QUESTION, SUMMER? WHAT IS WRONG WITH YOU?!
IT'S BAD ENOUGH I HAVE TO WEAR THIS STUPID WATCH WHILE WE'RE BEING MOVED, WHICH IS A VIOLATION OF THE TREATY WITH MY COUNTRY'S GOVERNMENT, BUT THEY'VE GOT US PENNED UP IN HERE LIKE DOGS.
OH, KAT, YOU'RE MY BEST FRIEND AND YOU JUST WOULDN'T BE YOU IF YOU WEREN'T GRUMPY ABOUT EVERYTHING! EVEN TRAIN TRAVEL!
YEAH AND YOU'RE EVEN HAPPY ABOUT HAVING TO PACK UP AND MOVE OUR SCHOOL BETWEEN SEMESTERS.
WE SHOULD HAVE A SITCOM.
NYET. I WOULD NOT WATCH IT. IT WOULD BE VERY DISTRACTING.
COUNT ME OUT AS WELL... UNLESS THERE'S MURDER.

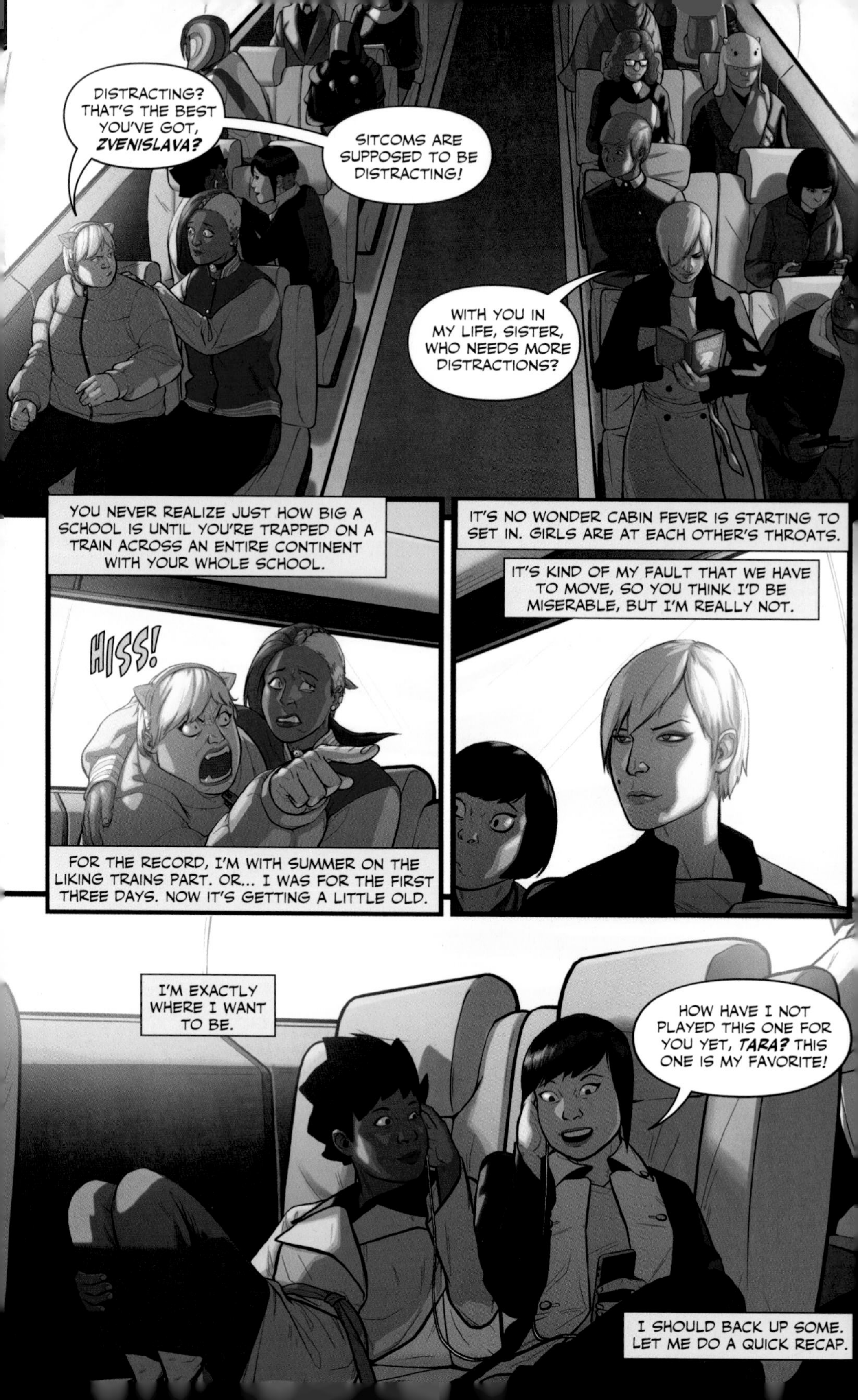
DISTRACTING? THAT'S THE BEST YOU'VE GOT, ZVENISLAVA?
SITCOMS ARE SUPPOSED TO BE DISTRACTING!
WITH YOU IN MY LIFE, SISTER, WHO NEEDS MORE DISTRACTIONS?
YOU NEVER REALIZE JUST HOW BIG A SCHOOL IS UNTIL YOU'RE TRAPPED ON A TRAIN ACROSS AN ENTIRE CONTINENT WITH YOUR WHOLE SCHOOL.
HISS!
FOR THE RECORD, I'M WITH SUMMER ON THE LIKING TRAINS PART. OR... I WAS FOR THE FIRST THREE DAYS. NOW IT'S GETTING A LITTLE OLD.
IT'S NO WONDER CABIN FEVER IS STARTING TO SET IN. GIRLS ARE AT EACH OTHER'S THROATS.
IT'S KIND OF MY FAULT THAT WE HAVE TO MOVE, SO YOU THINK I'D BE MISERABLE, BUT I'M REALLY NOT.
I'M EXACTLY WHERE I WANT TO BE.
HOW HAVE I NOT PLAYED THIS ONE FOR YOU YET, TARA? THIS ONE IS MY FAVORITE!
I SHOULD BACK UP SOME. LET ME DO A QUICK RECAP.

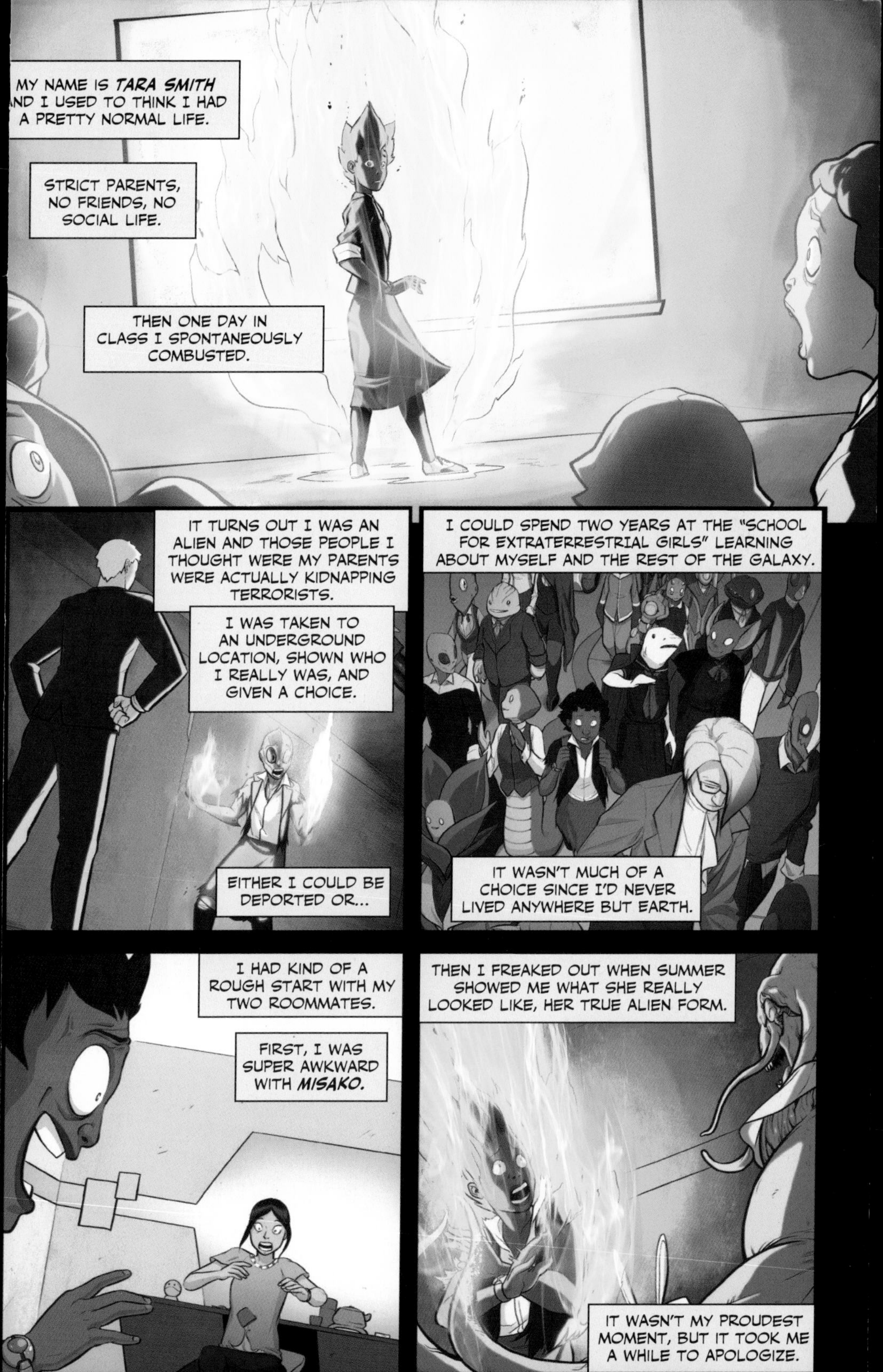
MY NAME IS *TARA SMITH* AND I USED TO THINK I HAD A PRETTY NORMAL LIFE.
STRICT PARENTS, NO FRIENDS, NO SOCIAL LIFE.
THEN ONE DAY IN CLASS I SPONTANEOUSLY COMBUSTED.
IT TURNS OUT I WAS AN ALIEN AND THOSE PEOPLE I THOUGHT WERE MY PARENTS WERE ACTUALLY KIDNAPPING TERRORISTS.
I WAS TAKEN TO AN UNDERGROUND LOCATION, SHOWN WHO I REALLY WAS, AND GIVEN A CHOICE.
EITHER I COULD BE DEPORTED OR...
I COULD SPEND TWO YEARS AT THE "SCHOOL FOR EXTRATERRESTRIAL GIRLS" LEARNING ABOUT MYSELF AND THE REST OF THE GALAXY.
IT WASN'T MUCH OF A CHOICE SINCE I'D NEVER LIVED ANYWHERE BUT EARTH.
I HAD KIND OF A ROUGH START WITH MY TWO ROOMMATES.
FIRST, I WAS SUPER AWKWARD WITH ***MISAKO.***
THEN I FREAKED OUT WHEN SUMMER SHOWED ME WHAT SHE REALLY LOOKED LIKE, HER TRUE ALIEN FORM.
IT WASN'T MY PROUDEST MOMENT, BUT IT TOOK ME A WHILE TO APOLOGIZE.

SOON, MISAKO AND I WERE BEST FRIENDS.

WE HAD ALMOST ALL OF OUR CLASSES TOGETHER.

WHICH IS WHERE I FOUND OUT THAT MISAKO WAS FROM A RACE OF INTERDIMENSIONAL MAGICAL FAIRIES.

AND WHERE I FOUND OUT THAT MY PEOPLE WERE RESPONSIBLE FOR NEARLY COMPLETELY ANNIHILATING HERS.

WHICH I HID FROM HER UNTIL THE HEADMISTRESS FORCED ME TO REVEAL MY TRUE FORM IN FRONT OF CLASS.

IT DIDN'T GO WELL AND SHE RAN AWAY... LIKE FROM THE WHOLE IMPENETRABLE BUNKER OUR SCHOOL WAS IN.

WHICH IS HOW WE ENDED UP WITH A NEW ROOMMATE, EKATERINA. SHE'S A GIANT CAT ALIEN WHO GREW UP IN RUSSIA AND LOVES AMERICAN MOVIES AND TV.

SHE GOES BY KAT AND SHE AND HER SISTER ZVENISLAVA USUALLY HAVE AN EXEMPTION FROM HAVING TO WEAR THE WRIST WATCHES THAT MAKE US ALL APPEAR HUMAN... RIGHT NOW IS AN EXCEPTION.

ANYWAY, MY EVIL FAKE PARENTS CAUGHT MISAKO AND FORCED HER TO LEAD THEM TO THE SCHOOL... WHERE THEY TRIED TO TAKE ME BACK.

WHICH IS WHEN I DISCOVERED I, FOR SOME REASON, AM A LOT STRONGER THAN THE PEOPLE WHO PRETENDED TO BE MY PARENTS.

PARTIALLY DESTROYING THE SCHOOL IN THE PROCESS.

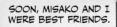

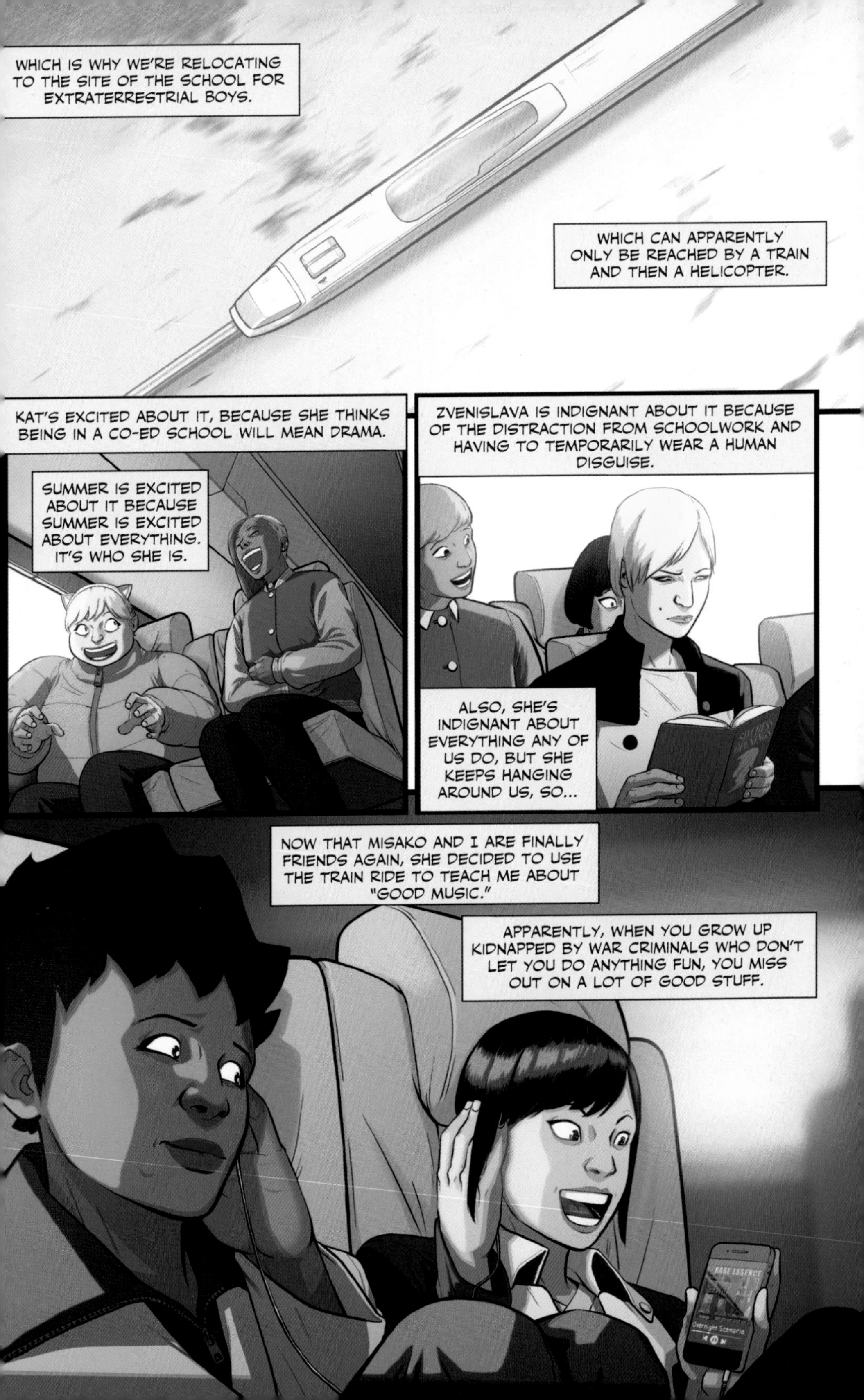
WHICH IS WHY WE'RE RELOCATING TO THE SITE OF THE SCHOOL FOR EXTRATERRESTRIAL BOYS.
WHICH CAN APPARENTLY ONLY BE REACHED BY A TRAIN AND THEN A HELICOPTER.
KAT'S EXCITED ABOUT IT, BECAUSE SHE THINKS BEING IN A CO-ED SCHOOL WILL MEAN DRAMA.
SUMMER IS EXCITED ABOUT IT BECAUSE SUMMER IS EXCITED ABOUT EVERYTHING. IT'S WHO SHE IS.
ZVENISLAVA IS INDIGNANT ABOUT IT BECAUSE OF THE DISTRACTION FROM SCHOOLWORK AND HAVING TO TEMPORARILY WEAR A HUMAN DISGUISE.
ALSO, SHE'S INDIGNANT ABOUT EVERYTHING ANY OF US DO, BUT SHE KEEPS HANGING AROUND US, SO...
NOW THAT MISAKO AND I ARE FINALLY FRIENDS AGAIN, SHE DECIDED TO USE THE TRAIN RIDE TO TEACH ME ABOUT "GOOD MUSIC."
APPARENTLY, WHEN YOU GROW UP KIDNAPPED BY WAR CRIMINALS WHO DON'T LET YOU DO ANYTHING FUN, YOU MISS OUT ON A LOT OF GOOD STUFF.
RARE ESSENCE
Overnight Scenario

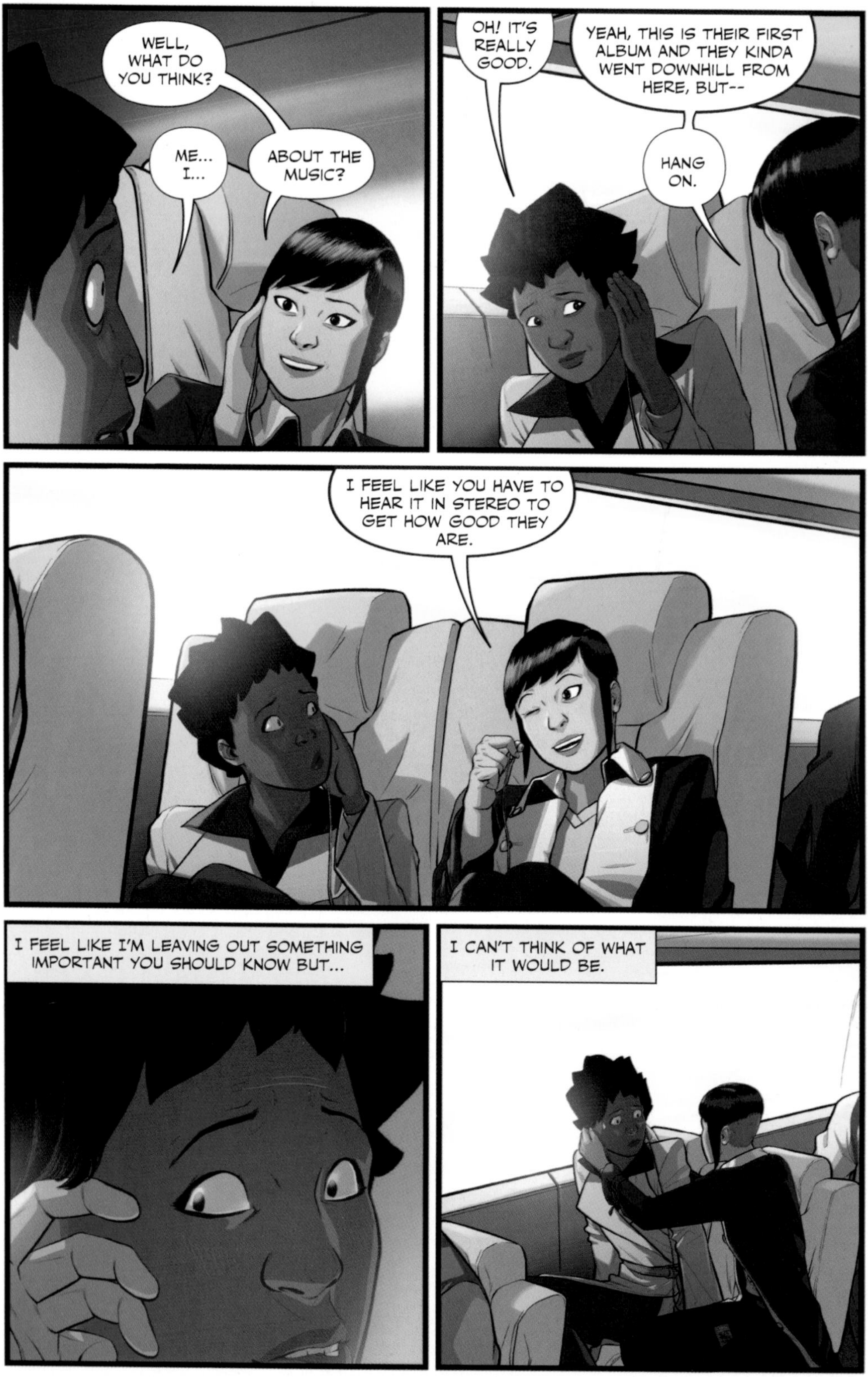
WELL, WHAT DO YOU THINK?
ME... I...
ABOUT THE MUSIC?
OH! IT'S REALLY GOOD.
YEAH, THIS IS THEIR FIRST ALBUM AND THEY KINDA WENT DOWNHILL FROM HERE, BUT--
HANG ON.
I FEEL LIKE YOU HAVE TO HEAR IT IN STEREO TO GET HOW GOOD THEY ARE.
I FEEL LIKE I'M LEAVING OUT SOMETHING IMPORTANT YOU SHOULD KNOW BUT...
I CAN'T THINK OF WHAT IT WOULD BE.